MIDDLE OF THE NIGHT

SHELBY LEWIS

MIDDLE OF THE NIGHT

Cover design and graphic design by Stephanie Drew Davies.

eBook ISBN: 979-8-9930481-1-6
Paperback ISBN: 979-8-9930481-0-9
Hardcover ISBN: 979-8-9930481-2-3

First Edition: November 2025

10 9 8 7 6 5 4 3 2 1

CONTENT WARNING:

Middle of the Night is a fictional world that contains adult themes throughout. Please see below for potential trigger warnings, which may also contain spoilers for the book.

<u>Content warnings include</u>: violence, blood and gore, sexual assault, death, prostitution, death of a parent(s) and themes of grief, mentions of suicide, violent nightmares, drug and alcohol use, and on-page death.

Please protect your mental health.

this one is for me

PROLOGUE

THE PHANTOM

The man they called the Phantom watched his blade sink into the soft flesh of the woman's stomach.

He didn't have a choice in killing her–the only woman he had ever loved.

He had become the Phantom to make a *difference*, to help people, to try to save the city from itself. To save people, not hurt them. He had never killed, not once in two years of being a vigilante. Until now. Now, with her blood on his hands, all he could think was *I wish I had never met her*.

If he had never met her, she would still be safe. If the choice was to damn the city or save her, it wasn't really a choice at all.

But that choice had been taken from him, ripped away by the very men watching as his blade sank into her flesh.

A single tear rolled from under his mask. Her eyes were blown wide, but she wasn't afraid.

She had never been afraid of him. From the very moment they met, she had seen the good in him, had seen the good in his mission to help the city.

And now the city was going to be responsible for her death. *He* was going to be responsible for her death.

CHAPTER ONE

EMMA

It was the middle of the night and Emma Warner was being followed.

It took two winding city blocks before she noticed the man, something she silently cursed herself for. From the furtive glances cast over her shoulder, she saw he was in a tattered hoodie, shoulders hunched, jeans ripped and dirty.

New Atlas already possessed more than its fair share of darkness, and the relentless rain of the past few days only made it worse. The flooded subways and sewers drove those who thrived in the underbelly of the city up into the weak streetlights above ground. The half-cobbled, half-asphalt streets were a rat maze that only natives knew well enough to navigate.

It was already a shit day. The creeps had come in droves to the Crescent Club. The rain was really bringing out the worst in people, almost as bad as the extreme heat wave two summers before. Even though the club was a mob spot popular with the rich and powerful (and the extremely corrupt), some days were much, much worse than others. Today was one of them.

Her shit job at the nightclub to pay off her debts became even shittier when a man spilled a drink on her and then pawed at her chest in a thinly veiled attempt to feel her up while pretending to help.

Things only worsened from there.

She probably shouldn't have hit him. But she had. And after a meeting with the Wolf–the owner of the Crescent Club and a crime lord–another ten thousand dollars got added to her debt. So not only had she been sexually assaulted, she also had to spend God-only-knew-how-long at the club working off the debt simply for sticking up for herself. And that was on top of working off the debt for her mother's medical bills–which hadn't made a difference, in the end. She'd still died.

Emma screamed as a hand grabbed her elbow. The sound abruptly cut off as the man's other hand, cold and clammy, covered her mouth. Now, to top off her exceptionally shitty day, another man caged her in against a brick wall, his breath hot on her face.

Her first thought was a silent plea for help from the man they called the Phantom, the city's infamous vigilante of the past two years. Something about the bad weather made the criminals in the city overactive, but the vigilante was usually there to stop them.

Not that it deterred the criminals in the slightest.

Her second thought was, *Shit.*

His rough grip made her drop her umbrella. Her fingers were slick with rain as they fumbled for her taser. Her gun was buried at the bottom of her bag, unused except for when she went to the range to practice–and those days were fewer and farther between. Thankfully, she always kept her taser at least in her pocket, if not in her hand.

He hadn't expected her to be armed. The prongs dug into the soft skin underneath his arm, blue light igniting the darkness of the alley as the man cried out.

Emma ran.

The rain was up to her ankles in most places, trash and the bodies of drowned rats spilling out of overfull drains and washing down the streets. Her heart pounded in panic, but it was a clear-minded sort of panic that made her realize she didn't want to lead her attacker straight to her apartment.

So she turned a sharp corner, slipping as she went, the noise of the storm making it impossible to hear if she was still being pursued.

She chanced a glance behind her and–

"*Oof.*" Her breath left her in a rush as she crashed into something.

No, some*one.*

With a shriek she quickly tried to quell, Emma pressed the button on her taser and it crackled back to life.

It was a man.

A man had fallen from the sky and somehow landed nimbly on his feet.

But then he abruptly sank to his knees with a splash, then over onto his side.

"What the...?" she mumbled when the dark lump of a man hadn't moved after several long seconds. She glanced up at the buildings around them but saw nothing.

That's when she noticed he was wearing armor. Armor and a cape that the flood of water dragged away from his body. A hood and a mask covered most of his face, leaving only his eyes and the lower half of his jaw exposed.

She recognized him from various internet forums, news stories, and grainy security pictures.

It was the Phantom.

Emma glanced up at the rooftops and back down again.

Something had knocked him from a nearby roof. That couldn't be good.

He still wasn't moving.

Without thinking, she hurried over to him. She had to get him out of the middle of the sidewalk. She had to wake him up, help him, even though she was probably being pursued.

Maybe if he woke up...he could help her. She looked over her shoulder again. Her heart beat an erratic rhythm in her chest. But so far, the man hadn't followed her.

Was she being stupid? She hesitated before crouching beside him. In New Atlas, people pretty much kept to themselves. Getting involved in other people's business never ended well. Good Samaritans weren't a *thing* in the city. Except for the vigilante at her feet, that is.

No, Emma decided. He was the Phantom. He protected the city. How he did so may have been a bit questionable, but he *helped* people. She'd seen the cellphone videos and news stories more times than she cared to admit. For two years straight so far, he protected the city. He even helped catch a serial killer the year before.

"Hey," she said, shaking his shoulder. "Wake up." She shook him again. Her fingers were still wrapped tightly around the taser, just in case.

The Phantom groaned and then sat up in one quick movement. He pulled back a fist as if he was going to punch something. Punch *her*.

"Hey! It's okay! You're okay! Well, I mean, you fell off a roof or something, but I'm *trying* to help you."

His eyes fluttered open, struggling to focus. He barely managed to sit all the way up before he swayed again. She couldn't help but notice the sharp line of his jaw as the rain slid off it. And that his eyes were green, maybe blue. It was a bit too dark to tell.

"My apartment's not far. Let me help you." She held out a hand. Still no sign of the man who'd tried to attack her. Maybe since she'd shown herself not to be easy prey he'd given up.

The Phantom stared at her outstretched hand for a long moment, then let her help him to his feet with a sigh. He was…tall. Really tall. She wondered, briefly, how padded his costume–armor?–was, or if he really was that muscular and broad-shouldered.

"It isn't safe," he said in a gravelly voice that was half whisper, half growl. "I–damn it." He abruptly leaned his weight onto her. "I heard you scream, saw that guy attack you but I couldn't make it in time."

"No shit," she said, thinking of the flash of her taser in the dark. "I handled it though."

That's when she noticed the blood being washed away by the rain. It wasn't much, but it was definitely more than what should come from a person who had just fallen from the sky.

"You're hurt," she said. "It isn't far. Let me help you."

There was another moment of hesitation. But she was already tugging him along, holding more of his weight than he was. The blood seemed to come from a wound in his side between the kevlar plates that covered his torso.

The Phantom hissed in pain after a few steps. He was limping, too. She didn't miss how he constantly surveyed their surroundings. Probably looking for whoever had tried to kill him by tossing him from above. Or maybe he tried to fly and landed badly? Or jumped between roofs and miscalculated? She'd seen parkour videos where people misjudged distances and–

God, she was freaking out, wasn't she? She couldn't stop the torrent of thoughts from churning in her mind. She was helping the fucking Phantom. Taking him to her apartment.

"Don't worry," she said. "I have a gun. And a taser. And pepper spray."

He glanced down at her from his towering height. She was practically tucked all the way under his armpit. That sharp jaw of his was tight with pain. But there was a twitch of amusement from his lips.

"It's up here." Emma pointed. He surveyed the streets again, the skyline, the alleyways. She paused for a second and surveyed the surrounding shadows, too. No sign of her attacker–hopefully she'd scared him off. Or maybe the Phantom's presence had. She was hesitant to potentially lead him to her apartment, vigilante in tow or no.

"Why?" he asked in that deep, quiet voice of his as she helped him into the building. The light out front was out again, and there was broken glass at the bottom of the stairs. It crunched beneath their feet as they stepped inside.

"The elevator's busted, I'm sorry," she said as she helped him up the stairs. "It's just one floor up, though."

"Why help me?" he continued as if she hadn't spoken. All things considered, she thought, he was really taking it like a champ. He was bleeding, had been unconscious, and apparently had had the shit beaten out of him before being tossed off a roof. Or falling off a roof. She still didn't know.

"Because," she grunted as they finally reached the second floor landing. "That's what *you* do. Help people. Who else is going to fight for us?"

And she meant it. From all the videos she'd seen, the Phantom helped people, no matter who they were. The poor, the homeless, the struggling. He kept their shitty, crime-riddled city just a bit safer. And God, did New Atlas need someone like that.

"Plus, you're not like that guy in Meridian City. You've never killed anyone." She propped him against the hallway wall as she spoke and fumbled for her keys. The door opened with a creak. She reached out to help him again, but he seemed to rally and straightened, shuffling forward a couple of steps.

Emma stared at him for a moment. "Come on in," she said after a beat. "Don't bleed all over my couch."

She meant it as a joke, but he slumped into the one rickety kitchen chair she owned. The kitchen was basically the entryway to the apartment, made up of a small counter, a stovetop, and a fridge with a tiny table and chair separating everything from the living room, which was a loveseat and a TV on a stand. Barely enough room for one person, let alone two.

His eyes closed for a second. Thankfully, he didn't seem to be bleeding that badly anymore.

She went into the tiny bathroom, got her outdated first aid kit, and then brushed past the Phantom to get him a glass of water to wash down ibuprofen with.

His eyes were still closed when she turned around from the sink. The kitchen was so small their knees were almost touching. She studied the lower half of his face again. She ached to take off the mask, to learn what no one else had figured out. But no. That'd be rude. Besides, he was probably just a random guy with too much time on his hands and an axe to grind with the criminal underworld of the city. She guaranteed she wouldn't recognize him without the mask no matter how badly she itched to take it off.

Emma nudged him with the glass and his eyes opened. She'd forgotten to turn on the lights. All that lit the apartment was the faintly buzzing light above her oven. But lights cost money, and she was pinching pennies right now. Especially after tonight. An echo of the Wolf's cruel laughter flashed through her mind.

She pushed the thought away and watched the Phantom down several pills in one go with a wince.

The Phantom was in her shitty apartment. It didn't feel real. "You're bleeding," she murmured. She really hadn't thought this through. Cellphone videos or not, the Phantom could very well be a psychopath. She pushed those thoughts away, too. In his current state, she could probably tase him before he got very far.

He tensed up. "I'm fine. I just need to rest for a few minutes and then I'll be gone."

She could almost feel the roughness of his voice in the small space between them, like sandpaper against her skin.

She shivered. She was still dripping water. So was he.

"Let me just–Let me look at it. If you don't mind. I want to help." Emma kept her voice soft.

His eyes flickered up to hers and then back down again.

He was so…still. It was almost unnatural. Who *was* this guy?

Finally, he shifted and began peeling off the armor. He first removed his thick gloves. His knuckles were bruised, his fingers long. His skin looked rough to the touch, like one big callus. The armor from his torso thunked to the floor next, piece after piece.

He wore a long-sleeved black shirt underneath it. There was a gash on one side, revealing a bloody line. It didn't look too deep, but Emma really had no idea what she was doing. Caring for her mom had been different. There had never been any blood. She'd really only had to help her mother as the cancer and chemo made her weaker and weaker. Emma had never stitched anything in her life, not even the holes in her well-worn clothes. Her mother had done all the mending. Emma never learned how.

"It's not too deep," he said, echoing her thoughts. "I've had worse."

His *voice*. In all the hundreds of grainy videos she'd watched, they had never captured his voice. Emma realized, all at once, with the vigilante of New Atlas sitting in her apartment just how desperately *lonely* she was. The last person to be in her apartment was the landlord showing her around.

She was so utterly, achingly lonely.

Emma glanced at the man before her, heart thudding almost painfully in her chest. "I'll just clean it real quick and bandage it then. If you…if that's okay."

He gave a curt nod.

She grabbed the first-aid kit and knelt before him. She lifted his shirt, just far enough to see the cut. His whole body was tense. Like he was ready to flee at a moment's notice.

Her thoughts stuttered to a stop when she saw a flash of abs.

So he *was* that muscular underneath the suit. Heat spread across her face. Between that, and the voice, and that sharp jawline... She made herself focus on the task at hand and not the abs before her. But the warmth of him was distracting for someone who was as terribly lonely as she was. It had been a long time since she'd been attracted to someone, and it was off-putting not only because she couldn't see his face, but because he was so...docile. His hands were fisted loosely at his sides. It had been a while, too, since a man had been this respectful of her.

She hated the bar was so low, but there she was.

"I'm Emma, by the way. Emma Warner. Not that you asked, but..." She cleared her throat awkwardly. "So...did someone throw you off the roof?" she asked as she pulled out the small bottle of rubbing alcohol and a few cotton balls. She really hoped he didn't need stitches, because she really didn't think she could do that. Imagining a needle in his flesh made her stomach quiver nervously.

He sucked in a breath as she dabbed at his bloody skin.

"Something like that," he murmured after a moment.

She applied more of the alcohol on his skin with another cotton ball and lightly scrubbed away the blood around the wound. She was careful not to press too hard. "Will they come after you?"

"They won't be a problem for you, if that's what you're asking." She glanced up and met his searing gaze. "I swear." There was an almost wild intensity in his eyes. He meant it.

Satisfied with the answer, she nodded, cheeks still hot, and set about bandaging the cut. She had to sort of Frankenstein two bandages together to make one that was long enough. His skin was hot where she touched it.

"What were you doing out so late, alone?" the Phantom surprised her by asking. He didn't seem one for small talk.

"I was coming home from work. I'm a...bartender." She bit her lip. Her earlier frustration still simmered under her skin. She carefully put the two separate pieces of the bandage together and set it aside. Almost absently, she spread a bit of antibiotic ointment over the cut while she talked. "It's a shitty job and I got sexually harassed tonight, but I have to have this job because it's the only one available." His chest rose and fell in a steady rhythm. She noticed another, much thicker scar under one of his pectorals and blushed. "Unemployment is sky high, and I have a ton of debt, so much that I need a second job, but I can't–" She cut herself off with a sharp breath. She tugged his shirt back down and stood. "Sorry. You don't need to hear about my problems. Obviously, you have bigger problems than me." She gestured at the knife wound. She'd said too much. He didn't care about her shitty job or her shitty night.

The Phantom stared at her. Seated, he had to tilt his head up just a little to meet her eyes. "No one's problems are too small," he said softly. His voice was like distant thunder, deep and rumbling. "That's why I do this."

Something fluttered in her chest.

"Good as new," she said to shake off the silence that stretched between them. "Feel free to stay as long as you need. I can get some sheets for the couch if–if you want to sleep awhile. I'm going to shower and go to bed."

He shook his head. "You've done enough. Thank you."

Feeling brave, she caught his bare hand in hers. A couple of his knuckles were scabbed over. "Thank *you*. I know you probably don't hear it a lot, but the little guys like me in New Atlas see you. We see what you're doing. And we need it."

His blue-or-green eyes blazed with an unknown emotion for a moment. She let go after a second, embarrassed. The spell was broken, and they both looked away at the same time.

"Anyway...stay as long as you want." She walked into her bedroom, skirting the narrow space around her full-sized bed with ease. There was only room for one skinny nightstand and the dresser. As it was, her bathroom door banged against the dresser every time she opened it too far. She kicked off her rain boots as she went. Everything was so close together that she could start the shower in the tiny stall from the bathroom doorway. While the building's ancient hot water heaters worked overtime, she grabbed a pair of pajamas and

called out, "There's leftover takeout in the fridge if you need something to eat before you go." She imagined the Phantom sitting at her
small, thrifted table eating noodles with chopsticks and almost
laughed. She pressed her forehead to the edge of the dresser and took
a moment to steady herself. There was a smear of the Phantom's
blood on one hand.

A soft thunk came from somewhere behind her.

She peered out, hoping he hadn't fainted.

But he was gone. Armor and all. The front door was still locked
and–there, at the window, a shadow. The edge of a cape, heading up
the fire escape and into the night.

CHAPTER TWO

A week had passed since the Phantom had been in her apartment, and Emma's nerves were frayed. Her leg bounced, her palms sweated, and her heart thundered so loud in her chest she was certain the people around her could hear it. She was currently waiting to be interviewed for a job she was barely qualified for but desperately needed. A job that could change everything. The alert for the posting had been like a lifeline thrown from a sinking ship to save her from drowning. She rarely got alerts for jobs anymore with the awful rate of unemployment in the city. And she desperately hoped to catch the life preserver this job offered so she could stay afloat just a little while longer.

To calm herself, she sank into one of her favorite pastimes, especially in the past week: looking up sightings of the Phantom.

The past week only served to further her obsession. She'd been interested before, following along with the frequent news stories, watching grainy videos posted on social media. But now she actively sought them out. Now she looked for any and every bit of information she could get her hands on.

She couldn't stop thinking about how he had been in her apartment. How real he was, a man made of flesh and blood beneath the suit. She'd always *known* he was a real person, but now she'd gotten a glimpse of him. The *real* man. The real Phantom. She wished it had been brighter in her apartment so she could have seen more details. Were his eyes green or blue? Something in between? Would she have recognized him in more light?

Thinking about the vigilante helped with the anxious feeling spreading through her chest.

If she was going to survive–to be able to pay off her debts, to be able to leave New Atlas, to ever be able to have a future again–she needed a second job, so she'd been monitoring every listing.

Two days ago, Kane Industries–a pharmaceutical giant that had a hand in most products around the world–posted a job. Elusive billionaire James Kane was looking for an assistant. He was only a few years older than Emma's twenty-six years but already CEO. Almost twenty years ago, someone murdered his mother, and his father, the primary suspect, committed suicide shortly after. James barely appeared in public after their funerals. It was a tragic story, one that always made Emma's heart clench with empathy. Especially now, now that she was an orphan herself.

The job was a long shot, Emma knew, but she applied anyway. Before her mom got sick, Emma completed an associate's degree in business management. Hopefully that would give her at least a bit of a leg up, despite her lack of experience in the field. She needed *something*, anything, and this was the first viable option in more than a year.

Anything was better than working at the club. Anything, *anything* to help pay off her debts to the Wolf. The Wolf's real name was Wolfgang Meyer, but the nickname was much more fitting. He was an apex predator, cunning and shrewd. He was a man who only accepted payments on time. Otherwise, well, there was a reason people very, very rarely paid late. A reason he had earned the nickname the Wolf.

Applying to work for James Kane would help her in more ways than one. She wouldn't have to suffocate at the club almost every night and she would have a second avenue of income that would keep her payments on time. And maybe, possibly, pay off her debts more quickly. And if she was really dreaming, maybe she could eventually go back to school and finish her bachelor's degree.

But Emma knew better than to hope.

Hope had gotten her involved with the Wolf in the first place.

Now here she was, hoping anyway, waiting in a room with a dozen others to interview for the job.

The building's interior was sleek and modern, exactly as Emma had expected. She wondered how they kept the gleaming marble floors so clean, especially with the terrible weather lately. She wanted to tiptoe so as not to scuff it. There was tasteful modern art on the walls and a couple of seating areas composed of uncomfortable-looking chairs. It looked exactly like the building for a pharmaceutical and technology giant like Kane Industries should.

Name after name was called. Even with appointments for interviews, the number of people applying surprised Emma. Mostly women.

Those waiting whispered among themselves. They craned their necks every time the door to the office at the end of the hallway opened and closed. Emma listened to their idle gossip without participating. She didn't particularly care about James Kane. Just the job.

"Do you think he's hiring based on looks?" one woman asked with a smirk as she tugged her low-cut shirt even lower. Emma hoped he wasn't. Mostly because that was what guys like the Wolf did. It wouldn't surprise her, though, and a small part of her mind started wondering if her simple business attire was good enough. Maybe she should have put more effort into her looks. Maybe she should have dipped into her emergency funds for a new outfit. The thought made her feel sick, but she was desperate.

"I wonder how much I could get for a photo of him from TMZ," another woman said. There was a chorus of nervous laughs. They all had to leave their cell phones behind in little baskets at the reception desk, but that didn't mean that everyone complied.

When her name was finally called, Emma stood on shaky legs.

She entered the office to find an older man, in his forties or maybe fifties. She knew what James Kane looked like the same way anyone in the city did, from paparazzi photos on his extremely rare outings, and this man definitely wasn't him. The man before her had the beginnings of salt and pepper in his hair, a trim beard, and was dressed immaculately, not a single wrinkle or piece of lint to be found. He even had cufflinks at his wrists that glimmered as they caught the light.

"Have a seat, Ms. Warner," he said in a pleasant voice. "I'm Douglas Ramos, Mr. Kane's cousin and COO here at Kane Industries. I'll be conducting your interview today."

Emma wasn't sure whether or not she was disappointed that James Kane wasn't there. It *was* a position as his personal assistant, after all. She'd heard of Douglas Ramos, too, the same way she knew what James Kane looked like. The paparazzi like to bring up how brave Douglas had been at age twenty to step up and take over as legal guardian after the shocking murder-suicide of the Kanes.

Douglas started telling her the job requirements, most of which required discretion, several NDA contracts, and regular hours during the week. Then he asked her all typical job interview questions, went over her resume, and asked what her expectations were for pay and benefits. He didn't even stumble over her listed position at the Crescent Club despite its bad reputation. She thought she did well listing her strengths and how a job bartending would help her be a personal assistant to a billionaire, on top of her degree. It was all bullshit, really, but she hoped it convinced Mr. Ramos of how hard she would work.

When she told him the pay she'd like to make—after having looked up similar jobs online—Douglas Ramos smiled. To her, eighteen dollars an hour sounded like the top end of reasonable, especially since she had a college degree. But the man's smile unnerved her. Had she asked for too much?

"I believe Mr. Kane would also agree that twenty-four an hour would be acceptable."

Emma stared. And stared. She realized she had been staring, speechless, for too long. Her heart pounded in her chest. Twenty-four dollars an hour, even with barely any shifts, would change her *life*. To some, it wasn't much, but to her it was unbelievable.

"I wow, yes, that's—that's perfectly acceptable," she finally managed to stammer.

"I have to say, I really think I've found the person for the position," he continued, as if her heart rate wasn't high enough already. "I have to finish today's interviews. Then I'll have to clear it with Mr. Kane first, of course, but your application seems very promising." He smiled kindly as he stood.

"I–thank you. Wow, thank you," she said, words tripping over themselves in shock. She stood and shook his hand eagerly. "You have no idea how much this means to me. Really."

"I'll give you a call tomorrow most likely, as long as Mr. Kane is amenable." Douglas stood and gestured to the door.

Emma hesitated and then blurted, "Why me?" She immediately clamped her mouth shut. Heat settled in her cheeks. "I'm sorry–I don't mean to sound ungrateful. I just…my resume doesn't exactly scream prior experience." She winced. What she didn't add was that it seemed too good to be true. And she'd already learned the hard way that when things seemed too good to be true, they were.

Douglas seemed to soften a bit. "My dear, you seem plenty qualified. And, most importantly, you're the only one who didn't ask after Mr. Kane upon seeing me." He chuckled to himself. "I'll call you tomorrow and let you know if the position is yours."

She thanked him again and walked to the elevators with her head in the clouds.

Emma couldn't help the bubble of hope that grew in her chest. With the hours and the pay and the benefits…she would be doing so, so well. She could still work at the club one or two nights on the weekend, and she would pay off her debts in–she quickly tried to do the mental math. Two or three years, maybe. And that was if she found a nicer apartment to rent. If she continued living in her shitty apartment, she could pay off the Wolf even sooner.

She barely slept that night.

Because, despite her best efforts, hope sank its sharp claws within her and wouldn't let go. She imagined how she would spend her first paycheck, all the things she needed but could barely afford with the meager remains of her checks from the Crescent Club. Her mind swirled with one imagined budget for spending more on herself and one for paying the Wolf the most.

But–*but*–what was she willing to deal with in exchange? A handsy billionaire? How far would she go for the money? Not far, she decided. Just because he was rich didn't mean he could get away with anything he wanted. She would only put up with what she did at the Crescent Club, and nothing more. She didn't want to compromise herself just to get out of debt. Not anymore than she already had.

The next morning, a call from an unknown number woke her early.

"Hello, Emma Warner speaking," she answered breathlessly. She squinted at the weak light coming through her broken blinds and rubbed the sleep from her eyes. She sat up straighter. This was it, the phone call where they said they made a mistake, that they had chosen someone more qualified and experienced for the position.

"Good morning," Douglas Ramos's warm voice answered. "I'm calling to formally offer you a position."

Shock reverberated through her body like a splash of ice-cold water.

"Are you there?" Douglas asked after a full minute of silence.

"Yes! Sorry, yes, I accept, absolutely." Tears pricked her eyes. She was still dreaming, right? This wasn't actually happening?

"You haven't even heard the full offer yet," Douglas said with a light laugh. "Mr. Kane would like to offer you not only the pay we discussed yesterday but also comprehensive health benefits and…well, I understand it's rather unusual, but he also offered one of our many guest suites for your use. You would still work the same hours, but live on the property."

Her jaw fell open with an audible pop. "I–That's very generous of Mr. Kane, but I couldn't possibly afford–"

"Rent free, of course," Douglas continued as if she hadn't spoken. "And it would not be taken from your pay either. The rest of the staff live on the property as well, myself included."

Something in the way he said it clicked in Emma's brain. "You mean Mr. Kane wants to keep an eye on everyone to better protect his privacy. Don't you?" Hastily she added, "I don't mean to be rude." Emma clenched her jaw shut. Her mouth always got her into trouble. Thankfully, she didn't add the *rest* of the thought–that maybe keeping her close came with other expectations as well.

"No, not rude at all, but perceptive. Yes, I believe that that is Mr. Kane's thinking in his offer. That, and he *is* actually quite generous, once you get to know him. No need to accept the offer right away. You have my direct number. Please let us know by next Monday your decision, in case we need to fill the position elsewhere."

Brain whirring a mile a minute, she said, "No. I mean, yes, I accept. When can I start?"

Rent free and not deducted from her pay. Health benefits. Regular hours. Weekends off. Living in a fucking *mansion*. It was definitely too good to be true. If something bad happened, she could always quit. She just needed to go over the termination clauses in her contract before she signed. She could survive on what she made now at the club, had been doing so since her mother died. Plus, she'd paid her rent through the end of the month, so she had a couple of weeks to figure it out. After that, though…her landlord loved to remind her any time her rent was even a second late about the "dozens of people" who would snatch up the apartment at a moment's notice.

"I can pick you up Monday, give you time to pack and get your affairs in order. Unless you need to work out a notice with a previous employer?"

"No, I'm–Monday is perfect. Thank you so much." Even if she needed to work out a notice with the Wolf, her shifts were always late nights and weekends, which wouldn't interfere with her starting Monday.

They hung up, and Emma had to bite her lip to keep from cheering aloud.

Things were really starting to look up.

Her next order of business was to request a meeting with the Wolf before her shift that night. She needed to explain her job situation and ask to quit. There was no such thing as a two week notice with the Wolf–he either let you quit, or he didn't.

If shit was going to hit the fan, it would be in this meeting.

Surely, *hopefully*, the Wolf loved money enough to let her do this in exchange for paying him more quickly. She didn't care if he raised her debt or interest rate, either. Anything to get out from under his thumb. It would be worth it. Especially now that she didn't have to worry so much about pay. She could be free from the Wolf, from the Crescent Club. From men who thought she owed them something.

For the first time in years, Emma let herself imagine it. She could be *free.*

The Wolf's reputation, though…she knew he didn't like to lose what was his. And even though she wasn't *really* his, she was his employee and owed him a severe debt, which made her beholden to him.

Her hands shook the entire way up to the Wolf's office. It was a plush space with a wide two-way mirror that allowed him to look out over the club without being seen. Unlike the Art Deco themed club proper with its patterned marble floors and golden accents, the Wolf's private office was understated and comfortable, yet luxurious. Lots of dark, thick carpets and velvet couches and chairs.

The Wolf was a tall, skinny man with too many scars to count. He was ugly and he was mean, but he was also the smartest person she had ever met. There was a reason his business flourished, both the legal and illegal kind. And there was a reason he'd never been caught. Emma never saw him give orders, but his orders were followed all the same. The only things he directly had a hand in were "legitimate" businesses, like the club itself and the chain of pharmacies he owned.

All of this was based on rumors, of course. The Wolf's reputation preceded him everywhere he went.

After she explained the situation, all the Wolf did was lean back on his velvet couch and look her over with a smirk. He was so skinny he looked unhealthy. His skin stretched tight over his bones, his flesh more scarred than not. Every flash of the lights from outside the two-way mirror threw the scars on his face into sharp relief. "Sucked James Kane's dick for a job, did ya? I thought you were too good for that sort of thing."

His tone was casual. So casual that Emma felt a tiny spark of optimism in her chest.

The Wolf sat forward in one easy, predatory movement. He rested his elbows on his knees, fingers steepled beneath the sharp jut of his chin. "Here's how this is going to work," he said in a flat tone that sent a chill skittering over her skin. "You'll still work for me, but in more limited shifts. And since your new job is so cushy, I'll be adding seven percent interest to your debt. How does that sound?"

Emma's throat went dry. It didn't sound good, not at all. The freedom she had just gotten a glimpse of was gone like the snap of a finger. But what choice did she have? She'd heard the rumors of people who wronged the Wolf. Missing in the middle of the night, returned with fewer fingers or toes or eyes.

She swallowed hard around the dryness in her throat. There was nothing she could do except to say, "That sounds great. Thank you, sir."

The Wolf smiled without it ever reaching his eyes. She was reminded suddenly, vividly, of a shark documentary she and her mother watched near the end of her mother's life. The Wolf's gaze looked dead-eyed, just like the sharks in that documentary. He glanced over at the thug who'd slapped her the other night after the incident with the handsy man.

"Well, good for you. Got yourself an extra job sucking dick and I get myself an extra seven percent interest."

Emma clenched her teeth so tightly it hurt. "Thank you for your generosity." Because that's what he wanted, what he liked. The ass-kissing. The gratitude. She told herself that seven percent didn't matter, not in the long run. It could be much, much worse. And she told herself, too, that the rumors about what she did for James Kane didn't matter.

But of course it mattered. It all mattered, because somehow she'd gotten more tangled up in the Wolf's web than ever.

The Wolf laughed. "Have fun working for that pretty boy. He's too busy partying to run his own company, so being his *assistant* should be a real treat. At least he isn't trouble, like his mother." He winked as he heavily emphasized the word *assistant*. "As long as his bed's kept warm, right?"

He waved a dismissive hand for her to leave.

Emma ignored the pit of worry in her stomach. James Kane couldn't possibly be as much of a creep as the Wolf.

The rain started up again in the early hours before dawn on Monday morning with no signs of letting up. Emma barely slept, her nerves wound tight. She was waiting for the other shoe to drop.

It happened with school, when she had to stop after two years when her mother got sick. It happened when she first approached the Wolf and gotten a loan so they could pay for her mother's treatments, only for her to die anyway. It happened when she was offered a position at the Crescent Club, only for it to be a job full of sexual harassment and punishment for sticking up for herself.

It seemed natural that it would happen again now. The Wolf had her in his snare but let her off too easily.

Either way, Emma's bags were packed. Her meager belongings waited patiently by the door. She resented her tiny, shitty apartment since circumstances forced her out of the one she had grown up in—just her and her mother, all those years. Now her mother was gone, and all that remained of their life together was crammed into a small cardboard box. That box was really all that mattered. Emma had only bothered to pack it, her clothes, and her quilt and pillow. Everything else was staying in the apartment. She wouldn't tell the landlord until the end of the month that she was moving out. Just in case that shoe did finally drop.

A soft knock sounded at the door.

She opened it to see Douglas, who was startlingly dry for all the rain roaring down from the sky outside.

"Good morning," she said. Her heart raced. She half-expected him to be there to tell her he was on his way to pick up the *real* candidate, that they made a mistake in hiring her after all.

"Good morning. Shall I help you with your belongings?"

She wondered, briefly, at the fucking COO of Kane Industries helping her move, but then again, he was her new boss's cousin. Douglas raised James Kane after his parents died. So maybe it wasn't so strange, when she thought of it as family helping family.

Douglas's car was understated in the way that only a really expensive car could be. Even with the terrible weather, it gleamed as if new. Maybe it was. Emma didn't know enough about cars, and especially the more expensive ones, to be able to tell if it was.

They loaded her things in a flash, barely long enough for either of them to get wet.

The ride to her new job, her new life, was quiet. Soft classic rock played underneath the drumming of the rain. Douglas didn't ask her questions. She didn't know if it was because he wasn't a talkative guy or if he could sense her nervousness from a mile away. And, to her relief, he didn't try to flirt with her, didn't try to touch her. Nothing. She didn't feel uneasy around him like she did with so many of the patrons at the club.

Kane Manor was just barely inside of city limits, close to everything while still separate enough to scream *wealthy*. A wrought-iron gate, connected to a brick wall that stretched around the property, swung open to reveal a long driveway lined with trees. In front of the gate was a guard hut; the guard waved them by when he saw Douglas.

As they wound their way up the drive, Douglas explained the security system to her. Cameras all along the walls, alarms, security guards patrolling and watching the gate. Security never came near the house except in an emergency. He also gently explained that she likely wouldn't see much of the master of the house. He tended towards the nocturnal and often went out for most of the night and slept during the day. The way Douglas said it was almost affectionate. A pang of loneliness went through Emma at the tone that made her miss her mom.

All at once, the long driveway revealed a massive structure made of beautiful, gloomy gray stone. White trim adorned the windows, and stained glass framed the heavy front door made of dark, carved wood. She noted that the hedges were slightly overgrown, the grass of the extensive lawn just shy of unkempt, and the fountain at the center dried up despite all the rain. The manor loomed over them, the gray of its walls blending in with the angry clouds.

They pulled around to the back of the house.

"I've given security your information and identification. You're free to come and go as you please, of course, but we ask that you simply alert the guards at the gate each time you leave and come back for your own safety." Douglas parked the car in a small spot near a door in the back. There was a large lawn behind them, leading into a line of trees. "Your rooms will be on the second floor. My rooms are on the same hall, while Mr. Kane's are on the first floor. The kitchen, library, pool house, and stables are free for you to use whenever you would like. The basement, however, is completely off limits. There is a code to enter, but I figured I would warn you. It's Mr. Kane's private study and he doesn't like to be disturbed."

They grabbed her meager possessions and entered through the back door into a massive pantry. It led into a kitchen that was, by itself, larger than the apartment she just left behind. Emma tried to surreptitiously wipe sweaty palms on her jeans. Everything smelled clean but there was an underlying scent of dust and decay that made her think that few people ever visited the mansion. Nerves jangled inside her, and she had to wipe off her hands again. She'd never been in a place so big, so old, so blatantly made of money. She tried to take a moment and look it all over like it didn't overwhelm her.

"We'll pause for some paperwork, if you don't mind. Then I'll take your things upstairs for you to get settled."

Waiting on the kitchen island was a stack of paperwork that included the typical employee and tax forms, health benefit contracts, and a thick stack of contracts that included heavily binding NDAs. From what she gathered, she could say she worked at Kane Manor and her job title, but that was it. She couldn't mention James Kane, his comings and goings, or anything else about the house or the company to anyone other than James Kane himself and Douglas. Posting any photographs of the house, grounds, or the occupants was entirely forbidden, unless it was of her private rooms. Breaking the contract would result in her immediate firing pending a lawsuit.

Maybe even killed, Emma thought almost hysterically as her head swam and she signed all the forms.

Thankfully, there was nothing in the many, many forms preventing her from quitting on a whim.

Douglas made them tea while she signed paper after paper. She preferred coffee but would take whatever caffeine she could get to help her through the intimidating forms. He remained silent, reading a newspaper with his own cup of tea. Not talkative, she decided. She didn't mind the quiet because it helped her focus on the legal jargon. She wished she had a lawyer to help, but could never afford one. She was paranoid that she was missing something important in the contracts.

In the midst of signing, she caught a glimpse of black in her peripheral vision in time to see a figure disappear down the hallway. Somewhere in the house, a door slammed.

Her new boss?

Douglas didn't seem to notice, still engrossed in his newspaper. Emma mentally shrugged and went back to the task at hand.

By the time she finished the contracts, the dregs in her cup had gone cold.

Her neck cracked as she looked up. "All done. I think."

Douglas flipped through the papers and seemed satisfied. He didn't look too carefully at them. Maybe he was saving that for later, she decided, for a lawyer they no doubt had on retainer. "Now that's done, let's get you settled," he said.

As they made their way up a staircase tucked into a corner of the kitchen, Douglas's soft voice kept up the narration from earlier. "I would also ask you not to disturb the late Mr. and Mrs. Kane's rooms on the third floor. They have been...kept the same since their passing."

"Of course," she murmured. Obviously, the mention of forbidden rooms–including the basement–piqued her interest, but she needed this job more than she needed to satisfy her curiosity. Besides, she wouldn't want anyone poking through her mom's things either.

They stepped onto the first landing at the very end of a long hallway. There was a round stained-glass window that overlooked the estate below. Far down at the opposite end of the hallway was another matching window, both done with intricate patterns of deep blue and red. The inside of the house was all wood and stone, the interior as cold and gloomy as the exterior. The smell of dust permeated the air, stronger than downstairs. Emma felt a cool breeze and thought that she wouldn't be surprised if a ghost drifted past her.

"You'll have the rest of the day to get settled and explore, if you'd like. You'll officially start tomorrow morning. We can get you set up in an office then. This door here belongs to me. And...here you are."

Douglas stopped at the next door on the hallway.

"I'll leave you to it. Text me if there's anything you need." He set her stuff politely beside the closed door. "Oh—we all usually fend for ourselves with meals. The kitchen is fully stocked, so help yourself and use whatever you need. We have groceries delivered every Monday, so let me know if there's anything in particular I can get for you." With that, Douglas disappeared back down the stairs.

Emma opened her mouth then closed it again. Free groceries, too? That seemed like too much. She could get her own things, maybe a small fridge for her room to keep them in. She didn't want to be a burden to them, to be beholden to them. Her luck had changed, but she didn't want to push it.

Pushing open the door to her home, Emma swallowed her apprehension.

She had to use the doorjamb to hold herself up when she saw what was before her.

The plural of *room* hadn't been a mistake. Besides the bedroom there was a giant bathroom and walk-in closet. It was the size of at least two, if not three, of her apartments. Someone had recently cleaned it, so it was free of dust, though the furniture was a bit out-dated. There was a thick comforter and set of pillows on the bed that looked to be the newest things in the room. Everything was a muted gray with blue and green accents, perfectly matching the gray stone and ivy of the façade outside.

There was a small couch, an armchair, a desk, a fireplace…her head spun. This alone was such a luxury compared to what she had just come from. And she had the run of the house when she wasn't working, save for a few off-limits areas. Kitchen, library, all the grounds, pool house, *stables*…

Taking a deep breath, Emma began unpacking her things. Her clothes barely took up a quarter of the closet.

She set her photographs on the dresser and bedside table. One of her as a baby with her mother—still glowing with youth and young love, not long before her father left them. Another of them when she was a teenager, at one of New Atlas's music festivals. High school graduation, a "vacation" they had taken that was just two days in a row at the park nearby. Another from when her mother was sick, the last photograph of them together. Around the photos went other various sentimental items, including a little toy her mother won at the music festival, and cards from an old boyfriend of her mom's, a cop named Oscar Kendrick who had always doted on them both. The breakup had been amicable, but he still tried to keep up with Emma. He'd been her only friend at the funeral. He still sent her Christmas and birthday cards, still teased her for calling him by his last name as if she were a cop, too.

Already Emma could tell that the house was gloomy and barely lived in. The pervading smell of dust in the air, the oppressive silence, the lack of any other people, even staff. She flung open the heavy drapes in her new room. With a satisfied nod, she resolved to open more curtains in the house. Maybe bring in some fresh flowers to her room once in a while. Douglas told her that the gardener and groundskeeper–a married couple–lived in a cottage farther out on the property. Maybe she could ask one of them for permission to pick flowers sometimes. If not, a cheap bouquet here and there wouldn't break the bank. Not anymore.

It would take some getting used to. But she would work hard. She would save money. She would pay off her debts. Then Kane Manor would become something in the rearview on her way to something better.

It wasn't a Cinderella story, but it was a good stepping stone into the rest of her life.

CHAPTER THREE

It was the middle of the night.

Emma couldn't sleep.

She spent the rest of the day in Kane Manor exploring and wishing she had billions of dollars. While she explored the library, the kitchen, the rest of the house, and the grounds outside, she hadn't seen another soul.

After such a busy day, she should have been able to sleep.

But her first day working for James Kane loomed before her, and the bed was too soft and unfamiliar. She slept fitfully for a few hours and now, with dawn closing in, she couldn't go back to sleep. She could feel the emptiness of the manor pressing down on her like a weight. In her apartment, she always heard noises from the other tenants and from the city outside. It was pitiful, but hearing others live their lives nearby helped ease her loneliness most nights. Here, there was nothing other than the occasional gust of wind or softly closing door. Even during the day, a strange, heavy silence pervaded. If she believed in ghosts, she really might think the place was haunted.

Even her usual trick of perusing social media for grainy clips of the Phantom wasn't lulling her back to sleep. In fact, it only made things worse. She thought of him in the lights from her tiny kitchen, his deep voice soothing like waves over sand, the warmth of his skin. She imagined him showing back up to the apartment–to see her, to thank her–and finding it empty.

Those thoughts only made her more awake.

Resigned to working on only a handful of hours of sleep, Emma slipped from between the warm blankets. Bare feet touched icy hardwood floors. She shivered. Might as well take the quilt with her.

Sufficiently bundled, she unlocked her door and quietly padded down the hallway to the stairwell and into the kitchen. She was going to need a lot of caffeine if she was going to survive the day.

A quick raid of the immense pantry revealed absolutely no coffee anywhere. There wasn't even a coffee maker.

With a sigh, Emma found a container of tea bags and set to work with the kettle. At least there was *something* with caffeine in it. She made a mental note to buy herself her own coffee maker with her first paycheck. There was absolutely no way she could live on tea alone. How could anyone live without coffee?

She sighed again as she watched the kettle and waited for it to boil.

There was a creak of floorboards behind her.

She whirled and swallowed a scream.

There was a man standing in the shadows.

"I'm sorry," a low voice said. It was half-familiar. Like a dream that faded upon waking.

James Kane stepped into the soft orange glow of the oven light. His hair was dark and unkempt, but the line of his jaw was sharp. He looked…rumpled. His clothes were too big for his frame. His feet were bare. There was a smudge of darkness under his eyes. She averted her eyes, the NDAs she signed looming in her mind.

He seemed to see her fully for the first time and startled. "What– what are *you* doing here?"

Emma flushed. Not a great introduction if he was asking what she was doing in his house. "I'm–I'm your new assistant. Emma. Warner. Mr. Ramos moved me in earlier and–" She bit her lip. This was the part where she got kicked out.

But James Kane just blinked slowly at her and then nodded once. "I'm sorry I startled you," he said as if he hadn't just taken offense at her presence. He still looked a bit stunned to see her, but continued, "Typically everyone else is asleep at this hour."

"I'm sorry!" Emma said in a breathless rush. She was still bundled up in her quilt. Her face heated even more. Leave it to her to meet her new boss in the most unprofessional way ever. "I can go back to my room, Mr. Kane." She took an uncertain step away. "Mr. Ramos said it was okay to use the kitchen, but I can go."

"James, please," he said so softly she barely heard him. He didn't comment on anything else she said.

"Jamie?" she repeated dumbly. She misheard him, but he didn't correct her.

This was the strangest first meeting with anyone, ever, she decided.

"I'm sorry I startled you," he repeated. "Douglas was right–use whatever you need, whenever you need to." Emma relaxed marginally. The light caught the sharp angle of his jaw. Emma had the strangest feeling that he looked…familiar. But that was stupid. Even as a recluse, his face was recognizable. Mostly because the few times a year he actually showed up in public, the press ate it up. There would be tons of pictures from a single spotting of him, recycled over and over again for months. Of course he looked familiar. He was *James Kane*.

Awkwardly, Emma shuffled in her pajamas and quilt and nodded towards the kettle. "Would you like a cup of tea? I don't–well, I usually drink coffee, but this is all you had."

"No thank you," he said in his quiet, polite voice. "I'm just getting something to eat really quickly."

Something came over Emma in a rush. Before she could think it through, she blurted, "I can make you something." Maybe it was because she felt the need to smooth things over. Maybe it was because she liked to cook for people and hadn't had a chance to in a long, long time. Or maybe it was simply temporary insanity. The entire interaction felt like a dream already. She was his assistant, not his housekeeper or his cook or anything else. She was supposed to do *office* work for him. But she couldn't take the offer back now.

James stopped in surprise. He stepped fully into the meager light. It softened the hard angles of his face. She noticed he was handsome, even rumpled as he was. Pictures didn't do him justice. And he was taller than she'd expected. He was so much more…human in the weak kitchen light.

"You don't have to," he finally said after a long silence.

Emma barely noticed that the kettle had started boiling. Hurrying to fix her tea, she said, "I don't mind. I actually love cooking. Or I did, before…" She trailed off. Before her mom had gotten sick. Before the medical bills piled up. Before her debt to the Wolf.

Before, before, before.

That girl existed a lifetime ago. "Anyway, I don't mind."

She set the tea aside to steep and ungracefully shed her quilt onto a barstool at the kitchen island.

"What do you like to eat?" she asked. She could feel his stare between her shoulder blades as she opened the fridge to see what she had to work with. Everything about this was weird, but at least things seemed to go more smoothly. The fridge–twice the size of the one in her old apartment, of course–was well stocked with almost everything she could ever need.

When she turned, waiting for his answer, she found him squinting at the bright light pouring out of the fridge. Maybe he was drunk?

"Anything, really," he mumbled. He turned his head away from the light.

Emma decided to make hangover food. An omelet was always a good bet. Easy to make, but easy to show off with. She quickly found everything she needed in the neatly arranged cabinets and started chopping vegetables and cracking eggs. Might as well make one for herself, too, she decided. It was close enough to breakfast time.

Emma lost herself in the simple tasks.

Within minutes, she was finished. James had taken a seat on a bar stool. His shoulders were hunched, as if bearing immense weight. For a second, he hardly seemed to notice the omelet in front of him. Then, with a blink, he straightened.

He was almost definitely drunk or had the beginnings of a hangover, she decided, though he didn't smell like alcohol as she might have expected.

"Thank you," he said in his low, deep voice. He took the plate and was gone on silent feet before she could so much as respond.

"You're welcome," she said to the empty kitchen.

Douglas warned her that James went out a lot at night. Maybe he was an alcoholic. The Wolf made a comment about him partying too much to run his own business, too.

She shook herself. It was none of her business. He valued privacy above all else. That much had been clear from the stacks of contracts she signed.

She ate her own omelet and drank her tea in silence.

Once she finished, she headed upstairs to change into something suitable for the rest of the day. She decided to use the main stairs, mostly because the dark back stairway creeped her out a little, at least in the dark.

The sound of raised voices made her pause at the foot of the stairs.

"–obviously not who I expected, Douglas," James Kane was saying. His voice must have carried from his rooms down the hallway underneath the stairs.

Emma barely breathed. His earlier words echoed in her head. *What are* you *doing here?* Maybe he was looking for someone prettier, someone more professional. Her stomach turned over.

"Obviously not," Douglas said. "But don't take your anger out on me. Either be more careful, or fire the girl. Don't string her along if you think you can't do this with her here."

Fire her? James Kane wanted to fire her already? She hadn't even *started*. They'd had *one* interaction, an admittedly weird one, but that was it.

"I'm not going to fire her," James practically growled. "I just–" Whatever he said next was too low for her to hear.

Emma closed her eyes and released her breath in a rush. That's what she got for eavesdropping.

When Emma finally reemerged downstairs for more caffeine, she found Douglas at the kitchen island with a travel mug and the day's newspaper.

"Good morning," he said kindly, as if he hadn't been telling his nephew to fire her an hour ago. "Sleep well?"

"Yes, thank you," she said, even though it was a lie.

"I have a bit of time before I have to head to the office, so let me show you where you'll be working."

Emma followed him up the main stairs, which were wide and led to a balcony that overlooked the foyer and front doors. They took a right, the opposite direction of her rooms, one of the stained glass windows illuminating the hallway red and blue and purple.

"It's a bit dusty, I'm afraid. This office hasn't been used in years."

He wasn't kidding. As soon as he opened the door, she saw boxes and dust everywhere. There was a desk with a computer and a landline phone that were the newest things in the room.

"Part of the issue is that a lot of information needs to be organized and digitized," Douglas explained. He went over her expected duties. The onslaught of new information and the amount of work looming before her quickly overwhelmed her. But they were paying her really, really well, so she would do her best.

Douglas explained that she likely wouldn't deal with Mr. Kane in person—she would simply send requests, questions, and comments to his work email. Or she would consult with Douglas on more urgent matters, and he would pass it along.

After showing her a few more things, Douglas left. He worked in the main Kane Industries building in the mornings and from home for the rest of the day. She wasn't sure which floor his home office was on. Maybe it was the door across from hers. Or, with how extensive her own set of rooms was, maybe he had an office set up in there.

Alone in the dark, dusty office that would become her second home, Emma blew out a breath. Her eyes tracked over the boxes, the desk, the scuffed floor.

Then she yanked open the curtains, revealing a long expanse of grass and trees outside, and got to work.

It was the middle of the night again the next time she saw James Kane.

Her first full week of work passed quickly, busy with setting things up and diving into her new duties. She learned quickly that Douglas did most everything by himself for years–personal assistant work, the kind of stuff a butler did, being the legal guardian for James until he came of age, on top of his job at Kane Industries. So not only was he running an actual business, he was also running the house. No wonder they were hiring someone else.

It was Saturday night. Emma indulged on a rare night off and stayed up late reading. It was a luxury she rarely had while working nights at the Crescent Club. So she'd lost herself in a book and for-gotten dinner. Now it was three in the morning and she was starving.

Bleary-eyed, she stumbled into the kitchen.

She startled silently.

James Kane sat on a stool, slumped onto the counter. It looked like he was…asleep.

Maybe he really did have a drinking problem.

A cup of water and a bottle of painkillers were next to him.

Emma warred internally with herself over what to do. She planned to heat up leftover pasta she'd made the night before. Was it more polite to wake him up first or simply try to be really quiet?

One of his arms was stretched out. His cheek rested on that arm, mouth slightly open. His other hand hung limply in his lap. She stud-ied him for a minute, torn. His lips were full, his dark eyelashes long.

She decided to gently nudge his shoulder.

"Mr. Kane? Sorry–Jamie?" She nudged him again when he didn't move.

He sat up in one sharp movement that had her scrambling back so as not to smack heads with him. He peered around the dark room for a moment. Then he relaxed. His fists unclenched.

"Sorry–I'm about to heat something up to eat and didn't want to startle you. Are you okay?"

His eyes settled on hers. There was something heavy in his gaze. Something almost…wild. She swallowed around a suddenly dry throat. His eyes were green, or maybe blue.

He nodded. "I'm okay." The words rasped out. His voice was used up, as if he'd been shouting. She wondered where he went all the time to party that no one reported on it. Maybe he paid them off.

Her mind flashed to the VIP lounge downstairs at the Crescent Club. If there was any place in this city that wouldn't give out information on its high-profile clients, that was it. Surely she would have heard the rumors though, at least from employees.

James stood with a long groan. For a moment, he leaned his weight on his forearms and seemed to gather himself. Then he pushed himself up and walked away.

She watched him go, wondering at the weird encounter.

But she couldn't deny that she wanted, just a little bit, to solve the mystery of James Kane.

CHAPTER FOUR

JAMES

When James Kane put on the mask of the Phantom, he became someone else entirely.

Maybe that was what drew him to a disguise in the first place. After all, even money could only go so far. And in his experience, money usually only led to more problems, to corruption.

But *fighting*–investigating, stopping crime before it got too far, taking down the corruption and evil in the city night after night–that got him much farther than money ever could.

James had firsthand experience that the justice system, that the *cops*, couldn't be relied on for change. They accused his father of his mother's murder, after all, which drove Jack Kane to suicide shortly thereafter. It didn't matter that James *knew* his father hadn't done it. It didn't matter that he told the cops that. They'd laughed him off, called him "kid" and kept investigating the wrong person.

Now James had no parents instead of at least one.

Now he took justice into his own hands so that no child would ever have to go through what he went through.

James would never admit that a part of him reveled in it, and especially not to Douglas, who already worried constantly about his "nightly activities." He never purposefully killed, never crossed that line, yet there was still something satisfying about the sound of his gloved fist connecting with flesh. He had always been angry, even before his parents, and he had finally found a *good* outlet for that anger.

And for two years, he painstakingly created change in the city as the Phantom. He was removing its corruption brick by brick, every single night for two years.

He stared out over the city from the half-finished steel tower conveniently owned by Kane Industries as he waited for his police contact to show up. The tower was unfinished and would stay that way for eternity, or at least as long as the Phantom needed it for a secret meeting spot. He started working with Detective Oscar Kendrick about a year prior when their paths kept crossing. Kendrick was someone who believed in doing what was right, no matter the cost. In a city as corrupt as New Atlas, Kendrick needed all the help he could get, even if it was in the form of a vigilante who had them meet in secret via burner phones.

James wondered as he waited, not for the first time, if hiring Emma was a mistake. He had to be so much more careful in his own home now. He had to keep things wholly separate when he usually let the lines blur—at least in his home. He knew that when he agreed to hire an assistant and let them live in the manor, but knowing it and living it were two different things.

And he never in a million years expected to see *her* in his kitchen that night. Douglas informed him of the new hire of course, a promising young woman, but it was *her*.

"What are *you* doing here?" He'd asked before he could rein the words in.

That night, the night they'd first met unbeknownst to her, he'd come across a woman several men were trying to rape and managed to stop them—but not before taking a baseball bat to the head and a knife to the side. As he escaped to the rooftops, he saw *Emma*, caged in by a man. Heard her scream. But after he made sure the first woman was safe, he'd come across a burglary suspect who had taken him by surprise. There had been no time to get to Emma.

He'd woken up on the sidewalk aching all over. And there she had been.

Emma.

Her dark hair had been stuck to her forehead, her skin a warm tan, her eyes an even warmer brown. She had a smattering of freckles across her nose, visible in the streetlight that surrounded her with its buttery glow and made all her edges hazy due to the rain or maybe his head injury. She'd saved herself first, and then had saved him.

It was tempting–to bask in her kindness when the city was so often cruel. But he was a danger to her. So, after lingering much too long in her presence, he had hurriedly put his armor back on and slipped out onto the fire escape, becoming another of the many shadows in the night.

But there she was, in his house, no longer a figment of his imagination.

He couldn't get her out of his head since that night, her kindness, her warmth, haunting him. It was a shock to see what was essentially a dream come back to life in front of him.

The rickety elevator behind him rattled its way upwards, bringing him out of his thoughts of Emma. James didn't move. Only he and Kendrick had the code to the elevator, so he wasn't worried about any sneak attacks. Besides, he also had security footage streaming live to his phone and had already seen Kendrick get out of his police car.

"We found a body," Kendrick greeted by way of hello as he stepped off the elevator a minute later. "That makes three missing, one of them dead. She was the second to disappear, a woman named Rebecca Goodwin. They called her Becks."

Something inside James's chest tightened. Three women missing and no one was batting an eye.

Just like when his mom was murdered. Two other women, besides her, had been strangled to death in their cars. But instead, the NAPD focused on Jack Kane. Jack Kane, who had alibis for the first two murders.

The familiar anger stirred within James.

"We found the connection, though, once we got her identity," Kendrick continued. They stood shoulder to shoulder now, staring out over the city they loved that would never love them back. The city that had broken them both, and bonded them in their impossible quest to save it. Kendrick's brother had been murdered, too. He was one of the very few cops who *weren't* corrupt. One who believed in the Phantom, believed in saving the city from itself in any way possible. One who would have looked beyond Jack Kane to figure out who had killed Katherine Kane, had he been the one working the case all those years ago.

"What's the connection?" James asked, his voice pitched unconsciously lower. It was a habit he'd started to round out his disguise, one he never gave thought to anymore. When the mask was on, his voice changed. His posture changed. *He* changed.

"They all worked at the same place. The Crescent Club. Run by a man named Wolfgang Meyer that we've never been able to *formally* connect to anything." The detective's voice thickened with disgust. "He must have connections, because nothing ever sticks. It's impossible to find a judge to sign a warrant for anything relating to him or the club."

James knew of the man that they called the Wolf, and of the club. A vague bell rang in the back of his mind at the mention of the club, but he ignored it.

"Looks like I should go talk to the Wolf," James said, his jaw set with determination. If the police couldn't talk to the Wolf, he would, and he would get answers one way or another.

EMMA

Emma's leg bounced as the Wolf counted her cash, her monthly payment plus seven percent interest. All there, all accounted for, all provided by her new employer James Kane. It was an ungodly amount of cash to carry altogether. She ignored the way the Wolf's bodyguard raked his eyes up and down her bare legs. The Wolf expected a certain level of excellence from everyone and it started with looks. Her shirt was tight with a couple of buttons undone, her black skirt shorter than she would have liked. Yet her uniform—and those of the other servers and bartenders—was a lot more modest than those of any dancers, performers, and everyone else who worked in the VIP club downstairs. They were easy to spot in a crowd because they wore the least amount of clothing.

The Wolf lounged on the cushy velvet sofa in his office. He sat back as if he had absolutely no cares in the world. Emma supposed he didn't. Not when people like her brought people like him envelopes of cash.

"James Kane's paying you well to keep his bed warm then, eh sweetheart?" He chuckled, and the surrounding thugs chuckled right along with him. "Is the house as empty as they say?"

Emma blinked, unsure why the Wolf was asking.

"Yes," she finally said, because there was no use lying. "Besides the security," she added, something uneasy coiling in her stomach.

"And the master of the house, is he always gone?" His dead, shark-like eyes sparkled with a hint of amusement and something else.

Emma hesitated again. "I have no idea," she said, which was pretty much the truth. "I never see much of him whether or not he's home."

"You get your own room or do you have to…share?" The corners of the Wolf's lips curled up slightly at the implication. She opened her mouth, face hot with embarrassment and something worse, but closed it again. The Wolf waved her off. "No matter, long as I get my money some way or another. Get to work. You're at the bar with Ricky tonight."

"Yes, sir," she said through clenched teeth. She hoped the hate didn't show on her face. The fact that she could have been free of him made her want to hit him right in the mouth for telling her *no*. She wished she were someone like the Phantom, able to take care of herself and hurt men like the Wolf. Men who deserved it.

But all she did was smile and *get to work*.

Her shift passed achingly slowly. As she worked, she wondered if the regular patrons were spreading rumors about her. Were they whispering that men who touched her got punched in the face? Or were they whispering that she was James Kane's whore? She hoped it was the first one–because then maybe they would think twice about touching her.

She felt eyes on her, all around her, their gazes heavy and unsettling as she cleaned a thin champagne glass. She imagined she heard them whispering. If James Kane paid her, what could *they* get her to do for money? The people who frequented this club were not good people, no matter what jobs they held during the day. Police officer. Lawyer. Councilman. Doctor. Politician. In this club, they were all the same. Her hand clenched tightly around the glass, tight enough to hurt. They were all men who thought they were owed certain things. Things they paid men like the Wolf to provide for them. She watched as one of those men ran a hand over the ass of a waitress on her way by.

The champagne flute in Emma's hands shattered from the force of her grip.

With a muffled curse, she bent to clean it up. A thin slice opened on her palm and began to sting from the residual alcohol. A drop of blood beaded on the wound, red in the strobing lights of the club.

"Clumsy girl," a man drawled from the bar. "Though I can't say I mind the view."

She could feel his hungry gaze on her ass. It was hot on her skin. The club went quiet, drowned out by the rush of her own rage in her ears.

When she straightened, bloodied palm cradled in her good hand, she realized that the surrounding club had actually gone quiet, as quiet as it could get with blaring music.

On the steps leading up to the Wolf's office was the Phantom.

She blinked furiously. Strobe lights flashed red and white and red again. She saw snapshots of him moving, throwing a punch, catching a blow on his forearm. It was like watching a stop-motion movie. Like flashes of a half-remembered dream. The Wolf's bodyguards were stopping him from pushing his way up the stairs to the office.

He was *here*, in the Crescent Club.

In the next flash, the Wolf was there. He was smiling. The pair exchanged words. Or maybe Wolf spoke while the Phantom listened. Rolled-up sleeves revealed the Wolf's thin forearms, corded with muscles and covered in scars. He pushed his hands into his pockets, the picture of utter ease.

Within a minute, the Phantom followed him up to his office.

What could he *possibly* be doing here?

"Now that's something you don't see every day," the same sleazebag slurred. He smiled up at her from where he drooped over the bar. He had thick eyebrows and a receding hairline. "Reckon he's coming to buy something?" He waggled his eyebrows.

Emma scoffed. "He's probably threatening my boss." She hated calling him that, "her boss." But here, image was everything. And words counted for that, too. She owed an extra five thousand for bad-mouthing the Wolf to one of the other girls back when she'd first been hired after her mom died. It was the reason she was always care-ful here. And the reason she didn't trust any of her fellow employees. The reason she didn't have any friends. Most of them traded infor-mation for the Wolf's favor, for the smallest chance of their debts being lowered, without a care for anyone else. She couldn't blame them. If she were any more desperate, she would do the same thing. Instead, she kept to herself.

"Hey, you're bleeding there, baby," the man cooed. "Let me take you somewhere to patch you up."

She gave the man a tight smile. "No, thank you."

She quickly finished sweeping up the glass and then called to the other bartender, Ricky. She held up her bloody hand in a wave and indicated with her other hand she'd be back in five minutes.

She made her way around the perimeter of the crowd towards the shitty employee bathrooms in the back. At least they were quiet. She grabbed a bandage from her bag in her employee locker and shoved the bathroom door open with her foot.

A drop of dark red blood splashed against the dingy white sink. In the harsh fluorescents, Emma's reflection looked haggard. What was the Phantom doing *here*, of all places? She wanted to burst into Wolf's office. Damn the consequences. She'd thought about the Phantom more times than she cared to admit to herself since that night. She couldn't get him out of her head. What was he *doing* here?

She cursed colorfully as she struggled to bandage the cut one-handed.

The door banged open behind her.

"Occupied, asshole!" she shouted over the music that came blaring through the open door.

The Phantom was a dark shadow against the single bright white light buzzing above them.

It was as if her thoughts had summoned him.

She hated that her heart stuttered the way it did.

"What are you–what are you doing here? You're not supposed to be in here."

"I could ask you the same thing, Emma," he said in a low growl. She closed her eyes and let the sound of his voice wash over her. He remembered her name. He carefully checked outside before shutting and locking the door behind him. "You work here?"

"You remember me?" she asked.

"Of course I remember you." He slid his gloves and gauntlet-looking things off and took the bandage from her. "Did someone do this to you?"

Had someone slipped her something? Why did it feel like a hallucination when she looked at him? The sheer darkness of him, like he was made of shadows, clashed with the brilliance of the fluorescents.

He took her injured hand in both of his. His skin was warm, almost hot. Electricity zinged up and down her arm from the connection of skin on skin. His fingers were rough with calluses but gentle as he fixed the bandage over her torn skin. A bruise marked one of his knuckles.

When was the last time someone touched her so gently? So innocently?

She realized he asked a question. "I broke a glass." Dazed, she watched his long fingers deftly patch her up. "Is this a dream? Is a vigilante really putting a bandaid on me right now? I guess you *did* owe me."

A corner of his lips turned up in a half smile.

"I recognized you," he said quietly. He stepped back from her, which wasn't far in the small bathroom. "I needed to ask if you knew anything about the women who've been disappearing."

She blinked. "What?" she said stupidly. "What women?"

"Three women have disappeared in the past month. Only one body has been found. They all worked here."

Emma slumped against the dirty tile wall. "Three?" she echoed. Her eyes traced the line of his jaw of their own accord. She watched, enraptured, as he put his gloves and gauntlets back on. His eyes were hidden in the shadows of his hood. "I don't–I didn't know anything about that. Is that why you're here? Questioning the Wolf?"

"Yes. He swears he knows nothing. Asked why he would waste a valuable resource."

Her skin crawled at the word. *Resource*. Not *employees*. No care at all for the women themselves. New Atlas had a bad habit of chewing up women and spitting them back out, usually dead, while men like the Wolf looked the other way.

"The Wolf's a piece of shit," Emma spat, "but he's got a point. He values his employees for what they can bring him. And if I didn't know them or about their disappearances…" She hesitated. She could get in a lot of trouble if the Wolf knew she was telling him anything at all. Trouble that got girls killed. But this was the Phantom. He wanted to help. He *would* help. "That means they worked downstairs. There's…that's where…"

The Phantom studied her without expression.

She shouldn't say anything else. He could figure it out from there. She was already too deep in debt to get into any more trouble. "I have to get back to work. See you around."

He moved out of the way as she opened the door. As Emma stepped past him, she realized that the entire time they'd been crammed in the tiny bathroom, he'd stayed out of her personal space, had made an effort not to crowd her.

She quickly made sure no one else was around before hustling back to the bar.

The creep from earlier was gone now, thank God, but now there was the end of the night rush to contend with. Everyone wanted one last drink before closing. A couple of patrons were shown downstairs while everyone else cleared out. Emma's gaze skipped past them with well-practiced ease. She was used to ignoring faces here. If she recognized anyone, if she ever tried to tie them to this place, she would be one of the women who disappeared. No one talked. *No one*.

Her thoughts turned to what the Phantom told her. *Three* women had disappeared? And one was dead? There was no indication that something sinister was happening. At least, nothing more sinister than usual. And something bad was happening if three women had already disappeared. Emma heard about the sort of things that happened downstairs. The sort of men who frequented the space. The meetings that happened between them. The expectations of the women–and a few men–who worked there every night.

As Emma fielded orders and catcalls and mixed and poured drinks, she found herself watching every shadow for a sign of the vigilante. She knew he was long gone by now. But she hoped for one more glimpse of him. Just one.

At least there was one person interested in finding those women.

Finally, finally, last call was over. She cleaned up while Ricky cashed out the register. All of her tips went to the Wolf, of course. And she wasn't totally sure they went towards her debts. She was afraid to ask, in case they didn't. Better not to know.

It hit her then, fully hit her, that those were problems of the past. A single paycheck signed by James Kane had already made a tremendous difference in her life. Exhausted tears pricked her eyes. She only had to do one more night of this for the next week, instead of five more nights. Though she wished she didn't have to work at the club at all, at the very least she got to work there *less*, and that in and of itself was something good.

Emma leaned heavily against the storeroom shelves for a minute, letting that sink in.

She finished restocking the bar feeling lighter than she had in years.

As Emma changed and gathered her things from her locker, her thoughts turned to her encounter with the Phantom. The feeling of his bare hands on hers. The intensity that emanated from him. His quiet, deep voice. She hoped she saw him again.

Her thoughts were still wrapped up in the vigilante as she stepped into the back alley. The bouncer at the back door nodded at her from his post right inside the door. He held his phone in one hand and a small cup of coffee in the other.

Cool air wrapped around her shoulders. The air was as fresh as it got within city limits. A hint of summer came with the breeze. Emma paused and inhaled deeply. She loved this moment every time she left the Crescent Club. The moment she could shake off the night, forget for a little while that she worked there and why.

Someone roughly grabbed her wrist.

"There you are, baby," a voice said. "I've been waiting half the night out here for you."

It was the man from earlier. The one who'd had such a good time watching her clean up broken glass. Emma tried to yank her arm out of his grip. He held on tighter. It seemed as if he'd sobered up quite a bit while waiting. The bones in her wrist ground together painfully.

"Let me go," she said in a low voice. She moved her other hand slowly around to where the taser waited in her back pocket.

"Aw, come on, don't be like that. I heard about your little deal with James Kane." So fast she couldn't act, he grabbed her other wrist. "How much does he pay you for a night? I promise I can compensate you for your time."

"I'm not for sale, asshole," she spat in his face. Fear wrapped ice-cold tendrils around her heart, so tightly she could barely breathe. She should have kept her taser in her hand. She should have kept her gun at her side and should have punched the asshole at the bar earlier and dealt with the consequences later. *Should have, should have, should have.* "If you want to buy someone, you have to be invited downstairs! Now let me *go*."

The man growled and shoved her roughly against the bricks. Pain exploded from the back of her head where it collided with the wall. He still held fast to her wrists. "You bitch," he practically crooned, voice at odds with his words. His lips nuzzled against her ear. She wanted to vomit. To scream. But this was New Atlas. No one came running when someone yelled for help. She had to get free. Had to get to her taser. Had to, before—she couldn't finish the thought. "Fine. Don't accept my generous offer. Besides, what's the saying? Why buy what you can take for free?"

He kissed her full on the mouth right as she tried to scream. He bit her lip, hard, and coppery blood filled her mouth. She thrashed against him. Her struggling was making him more excited. He *liked* feeling powerful.

One of his hands finally gave up one of hers to paw at her chest. She reared back and headbutted him, then made a grab for the taser while he howled in pain and called her every curse word he could think of.

Right as Emma's taser lit up the flesh on the inside of his thigh, he was yanked roughly off his feet from behind.

The Phantom's fist connected with the man's face once. Twice. Three times. Four.

"You couldn't have stepped in *sooner*?" she shouted at the Phantom as he tossed the now-unconscious man to the ground. "You fucking—he could have—he—"

The Phantom turned to face her. Her words stuttered to an abrupt halt.

"I'm sorry," he said, the words half a growl. His jaw was clenched tight. She couldn't see his eyes under the shadow of his hood. "I couldn't tell that anything was wrong at first. I saw him waiting out here, but—"

She shoved both of her hands into his chest. "You asshole!" He didn't budge in the slightest. All at once, the fight left her. She wiped furiously at her neck where the man's disgusting lips had touched her, then at her bloodied lip. She needed a shower. Or some bleach. Or bleach and then a shower. She spat out a mouthful of blood. She may or may not have aimed it at the man on the ground. Then she aimed a vicious kick at his side.

"I'm sorry," the Phantom said again in his low, gravelly voice. "Although I am impressed with how you handled yourself."

Emma huffed a humorless laugh. "Yeah, well. It's New Atlas. People who don't *at least* have pepper spray are idiots. Especially because *you* can't be everywhere at once." Did she imagine it, or did something like hurt pass over what she could see of his face? Backtracking, she quickly added, "Thank you. By the way. Feel free to hit him a few more times if you want. And…thanks for patching me up earlier."

He stared at her for a long moment. "You're welcome," he finally said.

"I should let you get back to…crime fighting. I have to get home." She didn't want to leave, but she was starting to feel this long night in her bones. She wanted to sleep all day, to sleep until her next shift. She wanted to quit this job. She tried to hide the shaking of her hands by clenching them into fists. The one with the cut gave a throb.

"Be careful, Emma," he said. The neon from the club's sign out front sliced down the alley and lit his profile in yellow and purple.

"I will." She pressed the button on the taser for emphasis and watched its satisfying zap. She thought she caught the ghost of a smile before he disappeared into the darkness at the end of the alley.

She didn't notice his shadow following her to the subway station, making sure she arrived safely.

CHAPTER FIVE

Emma made it all of two steps into the kitchen of Kane Manor before she sank into a crouch. The adrenaline wore off somewhere on the subway. She made the rest of the trip back in a daze.

Now, on the floor of a billionaire's kitchen, she struggled to get breath into her lungs. Her head ached. She still tasted blood. Her skin prickled as if it were covered in ants. She would never get the feeling of that man's lips and hands and *teeth* off of her. Even remembering the sound of the Phantom's fist connecting with flesh didn't help.

She slid further onto the floor, head on her knees and arms over her head. She couldn't breathe.

If the Phantom hadn't been there, what would have happened? What if the taser hadn't worked? What if she had dropped it? That man was going to–to–she couldn't even think it. It was a reality in New Atlas, and especially working at the Crescent Club, but the danger had never been so *close*. And it was the *second* time recently, the first being the night she'd met the Phantom. How could she have been so stupid?

"Emma?" came a familiar voice. She had no idea how long she'd been on the floor. She looked up at James through blurry eyes. He was crouched before her, a line of concern etched between his eyebrows. She hadn't heard him come in. "Are you alright?"

"I'm fine," she croaked. But she wasn't. What person who was "fine" would be curled up on the floor crying? "I just had a shitty night." She scrubbed furiously at her eyes. God, he was going to think she was nuts.

He was quiet for a long moment. He stayed crouched there, silent, simply watching her and letting her gather herself. Something about his presence was reassuring. Steadying.

Finally, she said, "I was just reminded tonight how—how fucked up New Atlas can be. And it wasn't even that bad." She bit her lip then winced at the pain. "It turned out okay. I'm just…shaken."

James watched her with eyes that missed nothing. "Are you sure you're alright? Would you…like something to eat?" His dark hair was mussed and slightly too long. She almost laughed. The words seemed to pain him. Like he had no idea how to comfort someone who was upset.

"No, thank you." She struggled awkwardly into a standing position. James rose in one fluid, graceful motion and offered her a hand. She stared up at him before taking it. His palms were callused and cool to the touch. Standing after so long had the blood rushing back to her feet. "Ow," she said. She gingerly poked the back of her skull. There was already a decent lump. A flash of memory of her head hitting the brick wall came and went.

James went to the freezer, squinting at the light, and came back with a bag of frozen peas.

"May I?" he asked. She nodded. He was standing close, so close she could feel his body heat. He smelled of fresh soap and men's shampoo. She let her eyes close as he gently pressed the frozen peas to the back of her head. His breath stirred her hair. His other hand fluttered to her shoulder and then away, like he wasn't sure whether or not to touch her.

"Thank you," she said in a whisper. She opened her eyes again to see him watching her carefully. *This is not a Cinderella story*, she firmly reminded herself. Their lives could never mesh. They would never be equal.

He gently took her uninjured hand in his free one. Her heart stuttered to a stop. But all he did was put her hand on the bag of peas so that she was the one holding it. Then he took a step back.

"New Atlas might be fucked up," he said. "But it's not all bad."

Her thoughts turned to the Phantom. No, New Atlas wasn't all bad.

Her gaze flickered to James. And maybe not all of those with money and power were bad, either.

James was still watching her.

"You're a mystery, James Kane," she murmured. A mystery she wanted to solve. She wanted to find the cracks in him and press until she saw what was underneath. What kind of man was he really?

"Goodnight, Emma," was all he said. And like every other time they'd crossed paths, he was gone as quickly as he'd come.

Emma scrubbed the night off in the shower and then slept for several blissful hours. She spent the day in bed with a headache and only got up when it was time to go back to the Crescent Club. She would keep her taser in her hand this time. And she wouldn't expect to be saved by the Phantom again. As she told him, he couldn't be everywhere at once.

When she arrived at the club, the Wolf's right-hand man, Murray, was handing out their assignments for the night. The Wolf was in charge of finalizing shifts, assignments, and everything else. Murray was the one who carried it out.

She was a server that night. That meant walking to the tables around the edges of the walls. Making small talk. Smiling prettily when men gave her disgusting *compliments*. She clenched her fists so hard the cut from the previous night started bleeding again. She'd been lucky bartending more often than not as of late, but had known that luck wouldn't last.

This shift wasn't as long, though, thankfully. Time to clock out came quickly; she changed and left in less than five minutes. She peered out of the back door before exiting, taser firmly in one hand.

As Emma walked down the alley, a figure dropped from the fire escape above her. She had the taser up and crackling before she noticed the mask and cape.

"It's you," she said with obvious relief. "Are you following me?" She didn't lower the taser.

"Yes," the Phantom said. She blinked in surprise. "I need your help."

She lowered the taser, curiosity blazing just as brightly in its place. "With what?"

"These disappearances. I tried to get more information about the downstairs part of the club you told me about. No one will bite." He fell into step beside her as she continued to the subway station. Well, at least no one would bother her now, she thought with a wry smile. Not with her scary companion. "Can you get down there? Get information for me? I tried finding another way in, or someone else to give me information, but I can't." He sounded frustrated by the fact.

She stopped walking. "I…" A million thoughts churned in her mind at once. "I don't think so. It's…not…a good place to work for someone like me. For anyone, really. Those girls that work down there, they're either desperate for money or power or both. Or Wolf has something on them and forces them to. It's not…it's not as simple as just waitressing and bartending down there."

She only knew any of it from rumors. It was a mix of the club upstairs, but where the patrons–the richest and most powerful people in New Atlas–could get sex or drugs or a lap dance or anything else they wanted. The women who worked down there supposedly didn't *have* to do anything with the patrons, but they could keep their tips from whatever *activities* they participated in. And those tips were always significant.

The Phantom stared down at her. His eyes darted over her face. "Alright."

"I'm sorry," she said, and she was. "I want to help. Just, after last night–"

"I understand," he said. She was relieved that he didn't push her. Her mind whirled with thoughts of the patrons downstairs, who were like the ones upstairs except *worse*. She remembered the man cornering her outside in the alley and shuddered.

"Can you teach me to fight?" she blurted after a moment of walking in silence. She vividly remembered the ease with which he took out the Wolf's men inside the club. "When you're not too busy, I mean. Fighting crime and whatever else you do. I work here pretty much every weekend. Or we can exchange numbers? No, that'd be weird. Secret identity and all." She wanted to smack herself. She had to grit her teeth to keep from continuing her rambling. "I'm sorry. You make me nervous."

"Do I scare you?" he asked.

Emma blushed. No, he didn't scare her. He *mesmerized* her. She thought about him constantly. "No," she finally said. She hoped he couldn't tell how hot her face was. That he couldn't tell what she was thinking.

When she finally braved a glance at his face, he seemed almost…bewildered. But it was hard to tell with the mask covering most of his face and the hood throwing shadows on the rest. She wondered how it stayed on his head. Was it attached to the mask? She almost asked.

"I don't want to feel helpless," she said instead. "I don't want a hero to have to save me next time."

"I can teach you some things. But don't get rid of that taser."

She smiled up at him. "Don't worry, I have a gun too."

He *definitely* looked bewildered, his eyes wide and full lips slightly parted.

Emma lay in bed later that night unable to sleep. A thrill of excitement kept shooting through her at the thought of spending more time around the Phantom. Him teaching her to fight. Watching out for her. Her mind kept bouncing back and forth between the memory of him in her tiny apartment kitchen and his steady hands bandaging her in the bathroom at work.

When she eventually fell asleep, she dreamt of a man in the shadows watching over her.

Emma was in the middle of drafting three emails the following evening when she sensed someone standing at her shoulder.

She glanced up at James with cheeks already heating in embarrassment just from his presence. She was *almost* getting used to him sneaking up on her. Normally they communicated by sticky notes. His handwriting was slanted, sloppy, like he was in a hurry. She had also recently implemented an inbox and outbox outside her office door on a small shelf. The next day, a sticky note appeared in her inbox that said she could leave stuff on a shelf outside James's bedroom in a similar setup. So far it was working well. He apparently responded better to the clutter outside his bedroom than to that within his email inbox.

"Can you move the meeting tomorrow from five to three?" he asked slightly guiltily. He shuffled nervously from foot to foot.

She blinked dumbly at him for a second, unused to actually seeing him *in* her office. "Um, yeah, sure, no problem," she finally said and scrawled herself a note to do so right after she finished her current task.

He was staring at her intensely when she looked up. She flushed again and pushed back the bangs she was still growing out. He glanced away and gently touched a fingertip to one of the flowers she'd picked that morning. The gardener had been all too happy to show her around and let her take whatever she wanted for a bouquet. She had one on her dresser now, too. She had greatly enjoyed the company along with the quiet lesson on various plants, herbs, and flowers.

Emma turned back to her computer and typed another sentence in her email.

"Thank you," she said after a moment. It was easier to say the words without looking at him. "For the other night. For checking on me."

There was a long moment of silence. She glanced over her shoulder. James had his back to her. She opened her mouth, then closed it. Maybe he hadn't heard her.

But then he said, "You're welcome."

After a few minutes, she switched over to their joint calendar and started rearranging stuff to make the meeting happen at three instead of five. She expected him to leave. To disappear like he had every other time their paths had crossed. But he didn't. He shifted the vase of flowers into a sunnier spot.

He looked up and caught her watching him. "Sorry," he said with another guilty expression. "These are nice."

"Thanks. Well, I guess I should thank you, as they're from your garden." She swiveled in her chair to face him fully. "Mr. Banks is really nice. Said he's been here since before you were born."

James smiled faintly. "Yeah, they're both great. I don't visit as much as I used to."

Emma smirked. "They might have mentioned that a time or two." From what she could tell, Mr. and Mrs. Banks were very fond of James and Douglas both. They had dinner with Douglas almost every week.

An alert pinged on her computer with an email reply.

They sat in companionable silence for a few more minutes while she responded.

"Why do you work at the Crescent Club?" James asked. She almost choked in surprise.

"I–What? How do you know I work there?"

He blinked. "Your resume."

Idiot, she chided herself. Of course. "I–" She struggled against a lie for a moment. She didn't want him to know about her debt to the Wolf. So she settled for a half-truth. "It was the only job I could find after my mother died. And I…still need the extra money. Her medical bills decimated our bank account. And these days it's hard to even find one job, let alone two…so I decided to work there on the weekends, too." She swallowed. It sounded better than the real story, where the Wolf wouldn't *let* her quit, where her debt increased simply from trying to make her own life a little better. She hoped it wasn't an issue. Douglas hadn't seemed to mind, but James was her actual boss.

"Of course," he murmured. He stared blankly at the flowers. "I lost my parents, too. As you probably know. I'm…sorry that happened to you."

"It sucks, doesn't it?" she said with a humorless laugh.

He gave her a soft smile. "It does."

Feeling a bit brave with his gaze still turned away from her, Emma said, "I can't thank you enough for this job. I…I really need it."

He nodded but said nothing. There was tension in his shoulders. She couldn't help but think of the conversation she overheard between him and Douglas. *I'm not going to fire her*. She really hoped so. She couldn't imagine going back to the Crescent Club full time. Not now.

"You're doing a good job," James finally said after the silence had stretched between them for an indeterminate length of time. And just like that, he was gone.

Emma rested her head in her hands for a minute. Would she ever truly get used to him appearing out of thin air and disappearing almost as quickly?

Probably not.

CHAPTER SIX

Emma started running again over the next week. Not only did she want to learn how to fight with the Phantom, but she also replayed that night outside the Crescent Club on a loop. It snuck up on her in unexpected moments, chilling her blood. She wanted to be able to fight back. She wanted to be stronger. To not be so…afraid.

She used to run when her mother was healthy, when they lived closer to a park, before everything had gone to hell. Despite all the difficulties over the past couple of years, she still tried to exercise when possible, but half the time she only used the stairs in her building because it was safer than any alternative.

She barely saw James Kane, their communications limited to sticky notes and emails once again.

It was time for a shift at the Crescent Club before Emma knew it. She left a bit early, hoping to find the Phantom waiting for her. But there was no sign of him before she went inside and no sign of him after, either.

She pretended she wasn't disappointed. She waited a bit too long outside for him, eyes trying to decipher every shadow.

The news channels finally got wind of the disappearing women. But they glossed over their connections to the Crescent Club, and therefore the Wolf. Paid off, most likely.

There was a fourth woman missing now.

No wonder the Phantom was MIA. He must have been working on the case.

Emma wished she could do something. Wished she could help. Wished she could put on a mask and cape and fight her way through the underbelly of the city until she got answers.

A week after asking him to teach her to fight, the Phantom finally emerged from the shadows after she stepped outside.

"Hi," she said. She hoped her excitement didn't shine through that one word. Her eyes roamed over him greedily. He seemed uninjured. She told herself that her excitement to see him was because she was lonely, because she missed having friends. "Been busy?"

"Another woman disappeared. The cops are involved now. Finally." He stepped closer to her. Too close. Her eyes trailed across his chest, up to his face. "I've been helping."

"I heard."

"Still want me to teach you a few things?" he asked. This close, she had to crane her neck to look up at him, her mouth dry. Wordlessly, she nodded. She didn't trust her voice at that moment. The sheer physicality of him overwhelmed her. Something about him was so solid, so…immovable.

"Hang on tight, then." He wrapped an arm around her waist. His other arm raised to the sky. There was a small noise, and then they were shooting upwards without warning. She screamed.

"Asshole!"

When they landed on the roof of the building next door to the club, the Phantom was *almost* smiling. There was some sort of small grappling hook attached to his arm. Like something from a movie, she thought.

A grin spread across her own face in answer. Her body was electrified. Alive. The night was cool and dark and quiet around them.

"What is that?" she asked, nodding towards the gauntlet thing around his wrist.

"One's for the grappling hook we just used. The other has smoke bombs. And both are equipped with tasers."

"That is…so cool," she said with another grin. "Like…Bond gadgets. Did you make all of it?"

"I don't have long," he said instead of answering. "It's best if we stay out of sight. I don't think it's a good idea for anyone to see you with me."

That wiped the smile off her face. Yes, many people rooted for the Phantom. But he made a lot of people angry. That is, criminals hated him, and New Atlas had no shortage of those. Someone might use any of his connections to punish him. Better to be careful, which was pretty much the motto for any citizen of New Atlas. Honestly, she should have thought of it herself.

"Since you're smaller than most of your opponents will be," he said without preamble, "It's important for you to stay steady on your feet. Use your smaller stature to your advantage. You'll probably be faster than most of them, too. Men will use their strength against you." Emma remembered the way the man in the alley below them grabbed her by the wrists. The way he pinned her against the wall. A flash of hot anger roiled through her veins.

She would make sure she was never that helpless again.

He showed her how to hold her feet, how to find her center of gravity. Again and again, he corrected her posture. He swung his fists at her slowly to show her how to read a person's movements. How to duck. How to get inside their guard. He instructed her on the best way to get out of someone's hold. He suggested watching videos online, too.

"Use your elbows, feet, and knees and put all of your strength behind them," he said as he demonstrated a simple move using his elbow. "Aim for the softest parts—nose, neck, gut, groin. And if they've already grabbed you, strike at their instep—"

"The acronym S.I.N.G., right?" Emma asked, the information surfacing from a movie she'd watched with her mom. "Solar plexus, instep, nose, groin?"

The Phantom blinked. "Exactly," he said after a pause. "Like this." He grabbed her so suddenly she yelped. "Go ahead. You won't hurt me."

Emma frowned, unsure whether or not she should be insulted. But she wasted no time stomping on his booted foot and digging her elbow into his chest in the same movement.

"Good. Your first aim is not to get grabbed like this—be faster than they are. But if you aren't, fight immediately and fight like hell."

Emma imagined the face of the man who'd shoved her against the bricks in the alley below them. Next time—there wouldn't be a next time, she decided. That's what all of this was for.

"The instep and solar plexus hits might not make them release you," he said, grabbing her again. "That's where the nose and groin come in. If you can, headbutt your attacker and try to break their nose. Or grab his balls and twist like hell."

She almost snorted, though he was being utterly sincere. There was something amusing about hearing a serious vigilante like the Phantom say *balls*.

"Please don't make me grab your balls," she said teasingly, cheeks hot. Even with the kevlar armor, their position felt too intimate. His arm around her, her back pressed to his chest, his breath in her ear.

She felt rather than saw him go very still. "No," he said slowly, carefully. "But I want you to try to get out of the hold. Let me know if I hurt you."

Emma almost yelped again as his armor suddenly dug into her back. She twisted like mad, stepped on his foot again, and reared her head back and still couldn't break away. Maybe she *should* grab his balls—he definitely wouldn't be expecting it, at least.

"Good," he said softly, though she still hadn't escaped. She tried one last time to headbutt him, throwing her whole body into it. His grip loosened ever so slightly and she managed to slip away.

She grinned triumphantly. His expression didn't change. But after a moment, he gave her a nod.

"Again," he said. And so they went again, and again until Emma was out of breath and made the time-out sign with her hands. The Phantom immediately stepped back.

"Can I ask, why did you start…doing this? Fighting crime? The mask? All of it?" she asked, trying not to let on that she was breathing as heavily as she was. Mostly from physical exertion but also from the proximity of the Phantom. Of how close they kept having to get as he taught her. They'd moved on from escaping being held by an attacker to how to properly throw a punch and other ways to effectively hit someone. Feet, knees, elbows.

He straightened and paused for a long moment. "Something…terrible happened to me as a kid. It opened my eyes to a need in this city. It only got worse as I got older. One day, I just couldn't take it anymore. I stopped a woman from getting mugged. And the more I do it, the more I see how much someone like me is needed. As for the mask…it's best if no one knows who I am. It's more effective to be anonymous."

"I'm sorry for whatever happened to you. And I'm glad you're doing it. Keeping New Atlas safe."

He nodded once. His mouth opened, but he stopped and pulled something out of the many pouches he had on his belt. A phone. He had straps across his chest too, full of more pouches and several knives of varying sizes. She wondered what else he had hidden on his person. Maybe he had snacks.

Something in his expression went cold, or maybe angry. It was hard to tell underneath the mask.

"A fifth woman was reported missing," he said softly. His eyes glittered in the dim streetlights around them. Her heart sank. *Five women.* And all from the Crescent Club. "I have to go now, Emma." His voice softened around her name from its usual deep growl.

Her breath hitched. "Alright. Thank you. Really."

"Hang on tight," he said. He stepped closer to her and wrapped an arm around her waist. This time she wrapped her arms around his neck and ended up pressed fully against the hard planes of his suit. He smelled like sweat, like something undeniably masculine.

Her stomach dropped as he lowered them too fast over the edge of the roof and to the alley below. Heights didn't normally bother her, but dropping off the side of the roof that fast felt like a rollercoaster, and not in a good way.

They held each other for another moment. Emma stared into his eyes. Green, or maybe blue, ringed in black to blend in with the mask. His jaw had the barest hint of dark stubble along it.

The Phantom took an abrupt step back.

Emma's entire body flooded with embarrassment. She bit her lip hard enough to bring herself back to her senses.

"Goodnight," he said to her. And then he was gone, back into the night.

Emma spent brief periods with the Phantom over the next several nights as he taught her more about defending herself. It wasn't much, but she was already improving. She could feel her body slowly becoming more capable. Despite the exhaustion from meeting the vigilante even on nights she wasn't working at the club, she ran or exercised at Kane Manor when she could. A pleasant side effect of running on the grounds meant visits with Mr. and Mrs. Banks, who always at least said hello but sometimes picked flowers with her or invited her in for a snack or a drink. That, and the grounds themselves were beautiful, not to mention much safer than the city streets.

She also spent a few meals with James and sometimes Douglas. Mostly James was silent, seemingly content to let his cousin do the talking. It seemed both men were growing fond of her cooking. Some evenings she barely got a few minutes into making a meal before one or both of them showed up. When she didn't cook, Douglas did and always invited her. She had missed cooking for other people. Every time one of them complimented her, a small knot of warmth grew in her chest. It took the edge off the harsh loneliness that lived in her chest.

By Friday, Emma's body was begging for a night off. On top of her shifts at the club, training with the Phantom, and exercising at the Manor, she was working every day. Even outside of normal working hours she waded through a million and one emails, files, phone messages, and sticky notes from James.

She went to bed early for once but slept fitfully. She kept dreaming of taking off the Phantom's mask. Of bodies in the river. Of the stairs leading down beneath the Crescent Club. Of shadows coming alive.

A door slamming woke her sometime in the middle of the night. She blearily reached for her phone to see what time it was. Almost four in the morning. *Fuck*, she thought, too tired to say it out loud.

Her throat was dry. The house was colder than usual, the shadows around her ominous. She turned on the lamp and blinked them away. A groan slipped from her lips as she sat up. She needed water. And maybe something for the blooming headache between her eyes.

Emma shuffled out of bed and went downstairs. Moonlight poured through the stained glass at the opposite end of the hall.

Whatever had woken her had already faded, perhaps part of a dream. The only thing she could hear was wind whipping through the trees across the estate outside. She finally started to get accustomed to the unnerving quiet away from the city.

As she drank a glass of water, there came another clatter of noise.

She froze, heart pounding, straining to hear anything else before gently setting the glass on the counter. Her feet crept on silent tiptoes towards the main staircase. She paused in the doorway of the formal living room, every shadow alive with imagined threats.

She wavered for a second before grabbing the heavy iron fire poker from the fireplace.

Another loud noise came from down the hallway. She nearly jumped out of her skin.

Had someone broken in?

She crept forward. James usually wasn't home at night, and Douglas was all the way upstairs at the end of the hall.

Emma was on her own.

Fear threatened to choke her. She inhaled deeply. She could do this. The Phantom taught her how to defend herself. All she needed to do was see what was going on, maybe whack a burglar over the head, and scream for Douglas. She silently cursed herself for leaving her phone upstairs.

She heard a muffled curse somewhere from the direction of James's bedroom. The door was slightly ajar. In all her time in the manor, his bedroom door always remained firmly shut.

If someone was breaking in, how long had they been in the house? How had they gotten past security? How long had they been searching for valuables to take? Or worse, what if James *was* in his room and someone was here for *him*? To kidnap him for ransom–or something more sinister?

She swallowed her fear and gently nudged the bedroom door further open.

There was a man standing over the bed.

"Hey!" she shouted, which was probably the wrong thing to do when there was an intruder. She raised the fire poker above her head and swung it down with all her strength.

The figure whirled and caught her makeshift weapon in one hand with a grunt.

In the darkness she could make out James Kane's face, if only barely.

"Oh *shit*. I'm so sorry! I thought–I heard a lot of noise and thought someone was breaking in to kidnap you or something!" She stumbled away from him. Oh, she was *definitely* getting fired now. Good thing he caught the fire poker before she managed to hit him.

"Is this…from the fireplace?" James asked in a gravelly voice. The room's shadows caressed and nearly swallowed him. "You came in here to fight off an intruder?" Disbelief and something else, something tighter, like pain, colored his voice.

"Yes?" she said. Her voice was barely a squeak. She waited for him to fire her. To yell. To curse at her. All three at once. Oh God, what if she had actually hit him over the head with the fire poker?

Instead, her makeshift weapon clattered to the floor and James swayed on his feet. He barely managed to catch himself against the post of his immense bed.

Emma lurched forward to help. "Are you alright?" Her hands fluttered around him, unsure where to touch, how to help.

James was breathing heavily. He grunted. She had no idea what he was trying to convey. He swayed again and she grabbed at his bare waist.

Something wet slid across her palms.

"Are you–bleeding?" Panic laced her words.

"It appears so," James said, seemingly unconcerned. He started to slide to the floor. She caught him around the waist again. He made

a soft noise. The only light came from what little the open door offered, barely enough for her to see him by.

"Let me turn the li–"

"No! Don't turn the light on." His sudden vehemence startled
her.

She paused. "Okay. Fine. Let's get you on the bed at least."

He smelled like sweat and something else. She sniffed discreetly. Alcohol. Had he been…in a bar fight or something? Was he
drunk? Her eyebrows raised as she helped him sit on the bed.

"Where are you hurt?" Emma asked more calmly. If he wanted
to be stupid and get in a fight while drunk, so be it. But she wasn't
going to let him bleed to death. He shifted to lie on his stomach. She
could barely see the paleness of his skin in the darkness. There was
blood on his back, but she couldn't tell where it was coming from,
not without turning the light on. Her hands ghosted over the skin. The
muscles beneath her palms were tense. And there were…a lot of muscles. A surprising amount of muscles. *Stop thinking about the muscles, Emma*, she told herself firmly.

"Just get Douglas. Please." His voice was muffled. Tired. Tight
with pain.

"Are you sure? Maybe we should–"

"Just get Douglas." There was a note of steel in his voice. Right.
A billionaire probably didn't want to go to a hospital unless he had
to. Too much bad press. She imagined the calls and emails that would
come if it leaked that James Kane went to the hospital after a bar
fight. She would worry about that later.

She hesitated, then said, "Okay. Yeah. I'll get him." If only to
save her own sanity, she thought, but when she turned back to where
James lay on his bed, eyes more adjusted to the darkness now, there
was a vulnerability to him that softened her. He turned his head to the
side, cheek slightly smushed by the mattress.

She hurried upstairs to Douglas's door. The door opened moments after she knocked.

"Emma? What's wrong?" he asked. He was in an old-fashioned
striped pajama set that would have made her smile at any other time.

"I think Jamie got into a bar fight or something. He's in his room and he's bleeding." She barely finished the sentence before Douglas pushed past her and hurried down the hallway.

"Thank you, Emma. I'm sure he's fine. Go back to bed."

She followed him anyway. "Are you sure? Can I help at all? I mean, I can't stitch anyone up, but I can…"

Douglas paused on the stairs and stared up at her. "Thank you, but no. I've got it from here."

She stood there for a long minute after Douglas disappeared. Part of her wanted to march down there and demand answers. To see for herself that James would be fine. But another part of her, the stronger part, reminded her that James valued his privacy above all else. What business of hers was it if he got into bar fights? What did she care if he went out every night and did God only knew what?

She sighed and went to wash his blood off of her hands.

CHAPTER SEVEN

Another of the missing women was found dead.

Emma watched the news on her phone in the kitchen with a cup of tea gone cold beside her. So far, they had found and identified three bodies. Two were still missing. Rebecca Goodwin, Jackie Mane, and Heather Samos were all dead. Lainey Dominguez and Sofia McLean—the most recent victim—were still missing. Emma didn't recognize any of them, which made her feel guilty.

"Good morning," Douglas's voice said from behind her. It was actually lunchtime, but she didn't mention it. "Sleep well?"

She raised an eyebrow. Was he going to pretend that the night before hadn't happened? "Yes, thanks. How's…Jamie?"

"Oh, he's fine," Douglas said breezily. He started fixing himself a cup of tea. "It was minor."

"Was he in a bar fight or something?" she asked. She bit her tongue as soon as the words were out. She shouldn't pry. But she also really, really wanted to know.

"Yes."

Interesting. Not only did James spend most of his nights out God-only-knew-where, but he also sometimes got into fights.

Douglas left shortly after.

Wishing she had a coffee but not wanting to make a trek to get one, she sighed at her cup. She'd forgotten to get a coffee maker for herself. She sighed again. How she survived this long on tea, she did not know.

"Good morning," said another voice.

Emma whirled and nearly dropped her mug. Her face immediately went hot, her body reacting with a strange mix of embarrassment and shyness.

"I–hi–good morning," she stammered. James definitely looked fine in the weak noontime light, so maybe his wound wasn't that bad.

She watched as he went to the fridge and rustled around.

Say something! she commanded herself. Her tongue was thick with humiliation. She had almost hit him with a fire poker in his own bedroom that she wasn't allowed inside of. Her boss!

"I'm–I'm sorry about almost hitting you with a fire poker," she said, then cleared her throat. "Thank you for not firing me."

She thought she saw the edge of a smile as he closed the door of the fridge.

"You're welcome," he murmured, but there was a bite of humor in the words. He didn't look at her as he left.

She put her head in her hands and groaned.

Summer settled into the city and brought more storms instead of heat. New Atlas was always a dark, dank city no matter what time of year it was. In the summer, rain and humidity ruled throughout the occasional heat wave. In the winter, snow piled up in all the crevices it could reach, seeping cold and wet into the very bones of the city. It was no wonder the city was rotten to its core.

Every time Emma met the Phantom she couldn't get those five women out of her mind. He hadn't asked her again about getting information for him, though she could tell it was a weight on his shoulders. She had gotten better at reading him, even with half of his face obscured.

He threw himself into their practice sessions, usually cutting them short so he could get back out into the city. More than she could say, she appreciated that he made time for her, even if it was only a few minutes.

"Do you have any leads?" she asked him after her Friday night shift. Their lesson only lasted ten minutes this time.

"No," he said curtly. He was gone with barely a goodbye.

It shouldn't just be up to him to help the city, Emma thought on her way home that night.

She wished she could do something. She wished New Atlas's *police* could do something, but sometimes it seemed like the Phantom was the only one who really cared.

And maybe there *was* something she could do. She could ask questions. She could get answers that the Phantom couldn't. As long as she did it carefully, that is. The Wolf didn't like snoops.

She took extra caution with her appearance that night. Her makeup was darker, her own kind of armor. It made her feel like a different person, someone stronger, more capable.

Her shift started normally. They had her serving tables again. The club was extra packed. She saw members of the DA's office. Several high-ranking police officers. A few city councilmen. It was only a matter of time before the most important of them disappeared downstairs. She tried to ask Ricky at the bar about the missing women, but he swiftly shut her down. She didn't press, afraid it would get back to the Wolf.

Her shift was almost over when she knocked a drink over in front of a man who had been sitting in her section leering at her for almost two hours. The man was the same one from weeks ago, the one who'd cornered her outside of the alley, the one the Phantom had beaten. She could still feel a ghost of his teeth on her lips. Throughout the night she had done her best to ignore him, to ignore the memories, but her anger was on a tight leash, which led to the sloppiness of a dropped drink.

Emma bent over to pick up the glass.

A hand caressed her ass. She grit her teeth and gave in to the anger. "Hands off, asshole!"

"Oh, don't be like that, baby," the man said, a flash of something sinister in his eyes. "I just came back to finish what we started."

"I'm not interested." Emma said with a sneer.

The man wrapped a hand tightly around her wrist. She yanked away, her blood no longer cold but boiling instead. The man's eyes narrowed. "All I have to do is slip some cash into the right pocket and you're *mine*."

She kept quiet, bent over again, and quickly snatched the glass from the ground, only for the man to touch her again.

The anger she held at bay broke like a wave over her head as the lights flashed faster and faster around them to the beat of the music.

Emma broke the glass over his head. Then she hit him. Once in the jaw, then once in the nose for good measure. The explosion of blood from his nose was satisfying in the red lights of the club. The sting of her knuckles was more pleasure than pain.

Her rage made her feel powerful.

Two of the Wolf's thugs were already converging on her.

The man was on his feet. He was in her face. Calling her all sorts of names. She clenched her fists tighter to keep from hitting him again. Kept herself centered and her feet planted, like she'd learned.

"Hey, hey, let's all cool off," one of the bouncers said. "We'll take care of it, sir, don't you worry. Let's go upstairs, Emma."

She inhaled deeply as they led her away. The fear tried to settle into her bones. She knew what was coming. She couldn't be afraid, not now. It was too late anyway. She should have kept her head, but she hadn't.

Now she had to live with the consequences, no matter what they were.

The Wolf lounged on the couch in his office with a pretty, young-looking girl beside him. She looked drunk or high out of her mind. Maybe both. She probably had to be to stand an ugly bastard like him.

Emma wanted to stand tall. To not show her fear. But instead she cowered, because defiance would only make things that much worse. Men like the Wolf wanted to feel powerful, to feel feared. And even though she *was* afraid, she was going to make sure it showed, because being brave would only make him angrier.

"Emma," Wolf said. He inspected his nails for dirt. A thick ring on his pinky flashed in the light. "We've already had a conversation about how you treat our patrons." He glanced over at the man who'd hit her in the face all those weeks ago. The night she first met the Phantom.

"I'm sorry, sir–I've met the guy before and he–"

With a gesture from the Wolf, she was knocked to her knees before him. She kept her head down. Fear locked icy spikes in her heart. The lights in the club below flashed from yellow to red.

"Please don't fire me," she whispered to the Wolf's expensive leather shoes. Because even with her job working for James Kane, her debts were crippling, and not even the Kane name could protect her when the Wolf came collecting.

"I'm not going to fire you. But I *am* going to add more to your debts to teach you a lesson, sweetheart. You understand." Wolf looked down his nose at her. The red light from the windows threw his scars into sharp relief. He looked every inch the predator he was. "After I teach you another lesson. Fifty thousand and ten percent interest."

Emma cried out. That was much worse than she'd thought. Years of work added to her debt, even with two jobs. "Please, I'm sorry, I'm sorry! Please sir, even with my job with James Kane I can't–I can't afford that!" She practically bowed before him. She wanted to throw up. To fight them all. To get their blood on her hands and be the last one standing. But even with a few lessons, she couldn't fight them all.

Her pleading was a mistake.

"James Kane. He caused me enough trouble." The Wolf spat out the name as if it had a sour taste. Then he sighed. "Well, there *is* a way you can make more money, if whoring yourself out to Kane isn't enough. Your weekend shifts can be spent downstairs. I know you think you're too good for that sort of work, but it'd come with a pay increase. You understand. Solves a problem for both of us. We've been a bit…short-handed lately."

Short-handed because five women were missing, and half of them had turned up dead. Their names went through her head, mixed with guilt and fear and anger. *Rebecca Goodwin, dead. Jackie Mane, dead. Heather Samos, dead. Lainey Dominguez and Sofia McLean, missing.*

Even as fear zipped through her like an electric current, she found herself saying, "Yes, I'll take it. Thank you, sir." Whatever happened downstairs, she could handle it.

She had to.

But every rumor she'd heard swirled like a storm within her mind.

"Next weekend. I'll have your new uniform dropped at your fancy digs, eh?"

Emma closed her eyes. The easy part was over.

But he still was going to teach her a lesson. In the past, one hit was enough. But tonight…one hit wouldn't be. Not this time.

"Now, you know what happens when you disrespect our patrons, Emma. I want you to keep my generosity in mind. *Learn* from your mistakes. That's how you grow. That's how I got where I am today. Understand?" He leaned forward, elbows on his knees. She looked up at him with tear-filled eyes. She nodded. "Not in the face, boys."

The first blow hit her squarely in the back of the head and sent her sprawling. Her face hit the floor before she could catch herself. Blood exploded into her mouth as her lip split on her teeth.

A blaze of pain on her right side as a foot connected with her ribs. Two men hauled her up by her shirt and held her while a third landed punch after punch to her midsection. She screamed as something popped. Her shoulder. Fists hit her ribs, her hips, the softest parts of her middle. Her vision darkened as pain overwhelmed her. Fire consumed her torso. Each blow landed and blended into one haze of pain, with an extra bright blaze from her shoulder. She couldn't think beyond the pain.

"Enough," Wolf said what could have been minutes or hours later. She collapsed to the ground as the men released her. Without them to hold her up, she landed on one hand and her knees. She couldn't breathe. Couldn't see. She coughed. Spit out blood as the Wolf came and knelt before her.

"You see this scar?" he asked quietly. He turned out his arm so that a thick scar on his forearm caught the light. "You know how I got it? In school, I was bullied. I had immigrant parents, a funny name, and I was dirt poor. No matter how many times I reported it, the school did nothing. One day, the leader of the little group of torturers and I were alone outside during lunch. Scott Miller was his name. I'd taken to bringing a knife wherever I went. For protection, you see. And as soon as the bell rang…." The Wolf rested his elbows on his knees as he squatted and stared down at her, emotionless. "I put that knife in my own arm and started screaming. And when my parents sued the school, we won. All those reports added up to show Scott Miller in a very bad light. I used that money to eventually buy this place. Those reports did nothing until I took matters into my own hands."

Emma somehow managed to ask, "Why are you telling me this?" The words were barely a whisper.

"I'm trying to show you that I would do anything to win. That I get what's owed to me, one way or another." Something flashed in his eyes. He stood and pushed his scarred hands into his pockets. "I hope you learn from this, Emma. Because I will not be so generous a third time. Now get out of here. You start downstairs next weekend." He gave her a look of disgust as she struggled to her feet. She wobbled and nearly fell, and every breath she took caught.

God, it hurt. She probably had broken ribs. She licked her lips clean of blood.

It took her ages to get down the stairs. She didn't even bother changing. She could barely lift her backpack. Didn't think to get out her taser. She wrapped one arm around her center. The other dangled limply at her side. Her eyesight flickered in and out as the pain threatened to overwhelm her. She usually took the subway most of the way home to save money, but she couldn't make it that far. She would have to take a taxi the whole way.

The bouncer at the back door sneered at her. She tried to push the door open but it hurt too much. He watched her struggle with it for several minutes with a grin. Then he finally shoved it open and hissed "cunt" in her ear.

Outside, Emma let the cold air wrap around her. It had stormed again, cooling summer back into spring. She leaned against the bricks. She didn't know how she would make it to the end of the alley, let alone all the way to Kane Manor.

She must have blacked out for a second. She somehow caught herself before she slid to the ground. Or maybe she *had* blacked out. She wasn't sure how much time had passed.

"Hello," a familiar voice said. "Were you waiting very long?"

Emma peeled her eyes open. The Phantom was standing across from her, half in the shadows of the neighboring building. She shook her head. It wasn't an answer to his question, but a plea. If he touched her, she would scream. Her good arm was the only thing holding her insides together. And her other shoulder was dislocated.

He must have noticed the pain on her face. He stepped forward. "Are you alright?"

"I'm okay," she said. But the pain in her voice was hard to hide. The words rasped out of her. Her voice was raw from crying. All she could taste was blood.

"Are you hurt?" He stepped closer. Reached out a hand.

"No!" she cried out. "I'm okay. I'm okay." If she said it enough she would be fine. She just had to make it to a taxi. Make it to her bed. She was *fine*, she told herself, but the words faded from her mind in a haze of pain.

She managed to push off the wall and started walking away. She couldn't hear his footsteps but knew he was following her.

"I can't tonight," she ground out. Her vision flickered again. "I— I'm sorry. Maybe next weekend."

She didn't want him to know what happened. Maybe he wouldn't care. Maybe he would call her stupid. So she kept her mouth shut. This was her burden to handle, not his. He had enough going on to worry about her.

"Emma," he said. He caught her arm. The one that was dislocated. She cried out. The simple touch sent pain screaming up and down her spine. Black spots flickered across her vision. She had no idea how she was even upright, let alone conscious. It hurt so much. "You're hurt."

A few tears slipped out before she could stop them. "I'm okay. Really. Just a bad night, okay? I'll see you around."

She stepped away and he let her go.

She found a taxi. Half fell into the seat. Gave the address and…

"Miss. Miss. We're here. Wake up."

A gentle touch on her knee.

Emma jerked awake with a shout of pain, uninjured arm coming up to deflect an imagined attack.

The taxi driver was staring at her with owlish eyes. They were at the front of Kane Manor. The guards at the gate must have seen her passed out and let the taxi driver go on through. She looked out of the window. One of the guards was behind them on a golf cart.

"Thank you," she mumbled. Managing to push the door open with her foot, she handed over a few wadded bills of cash. She had to take a breath–which hurt like hell–and pull herself out with her good hand. She groaned through gritted teeth. "Thank you," she said to the guard. He gave her a half-wave as he followed the taxi back out.

By the time she made it around to the back door, she was about to pass out again. She just needed to make it a little farther.

Put the key in the door. Open it. Close it. Lock it. She gave herself step-by-step instructions. Walk. One foot. Next foot. Breathe. *Oh*, deep breaths hurt. Breathe again. Again. Eyes open. *Keep your eyes open*. Almost there.

She blinked, and had somehow made it to the kitchen.

The pain was overwhelming. Her ribs were probably broken. Maybe she had internal damage. But–no. The Wolf had been doling out beatings for years. He knew how to make it hurt the most without permanent damage. The dislocated shoulder was the worst–it dangled limply from its socket. Her head was next, which was probably why everything was fuzzy around the edges.

Emma's breath hitched. The pain was taking over her senses.

She gently touched her shoulder with her good hand and nearly screamed. Blackness overwhelmed her vision.

She opened her eyes.

James Kane stood above her. His hair looked mussed as if from sleep.

"Emma?" he asked. "Are you alright?" Her vision blurred.

"I'm okay," she said in the barest whisper.

Her eyes closed again. The last thing she saw was strange: smudges of black around his eyes.

CHAPTER EIGHT

Emma opened her eyes to sunlight and an unfamiliar face.

"Ah, you're awake," said a man she'd never seen before. He was tall and thin, with short, dark hair and brown skin. "Had to give you some pain medication so I could get a look at your injuries and set your arm. You're lucky Mr. Kane has such an extensive set of medical equipment at his disposal."

"What–where–" Her mouth was so dry the words barely made it out. But flashes of memory came back to her–this same man's face over hers, something metal glinting in low light, a gentle murmuring of voices around her while she lay on the kitchen floor. Pain and anger as she lashed out at the threat around her.

"You're in your own bed. I'm Dr. Torres. Mr. Kane called me. Drink this."

Emma struggled to sit up. Doctors always meant bad things, like her mom's health getting worse, like the news her mom was dead. She tamped down that panic. Whatever medication they had given her dulled the painful pulling of everything in her torso. "I can't–afford concierge medicine. I–"

The doctor gently pressed her good shoulder to keep her down. Her other arm was in a sling. He held a glass out until she sipped the water. "Don't worry, Mr. Kane took care of the bill already." She let herself sink into the mattress. "Miraculously, you only have one cracked rib. You have quite a bit of severe bruising though, so I would suggest taking it easy for the next four to six weeks. You can remove the sling in a couple of days. But avoid heavy lifting and strenuous activity with that arm for a few months at least."

Emma nodded, his words sinking in slowly. *Took care of the bill.* She wore an unfamiliar button-up shirt, her bra, her underwear, and nothing else. That meant someone had undressed her. That someone had put the new shirt on. Her breathing hitched. It was too much, all at once. Someone else taking care of her. Someone else *having* to take care of her.

There was a gentle knock at the door. The doctor looked to her for permission before opening it at her nod.

It was hard to string two thoughts together. James Kane had called a doctor for her. He had *paid* for a doctor for her. She wondered how much it cost, if it was something she could feasibly pay back.

Douglas stopped at the end of her bed.

"Emma. How are you feeling?" he asked. He came around the side of the bed and placed a tray in her lap. Breakfast and—

"*Coffee*," she breathed.

Douglas smiled. "Thank you, Dr. Torres. We'll call you should we need anything else."

Emma scooted so she was sitting up. She took a careful sip of the coffee. Not enough sugar or cream, but she had missed it so much she didn't care. She took a bigger gulp. The taste helped clear the fuzziness in her mind.

"What happened?" Douglas asked without preamble.

She sipped the coffee again to buy herself a moment to think. "I was mugged," she eventually said. "I barely even remember it." Lie, lie, lie. Shame threatened to choke her. They didn't need to involve themselves in her mess anymore than they already had.

"Should I call the police? Did they steal anything?" She shook her head vehemently. Douglas hummed. "Well, I'm glad you're alright. I'll let James know. Needless to say, you can have as many days as you need to recover."

She thanked him and was glad when he left shortly after.

She pressed a hand to her chest. What was that emotion she felt, she wondered?

Then it hit her. Disappointment. James had helped her but was nowhere to be found. Maybe he was upset with what happened. With having to pay for a doctor for her. The pain in her body that flared with every breath underscored the sentiment. But maybe, she told herself, James Kane was just being a decent person and helping her out.

She finished her breakfast and coffee and set the tray aside. Every movement hurt her ribs and abs and shoulder. The Wolf wanted her to start her new position in a week. She wasn't sure she'd heal enough, but maybe it would help. Maybe her injuries would be a good excuse to beg off anything that was expected of her beyond serving or bartending. She couldn't help the small stirring of fear in her gut.

Her thoughts turned to the Phantom, to how she had essentially run away from him. She was certain he knew something was wrong with her. She closed her eyes. At least now she could help him, right? Working downstairs would offer her a lot more opportunities to find some answers. It was what the vigilante wanted her to do all along, after all.

Another knock sounded at her door.

"Come in," she called, assuming it was Douglas again, or perhaps the doctor.

James stepped into the room and paused on the threshold. "Hello. How are you feeling?"

"I'm okay," she said, straightening in surprise. "Thanks for–everything."

He gave her a small half-smile. Today he wore jeans and a tight black t-shirt. He was surprisingly muscular. *Really* muscular. The sunlight from her windows bathed him in gold. "You're welcome. I was glad to hear you weren't more seriously hurt. You scared me for a minute there."

Her face was hot. She had an image of herself passed out on the floor and him tripping over her, even though she was pretty sure that wasn't how it had happened.

"Douglas said you were mugged?" Did she imagine it, or was that a brief flash of anger in his eyes? Did his jaw tighten? "Did you see who did it?"

"No," she lied. "I didn't see his face. I barely remember it, really." James made a noise that she couldn't interpret. She remembered finding him in his room, covered in blood. "Maybe I'm not the only one getting in bar fights." She smiled at him.

His dark brows furrowed in confusion. "A bar fight?" He leaned against her closed door.

"Don't tell me you forgot about me threatening you with a fire poker? Finding you covered in blood? I thought you were in a bar fight." She kept her tone light, teasing. "Actually, please tell me you forgot, because it was pretty embarrassing."

Finally, he gave another half-smile. "Ah, yes," he said in his soft voice. "When you so bravely came to fight off my potential kidnappers."

She laughed. The noise seemed to startle him. Then he smiled–a real smile. It dazzled her. She didn't think she'd ever seen him smile like that. It changed his entire face. His eyes were a beautiful, unique green in the sunlight. The color of fresh summer grass.

It suddenly hurt to breathe for an entirely different reason. "Yes, I *was* pretty brave. Not so much when a mugger came at me." She fiddled with a button on her shirt. She frowned at it. "Whose shirt is this anyway? I definitely wasn't wearing this when I left work last night." It was too big for her, too.

James rubbed the back of his neck. The tips of his ears were pink. "Ah…mine. The doctor had to cut yours off downstairs to make sure you weren't bleeding while you were fighting him…then he needed you in something loose while he checked for internal injuries. The easiest thing to find was something of my own. I didn't–I didn't see anything if that's–" He looked uncomfortable.

Emma's face was on fire. She fought the doctor? He'd cut her shirt off? She remembered a flash of metal–scissors. A calming voice telling her to hold still. And–oh, God, she *had* fought the doctor. "No, that's–I mean, thank you."

James took a step further into the room. "I—let me give you my personal number in case you need anything. It's a big house so…yelling probably wouldn't be the best idea." He rubbed the back of his neck again. "Besides, I keep seeing your email requests a week late." He laughed softly.

Emma scrunched up her nose as she unlocked her phone and handed it over to him. He *did* have a terrible habit of responding to anything work related annoyingly slowly. Thus, the sticky note system and the inboxes outside their doors. He quickly typed his number and handed the phone back to her. Their fingers brushed. His hands were cold. Electricity sparked up her arm, causing her to shiver at the touch.

"Let me send you my number," she said to cover up her reaction to his proximity. She typed quickly. *This is Emma. Text me in case you need saving from a kidnapper.*

She tried not to notice how his jeans showed off muscular thighs as he pulled out his phone.

He read the text and chuckled softly. "Don't worry, you're the first person I'll call if someone tries to kidnap me."

She smiled. "Good. *Don't* text me if you're being mugged, though. Kidnappers I can do. Muggers…definitely not." She laughed then winced. Laughing hurt. Whatever the doctor had given her had started to wear off.

James's smile faded. "Are you sure you didn't see who did it? *Nothing*? Will you at least tell me what happened?"

She shook her head. "He came out of nowhere. He had a hood on, beat the shit out of me, and ran when something scared him off." She shrugged, then winced. "That's all."

"You're sure?" There was a note of steel in his voice that had her wondering why he cared so much. She nodded. James sighed. "Tell me if you remember anything. If you do…" He trailed off, lost in thought. He seemed to shake it off. "Then we'll go to the police, alright? People like that shouldn't get away with it."

"That's what the Phantom is for, right?" She said it without thinking.

James went very still. "What do you mean?"

"I mean, he looks out for stuff like that, doesn't he? Muggers, other criminals? Beats the shit out of them? So maybe if I remembered anything about who did it, I should take it to him instead of the cops." She shrugged. Damn, that hurt too. "Seems like he does a better job than they do."

"Yeah, well. Maybe you're right." He seemed lost in thought again.

"That happens sometimes," she said. He glanced down at her. Then he smiled. "You can sit, if you want. If you're not…busy." She tried to remember their shared work calendar but drew a blank.

James stood for a minute longer beside her bed. Then he sat on the very edge by her feet. He kept his back straight, hands on his knees, feet flat on the floor. He looked everywhere but at her. She was suddenly very aware that she was wearing nothing but underwear and his shirt. The warmth of him bled through the blankets.

"You know, you're not so bad, Jamie," she said to him. The rich men she knew at the club wouldn't be so polite while alone with a half-dressed woman. Especially an incapacitated one. And they certainly wouldn't have paid for a concierge doctor. She hated that he'd had to do it for her, but she appreciated it all the same.

He opened his mouth to say something, but his phone vibrated. He glanced at it. "I have to go," he said as he stood. He moved gracefully, like a dancer. "I'm glad you're alright."

He left her room as quietly as he'd come. She realized his feet hadn't caught any of the creaky floorboards that hers always did, like he was familiar with each and every one of the huge house's old quirks.

After the door shut, Emma sank against her pillows. She let her eyes close. Let herself remember the muscles underneath his shirt. The electricity between them when their fingers touched. The color of his eyes in the light. His laugh. His smile. She pulled the collar of the shirt over her nose and inhaled. But it smelled like fresh laundry and nothing else.

She thought again about his handwriting, for some reason, hurried and slanted. The sticky notes were always different colors, like he had an entire pack of them and grabbed whatever was closest.

Just for a minute, she let herself imagine what it would be like to kiss James. To let him take care of her. There was something sweet and protective about him. Something about him that called to her.

CHAPTER NINE

Emma was already awake when James knocked on her door the following morning. He looked like he hadn't slept. He had a breakfast tray in his hands.

"Good morning." Emma smiled up at him. Douglas had brought her lunch and dinner the previous day. "Oh, *coffee*." She made an eager grab for the mug before he settled the tray over her legs. She was glad she'd woken up extremely early–mostly because she spent most of the day before asleep–and taken a shower. This time she had pants on, thank God. "*Thank* you."

"I was just checking to see how you were doing," James said softly. He leaned against her dresser and watched her drink the coffee. He shifted awkwardly from foot to foot. Then he stopped, like he knew he was fidgeting too much.

"Better," she said truthfully. "It isn't too bad." That part was half-lie. It did hurt. But it was manageable.

James fiddled with a picture on her dresser. It was of her as a teenager with her mother at one of New Atlas's summer music festivals. James picked up the picture and studied it. "Is this your mother?"

"Yeah," Emma said around a sudden lump in her throat. "Maggie Warner." Saying her name felt like making her real again. She rarely got the chance to talk about her mother these days, and she missed her.

"You look a lot like her."

The lump grew bigger. "Thanks. She was…amazing."

"Where was this taken?"

"I forget the name, but it was one of those music festivals New Atlas used to sponsor, back before those riots ruined everything a few years ago. I was fifteen. Mom went so she could keep an eye on me. I think she ended up having more fun than I did." She smiled at the memory. It still hurt, that loss. "She was really protective, even when she was really sick. Right up to the end."

"She sounds great," James said. She could see her own sadness mirrored in his eyes. That's what she assumed, at least–he had lost his parents, was an orphan like her. If anyone understood that sadness, he did.

"What was your mom like?" she asked. "If you don't mind me asking."

He set the picture back in its place and leaned against the dresser. "She was a great mother," he said. He slid his hands into his pockets. "She spent a lot of time with me. And she always made sure we did things together as a family."

"Even as a kid, I remember how it shook the whole city when they died," Emma said. The news coverage had been endless. It was hard *not* to remember it, even though she'd been a kid at the time. She saw him tense up and decided not to mention the rest of it–the accusations against his father, the circumstances of his death. "Does it ever stop hurting so much?" She twisted her hands in the blankets.

"No," James said. Something shuttered behind his eyes. "No, it doesn't."

Emma held the mug of coffee under her nose and inhaled deeply. A small, satisfied noise slipped out.

"Not a fan of tea?" James asked. One dark eyebrow rose.

She made a face. "It's not *bad*, but I much prefer coffee. I'll take whatever caffeine I can get though. *Where* have you been hiding this, by the way? I've been through every inch of the kitchen and pantry. It's in your room, isn't it?"

James glanced at her and then away. He swallowed hard. "I, ah, purchased a coffee maker. You mentioned once that you preferred it, so…Think of it as my get well present."

She set her cup down on the tray. Her heart was beating against her ribcage. No one had ever done something like that for her. Ever. The wave of emotion would have knocked her over if she hadn't already been sitting. "You shouldn't have done that," she finally said. "You've done so much already. But thank you."

He flushed. The color in his cheeks made him look good. "I'm glad you like it," he finally said.

To cover up the awkwardness, Emma asked, "Wasn't your mom a reporter? I think I found some old articles of hers in the things I've been sorting through."

"I–yeah. She was an investigative reporter." His green eyes caught hers and darted away. "I should go," he said a little too hurriedly. "Enjoy your coffee."

She probably shouldn't have asked so much about his dead mother. Emma sighed as the door clicked shut. She was too curious for her own good.

To distract herself, she pulled out her laptop to see what work awaited her. Douglas told her to take time off, but working was better than the embarrassment currently threatening to swallow her.

The amount of emails in her inbox was worse, though. The longer she spent working for James Kane, the more people in his world realized that they had a much higher chance of contacting him through her.

Emma groaned, shut the laptop, and closed her eyes. Surprisingly, she fell asleep almost immediately.

The next day she tried to read instead of working, but she almost immediately started feeling stir crazy. Since her mom had gotten sick, free time was rare. She wasn't used to it, didn't know what to do with it.

So she answered the easiest emails.

By the third day, she told herself she would go to her office but take it easy. Everything still hurt but she was going to go insane staying in her room. She would do her best to work for the next two days and then have her first shift in the VIP section at the Crescent Club.

It helped that she could now have coffee every morning. James bought probably the fanciest coffee maker he could find, capable of brewing literally anything. She sighed happily when she first saw it and quickly figured out its tricks.

A package outside her room ruined her steadily improving mood Friday afternoon.

Dr. Torres had just left after telling her she was healing well and letting her get rid of the sling on her arm.

Whatever happiness that news gave her evaporated as she opened up the package.

Her new uniform.

The thought of what the uniform meant scared her. The sight of it was a weight in the pit of her stomach. She thought of every single rumor she'd ever heard regarding her new position, each one worse than the last.

Then her mind settled on one undeniable fact: women who worked at the VIP club were going missing. They were *dying*.

And now she could find out why.

With trembling hands, Emma pulled out the contents.

The pair of shorts and skirt were both *very* short, but the shorts were high-waisted. The two white shirts were basically pushup bras. It was…much different from her previous uniform. There was also a short black dress with deep cuts in the front and back. She didn't know how Wolf knew her exact measurements and she didn't want to ask. But it all fit perfectly when she tried it on.

Her skin crawled the first time she wore it for her shift. The shorts did a slightly better job of hiding the bruising all over her sides and abdomen than the skirt. As she dressed, she remembered the Wolf explaining the scar on his arm, telling her he always got what he was owed one way or another. That he did whatever it would take to win. The memory sank claws of fear and anxiety into her spine, the words an iron prison keeping her trapped inside. Her heart fluttered anxiously as if beating itself against the cage the Wolf had so skillfully made around her.

Emma did her makeup carefully, lining her brown eyes with dark liner. She tried to put her hair up but her healing arm hurt too much when she tried to use it. At least it hadn't been her dominant arm. She could still handle carrying orders. She hoped.

She put a long coat over her outfit and packed something to change into. Changing clothes was hard with only one good arm, but she didn't want to be in the uniform for any longer than she had to be.

The Phantom was waiting for her around the corner from the club.

She slowed to a stop when she saw him and glanced around to make sure they were alone.

"Hi," she called. He stepped into the light.

"Are you alright?" he asked without preamble. "Last weekend…"

"I'm okay." She smiled. "Really. Good as new. Saw a doctor and everything."

He gently caught her wrist in his hand. Thankfully it was her good arm. "Who hurt you?" he asked in a low, dangerous voice. A thrill went up her spine.

"I was mugged," she said, and the lie came easier now that she'd practiced it. "I didn't even see the guy. He had a hood on." She shrugged, then winced when it still hurt.

He released her wrist. "If you knew who did this to you, you'd tell me, right?"

She bit her lip. "Of course." Except there was nothing even the Phantom could do against the Wolf.

"I'm glad you're okay. Though I'm really not sure you should be back here so soon."

"It's not that bad, I promise. I'll probably just be behind the bar taking orders. Nothing strenuous at all." She crossed her heart for good measure. "Though it'll probably be a few weeks before I can go back to our lessons."

"Still got that taser?" he asked. She could practically feel his voice scrape against her skin.

Oh, right, he'd asked a question. She patted the pocket of her coat. "Right here."

"Good. I'll...let you get to work."

He turned to go. It was her turn to catch his arm. He paused and looked down at her. "Thanks for looking out for me," she murmured. Did she imagine it, or did his eyes flick down to her lips?

"Always," he said.

Emma stepped back to watch him go, her eyes locked on the shadows for a long minute after he was gone.

She had no idea that he was on the roof above her, watching her too.

As soon as she entered the club, the bouncer at the door showed her to an employees only elevator in a back corner. Before the door closed, he gripped her injured arm, hard. "Boss says to remind you of his generosity."

A prickling of apprehension crawled across her skin. "Of course. Thank you."

"Meet with Marie at the bar. She'll show you around."

The elevator door clanged shut.

Seeing the Phantom had stirred Emma's resolve. Women were disappearing from the Crescent Club, five total so far. If she could get information about what was happening to them, it would all be worth it. She would take what she learned to the Phantom. Let him get to the bottom of it. Because this was an opportunity he wouldn't have—a direct line to the place every woman had worked. The place where all of them were likely last seen alive. Lainey, Rebecca, Jackie, Heather, Sofia. Their names echoed in her mind.

When the doors opened again, Emma blinked. The downstairs club was smaller. Darker. The lights changed slowly between purple and blue. In the center of the space was a bar arranged like a stage with a dance floor was in front. Tables both small and large filled the rest of the room. They were almost like cubbies, made for comfort and privacy, surrounded by cushioned armchairs and couches. The Art Deco theme continued from upstairs with splashes of gold patterns, velvet upholstery, and dark-colored marble everywhere. It screamed opulence, wealth, but of a dark sort. Like upstairs, the lights flashed to the beat of the songs, turning everything a shade more sinister.

Across from Emma was the infamous staircase. There were two bouncers beside it, plus the two upstairs. There were a few more bouncers arranged around the room, watching and waiting. She had a feeling that there was less trouble downstairs than up. At least where anyone could see.

Around the perimeter of the entire space were doors, each with a green light beside it.

"Emma?" a soft, feminine voice said. She turned and saw a gorgeous, tall blonde in a skirt and white top that matched her own ensemble. Her blonde hair was loose around her shoulders in artful waves. Her full lips were painted a deep color that she couldn't quite make out in the lights. "I'm Marie. Let me show you around."

They shook hands. Marie's grip was stronger than she expected.

The rooms, it turned out, were soundproof. Each had a bed, minibar, and couch inside. Emma didn't have to ask what they were used for.

"When the light outside is red, it's occupied. Blue means they want to order. Green is empty. Everything is divided into sections, two girls to a section. Used to be more, but…we're short staffed. Let the girl you're with know if you're invited to one of the rooms or have been requested for a private party. Or if you're going on break. You're allowed to sit and dance with patrons as requested. You can even go home with them if you'd like. But I…don't recommend that. At least here, there are people to make sure you come back." Her gaze darkened as she looked around.

Emma nodded absently.

Marie chewed her lip, glanced at Emma. Opened her mouth then closed it again. Finally, she said, "I heard what they did to you. If you…don't want to accept any invitations, tell them you're otherwise occupied. That means someone else has already paid for your time, usually after your shift, or has paid for exclusivity. They won't argue. The money goes to the boss of course, but tips are yours. And they tip generously down here."

"Thank you," Emma said, truly grateful. If she could put off the patrons for the next few weeks, all the better. She hadn't missed what Marie said–at least here, someone could make sure girls made it out of the private rooms. That they were short-staffed. "I–"

"Look," Marie interrupted with a sharp wave of her hand, "I heard what they did to you but I also heard *why*. That doesn't fly down here. Okay? Some of these guys are dicks, and we usually try to let you know who to look out for, but you absolutely have to be on your best behavior. These men are powerful and don't like to be insulted, not even in the slightest. You'll make it hard for the rest of us if you pull shit down here like you did upstairs. Got it?"

Emma swallowed hard. "I got it. I promise to be on my best behavior."

Marie nodded, seemingly satisfied. "You're with me tonight in section three. It's not too different from upstairs, really. Just a little more…"

"Naked?" Emma joked. She gestured to her outfit. Marie grinned.

"Yeah. A *lot* more naked. Just wait until one of those lights turns blue." She laughed. Her hair cascaded like water down her back, illuminated in the purple lights.

Her first shift wasn't too bad. Within a couple of hours her ribs hurt terribly from standing for so long, and her bad arm ached even though she barely used it. Marie slipped her a few ibuprofen behind the bar.

Did she know about all the other missing girls? Emma wanted to ask but didn't have a chance.

It took longer than expected before someone laid a hand on her waist. "You're new," the man said pleasantly. His hand didn't move. Emma smiled blandly and didn't move a muscle. "Would you care to go somewhere a little quieter?" He inclined his head to the rooms behind them.

"I'm sorry," she said pleasantly. "I'm afraid my time is otherwise occupied. Maybe some other time?" She smiled wider, winked for good measure.

To her surprise, the man simply nodded. "They work quick, don't they?" He chuckled and left her alone.

She and Marie met at the bar to pick up orders for separate tables. "Another word of advice?" she said into Emma's ear to be heard over the music. "We still get breaks, so I recommend you go upstairs. It's…easier if they don't see you sitting around. Because then they expect your free time to be *theirs*."

Emma gave her a genuine smile. "Thanks."

Marie headed back to the waiting patrons, her hips swishing to the beat of the music. Emma followed her advice on her next break. Her sides ached. Her arm hurt. Even with the painkillers, it hurt. She was exhausted in a way she hadn't been in a while.

Back downstairs, her break over far too fast, Emma kept an ear out for anything about the missing women. But the men in her section were mostly talking about the upcoming election, some sort of charity gala, and a "groundbreaking new drug." She assumed they were insider trading or rigging the election. Or whatever powerful men did in private clubs like this.

Marie caught her eye near the end of the shift and inclined her head to the nearest room. Emma watched as the man who'd invited her earlier now took Marie by the hand. The light outside the room turned from green to red. Her stomach churned. She knew Marie had a choice but–did she really? Did any of them? If she didn't go into a room, would she be reprimanded and forced to, anyway? The Wolf had always been adamant that he didn't run a brothel, but now, faced with rows of red and green lights, Emma wondered if that was true.

It wasn't only the employees who went into the rooms. Some men brought dates. Some men disappeared into them together. Some women together, too. The lights changed from green to red to green again all around the room. Occasionally a room would go from red to blue to red again, but not often.

Emma tried not to feel frustrated when it came time to clock out and she'd heard absolutely nothing about the missing women. The only hint came from Marie–who still hadn't emerged from her private room. There was no sign of whatever might or might not have happened behind that red light and closed door. Emma waited until she saw Marie again before she left.

Emma sat on a stool at Kane Manor after her shift, her head cradled in one hand. It was the middle of the night and every part of her was tired. Just one night of men grabbing at her, touching her, asking her to go somewhere private with them, and she wanted to scream. She hadn't even bothered to change, she was so tired. She planned on yanking the uniform off and crawling into bed. But she needed a minute first. More than anything, she wanted something to erase her night. A hot shower, a kiss with a stranger, a shot of something strong enough to briefly erase her memories. Anything. She wanted something that was *hers* and hers alone.

When Emma looked up again, there was James, walking into the kitchen in nothing but a pair of sweatpants slung low on his hips.

Her mouth went dry. Her breathing hitched.

She'd seen a hint of those muscles before but…*fuck*.

He stopped short as if surprised. She tried her best not to stare but it was impossible. He was…gorgeous. After a long moment of staring, Emma finally dragged her eyes up to his face.

She was still wearing her work uniform. And as long as she'd been staring at him, he'd been staring back. The small top definitely did wonders to her chest. It seemed like he noticed. Her entire body heated. Just one kiss wouldn't be a bad thing, right? Enough for someone *nice* like James to undo all the bad she dealt with. Just one.

"I was just headed to bed," she said in an embarrassingly husky voice. It sounded like an invitation. Part of her hoped he took it that way. Of their own accord, her eyes traveled down again. Saw the vee of muscles at his waist. The defined abs. The…scars? She blinked. There were several scars, including one long thin one near the waist of his pants. *What* did he get up to in his spare time? Or had he been the sort of kid who loved adventure, loved climbing trees, who always ended up with scraped knees? But her eyes quickly returned to the muscles of his chest, his arms…

"Are you…alright?" he asked, breathing shallowly.

She bit her lip again. His eyes tracked the movement. "I'm alright," she said softly.

They stared at each other for a long moment.

Then, "Goodnight," he said, and the word was dangerously low. She stood and came around the kitchen island towards the stairs. He was standing directly in her way. At first, he didn't move. Their eyes locked together. The space between them was electric. Heated. Or was she imagining it?

But her outfit *was* revealing and he *was* a man. She could tell by the darkness overtaking his gaze that he *saw* her. That at least a part of him might want her. Warmth spread lazily across her abdomen and up her spine. She imagined reaching out a hand and tracing the muscles at his waistband. She missed human contact—at least, the human contact that *she* chose. She ached for a gentle touch.

James stepped out of her way. Cleared his throat. "Goodnight," he said again in a firmer voice.

"Goodnight," she murmured. She could feel his gaze on her as she went upstairs.

Emma leaned against the closed door of her bedroom and let out a long breath. She told herself she wasn't imagining it. That he'd been looking at her, too. But it was stupid. It could never happen. She worked for him, for fuck's sake.

After she showered she got in bed with no hopes of sleep. Every time she closed her eyes, she saw James. Saw him look at her. Saw the muscles that led beneath the waistband of his pants. Imagined they had both stepped forward and met in the middle. Imagined his hands on all the places that her clothes didn't cover. Imagined what his abs felt like under her hands.

She was in so much trouble.

CHAPTER TEN

JAMES

James couldn't stop thinking about Emma.

The second he'd met her, she'd fascinated him. What woman stopped in the middle of the night, walking home in the rain, to pick a vigilante up off the street? *After* someone attempted to assault her? What kind of woman then took the vigilante home and patched him up? Helped him? In *New Atlas*? In a city known for its crime and cruelty, there she was, a shining beacon of hope and kindness.

He couldn't stop himself from making excuses to be around her. It was easier with the mask on. Easier when she didn't have any illusions about who he really was. Emma thought James Kane was a good man. But he wasn't. Not even close.

He kept going back to her anyway. He'd felt such immense relief when she asked him to teach her how to fight. Finally, an excuse to see her more. No more hiding in the shadows watching her. No more letting himself get distracted by making sure she got home safe. No more hovering around the kitchen or near her office hoping for a glimpse. He'd even gone to her to ask her to move a meeting, for God's sake, simply to have an excuse to see her.

She did something to him when she was near. Hell, even when she wasn't. There was life in his home now. The smell of her cooking most nights. Flowers appearing on tables. Music from her office. *Light*. Every time he saw her, he became a little more human—a little more of James Kane and a little less of the Phantom.

And when she called him Jamie, something in him *ached*. She misheard him, of course, but he never corrected her because the last people to call him that had been his parents.

He hated it as much as he craved it.

And when he saw her outside of that club, holding herself and so obviously injured, his rage almost blinded him. He hadn't felt such unending rage in a long, long time, not since his parents.

Who had hurt her? That was the only thing that mattered. Finding whoever hurt her and making them pay.

He followed her home, barely paused long enough to take the armor off.

And seeing her like that on the floor…He couldn't describe the emotion that washed over him in that moment. The panic. The fear. The *anger* at whoever was responsible.

But she lied to him. She hadn't been mugged—he *saw* her go into the Crescent Club as usual and come out injured, had followed her all the way home. She was hurt *inside*. He wanted to burst in there and beat the shit out of every single person he could get his hands on. Hit them until he knew what exactly happened.

And she definitely hadn't fallen. He asked Dr. Torres, just to be sure. The doctor said the injuries were more consistent with a mugging than a fall. But *why* lie about it? Why didn't she want him—James or the Phantom—to know what had really happened? He had to force it out of his mind. The anger that came over him every time he thought about it almost drove him to stupidity. He told himself that there was nothing he could do except teach her how to protect herself.

And, God, seeing her in whatever *outfit* that was? It did unthinkable things to his mental state. He couldn't stop remembering *that* either. How she so openly stared at him. How her pupils had blown wide. How her breath caught and then sped up at the sight of him. He'd been struck dumb. Every thought had eddied out of his head.

All he could think about was what it would be like to kiss her. Touch her.

James lost sleep over thoughts of her. Woke up earlier in hopes of catching a glimpse of her. Went out into the city later so he could follow her to the Crescent Club every weekend. Guilt ate at him when he heard reports of something he could have stopped while he was with her. But the guilt was worse when he didn't have eyes on her entering the club or making it back to Kane Manor unscathed.

He told himself he was just checking on an employee. That there wasn't more to it. But if something happened to her when he could have protected her…

He was in trouble. It was only a matter of time before this, all of it, came back to bite him somehow.

He couldn't stay away from her if he tried. But he had to try. It was dangerous for him to be so consumed by her. It was dangerous for *her*. He had to keep his distance. He had to try to stay away from her. Because he always lost the things he cared about. The good things in his life always came with expiration dates. And with someone as embroiled in the criminal as he was, he automatically put those he cared about in far more danger.

But he really didn't want to keep his distance, didn't even know what that would look like. So why bother trying?

EMMA

Marie was crying.

In only two weeks of her new position, Emma had already found an easy, steady camaraderie with the other woman. Over the past few years, she had almost forgotten what it was like to have friends. Marie was quickly becoming exactly that: a friend. They even got dinner together at a nearby diner the night before, after their shifts ended at the same time.

Emma's injuries still bothered her, but she was slowly but surely getting better. And while her new position was suffocating–the threat of those green lights turning red haunted her every night whether or not she worked–she was slowly getting used to that too, with Marie's help.

"Hi," Emma said softly so as not to startle Marie. She finished storing her stuff in a locker, about to start her shift.

Marie startled anyway. "Oh! Emma," she said, hastily wiping carefully underneath her eyes so as not to smudge her makeup. "Your shift starting?"

Emma glanced at the time. "I have a few minutes. Are you…okay?" She shifted nervously.

"Yeah, I–" Marie blew out a breath, stirring the long blonde hairs that had fallen in front of her face. "I just…won't make my rent this month." She shrugged and pressed her lips together as another tear slipped from the corner of her eye. She wiped at it almost angrily.

Emma thought about the months before–and even after–her loan from the Wolf. Money had been tight most of her life, but that first year was the worst. A lot of times a spoonful of peanut butter was a full meal or a cup of instant ramen. She frequently went without breakfast in order to save money on buying food, and always, always gave up what she had if her mom was going to go without. They received final notices on rent and utilities so many times she lost count, power or water cut off for a few days here and there.

That was to say, Emma knew perfectly well the pain Marie felt at that moment.

"Here, I'll go down with you. Break's over," Marie said as if nothing happened.

"Where do you live?" Emma asked softly as they waited for the elevator.

"The apartments over off of Fifth." It was, in a city full of shitty areas, better than most.

"My mom and I lived there before she died," Emma said, surprised. Her childhood home. Another memory washed over her, the day her luck had run out and she'd been evicted. It was the only home she'd ever known. And in one fell swoop, she'd lost it and her mother at once. "I had to move. After."

"I'm sorry about your mom," Marie said as they stepped into the elevator. "I've only lived there about a year and "

"And it's nicer than the rest of the shitty apartments in the area?" Emma finished, because she knew the area with intimate familiarity, knew the reasons her mom chose it for them when she was a toddler, after her dad left them.

Marie laughed softly. "Yeah. I just hope…we don't get evicted." The other girl had mentioned at the diner that her boyfriend was sick with the flu and currently out of work until he was better. Even a week or two off of work was detrimental for their finances.

"Talk to the landlord. He usually gave me an extra week on rent if I asked nicely." *Until the end*, she added silently. Until she asked one too many times and gotten kicked out.

Marie grimaced and sighed heavily. "This *is* my extra week."

"Oh." Emma winced.

All night, as she worked and dodged wandering hands and offers for privacy, Emma thought about Marie's rent.

Towards the end of her shift, a younger man asked her if she wanted to join him for a private drink. He was someone she hadn't seen before, though she wasn't sure if that was because he just hadn't been in her section or if he was new.

At her hesitation, the young man winked one warm brown eye. "Just a drink, I promise. It's too loud in here, but I want company."

And when Emma glanced up, she saw Marie slipping from a doorway where the light turned from red to green.

Emma turned back to the customer before her and gave him a smile. "Okay. Just a drink."

Her heart pounded as she followed the man to the nearest room. They stepped inside, and she caught the edge of green light switching to red as the door closed.

It was so much quieter inside. Emma's instinct was to let out a relieved breath at the silence, but her heart pounded. If the man in front of her decided he wanted more than a drink….She didn't think she could fight it. Not without serious consequences. At the thought, her shoulder and ribs both twinged with faint pain.

"Sorry," the man said quietly. "I'm just trying to make my work friends think I'm cooler than I am." He smiled and Emma calmed ever so slightly.

Inside the room there was a minibar, a small bed, and a low velvet couch. The bar also had enough condoms and lube to sink a ship. The sight of it made her sick.

"Just a drink," the man said again as he turned from the bar. Shit. Had he slipped something in it? She hadn't been paying attention. He could be lying about his work friends. Dizzy anxiety caused her vision to fuzz. "I'm Cohen."

"Emma," she said automatically. She took the glass and pretended to drink without swallowing.

Cohen sank onto the couch with a small sigh and drank deeply. "Come. Sit. I promise I'm not…like these other guys. I was here for a work meeting and just needed a breather." He winked at her again. "I figured a pretty face wouldn't hurt, either. No need to be so nervous."

Emma sat. "It *is* pretty loud out there," she admitted. She tried to relax, or at least appear relaxed.

Cohen laughed softly. "It is. I don't know how you stand it."

"I'm used to it."

He lapsed into silence after that and seemed content to keep it that way.

Emma saw her chance and said, as casually as she could, "Been coming here much? I haven't seen you before."

He shrugged. "Here and there. It's not really my scene. I dance upstairs, sometimes, but…" He finished off his drink. "But appearances are important, as I'm sure you know."

She snorted. "Yeah, they are. Too important."

He flashed her a smile and she saw a little bit of a gap between his front two teeth. It was almost endearing. She relaxed a little more.

"You were right about me being nervous," she said. "I guess a few women went missing." She shrugged as if she didn't care that much.

Cohen frowned into his empty cup. "Really? I hadn't heard that." And either he was an excellent actor, or he really hadn't heard about it. Emma tried to quell her frustration. It would have been too perfect to go into a private room for *just a drink* and come out with information. But it would have been nice.

"It's probably nothing," she said after a moment. He didn't take the bait.

They fell back into silence.

After about fifteen minutes, Cohen checked his watch and sighed heavily. He stood and held out his hand to Emma.

Her own shook as she took it and stood.

"I better get back to my colleagues, Emma. Thanks for the break." He dug in his pocket and pulled out a black wallet. He pulled out a hundred dollar bill and held it out. "For the break, and as an apology for pretending with my colleagues that it was more." He smiled, then disappeared out the door.

Emma stared after him, sweaty hand clenching the money tightly.

It felt a bit like a miracle.

Her shift was over now, her break with Cohen having eaten up the last bit of time, so she was able to go clock out. She caught Cohen's eye as the elevator doors closed and he grinned wide at her like they were best friends sharing a secret joke. She grinned back. That he was likely lying to his friends about what they did didn't even bother her in the slightest. There were worse rumors about her, about what James Kane paid her for.

Marie was leaving as Emma stepped off the elevator.

"Hey! Wait!" Emma called, hurrying over before Marie could make it outside.

"Hey," Marie said almost cautiously. "Done for the night?"

"I still have to change and stuff," Emma said as she dug into her bra. In such a small uniform, it was the only place to store cash tips. "Here. Tonight's tips. For your rent." She held out the cash.

Marie stared, lips slightly parted. "You—What? Why?" Her eyes narrowed.

Emma blushed but held the money out insistently. "Because you need it more. Because I've been hungry, I've been late on rent, I've—I was evicted from those same apartments when my mom died. Just take it and forget about it. No strings attached."

Marie took the money, then crushed Emma in a hug. "Thank you," she said into Emma's neck. The words were watery. "Really. Thank you."

"You're welcome."

Marie released her and sniffled, her eyes extra bright. "I'm gonna–I'm gonna go wake up my landlord."

Emma laughed as they said their goodbyes.

Later that night, as Emma entered quietly through the back door at Kane Manor, she saw the edge of James's shirt as he abruptly left the room. The past couple of weeks had been the same. She barely saw him. Every time she entered a room, he left. When she offered dinner, he took a plate to his room. She even felt brave enough to text him once, but he never replied. He responded to her work emails and sticky notes, but that was it. Maybe that moment in the kitchen, the tension between them…maybe he thought she was unprofessional. Maybe she'd embarrassed him. She'd certainly embarrassed herself. But she didn't get a chance to apologize.

She didn't see the Phantom, either. He told her he was busy and since she was hurt, their lessons were on hold. She started exercising again, just a little. Enough to keep her strength up. She tried to go for a run and ended up resting at the Banks' cottage for an entire afternoon.

Her frustration grew with every shift that passed with no new information. It was hard to catch any of the other girls alone. And the patrons never seemed to talk about it, either, if they even knew anything. Emma *knew* the club had something to do with it. What she didn't know was whether it was a serial killer who chose his prey from the employees or something else. She started noting the people who showed up every single weekend, tried to flirt with them. Tried to eavesdrop on their conversations. She kept hearing the same things–the charity gala, the election, a new drug. Never more details.

Finally, on her third weekend downstairs, Emma had her break at the same time as Marie. Since the night she gave Marie her tips, they hadn't had another moment alone. Which was a shame, because Emma hadn't had a friend in years, and she really enjoyed being around Marie.

That night, Marie was discreetly counting her tips when Emma stepped off the elevator. She hid the money, then smiled and relaxed when she saw who it was.

"Table seven was asking for you," Emma said. "Are you 'otherwise occupied'?" She said it in a dumb voice to get a laugh, which worked.

"Yes, I am. Table seven is always asking for me." She laughed, but there was a heaviness in her gaze. "Plus I work six nights a week right now and sometimes…"

"You just need a break?" Emma finished for her. Marie sighed and nodded. They both leaned back in their seats. "Six nights? Why so many? Is your boyfriend still sick?"

"No, he's back at work. Haven't you noticed we're a little short-staffed?" Marie raised a perfectly manicured eyebrow.

"No, I thought I was just being hazed," Emma said. Marie tilted her head all the way back and laughed again.

"No, we're down a few girls."

Emma studied her carefully. Marie was definitely tense. "Please don't tell me the flu is going around here, too, or something."

Earlier, she caught the edge of a murmur at a table about that new drug, but when she got closer, the girl whose section it was—Lena—angrily ranted about Emma stealing her tips. She wondered if the women were being offered that drug, if it was a bad batch or something.

Marie went still. "No. Have you…seen the news?"

This was it. Emma tried not to seem too eager. "Yeah, why? I mean, not in the past few days, but yeah I have."

"Five girls have gone missing," Marie said. "And some of them worked here. Actually, they all worked here. Downstairs."

"Missing?" Emma repeated, voice shocked as if this was news to her. "Missing how?"

"I shouldn't say anything," Marie said quickly. She bit the side of her thumbnail. "Boss wouldn't like me spreading nasty rumors."

Emma caught the girl's wrist and lowered her voice to a whisper. "I won't snitch on you. Remember what he did to me? I promise I won't tell."

Marie's eyes darted around the room. She was nervous. Her breath was coming quickly. "I–"

A timer went off on Marie's phone. Break time was over.

Marie tugged out of Emma's grip and stood. "I'll see you later."

Emma nodded. She tried not to let her frustration overwhelm her. Weeks, and this was the closest she'd gotten to new information. And it was only confirmation of what she already knew.

"*Fuck,*" Emma muttered. She smacked her fist into the seat cushion then stood. Marie didn't trust her. Or she was too scared of the Wolf to say anything.

Or she knew exactly where those women were disappearing to and was too scared to say.

The regular patrons were getting impatient with her for constantly being occupied when they propositioned her. So she let two different men lead her onto the dance floor, let them buy her a shot of alcohol to soothe her nerves. If she didn't play this part right, she wouldn't be able to dig any deeper. Wouldn't be able to get Marie to trust her. To open up to her.

And worse, the Wolf might notice and step in.

Emma's thoughts drifted as she danced. She barely felt the hands of the two men on her. She smiled when she was supposed to, moved when she was supposed to, giggled when she was supposed to. It only registered when sweaty hands pressed to her chest, as they tucked in a couple of twenties for the dance.

She was busy replaying the conversation with Marie in her mind. It really seemed that the other girl knew exactly what happened with the other women. Or at least had strong suspicions.

A crazy thought passed through her mind, but she quickly dismissed it. No, letting herself be kidnapped would be stupid. If she got desperate, maybe she would. But she would have a contingency plan in place.

Her potential contingency plan met her outside the club after her shift.

She let her rain jacket blow open in the late summer wind. Her body was too hot after dancing with those creeps. Too tired, she hadn't bothered to change. She wanted to get home and shower the night off of her as quickly as possible. And maybe a small part of her wanted to run into a half-naked James again.

"Oh, hey," Emma said as she stopped in front of the Phantom where he waited at the end of the alley. His eyes flicked down to her clothes–or lack thereof–then back up again.

"I was…checking on you," he said quietly. "Since it's been a few weeks."

Warmth of a different kind bloomed across her limbs. "I'm…good. How've you been?" Was she really having such a…*normal* conversation with a vigilante? She almost smiled.

"Good," he said. "Are you…wanting to continue with your lessons?"

"I–yeah. Yeah. Definitely. I'm still not one hundred percent better, but I definitely want to." *I want to spend more time with you*, she added silently. She missed him. Every night she watched the shadows for him. Hoped she might see him. She'd taken to scouring social media and the news in every free second she had.

"I'll meet you here next weekend, if you have time." Was it her imagination, or did his voice soften?

"Okay. It's a date." She grinned at him. He didn't return it. "Were you…waiting out here all night for me?"

His eyes snapped to hers. "No. I just have a good idea of your schedule by now."

Emma raised an eyebrow but didn't comment. "You know, this would be so much easier if I had your cell phone number."

"Who says I have a cell phone?"

"Everyone has a cell phone. Plus, they have police scanner apps now, which I imagine you know all about."

That earned her a half-smile. "How do I know you're not a hacker who'll trace my cell phone back to me?"

Was that…a joke? Emma paused. No, he seemed serious. "I'm not, but that's fair. Fine, we'll keep meeting in the shadows like criminals."

He took a step closer to her. "The only thing you have to fear from the shadows is me," he said in his gravelly voice. She couldn't stop her small gasp of an exhale at his proximity. She remembered his long fingers patching her hand up weeks ago. Remembered the feeling of his arms around her waist as he took her up to the rooftops for every lesson.

"I'm not scared of you." It came out as a whisper. He stared down at her. The door to the club creaked open behind them. She whirled towards the noise. When she turned back, he was gone.

"Hey, you're still here," Marie's voice said from behind her. "Thought you'd be long gone as usual."

Emma turned with a smile. "I was just enjoying the fresh air for a few minutes," she said, though her heart was still pounding.

"Good idea." To her surprise, Marie linked arms with her. "Better not to walk alone anyway."

"I have a taser." Emma pulled it from her pocket and shook it.

Marie grinned and pulled out her own taser. "Great minds."

"Or just two regular citizens of New Atlas." They both laughed. "Are you headed to the subway?"

Marie nodded. "You?"

"Yep." They started walking together, arms still linked.

"I would have thought James Kane sent a fancy car to pick you up every night," Marie said as they rounded a corner.

"It's not like that," Emma said. She hated how defensive her voice was. "It's just a normal job. All the other staff live on the estate, too."

Marie hummed. "If you say so. Why are you working here then?"

She heard the unspoken words. Why work *downstairs*? "I…owe the Wolf a lot. Especially since I have a penchant for…you know."

"Hitting men instead of hitting *on* them?" Marie laughed again. "I get it. I work at a coffee shop part-time, too."

They fell into a companionable silence. The sign for the subway station came into view.

"Marie," Emma said. "You were going to tell me about the women who disappeared. I just need to know if I need a different job. You know?"

Marie stopped abruptly. She glanced around as if afraid of being followed. "I–I really shouldn't say anything."

Emma grabbed both of Marie's hands and squeezed. The girl was shaking. "*Please*. I just need to know what to look out for."

Marie sighed and tugged her along. She walked at a fast clip, hurrying for the subway station. "Just don't…go home with any of them, alright? Don't let them give you anything."

"You mean like money?" Emma asked. They started descending the steps into the station.

Marie lowered her voice to a whisper, though the space was mostly empty. "No, like drinks or drugs or…I don't know, just don't let them give you anything. There's something weird going on, and I think it's bigger than we realize. The others, before they went missing, they were all…*weird* at the end of the night. Like they were possessed. I think they'd been slipped something."

Emma's breath hitched with fear. "As in they were roofied?"

"No. Well, kind of. They were all *aware*. Not passed out. But…blank. I don't know how to describe it. I only saw one of them—Becks—before she disappeared, but the stories I heard about the others were the same. I don't know who they were with those nights, either. It could be a bunch of different men." Marie trembled as they stepped through the turnstiles. "Something bad is happening. So just be careful."

Marie's train was just arriving. "You be careful, too," Emma said. Her mind was spinning. She waved at Marie through the closing subway doors.

Within a minute, the train sped off and Marie was gone.

Five women were already missing. Emma was afraid the sixth would disappear sooner rather than later. There was something bad going on in New Atlas, alright. And she was going to get to the bottom of it.

CHAPTER ELEVEN

Finally, Emma had more information. But she had another week before she was going to see the Phantom. She didn't know if it would help at all, but now she could bring him into the loop. He could tell her specific things to look for. Maybe her information could help.

For a week, she turned the knowledge over and over again in her head. Marie thought more than one person might be in on it. That didn't bode well. None of it did, but that was the piece she kept coming back to. Different men. Five different men, five missing girls? Or one man, responsible for it all? That and that all five women were most likely drugged. Blank. Aware, but blank.

Emma admitted to herself that she was excited to see the Phantom not just because she finally had information for him. She thought about the last time she saw him. The electricity she felt. There was a tentative friendship blooming between them, and she wanted…more.

Was it stupid to want someone like him? The mystery of him, of his identity, made him even more appealing, she knew that.

James, on the other hand…James was *real* in all the ways the Phantom wasn't. He was a mystery, too, but so much more accessible than the vigilante. And apparently secretly ripped. She let herself imagine becoming friends with him, becoming something more. But no, it would never work. They were from completely different worlds.

Emma shook herself out of her daydreams as she got on the elevator at the Crescent Club, tied back her hair, and got to work as soon as she stepped off. She was in a routine now. She barely let the touches of patrons bother her. Most of the time it wasn't so bad–she'd gotten good at brushing their offers off. And when it wasn't so easy…it was going to be worth it, when she saved the girls she worked with.

She realized she hadn't seen Marie yet, but several of the lights on the private rooms were red already.

It was a busier night than usual. She was called twice to help behind the bar since she bartended a lot upstairs. She flirted with the men who ordered from her. Agreed to maybe dance with one later.

As the blue lights shifted slowly to purple, Emma's gaze swept across the room. She kept an eye on her section in case her partner Lena needed help. Which of these men could she target? Who could give her information? And how could she get it without putting herself in danger? It would do no good for her to become the next target *before* telling the Phantom what she knew. She needed to find out who the men had been, if there had been a different man with each girl when they disappeared.

Her vision snagged on something. She studied the room again.

Her gaze collided with James Kane's across the dance floor. She could feel their stares connect like two pieces of flint struck together to create a spark. His eyes widened almost comically in shock, and his lips parted. Her heart dropped to somewhere near her feet. No. No no *no*. He couldn't be one of these men. He didn't *come* to places like this.

But this place was known for its discretion, and she knew that was something he valued above all else. And she never had been able to figure out where he spent every night when he wasn't home.

He was sitting in her section.

Her partner, Lena, came up to the bar. She nodded to James, who was still staring at her despite the man next to him clearly trying to get his attention. "Hey, isn't that your sugar daddy or something?"

She grinned, dark eyes sparkling. "You do the honors. I'll get the other table and help back here. Maybe you can get some extra tips tonight, yeah?"

Emma barely heard her. She stalked over to the table. She never expected to see James Kane in a place like this. Her heart thundered in her chest, so loud she imagined she could hear it over the deep bass of the music.

"Hey there. Can I get you fellas anything?" she said in a falsely sweet voice. Years of working at the club had taught her to mask her emotions well. Right now, a strange mixture of searing anger and heavy disappointment roiled in her stomach. She cocked her hip to one side and tried her hardest not to look at James, who was still openly staring at her. The man trying to get his attention noticed.

"Like what you see, Kane?" the man sneered. She'd seen him around a few times. He had tried to get her into a private room before. Her anger flared. "This one usually ain't for sale, but maybe she'll make an exception for you. For the right price."

She finally turned her attention to the man she thought was above all of this. She looked him up and down as if she were considering an offer. But her eyes were hard on his. "What are *you* doing here, James Kane?" She couldn't entirely keep the venom from her voice. The longer she looked at him, the more her disappointment grew. Maybe she didn't know him that well. Maybe he'd hidden this part from her. They only worked together, after all. How was she to know what he did every night?

He flinched ever so slightly. His eyes hardened to stone. "I could ask you the same thing."

The other men laughed.

In a slightly more even tone, she said, "You don't usually come here." She boldly sat next to him. Placed a hand on his knee. He was still staring at her. Part of her wanted to make him uncomfortable, to push him. Maybe even punish him.

James's eyes flashed to his companions then back to her. "I heard this place values privacy." He leaned back. She could tell he was only pretending to be at ease. But every line of him was tense. He looked like he wanted to shrink from the attention everyone around them was giving him.

She couldn't think. There was no way in hell James Kane was one of these–these *creeps*. No way he *paid* for women like they did. No way he associated with men who made women disappear.

Right?

But she couldn't ask him that *here*, in front of everyone.

"Can we talk?" he asked quietly. She glanced towards his companions.

Emma bravely snagged his suit jacket. She had to admit he looked *really* good. He was in tight gray slacks and a matching jacket. His white button-up fit his muscled frame a little too perfectly. The top two buttons were undone. He had no tie. In any other circumstances, she would have been distracted to the point of pain by the sight of him.

Instead she gently tugged at the jacket. "How about a dance?" She said it low, leaned in as if it were a secret. He swallowed. Let her pull him to his feet. Followed behind her as she led him to the crowded dance floor. The song shifted to something slower, heavier. The music vibrated underneath her skin. She glanced over her shoulder with a flirty smile.

James's hand ghosted across her waist.

She stopped and turned. Stepped closer. Pressed herself against him. Both of his hands settled against her hips, but otherwise he didn't move.

"It'll look strange if you don't dance," she said into his ear. His fingers tightened. He held her close while her hips moved. The lights changed from blue to purple and back again with the beat of the song. "What are you doing here?" she repeated. One of his hands flattened against her back.

The light caught his jaw in a way that was almost familiar. His pupils expanded as he stared down at her. "I had…a meeting. I didn't choose this place, I promise. I don't–normally, I don't–come to places like this. What are *you* doing here?"

Emma wanted to cry with relief. Of course he didn't choose this place. But then she asked herself why she cared so much. "I–I–"

"I thought you worked upstairs." He leaned in. His breath brushed against the shell of her ear. She shivered against him. There was a shift in his eyes. His movements became surer. "What are you doing down *here*?" His voice was deep. The words ghosted across her skin. She closed her eyes and kept moving against him. She had never seen him like this. So…confident. He was actually kind of a good dancer.

"Touch me, James Kane," she said instead of answering his question. "You have my permission. Have to put on a good show, right?"

His grip tightened again almost painfully. She turned so that she was facing away from him. Ground herself against him and the muscular planes of his chest and thighs. His hands moved with her. One pressed flat against her lower stomach. It sought the bare skin between her top and her skirt as their bodies moved together. She was going to burst into flames already and he was barely touching her.

His other hand skimmed across her shoulder and came to rest against her neck. He loosened her hair and stole the tie. His fingers wrapped around her hair as it tumbled over her shoulders. She turned back around to face him. Ran her fingers through his hair. She gave an experimental little tug.

He groaned.

The sound burrowed into her and turned her blood molten. His hands moved to caress her ass, up to her ribs. Everywhere his skin touched hers she expected to see flames. She trailed one hand across his sharp jaw and down his chest then tugged his hair again with her other hand.

His gaze turned feral. Dangerous. He gripped her harder. Closer. It wasn't enough. His body moved against her, and she could feel his arousal. One of his hands spread flat against her ribs. His thumb traced the underside of her breast.

She gasped. She couldn't get enough air. If he didn't kiss her, tear her clothes off, take her to one of the private rooms, she didn't know what she'd do. She needed him. She'd never felt need like this before.

James stilled. "Did I hurt you?"

Her ribs were still tender but she hardly noticed. All she was aware of was that deep, fiery need under her skin. But she blinked, coming back to herself a little. The song was ending. James moved half a step away.

"No," Emma said. She gasped for breath. Sweat coated her skin. "Make sure to tip," she said without thinking. She pulled him close again. That little voice in her head still wanted to punish him somehow, though it was crazy to feel that way. "Dances get tips. It'll look strange if you don't."

He wordlessly pulled out a bill and went to hand it to her. She captured his hand in hers, guided it to her chest. He tucked the bill between her breasts. Emboldened by the way he was still looking at her, she pressed his hand with hers. Slid it down the swell of her chest. He was breathing just as hard as she was. But he looked ready to bolt at a moment's notice. Like he was suddenly uncertain about touching her.

"I'm sorry," he said, low enough that only she heard. Sorry for what?

She needed to get out of there.

She expected to see that everything around them had stopped. But the club was going on as usual. She was garnering a few extra stares, but not many. Mostly from men she had refused before and her coworkers, who knew James was her other boss.

"I have to go," she said. She turned and practically ran to the elevator. She passed Lena on her way and shouted that she was going on her break.

As the elevator doors closed, she caught sight of James standing right where she left him on the dance floor.

Upstairs, she locked herself in the employee bathroom.

"Oh, *fuck*," she breathed. She had to use the sink to hold herself up. Her legs were weak. She could feel every single place James touched her like it was branded on her skin. She bit her lip so hard she tasted blood. The pain did nothing to clear her head, so she splashed cold water on her face. Her neck. Her arms.

She closed her eyes and saw the way he'd stared down at her like a predator about to devour its prey. She would never be able to forget that look. It would keep her up at night. Wanting him. Needing him.

She cursed again and sank on top of the toilet.

She was going to get fired. If James didn't fire her, Douglas would as soon as he found out about…whatever that was. She had the feeling that James hid nothing from his cousin. So it was only a matter of time. She was relatively sure there had been an entire section about inappropriate conduct in one of the many papers she'd signed when accepting the job.

Emma spent her whole break locked in the bathroom trying to psyche herself up to go back downstairs and face James. Did he want her like she wanted him? Had he felt the heat between them? But—he'd given her money. She hoped he didn't feel like she was expecting anything from him. A wave of nausea rose at the thought. What did he think of her, dancing with him like that and then telling him to fucking *tip* her?

She would give the cash back. He didn't have to pay her to do whatever he wanted to her body. If he looked at her with that wildness in his eyes one more time, she would lose her mind. And probably her clothes. *For free.*

God, she couldn't think. No wonder she had said something so stupid like *make sure to tip*. He had stolen every brain cell she possessed with his touch.

"Get it *together*," she growled at herself in the mirror. She was already losing her mind and they'd only *danced*. He hadn't even kissed her. She went to pull her hair back from her sweaty neck, but James had her hair tie.

So she squared her shoulders and went back downstairs.

James was gone.

She went back to the table he'd been at.

"I wouldn't mind a dance like that, sweetheart," one of the men said with a shit-eating grin.

It wasn't necessarily a lie when she said, "I'm sorry, my time is otherwise occupied tonight." She smiled sweetly, picked up their empty glasses, and promised to come back with refills. A hand brushed against her ass on her way by.

She set her jaw and endured it. All the flames underneath her skin went out at that single touch.

"Let me at least buy you a drink," the same man said when she returned. She hesitated. She really *could* use a drink after—whatever that had been with James. But she relented. The man bought her a shot and one for himself. She watched who poured it and never let it out of her sight. She wouldn't forget Marie's warning not to take anything from the patrons.

Another man bought her another drink and gave her a tip for just sitting with him while she drank it. She kept her smile pleasant and flirtatious. Tried to see if he knew anything about the missing girls without seeming like she was asking. He either knew nothing or didn't bite. When he invited her to one of the rooms, she declined.

She focused the rest of her energy on getting through her shift. Her limbs were pleasantly heavy and buzzing with alcohol. She hadn't eaten anything in a while, which made the buzz worse. Thankfully, there were no rules about drinking on the job, not when they wanted the girls to be nice and loose.

Lena was grinning at her. "I don't think you were pretending to enjoy *that*, were you?" she asked as Emma rested against the bar for a moment later in the night. "He wanted to know what time your shift was over. I told him." She didn't have to ask who Lena meant.

Usually, they had an unspoken policy against telling men when another girl's shift ended. It was up to the girl if she went home with someone or not. But she couldn't get mad at Lena. Pretty much everyone knew she lived at Kane Manor and assumed that she was something more than James Kane's personal assistant. And after that dance…

Emma poured herself another shot behind the bar. Then another. She really didn't want to have to think anymore. By the time she got on the elevator at the end of her shift, she was definitely drunk. She hadn't eaten in…too long. But even the alcohol couldn't erase the heat in her limbs. The endless loop of memory playing in her head.

She didn't bother changing again. She needed the air on her skin before she went back to the manor. Needed to clear her head.

The night air was freezing. It was too early in the year for such cold, but she relished it. She stumbled a bit as she shoved open the door. The bouncer was grinning at her for some unknown reason. Probably because she was so obviously drunk at the end of a shift.

James was waiting for her. He leaned against the bricks opposite the employee entrance, one leg propped up, hands in his pockets. He looked positively sinful in the neon light.

"I–how'd you know where I would come out?" she asked stupidly. She had to blink a few times before he came fully into focus. She shook herself. And if Emma stood there a second longer, she was going to accost him there in the alley. Her eyes kept roving to his lips of their own free will. She dug in her bra and pulled out the money he'd given her. "Here–you don't owe me anything. See you at home."

She started hustling down the alley before he could catch up. But it was hard to hustle with so much alcohol in her veins and heels on her feet. She had to catch herself on the wall more than once. She wasn't doing a very good job of pretending to be unbothered and sober.

"Emma, wait!" he called. She heard him jog to catch up with her. "Let me at least drive you. It's freezing."

She stopped. She was so embarrassed by herself that she could scream. She quickly debated with herself how hard it would be to make it to the subway while drunk. How dangerous it might be.

"Okay." She stared at the ground to avoid looking at him. The night spun around her as she followed him around front to the valet. His car was small and definitely looked expensive. He held the door open for her.

The rumors about them would be everywhere by her shift the next night. Maybe it would keep the men downstairs away from her if they thought James Kane had a monopoly on her time.

They rode all the way home in total silence.

It was only after James parked in the garage that he turned to face her. "Are you angry with me?" he asked. He didn't quite look her in the eye.

She started. "What? *No*. You said you didn't choose to go there, and I believe you. You're–you're a good man."

His fingers tightened against the steering wheel. "I'm sorry for how I behaved," he said softly. He looked away.

"*What*? You're sorry? *I* threw myself at *you* and then took money from you and–"

"You gave the money back," he pointed out. "Besides, you have nothing to be sorry for."

She had a lot to be sorry for, and to be embarrassed about. And she *still* wanted him. Even as embarrassed as she was and as awkward as she was sure he felt…she wanted him. She pushed her way out of the car. Fumbled with the door handle twice before it opened. "Thanks for the ride."

It was only then that she remembered she was supposed to meet the Phantom after her shift. Damn. Too late to go back now. Besides, he probably saw her get in the car with James and thought the worst of her.

She half-fell up the few stairs leading into the house.

James was right behind her. His hand was warm on her hip where he steadied her. She tried her best to seem more sober than she was as they entered the kitchen. Tried to ignore what the feeling of his hand on her did to her.

"Tell me why you're working there." His voice was gentle.

"I don't have a choice." Voice small, she sighed and faced him. She knew he meant downstairs specifically, not the Crescent Club. The words came tumbling out. "When my mom was sick, we had no money. No insurance. She was too sick to work and I had to quit school and my job to take care of her. It was a full-time job, especially at the end. I'd heard through the grapevine that you could go to the Wolf to get a loan no matter your situation. So I did. There were no other jobs to be had after she died, and he offered me a position to pay back the debt." She swallowed. Closed her eyes so she wouldn't have to see his face as she said the next part. She wished she had another drink to get her through this. "I have…a problem with the patrons sometimes. They…you've seen them. They're entitled. Take what they want. Every time I act out, the Wolf adds more to my debt. I got angry one time too many and he…sent me downstairs. It pays better." She whispered the last part, the words making her feel small. The pain of losing her mom welled up and grief washed over her anew.

A light touch against her wrist. He took her hand. "Look at me, Emma," he murmured.

She did.

His expression was intense. He practically growled the words as he said, "You have *nothing* to be ashamed of. New Atlas creates bad situations for everyone. You're doing what you have to do. If there's any way I can—"

"No! I don't–I don't need any help. This job is enough. Though I'm surprised you haven't already fired me for earlier." She scoffed. He was still holding her hand. His skin was hot against hers.

"I understand," he said. He was standing too close to her but she didn't feel uncomfortable. "I'm not going to fire you."

It was so nice to touch someone *she* chose. An image flared in her mind of the way he looked at her in the club. He wore the same look now.

She gave in.

"Touch me, James Kane," she breathed, repeating the words she said at the club. His eyes locked on hers. She leaned forward, and he met her halfway.

When their lips met, she involuntarily groaned. His hand slid up her bare arm. He tangled his fingers in the hair at the base of her neck. She grabbed his hair in return and was rewarded with a moan against her lips. Every nerve in her body was aflame.

It seemed inevitable, this kiss.

She bit his lower lip. He growled. His hands cupped her ass and in one easy movement he lifted her onto the kitchen island like she weighed nothing. Her legs wrapped around him and trapped him against her. She could feel his hardness against the inside of her thigh.

More. She wanted more. The room was spinning in earnest now and it wasn't just because of the alcohol in her system.

Her jacket was gone and his hands were everywhere. Her bare arms. Her ass. The outsides of her thighs. One of his hands slid up to cup her breast, and she almost came undone right there. His lips moved to her neck while she rid him of his suit jacket.

"Please," Emma begged. Her hands shook as she unbuttoned his shirt. She couldn't get it untucked and open fast enough. She craved more of him. Her skin, her breath, every drop of blood in her body–everything was made of fire. "Please, Jamie."

"Emma," he said, like a plea against the base of her neck. Her fingers finally found the bare skin of his stomach, his chest. Her palms pressed against his abs. Dared to slip lower. She tilted her head back as his lips moved over her clavicle.

Her eyes closed. She swayed. Had to catch herself against the kitchen island with one hand. The room was still spinning.

The moment she regained her balance, she pressed her hands back to James's bare skin.

He captured both of her hands in one of his and took a very purposeful step back.

She practically whimpered. "Please, Jamie," she said again. She tried to escape his grip and reach for him. She wasn't above begging. She needed him more than she'd ever needed anything.

"Not like this," he said in a voice deepened by desire. "Not when you're drunk."

The sharp sting of rejection spread through her.

He dragged his free hand through his already messy hair. She couldn't catch her breath.

"Jamie," she said. He closed his eyes. He released his hold on her and stepped away again. Shook his head.

He didn't want her.

To her embarrassment, tears pricked her eyes. She closed them so he wouldn't see. She laughed humorlessly. "God, you must think I'm such a fucking mess."

"No," James said without hesitation. "I just—"

She continued as if he hadn't spoken. "First you catch me on the floor having a mental breakdown, then you find me passed out on your floor after getting a beating, and now I'm *drunk* and throwing myself at you."

At James's silence, she opened her eyes again. His fists clenched at his side. He was…angry?

She slid off the counter to make a run for it. She was a mess. Of course he was angry with her.

"What do you mean," James said in a low, dangerous voice, "getting a *beating*?"

Emma realized her mistake. She pressed herself against the kitchen island. She put her hands behind her back because they had a mind of their own at the moment. Her alcohol and kiss-addled brain struggled to come up with a way to talk herself out of it.

James stepped forward. His entire posture shifted into something more…dangerous. She swallowed hard. "What do you mean you *got a beating*?" he repeated. His voice was almost a snarl.

"It's no big deal," she said hurriedly.

"No big deal?" His voice lowered, every line of him tense with anger. "You were passed out on the *floor*. Your shoulder was dislocated. You had a cracked rib. You–"

"It's fine! It was my fault!"

She'd never seen him like this. So dark. So menacing. So *angry*.

"Who." It wasn't a question. It was a demand. A small part of her thrilled to see him like this.

She shook her head. "I promise you, it was nothing."

He grabbed her upper arm, but his fingers were gentle. Flames of anger practically danced in his eyes. "*Who*, Emma?"

"Jamie, I can't."

How could she explain that it was just part of working where she did? That she was enduring it to investigate the disappearing women? Part of her whispered that if he had meetings with the types of men who frequented that place, he might not be trustworthy. But that was stupid. James was *good*.

"You said you had no choice," he said as if to himself, as if the pieces were clicking together. He let her go. "It was the Wolf, wasn't it?"

Her silence was answer enough.

"There's nothing you can do about it," she said eventually. "And it won't happen again." Because she was afraid of the pain. Afraid of the Wolf. Even now, her shoulder ached.

"I have to go." He stalked away from her without another word. She heard a door slam.

She slumped against the counter.

It was too much. The dance. Their kiss. And whatever…*that* was. That anger. She thought James was a shy, mysterious rich man who partied too much. But that anger was something different. Something that felt as dangerous as it was electrifying.

Another door slammed. Glasses rattled in the cabinets around her.

Emma touched her swollen lips with her fingertips. She was far more sober than she had been only minutes before.

She had never in her life wanted someone like she wanted James Kane. Never wanted to *know* someone like she wanted to know him.

The more pieces of him she saw, the less it all fit together. The more pieces she craved.

She had a nagging feeling that James Kane had a secret. A big one.

CHAPTER TWELVE

JAMES

James hadn't been able to resist her.

He went to his room with a slam of the door to cool off. Decided better of it and stalked over to the basement door. Punched in the code. Slammed that door, too, just because it felt good.

He was angry. At himself, at the Wolf, at everything. Mostly himself.

Emma was vulnerable, and he had taken advantage of her. She was drunk, not to mention working in a place where so many of her choices were taken from her.

Part of him wondered if she'd given him the full story. James was the one to ask her if she could get more information. She'd said no, but had that been the end of it? She said she didn't have a choice, but could she have purposefully gotten the Wolf to send her downstairs at the club so she could get more information? If so, it was his fault. It was *his* fault she'd been beaten. He knew now that the Wolf ordered it. He needed to ask her outright.

But not as James.

He paced the small elevator as it made its slow descent. As soon as the doors opened, James strode forward into the space where he felt most like himself.

The area was a big, open basement, renovated to keep dry even though it was still dark and somehow dank. The space used to be a warehouse of sorts, back when Kane Industries operated partially from the manor. All kinds of lab equipment remained from their pharmaceutical pursuits. James got rid of most of it, but some was repurposed or updated completely. He liked to experiment on things, figure out how to make the perfect smoke bombs or tougher materials like kevlar. He used to take his CEO duties more seriously, too, and check on things the business was making. Not so much anymore, now that the Phantom took up so much of his time.

The lab equipment was against the far wall, closest to the elevator where it was brightest. The rest of the space was, as Douglas called it, an organized wreck. Workstations were covered in blueprints, prototypes, armor pieces, sticky notes, and computers, all arranged for easy access. Only one table had a chair in front of it. To one side were mats for sparring, usually with Douglas. To the other sat his armored car and two motorcycles, one of which was also armored. Mostly so he could slide it across the pavement on sharp turns without completely destroying it.

And at the far end was a giant garage door. It led to tunnels that were once used for discreet deliveries. All but one had been filled in throughout the past few decades. That one tunnel was used as a secret escape tunnel back when his grandfather was mayor.

James ignored all of it as his thoughts whirled, filled with Emma.

She said she owed the Wolf a big debt. He almost wrote a check right then and there. He spent the next five minutes searching for his checkbook, but it wasn't where he thought it was. When he couldn't find it, he gave up with a curse.

He needed to hit something.

Touch me, James Kane. How could he say no? How could he resist when he spent so much time aching with want for her? Kissing her had been…better than he could have ever dreamed.

But he could taste the alcohol on her lips, saw her stumble and sway and fall. She was drunk, and he had taken advantage of her. He hadn't wanted to stop and, for a moment, it had been almost impossible. He'd wanted her since…well, at least since he'd ended up in her apartment to get bandaged up.

He couldn't do it, though. He couldn't take anything from her that she wasn't one hundred percent willing to give. He saw the way the men in the club leered at her, reached for her, demanded her attention.

What if something had happened to her in the weeks she'd been working at that club? He'd had no idea. He was supposed to be *good* at figuring things out. He cursed himself for not seeing it sooner as he put his Phantom armor on. Piece by piece, he shed his identity as James Kane.

He could barely breathe. He was such an *idiot*.

He needed to–he didn't know what. Get out. Hit something. Feel the cold air on his face until he forgot about her touch. Her lips. He wanted to kiss her again. Wanted more than that. He simply *wanted*. In years, he had never wanted anything for himself like he wanted her. And it was selfish to want her like he did. She deserved someone *good*. Someone who wasn't angry, who wasn't violent, who didn't lie with every word out of his mouth.

But he still wanted her for himself.

His mind spun. He started his bike and let the noise roar through the tunnel around him.

What if she had been hurt worse? What if she had been the sixth missing girl?

He pushed the motorcycle to its limits as he rushed through the tunnel and out into the city. Hit the highway and sped faster. Faster. Didn't bother being careful. Didn't care what happened to him.

His mind was made up. He was going to do to the Wolf what had been done to *her*. But worse. He deserved worse. James would make sure he paid for it. He would find every single man who ever laid a finger on her and pay it back ten times over.

But what if that made things worse? What if the Wolf took it out on her? And if she didn't want James to pay her debts, she was forced to work there until the debt was paid. He had no idea how large her debt was, had no idea how long she would have to work both jobs to pay it off.

No matter how badly James wanted to make sure the Wolf paid…this wasn't the way to do it. He couldn't risk making things worse for her. She was in too much danger already.

With a frustrated growl, he yanked the motorcycle around until he was heading away from the Crescent Club once more.

James couldn't think straight. His mind was consumed by her. It had been a mistake to give in. To take advantage of her. To let that darkness within him have its way.

He would never touch her again. It was better that way.

EMMA

It took Emma hours and hours to fall asleep. She couldn't stop remembering James's touch. His kiss. The sound of his moan. His anger when she admitted to being beaten up. And when she finally fell asleep, her dreams were…filthy. Different iterations of how the night could have continued. How she *wanted* it to continue.

When she arrived for her shift the following night, she half-expected to see him in the club. Half-hoped she would. She had no reason to think he would be there again, but thoughts of their dance and their kiss seared her mind as she remembered.

Marie was her section partner that night.

"So all that stuff with James Kane 'isn't like that,' huh?" she teased.

Emma blushed furiously. She opened her mouth to retort, but Marie interrupted. "Don't tell me some bullshit line about him just being another customer. *Everyone* could see the spark between you." Marie leaned in with a salacious grin. "*Please* tell me you continued when you got back to that big, empty mansion."

Emma felt a flash of anger. "*No*. I–he didn't pay me for anything. Gave me a ride home *since I work there*. Then we went to bed. *Separately*." She didn't add that she *wanted* to continue things.

Marie hummed. "Well, at least all the regulars assume *he's* the one occupying all your time now."

Emma agreed. It was a relief, for sure. Every night when a man leered at her, touched her without permission, asked her to come with him…she wanted to scream. The rage would build and build and build until she couldn't contain it anymore. Exercising had become the best way to burn off the anger, even though her ribs and shoulder still hurt.

She looked forward to seeing the Phantom again.

Thankfully, he was waiting for her after her shift.

"I'm sorry I missed you last night," she said as he grabbed her around the waist without preamble. The air rushed past them. Emma barely noticed. She was getting used to traveling by grappling hook. "I was…drunk." She winced. It sounded more embarrassing out loud. They landed on the roof next door with practiced ease.

Instead of replying, the Phantom started her in a series of stretches to assess how her injuries were healing. Then had her practice certain things he'd already taught her. Was he…upset? He barely spoke to her other than to give instructions. She felt guilty for blowing him off and completely forgetting about him the night before.

Emma started throwing punches, which was simple enough. She could tell every time he caught her fists he was going easy on her. He made her practice using both hands, just in case. She liked that about him—he always prepared for the worst, which somehow made her feel extra safe. She knew he was teaching her as thoroughly as he could.

Emma was frustrated he was treating her so gently, though, especially when his mood was so obviously sour. She wanted to *fight*. She missed out on a lot of training because of her injuries, which meant she had too much pent-up energy.

So she kicked out with her right foot and hit him in the hip. He stumbled slightly with barely a grunt. His eyes flashed.

"Stop going easy on me," she said, hands on her hips.

He stared at her for a moment.

Then he lunged.

He was *fast*. She gasped, unprepared for just how quickly he could move. In a blink, he had her in a chokehold. But he still held her loosely. Carefully.

Emma knew how to get out of the hold since it was one of the first things he taught her.

She grinned triumphantly when she succeeded. He stepped back. She got the feeling he was raising an eyebrow at her underneath the mask. There was almost…amusement in his expression.

"Do you want to spar, then?" he asked in that low, gravelly voice of his.

"Huh?"

"Spar," he said slowly as if she were hard of hearing. There was a note of…something in his voice. He was still annoyed about whatever it was. "You need some practical experience at some point. Better with me than with someone who actually wants to hurt you."

She warily agreed. This was going to be humiliating.

"You try to hit me first," he said as he spaced his feet apart, arms loose at his sides. "Since you sprung it on me last time."

And it was one thing to kick the vigilante when he wasn't expecting it. It was another thing entirely to fight with him when he was paying attention.

Emma wasn't scared of him, exactly. He was just so…big. And a much, much better fighter. Plus he literally had armor on. It wouldn't be a fair fight. But it probably never would be, would it? That was the point, she realized. She couldn't fight fairly. But she wasn't really sure how to cheat short of pulling her taser or gun on him. Which defeated the purpose of learning to spar.

When Emma rushed at him, he easily sidestepped. He simply shoved her lightly from behind. She barely managed to keep her feet under her. Right. Center of gravity and all that. That had been *the* first thing she learned.

She took a deep breath and lunged again. He aimed a fist at her and swung. She ducked. She smiled proudly at the dodge. But she didn't see his other fist. He pulled the punch at the last second, but it still hurt as it landed.

He won, of course. She wasn't fast enough or sure enough of herself. His arm wrapped around her neck. He squeezed once to indicate that she was dead, and then stepped away.

They tried again. She let him come at her this time and ducked under his swing. Got a hit to his side, which hurt like hell because of the armor.

"Good," he said, not even winded. She managed to dance away from him again. Her shoulder ached a bit but she didn't want to stop. "It's harder when you aren't surprising me, isn't it?" He smirked. He was taunting her.

She made a face. "That's the only way I'll ever win," she shot back. Now she was the one getting annoyed. "Cheating."

"Or, if you pay attention to what I teach you…" He shrugged cockily.

She narrowed her eyes. "Or, maybe you aren't that good of a teacher."

He let out a surprised laugh, so she took her moment and struck. She decided to kick him instead. Even slightly distracted, he easily caught her ankle and pulled to knock her off balance. She jerked her leg away and stumbled, barely catching herself before she fell over.

Somehow he got one arm around her chest and his other hand around her neck. His grip was loose. He knew he had won, so why bother holding her tighter?

Her chest heaved. Her shoulder hurt, and she definitely still had some trouble taking deep breaths because of a lingering ache in her ribs.

Emma suddenly became very aware of him. Eyes closed, she reminded herself that she was getting annoyed with him. But she had been so lonely for so long, so touch-starved, so desperate for human attention. Her hands came to rest on his arms. She imagined his lips touching her neck and–

James had really done a number on her if a man in armor was making her horny with just his proximity.

The Phantom released her after a long pause.

He calmly told her what she did wrong and what she had done well.

They were both getting more and more frustrated, she could tell. They went for two more rounds before Emma finally smacked him in a spot on the thigh where the armor didn't cover and felt a small flare of triumph.

Then he just knocked her on her ass again.

She frowned and stuck her tongue out at his back as he walked away.

Emma was tired of losing. What she was doing wasn't working. She needed to fight dirty. Fight to win.

She silently got to her feet while he was still walking away, a sudden idea popping into her head.

She pounced, wrapped both her fists in his cape, and *yanked*.

Knocked off balance, the Phantom fell on *his* ass. She gave him a feral, satisfied grin. She laughed at the stunned expression on his face.

"I'm counting that as a win," she said smugly. He got to his feet in one fluid movement. His grace always surprised her.

"Never fight fair," he said after a beat. "Even if that was…a particularly dirty move."

She rolled her eyes. "Haven't you ever seen the movie *The Incredibles?*" He gave her a blank stare. "It's a kids' movie about a family of superheroes. There's this whole montage on why capes are bad?"

He obviously had no idea what she was talking about.

"All I'm saying is, don't be surprised if that cape gets you like…sucked into a plane engine one day or something."

He shook his head and sighed, amusement entirely gone from his face. Still annoyed then.

More than annoyed, actually. Emma realized the Phantom was…angry. Actually angry. A muscle ticked in his clenched jaw. Her brows knit together. Was he upset that she wasted his time the night before? She knew he had better things to do. She flushed when she thought about what wasting his time meant. It meant bad things happened to other people while he waited on *her*.

"Is there something on your mind?" she finally asked with a boldness she didn't feel.

"When were you going to tell me you started working in that VIP club?" The words were quick, harsh.

"Oh," she said. "How–?"

He simply stared at her, his eyes almost familiar. She was used to seeing them in shadow, and she wanted to see them in the light. Wanted to know the depth of their color, the variations, the way he *really* looked.

Of course he found out. That was pretty much his job. Plus her outfit change *was* kind of a giveaway.

She grimaced. "It's been…a while."

The Phantom whirled away from her in a blur of sudden motion as he stalked to the edge of the roof. "Why would you do something so *stupid?"* he growled.

"Because I had no choice!" The words burst from her in a near-shout. She lowered her voice with a glance at the streets below. "The Wolf pretty much made sure I had to. But now I have a chance to help you. And I'd do it again on purpose, if it meant helping figure out what's happening to these women. It's not that bad. It's…it could be worse."

She remembered the feeling of her shoulder popping out of place. She felt a ghost of that pain now. But she hadn't been forced to sleep with anyone. She was getting away with just flirting and dancing. It could *definitely* be worse. Because that was the expectation: the girls downstairs were fair game. Marie once told her about an incident right before Emma started where another girl was dragged by two men into a room for refusing. The Wolf had been downstairs, keeping an eye on things like he often did, and said nothing. When the girl came out, crying, the Wolf merely took her tip money from the encounter and left.

It could be so, so much worse.

"One of the other girls gave me some information. I was going to tell you about it last night." He didn't turn around. She continued uneasily, uncertain why he was so angry. "She said that the other girls were all…blank the nights they disappeared. Like they'd been drugged. She said it seemed like they were possessed. But they were awake. All five of them. And they might have all been with different men."

"Why didn't you tell me?" Finally, he turned. His eyes blazed with anger and something else she couldn't decipher.

"What good would it have done?" she demanded. "It took me until *last week* to get that information. Before I gained someone's trust enough for her to tell me even so little. Why would I waste your time chasing leads?"

"Because you could have been next!" The words were an angry growl. He clenched and unclenched his fists.

She blinked at the rare outburst. "Oh." She was startled. Usually he was so…calm. Collected. To have his ire directed at her was like a bucket of cold water over her head.

"You have to be *careful*. Five women are missing, Emma. *Five*." He stepped closer to her. "Do you even realize–" He stopped and took a deep breath. "I'll look into it, okay? Be *careful*. I'll check on you after every shift."

To make sure she wasn't next. Her face was hot. Was the Phantom really so concerned for her safety? Then again, that was his job. And she was the closest thing he had to inside information.

"Thank you," she said softly. "I'm sorry I didn't tell you sooner."

He waved a gloved hand in dismissal. "I'm just worried about you. There's something going on here, and you're right in the middle of it now."

"I know," she said. "I'm being careful, I swear."

It was the middle of the night already. Emma was becoming an increasingly nocturnal creature with every passing week. Her shifts at the club, plus working with the Phantom, and the fact that James never seemed to be awake during regular daylight hours were all influencing the change in her schedule.

"I should probably get going," she said hesitantly.

The Phantom took her back down to the street below then surprised her by walking with her towards the subway station.

"I think I finally have something," he told her as they walked. His cape rippled in the light breeze. Somehow his hood stayed on, even with the wind.

Excitement rushed through her. "What? You just now waited to tell me this?"

"I've been working with a detective friend of mine," he said, ignoring her, "and it seems like there's a new drug about to hit the streets. He says that of the three bodies they've found, all three had traces of the same unknown substance. They've been running tests for weeks trying to figure it out with no luck."

Emma stopped dead. "That's what Marie told me," she said. "It sounded as if they were all drugged. And I've been hearing talk about something new…" Apprehension bloomed in her chest. This couldn't be good. "I thought they were talking about actual pharmaceuticals, but…These types of guys are rich. Well connected. It can't be good if they're talking about a new *illegal* drug."

The Phantom took her wrist. "Be careful, Emma. Please. Let me know if anything–*anything*–is suspicious or if anyone pays you special attention."

"I will, I promise." She hadn't realized they were already at the subway station.

He stepped back. "Be careful," he said again.

On the train, her mind turned towards James, as it had all night. On a whim, she texted him. *I'm sorry for last night.* She was sorry she embarrassed herself. That she had thrown herself at him.

She fell asleep before he responded.

In the morning, she read the two words he sent after five AM. *Don't be.*

CHAPTER THIRTEEN

It was Sunday and she was exhausted despite sleeping late. New bruises bloomed on her skin from her latest sparring session with the Phantom. But unlike the bruises from the beating the Wolf had given her, she was…proud of them. She had *earned* them.

On top of the bruises, there were heavy bags under her eyes that didn't seem to go away. It was weighing on her that she was still no closer to figuring out what happened to the five missing women. She hoped she could make headway before a sixth disappeared.

And James was still avoiding her. She'd even given in and texted him again the night before, *You haven't been kidnapped, have you? You were supposed to let me fight them off for you. Tell them you need to answer your emails.*

Just busy with other stuff, was his only response. Then, *Please tell me you saved a plate of whatever you made at lunch. It smelled great.*

That was something at least. A bit of humanity from him. Maybe she could make something else that smelled really good to lure him out of wherever he was hiding.

What she really needed was something to take her mind off of everything. Something to keep her busy.

So Emma sat at the kitchen island and researched new recipes to try while thunder rumbled outside, settling on one from a favorite chef. Somehow Douglas always kept the fridge and pantry stocked with most things she needed, despite there only being three of them in the house. Had he always done that, or did he simply noticed that she enjoyed cooking? She still bought her own groceries, not wanting to be a burden, but Douglas insisted she use what was available if she was going to keep feeding them.

Cooking something new eased her mind. She focused on the food and only the food. The movements were familiar. Simple. It reminded her of the final year of her mother's illness. They occupied their time picking out ridiculous recipes and trying them. Or they invented recipes based on whatever meager groceries they had on a particular day. Since her mother hadn't been well enough to leave the apartment, it was a fun way to spend time together and do something new without having to actually leave. They even starrted feeding their neighbors if their creations turned out well. A popular favorite had been macaroni and cheese with sriracha sauce and bacon bits.

"Are you okay?" James's quiet voice asked from behind her. She startled. Thunder cracked loudly overhead.

She was crying without realizing it. She tried to discreetly wipe her eyes. "Yeah. I was just thinking about my mom."

"You miss her a lot," he said. It wasn't a question.

She nodded. "Some days more than others. Is that how it is for you too?"

"Yes. Some days are worse. Some are…better."

She turned while her food finished cooking. James was in a dark t-shirt with a flannel over it and dark jeans. He seemed to prefer dark colors. In fact, other than the couple of times she saw him in a suit, dark colors were all he wore.

James turned to leave.

"Jamie, wait!"

He paused. His face was more open than she'd ever seen it.

"I'm–I'm sorry about… that night. There's no excuse for my behavior, and I apologize. It was a mistake. It won't happen again." Her whole body was hot. It *had* been a mistake. It was, for one thing, unprofessional since he was her employer. But she had also thrown herself at him. More than once in one night. And she really, really didn't want to be fired. She'd checked her contract and read and re-read the section about inappropriate conduct. She *definitely* breached that part.

James's expression shuttered, but he didn't run off. "You have nothing to be sorry for."

"Can we just…forget it happened?" She bit her lip. Twisted her fingers in her shirt. The stove was warm at her back.

"Of course," he said.

"You can–join me. There's plenty."

He glanced at the food and then away. "Not this time, I'm sorry."

A crash of thunder hid the noise of his exit.

Douglas passed him on the way out. "James–" he started, but James kept going with a dismissive wave over his shoulder.

Douglas raised an eyebrow at Emma. She shrugged. "Care to join me, Douglas? It's almost ready."

He smiled politely. "Of course. Thank you. I'll fix *him* a plate too."

She wanted to pester Douglas with questions about James but bit her tongue. There was no use. Privacy and discretion were the foundations of her employment. No matter how badly she wanted to know more, wanted answers, she couldn't cross that line by asking for more information.

"You seem like you have something on your mind," Douglas said after they had spent several minutes eating in silence.

Emma blinked and slowly came back to herself. "Yeah, I guess I do."

"Anything I could help with?"

She snorted. "I doubt it." Douglas couldn't help her solve the problem of the missing women. Or the mystery that was James Kane. She would have to do both things on her own, if at all.

"He'll come around," Douglas said after a moment. She must have made a face, because he smiled knowingly and continued, "It takes a lot for him to trust anyone. He's still learning. He'll get over whatever he's upset about."

Emma flushed. "I–There's nothing–"

Douglas stood with his plate. Placed a hand on her shoulder almost affectionately. "It's alright," he said.

She opened and closed her mouth several times. God, had Douglas *seen* them kissing that night? Had James confided in him? She didn't think she could get any more embarrassed about it, yet here she was, about to combust on the spot from sheer humiliation.

"I'm sorry if this is rude," she said to change the subject, though she was curious, too. "But why aren't you the CEO of Kane Industries?"

Douglas chuckled as he washed his plate. "Because I didn't want it. I originally started premed, you know. But I ended up in business school because it was easier, with James, to do it at night or in my free time. Even after I finished school, got some experience…I didn't want it. I was young. I came home for the funerals and found out that no one had been appointed guardian…so I stayed, started working for the company."

"Because Jamie needed you?" she asked. Her heart ached. Two deaths and a child alone were too much tragedy for one family.

Douglas startled, then paused, something akin to grief flickering across his face at James' name. "Yes, exactly. And then I just…never went back to the life I had. We were each other's only family left." He paused again, seemed to way something in his mind before he said, "Did he tell you he was the one who found them? His parents?"

Emma sucked in a sharp breath. Tears pricked her eyes. Watching her mom fade away at the end of her life was the most painful thing she ever lived through. But she couldn't even begin to fathom the shock and terror of James finding his mother dead, and then days later finding his father dead. And as a *child*. Her heart cracked in her chest. She couldn't form the words, so she merely shook her head.

Douglas made a noise in the back of his throat. "He was only nine. He was…angry for a long time after that. I wasn't the parent he wanted, or even the parent he needed, but he did need me. And now he pays me to help take care of things." He laughed humorlessly. "But I would do it for free."

"I'm sorry," Emma said, because she had no idea what else to say. She knew the pain of watching a parent die, but her mom was sick for a long time first. They always knew the end was coming. For

James to be only nine, for him to find his parents dead only days apart…she shuddered.

"Like I said, it takes a lot for James to trust anyone. It took him almost ten years to trust me. He'll come around." Douglas winked at her, thanked her for dinner, and took a covered tray to James's room.

Emma's heart ached for them both. Another piece of the puzzle that was James Kane clicked into place. They were so alike, Emma thought sadly, but still so different. But she was thankful Douglas had given her another piece to understanding James.

"I have a problem," Emma said to Marie at the very beginning of her shift the next weekend. Ever since the night she helped Marie out, they had been inseparable. They texted and met up for dinner before shifts sometimes, though not as often as they'd like.

"Is it table eleven again, because–"

"I have a crush on James." She buried her head in her hands where she leaned against the bar. James was a popular topic between them–Marie was always curious, but Emma always tried to avoid it.

Marie raised an eyebrow. "And? This is not new to me."

"And I *work for him*. And he's…a bazillionaire! And I'm pretty sure he doesn't like me." Emma thumped herself in the forehead with a fist. "He's been avoiding me ever since–you know. That night. Here."

"If he *doesn't* have a crush on you, I'll cut off my left tit," Marie snorted. "Trust me, he's got it bad. I could see that just from how he looked at you."

Emma rolled her eyes. "I'm dressed in barely more than a bra and panties. *All* the guys in here look at me like that."

Marie placed a hand on her hip. "James Kane looks at you like he's never seen the sun. And *you're* the sun."

Emma playfully nudged her. "Pretty sure that's a line from a movie."

They talked a little more while they prepared drink orders for their separate sections. Emma didn't believe for a second what Marie was saying about James. Sure, he *wanted* her. But did he *like* her?

She wasn't so sure. Especially considering his tendency to run from every room she was in.

"What time does your shift end?" Marie asked.

"Two, why?"

"Same here. Meet me out back after? Table eleven has been hounding me about going home with him lately, and I want to make sure he doesn't do anything…funny." They both glanced at the man in question. He was one of the more…arrogant patrons. Emma was also pretty sure he was the assistant district attorney.

It had been a while since a woman had gone missing but… "Sure. Two tasers are better than one," Emma said.

Marie flashed her a smile and was gone.

The night was a busy one. It seemed like every man in Emma's section wanted something from her. And not just drinks. Her section partner, Lena, was invited to one of the private rooms and didn't emerge for an hour.

Plus, something in the atmosphere was…different. The men seemed…sharper, less drunk. More predatory. She might have been imagining it, but there was something…dark in the air. Something expectant.

She caught sight of Marie entering one of the rooms. Caught the edge of a flirty smile turned towards whichever patron was with her. Her teeth and hair were purple in the lights from the club. The lights flashed blue and Emma saw the man from table eleven. The assistant district attorney. In that brief flash, Emma saw something dangerous in the man's gaze. Something hungry. She wondered why Marie agreed to go with him after all. Maybe so he wouldn't bother her later, after work.

Emma averted her eyes. It was none of her business what any of the other girls did in those rooms. Though that didn't stop the protectiveness she felt towards them, all of them, but especially Marie. Upstairs, the girls were constantly backstabbing each other for the Wolf's favor. Downstairs, they looked out for each other. She wished she had even a speck of James Kane's money so she could help all the women she worked with.

She saw the Wolf, casually chatting with one of the security guards. Her blood went cold. No wonder the atmosphere was weird. Everyone was on their best behavior for the boss.

Emma finished up before Marie came out of the room. So she went upstairs to change and wait on her, away from the Wolf, away from everything. Maybe she could get more information from her tonight. Most shifts they talked as they worked. Their times meeting for dinner had been fun, easy. Emma had come to appreciate Marie's wry sense of humor and bold way of putting things. She always quoted movies and TV shows, even if Emma didn't get the references.

It was a quarter past two when the elevator from downstairs started humming, signaling its arrival. Emma waited near the employee lockers. She was supposed to work with the Phantom, but he could wait. She wondered if he would follow them to the subway station. Keep them safe.

The elevator doors came open and revealed Marie.

Emma instantly knew something was wrong. Her eyes, usually full of a spark of mischief, were dead. Blank. And she was too *still*. Marie almost always fidgeted, even standing still while waiting at the bar for drinks.

She rushed over to the girl, took her by the shoulders. "Hey, you okay? Did that guy do something?"

Marie seemed to look past her. *Through* her. Her face was utterly, completely blank.

Emma shook her friend. "Hey. What's wrong? Are you okay?"

Marie didn't react in the slightest. She blinked slowly and stood exactly where she'd stepped out of the elevator. As if she were waiting for something.

Marie's words from weeks ago came back in a rush. *All of them were…weird at the end of the night. Like they were possessed. I think they'd been slipped something.*

Something was wrong with Marie.

Desperation stirred in Emma's chest. Desperation and fear.

She slapped Marie hard across the face.

Still nothing. Not even a blink. If she hadn't been standing normally, with her eyes open, Emma would have thought that she'd been roofied.

The elevator started to descend. The light above it lit up. Someone was coming up.

And Marie seemed like she was waiting for them.

"I'm not going to let them hurt you," she swore to the girl in a low voice, even if she couldn't hear her. "I just need to see who it is."

Heart pounding so hard she was afraid she might throw up, Emma hid behind the lockers so the person coming up on the elevator wouldn't see her.

She heard the doors open. Footsteps. "Thanks for waiting on me," a low male voice said. Then he chuckled as if at some private joke. "Follow me, they're waiting for us outside."

The footsteps led to the back door.

Emma realized that the bouncer that was usually at the door was nowhere to be found. In fact, there was no one around at all. It was eerily quiet. Empty. Like everyone had been warned to stay away. She should have noticed that sooner.

She couldn't let them take Marie. Even if she needed to find out more information. She couldn't do that to another girl. She would find some other way to solve this mystery. Make herself a target if she had to.

Just as she stepped out from behind the lockers with her taser in her hand, the back door slammed shut.

She was a second too slow.

She shoved the door open and ran out. The hard edges of her gun bounced against her shoulder blade from its place inside her bag. The night air was unseasonably cold, autumn instead of late summer.

There was a car at the end of the alley.

A man was pushing Marie into the car.

The man from earlier. Table eleven. The assistant district attorney.

"Hey!" Emma shouted as she started running after them. It was a small blessing that she usually changed into running shoes and workout gear for her nights training with the Phantom.

The man stopped as he started to slide into the backseat. There was another man beside him, she realized. A bodyguard, probably.

A flash of metal in the streetlights caught her eye.

A voice from behind her yelled, "Get down!"

She acted on instinct, trusting that voice.

But again, she was a second too slow.

Pain exploded from her head. The sound of the gunshot reached her a moment later, the noise deafening in the alley.

The car at the end of the alley pulled away unhurriedly.

"Emma!" the voice said. Was it…James? But no, that couldn't be right.

She opened her eyes and saw the Phantom.

Her brain was…fuzzy.

"I'm not dead," she croaked. But she had definitely been shot in the head. With shaking fingers, she touched the wound. It was more like a scratch than a bullet hole. That was good, right? Blood started to pour into her right eye.

He grabbed her face with a gloved hand. Inspected her head. "It looks like just a graze. Might need sti–"

It all came rushing back to her. "They have my friend!"

Adrenaline was the only thing that allowed her to leap to her feet. The Phantom blinked at her. She didn't have time for this. She took off towards the end of the alley, towards that car, towards Marie. But the Phantom was running in the opposite direction.

"Where the fuck are you going, asshole?" she shouted. Urgent desperation dug sharp claws into her heart. She'd been too slow. Marie was in that car. Marie would *not* be the sixth missing woman. *"They have my friend!"* She barely recognized the sound of her own voice. It was animalistic. Anguished.

At the far end of the alley, a beast roared.

She swiped the blood from her eye.

Not a beast. A car, covered in armored plates. Headlights came on. It roared again.

The car came thundering towards her and stopped right before it hit her.

"Get in!" the Phantom growled over the sound of the engine.

She didn't have to be told twice. Before the door fully closed, the car lurched down the alley and screeched around the corner after Marie.

"Here." He shoved something dark at her. Cloth. A shirt. "Press it tight to your head."

She did as she was told. It smelled of sweat and something undeniably male.

The Phantom deftly wove through traffic. Why were there so many cars at two in the morning? She wanted to scream at them to get out of the way.

"They took her," she said. She could barely breathe, the panic too heavy in her chest. It was a vice around her lungs. "She–she was drugged. I hit her and she didn't react and–"

The man's face came back to her.

"It was the assistant district attorney."

The Phantom shot her a sharp look. "Are you sure?"

"I'm positive." She took a deep, shuddering breath. "It's my fault, I shouldn't have left her."

He cursed. "This is worse than I thought." His voice was dangerously calm. She let that soothe her, just a little. He wasn't worried. They would get to Marie. They would make it.

"No shit, stupid," she growled. Of course it was bad. They had *Marie*. Marie, who liked cheesy movies and quoted them often. Marie, who was strong. Marie, her *friend*.

A spray of bullets crashed into the back window. Emma shouted in alarm, threw her arms over her head, and ducked down. She expected a shower of glass, bullets, something. But there was nothing.

The Phantom seemed unfazed. The car merely sped up.

"Is that–bulletproof?" She gaped at the shatter pattern of several almost perfect circles.

"Yes." He jerked the steering wheel to swerve around an eighteen-wheeler. She smacked a hand on the dashboard to keep from being tossed into the floorboard. "Seatbelt!"

She did as he said and yanked the seatbelt on. She twisted to see two figures on motorcycles following them. Ahead, she could just see the taillights of the car Marie was in. The Phantom floored it, and she was pressed back into the seat as the car went even faster. There was a burst of pain from her head and then it was gone just as quickly as adrenaline surged anew through her body.

"What the fuck *is* this thing?"

The highway was mostly clear of traffic now. Only a couple other cars, their quarry, and their pursuers. There was another explosion of bullets against the car. One of the back windows cracked ominously.

"Take the wheel," the Phantom said.

Her body acted on pure instinct. They trained together so much these past weeks that she trusted him. Could almost read him.

She dared a quick glance at the speedometer as she reached over and took the wheel. He rolled his window down before easing off the gas ever so slightly. Blood still trickled into her right eye. The car swerved slightly as she tried to keep it straight while going over a hundred miles per hour.

The Phantom stuck his left arm out of the open window as a motorcycle pulled level with them.

A small sound, and his grappling hook shot out.

It stuck in the spokes of the front wheel of the motorcycle.

The Phantom yanked with both hands.

In one swift movement, he snapped the gauntlet from his arm and took the wheel back from her while accelerating once more. The gauntlet flew out of the window as the motorcycle smacked into the rear bumper of the car. The figure riding it disappeared into the shadows behind them.

She watched the bike crash through the cracks in the rear window. Sparks flew as it careened across the asphalt. Cars behind them swerved around it.

The second motorcycle was gaining on them too. The back window on her side cracked as more bullets hit.

Emma yanked her bag into her lap and dug through it until her fingers touched cold metal.

Her fury reached a frenzied level. She wouldn't let them have Marie. She wouldn't let them have any more women.

She rolled down the window. Wiped the blood from her eyes. "Keep it as straight as you can!" she called to the Phantom over the wind.

"Is that–is that a *gun?*" he shouted back. "Don't kill them!"

Did he really just crash the first motorcycle like *that* and tell *her* not to kill someone?

She leaned out of the window and used her hips against the door to steady herself. One hand cupped around the other like she learned at the range. She started going as a teenager at her mother's behest. Emma needed to know how to protect herself, her mother told her, especially because there were only two of them. No one else would protect them. Not in New Atlas.

A hand grabbed Emma's waistband as she leaned a little too far. The wind whipped her hair around her face, sticking in the blood on her head.

The other motorcycle caught up with them. The figure on it raised an automatic gun of some sort.

She raised her own weapon. She saw her distorted reflection in their helmet. With a smile full of bloodied teeth, she pulled the trigger once. Twice.

The first shot went into his side. The second hit the back tire.

She shoved herself back into her seat with satisfaction and rolled the window up. She heard the screech of the motorcycle crashing behind them.

"Let's get these bastards," she said.

The Phantom gave her another, longer look. He seemed a bit stunned. What must she look like, a crazed woman covered in blood, firing a gun at their pursuers?

Emma wasn't as helpless as she used to be.

But he nodded and hit the same button as before. The car went flying forward. Faster. Faster.

She found a water bottle in her bag and used it to wash some of the blood from her face with the shirt he'd passed her. She kept her feet and one hand braced as he took turn after turn practically on two wheels. The other car had gotten just enough of a head start. They bought themselves just enough time with the distraction of the motorcycles.

"Shit," the Phantom growled. The car slowed.

"What?"

"I lost them."

"What do you *mean* you fucking lost them?" She sat up straighter. They were in a quiet industrial area by the water somewhere outside the city. Lots of warehouses, docks, boats, and ships. At any minute, Marie could disappear for good.

"I took the turn right after them, but they're gone!" He thumped the steering wheel with a fist.

"They can't be far. If they take her somewhere else—"

"I *know*," he said. He glanced around for a second as if thinking. He flipped the headlights off. The car began to crawl forward in the darkness. In this area, the streetlights were few and far between. Most of the lights seemed to be near the doors of the buildings, each with a noticeable security camera.

He took a couple of careful turns, then swerved suddenly and cut the engine off. "There," the Phantom said and pointed. The car they'd been following was parked about a block away outside of a brick building. It had two huge bay doors and one regular door. One of the bay doors was partially open. There was weak light coming from inside. As she watched, Emma saw a pair of feet go past. Then another.

"Stay here. I'll get her." He was out of the car before she could protest.

She grabbed her gun with one hand and taser with the other.

"Like hell," she muttered, and went after him.

CHAPTER FOURTEEN

The Phantom had already disappeared by the time Emma got out of the car. Sticking to the shadows, she went further down the street and then crossed to the warehouse. Adrenaline was a fire in her veins. Her mind was sharp. Clear. She didn't feel the pain in her head anymore. There was only one thing she focused on: saving Marie.

Within a minute she had the beginnings of a plan. The Phantom was obviously the better fighter of the two of them. So the best thing she could do was raise hell and create enough of a distraction for him to do what he did best.

She ran in a crouch to the driver's side door of the car that took Marie. The passenger side was towards the big bay door, so she was able to use the car itself to conceal her movements. She waited with bated breath to see if anyone noticed her. When she tried the handle, it was unlocked. Lucky. She slid in and shut the door behind her with barely a click. The interior lights remained off, which was also lucky.

Even luckier was the fact that it had a push start. And the key fob was in the cupholder. She guessed bad guys were lazy. Or didn't expect anyone to steal their car.

She originally planned on merely setting the alarm off, but this would be even better.

Emma slid the driver's seat back to create space in the floor-board. She crouched low. The taser went in the cupholder and she gripped her gun tightly in one hand. She didn't stop to think whether or not it was a terrible idea.

She started the car. It came to life with a quiet purr. She shifted it into reverse. In one quick movement, she jammed her foot on the accelerator, backed up as far as she could, and then put it in drive. She shoved the pedal all the way to the floor. The car shot forward like a bullet.

Emma almost hit her head on the steering wheel as the car caught the edge of the door. The windshield cracked and shattered. With a screech loud enough to wake the dead, the car dragged the door par-tially with it before both got stuck. The wheels spun in place for a moment before she shut it off.

Bullets peppered the car. She covered her head with her hands and huddled in the space between the seat and the steering wheel. The windshield and passenger window both burst in a shower of glass.

She'd glimpsed the inside of the warehouse, barely enough to see several armed men, huge machines, storage crates, a metal walk-way. Most of it was in shadow but there was a bright spot farther back. A doorway, maybe. Her mind spun as she tried to think, to for-mulate a way out of this. It definitely had been a terrible idea, but it was too late now. She kept low and kept quiet while she tried to think of her next step.

"What the fuck?" she heard a man say. His footsteps crunched on broken glass as he approached the driver's side.

Emma cocked her gun. She rested her free hand on the door han-dle.

As soon as the man was close enough, she shoved the door open with all of her strength. He stumbled back a step with a noise of sur-prise as it smacked into him. Recovering quickly, he reached through the broken window to grab her. She let him. She stuck the muzzle of the gun against his side and fired. There was no time to think, only to act.

More gunshots rang out behind her. She ducked and scrambled to use the car door as cover, blindly shooting twice to cover her move-ments.

The man she shot moaned from the ground. He reached for his weapon with hatred in his eyes. She used the butt of her gun to hit him in the head. Once. Twice. Three times and he went limp. The sound of the gun hitting his skull made her sick, but she kept going.

The gunshots stopped. They were probably surrounding her on both sides. *Where the fuck was the Phantom?* The adrenaline made it impossible to tell how much time had passed. It could have been seconds or minutes for all she knew.

She peered over one shoulder through the broken car window just as there was a small explosion from above. A section of the metal walkway collapsed on top of two men.

The Phantom leapt to the ground with his cape blown wide like wings, his outline a dark shadow against an arc of flame.

Emma held her breath and watched as he landed easily and exploded into action.

The men around them clearly marked the vigilante as the greater threat and left her where she was. She tried to count them but they were moving too fast. Maybe a dozen. Maybe less, maybe more.

The Phantom in his element was a wonder to behold. He took hits like he didn't feel them. He hit back with a ruthless intensity that had her heart pounding. She'd never seen him like that, even in their sparring sessions. Had never seen him truly unleash himself. He seemed utterly unfazed by the men surrounding him. His suit must have been bulletproof, too, because he took three shots to the chest with barely a flinch. He was all predator, a wild animal with a sort of calm anger that should have sent the men around them running.

Emma grabbed her taser from the cupholder. She set her elbows on the hood of the car and carefully aimed her gun at the nearest man.

Two shots and he went down, a lucky shot with the fresh blood from her head wound obscuring her vision. She shot again, three times this time before she got lucky. The second man went down. She didn't think either of them were dead, but either way it was two the Phantom didn't have to deal with. She noticed he was disarming each man quickly and efficiently, forcing them to fight hand to hand with him. He moved powerfully. Gracefully. He took a hit to the jaw and merely re-centered himself and hit back twice as hard.

A couple of the men finally noticed Emma shooting. She shot one of them before he could get much closer, but two others were on her before she could get off another shot. She only had a few bullets left. Damn, she should have been counting. At the range, they taught her the importance of knowing how many bullets were in her magazine. Her particular model had thirteen bullets.

She decided to copy the Phantom and disarm her attackers. Her first hit was to the closest man's wrist with the butt of her gun. He dropped his weapon. She tased him in the neck. He went down.

Two more men replaced him, much too close. She whirled and shot wildly. One bullet hit the first man in the arm, making him drop his weapon. She ducked as the other returned fire. She crouched low and ran at him. As she got close, she pulled the trigger and–*Click*. Empty. Emma threw the gun, panic fluttering in her gut, hitting him in the head. He cursed.

Both men lunged for her at once. She slipped towards the one with the injured arm and tased him in the ribs. The world went white as her head erupted with sudden pain. She cried out, dropped to her knees. The wound on her forehead gushed blood. Black spots danced in her vision.

Get up, she told herself, but her body didn't cooperate, dazed as she was.

The larger man grabbed her by the shirt and hauled her up. She could barely see through the pain and the blood in her eyes.

"You bitch," he snarled at her.

He was abruptly yanked away from her. Off balance, she stumbled and almost fell. One of her ankles twinged with pain as she found her feet again.

There was an animalistic roar of rage. The Phantom smashed his fist into the man's face. Over and over and over. The man went limp, held up by his shirt collar by the Phantom. He hit him again. Again. Again.

Emma chanced a look around. There was no one left to fight.

She staggered over to the Phantom. Laid a hand on his arm. "It's over," she said in a rasp.

Finally, he stilled. His hood was down, more of his face in the light than she'd ever seen. The now unconscious man fell at his feet.

The Phantom's eyes met hers and, for a moment, there was nothing human left in them.

He seemed to come back to himself in a rush.

The Phantom grabbed her and pulled her close. "Are you okay?" he said in a voice roughened from shouting. "Are you hurt?"

"I'm okay," she said. She held his wrist to steady herself. One of her fingertips slid under the edge of his glove to bare skin and she shivered at the heat of it. "He hit me where the bullet got me earlier. I'm okay." There was pain in her side, too, but not nearly as bad as her head. She swiped at the blood to clear her vision.

"Where's Marie?" she asked. "Have you—"

The Phantom glanced over her shoulder. "There's a room back there. I'd tell you to stay here but—"

But she was already running for the light she saw earlier. She heard the heavy thud of the Phantom's boots as he followed.

Two more men guarded the room. A back door swung open and someone stepped out before she could see who it was. The assistant district attorney followed the unknown person. Emma didn't see Marie.

The Phantom's fist connected with the first guard's face. The second raised his gun. Emma leapt into action, pain dancing across her knuckles as they connected with his jaw. She brought her taser up with her other hand. With one press of the button, he convulsed and fell.

The Phantom was already after the others, but—

He stopped. She bumped into his back. She peered around him to see why he stopped so suddenly.

Trembling overtook her body before her brain could catch up.

The Phantom angled one arm to keep her firmly behind him.

The assistant district attorney held a gun to Marie's head.

"Please," Emma said, the word choked. "Please don't—"

Marie's gaze was still blank. There was a bruise on her face and blood in the corners of her lips.

"You have *really* messed things up for me here," the man said. His bald head was shiny in the dim light. "One more step and I'll kill her."

"You don't have to do that," the Phantom said in a low, calm voice. "It's over. Your friends left you. And there's no one left out there to help you."

"You think I'd survive *prison*?" the ADA shouted. The gun swung slightly towards them. Emma flinched. The Phantom moved to block her with his body.

If only she hadn't run out of bullets, she thought.

"I can protect you," the Phantom continued calmly. "Just put the gun down."

"Protect me?" The man's eyes were wild. Afraid. And not of the vigilante, Emma realized with a growing sense of horror. "It's so much deeper than you think. There's no way out. Not once you're in. You have no idea. New Atlas PD is in on it too. There's no way out."

"Not all of New Atlas PD." The Phantom shifted again as the man moved. Protecting her. She wished she could see his face and somehow communicate with him. Maybe she could distract the ADA so the Phantom could grab Marie. "There's at least one cop I trust. We can keep you safe until you can testify."

The man shook his head violently. He groaned and pressed both hands to his temples with the gun still in one of them. Emma tried to remember his name. Maybe if they called him by name, it would calm him. That was a negotiation tactic, right? But her entire focus was on Marie, on the blood on her lips, on her blonde hair, unbound and windblown. On the blank look in her eyes.

The Phantom took a single step. In the blink of an eye the man pressed the gun back to Marie's head. Emma gasped. "This is *all your fault!*" he cried. He shook his head frantically. "I won't even make it to jail."

The Phantom lunged forward as a gunshot echoed through the space around them.

The world around Emma seemed to slow. She saw the Phantom tackle the ADA to the ground. Saw him wrestle the gun away. Saw him knock him unconscious with a well-aimed punch.

In the mere moments it took for him to move, Marie's body collapsed to the ground.

Emma fell with her. She scrambled on hands and knees to her friend.

"Marie!" she cried out. "*Marie!*"

Emma pulled her to her chest. Her fingers hurried to put pressure on the wound. That's what you were supposed to do, right? But her hands tangled in Marie's hair. Something wet and thick soaked into the knees of her pants.

Blood.

Marie's unblinking eyes stared up at the ceiling. Blood slowly colored her blonde hair red. Emma felt for a pulse on her neck, her wrists.

Nothing.

She was dead.

Emma was too late.

A rage she had never known before crested within her on a wave. She clutched Marie's body and screamed.

The rage built and built and built until she couldn't see or hear or think. She wasn't herself anymore, merely an instrument for her rage and nothing more. She gently set Marie down and turned towards the unconscious man who killed her as the rage turned into an inferno.

Emma lunged and dug her taser into the soft flesh of his neck. She pressed it over and over and over and over. She watched as he thrashed, even unconscious. Watched as foam began to pour from his mouth. But that quickly stopped satisfying her so she let the taser drop in order to wrap her hands around his throat instead. Started squeezing. Harder. *Harder.* The give of his flesh under her hands wasn't enough. *He killed Marie.*

Strong arms wrapped around her and wrenched her backwards.

"That's enough," the Phantom said in her ear. She struggled against him. An animalistic snarl came from her lips. She was going to kill that man with her bare hands. Strangle him until the light went out in his eyes like it blinked out of Marie's. And then she was going to find the others responsible and kill them too. "*That's enough, Emma.*"

He pulled her out of the room.

"Let me go!" she shrieked. Her feet left the ground as she struggled to get free. She thrashed and kicked and tried everything to get free. But he was too strong. "*Let me go!* I'm going to kill him!"

He set her down but still gripped her so she couldn't escape. He shook her slightly. He ducked his head to look into her eyes. "That's not going to make it better," he told her in a low voice. He gripped her chin tightly and forced her to look at him. "That won't bring her back."

She stared defiantly at him for a long moment.

Marie was dead and it was her fault. If she had grabbed Marie back at the club, she would still be alive. She should have protected her, not used her to find out who was behind everything. Marie was her *friend*, and Emma had used her like every other person had used her.

And now she was dead.

All the fight left Emma at once.

A cry escaped her lips. Her legs gave out beneath her. The Phantom kept her from falling. He pulled her close and held her as she cried.

"I'm sorry," he said into her hair. He pressed her so close to him that his armor dug painfully into her. One of his hands cradled the back of her head. "I'm sorry."

She cried for a long minute before he stepped back. "I'm sorry," he repeated a third time. "But I have to—we have to take care of this, alright?"

She nodded. Tried to wipe the blood and tears from her eyes. But her hands were covered in Marie's—

The Phantom pulled a cellphone from his belt and dialed a number. She focused on him. Him, and not her hands, and not the open doorway beyond him. Just him. The line of his jaw. The green of his eyes. Not the color staining her hands and the floor and—

The Phantom raised the phone to his ear.

A bit deliriously, she hiccupped a laugh. At his quizzical look, she said, "I *knew* you had a cellphone." As long as she focused on that, on *him*, it would be okay. She wouldn't fall apart if she kept her eyes on him and not what was in the room beyond.

"Kendrick," he said after the phone rang only twice. "I need your help."

CHAPTER FIFTEEN

Emma sat on the hood of the beast of a car while they waited for the Phantom's cop friend to show up. Her now-empty gun sat next to her, retrieved by the Phantom at some point when she hadn't been paying attention.

The Phantom took his gloves and remaining gauntlet off and pulled a hefty first aid kit from the backseat.

Emma sat in silence while tears streamed down her face. He meticulously wiped the blood from her hands. His touch was gentle. Careful. She focused on the feeling of his calluses where they scraped her skin. The warmth of him.

"This is going to sting," he murmured as he inspected her head a minute later. He dabbed the cut with alcohol. Emma sucked in a sharp breath but welcomed the pain. It was her fault Marie was dead. All her fault. She had been too slow. She could have saved her at the club but–

"I don't have anything to numb it," the Phantom continued. "Hold still." One of his hands slid to the back of her neck and held her tightly. She closed her eyes and let his touch anchor her. Cold tears splashed her palms where they rested in her lap.

There was a sharp pain and an uncomfortable *yank* as he started stitching her forehead.

"It's supposed to be my turn," she muttered.

"What?"

"You patched my hand up at the club that one time. And before that, I patched you up in my apartment. That means it's my turn now."

She opened her eyes and watched him as he focused on her. "I'm sorry," he said. His voice was low. Deep. Exhausted. "I couldn't save her. It's my fault."

Emma gave a bitter laugh. "It's *my* fault. I could have saved her at the club. I told her–" A new pain washed through her. A pain in her chest. Cracking her open. Splitting her in two. She pushed the words out. She had to say them. She had to admit her guilt. "I told her I wouldn't let them hurt her." Her voice cracked. She sucked in another sharp breath. It hurt to breathe. This pain–this *guilt*–was worse than any physical pain she would ever go through.

The Phantom was already done stitching her up. He set the needle inside the first-aid kit then put his other hand on her neck too. He used the tips of his thumbs to tilt her chin up so she could look him in the eyes.

"I swear to you," he said somberly, the words weighted with anger and something else, "I will find out whoever is involved in this. And I will take them down."

She saw a reflection of her own rage and guilt in his green eyes. She grabbed onto that emotion. Stoked the flames of her anger. Being angry was better than this sadness, this crushing guilt.

"I'm going to help you," she said solemnly. "Whatever it takes. For Marie. For the other five women. *She was the last.*"

They stared at each other like that for a long moment.

That was what had drawn her to him, before she ever even met him. There was an edge inside of him, a hardness, that called to something within her. And this rage…she'd seen it in him, while he was fighting. She understood it now, better than she ever had before. She *saw* him now.

The Phantom gently ran one thumb over her lower lip. She shuddered. She leaned into the touch. "I'm sorry about your friend," he said softly. She closed her eyes. She wanted him to kiss her. To erase what she was feeling, if only for a moment.

An unmarked police car pulled up next to them, interrupting the moment. A Black detective got out.

The Phantom stepped away from her.

"Kendrick," he greeted the man. He slipped his gloves and remaining gauntlet back on. She wondered if he had spares at home, wherever he lived. "This is Emma."

Emma and the detective did a double take at the same moment as the name finally clicked in her head. "Wha–"

"What are you doing here, Em?" Oscar Kendrick said, beating her to the same question. Of all of the detectives in the city, the one the vigilante trusted the most was an old boyfriend of her mom's. Kendrick–she called him Officer Kendrick when he first started dating her mom, then shortened it to Kendrick–was one of the best boyfriends her mom had ever had, actually. The one whose birthday and Christmas cards decorated her dresser at Kane Manor. Her heart squeezed every time she looked at them, because they served as a reminder of what could have been. He'd been the shoulder she cried on at her mom's funeral. Even though things hadn't worked out between them, he still loved Emma, and had loved her mom.

"You know each other?" the Phantom said slowly.

"He used to date my mom when I was a kid," Emma explained. Kendrick inspected the new stitches on her head. She welcomed the familiar touch. Fresh tears spilled over. *Fuck,* was she glad to see him. It was the closest she had felt to her mom's presence since her death.

"What are you doing here?" Kendrick asked her again. When she didn't answer, he turned to the vigilante. "You two know each other? She was with you this whole time?" He shifted protectively in front of her.

"I want you to record a statement from her. Somewhere safe." He went on to explain who was tied up inside, what happened before Kendrick's arrival. What the ADA said about this going deeper than any of them had realized. Why he wanted Emma left out of it.

Kendrick cursed softly. "This is worse than I thought." His words echoed what the Phantom said earlier on the highway during their frantic chase.

"I want you to send me undercover," Emma said before the two men could disappear inside. She would stay in the car this time–actually would. Because if anyone found out she had been there, that she knew Marie and about what was happening, that she was a witness…she would probably be dead before the next sunset.

The Phantom froze. "Emma," he said with a dangerous note of warning in his voice. He glared at her. "You're going to be a witness for *tonight*. That you saw the ADA–saw what he did in there." She didn't miss how he didn't say exactly what happened. "You're going to testify after all this is over, once it's safe."

"No," she said. She stood and clenched her fists. Toe to toe with him now, he had to tilt his head down to look at her. Her chest brushed his. She glared at him. "You're going to send me undercover. Give me a wire, whatever. I'm going to make myself the next target and *we are going to finish this*. I don't care what happens. *They killed her*. I won't let it happen to anyone else!"

The force of her rage made her entire body tremble. Her nails bit into her palms. Anger emanated from him in waves, too, but she stood her ground. *Lainey, Becks, Jackie, Heather, Sofia*. Their names echoed through her with every beat of her heart. *Marie*.

The Phantom must have recognized her obstinance. "We'll talk more with Kendrick later. Somewhere safe."

"We should get going," Kendrick said. He was staring between them with obvious interest. He pointed at her. "Stay here, don't let anyone see you. We'll talk later."

The Phantom gave her one last look as the two men walked away.

Before she got in the car, she heard the detective say, "*How* do you know her?"

Emma didn't hear the answer.

From inside the car, Emma watched as tons of cop cars, an ambulance, the medical examiner, and many others showed up over the next ten minutes.

She watched through heavy-lidded eyes as they rushed inside. Saw Kendrick come out and take over the scene.

Her eyes closed. She didn't want to see them bring out Marie.

Emma jerked awake to the noise of the driver's side door opening. Had she fallen asleep?

"It's just me," the Phantom said as he climbed in. She saw that most of the vehicles outside were gone. She had no idea what time it was, only that it was well past the middle of the night. His hands clenched and unclenched around the steering wheel. "We can do this another time if—"

"I'm okay," she said. She sat up. Her head was hurting terribly, and her mouth tasted like a dumpster in a desert. But she wanted to do this. She needed to do this. "Let's go."

He drove them to a half-built tower in the city. He entered a code on a panel and led her up to the top in a rickety elevator. There were no walls at the top and the breeze was brutally cold. Kendrick already waited in the darkness, arms crossed.

"Is this…a secret hideout?" she asked. She peered around curiously.

A ghost of a smile on the Phantom's lips. "Something like that."

"Alright?" Kendrick asked when he saw them.

"I want you to send me undercover," she said again. She wasn't going to be talked out of it. She could feel the Phantom stiffen next to her. She ignored him. "I work in a secret VIP club downstairs at the Crescent Club. All fi—*six* women have gone missing from there. I want to make myself the next target."

Kendrick blinked at her. "Em, I'm not sure that's a great idea." He glanced between them. He was the only one, besides her mom, who called her Em. She resisted the urge to catch up with him, to lose herself in the familiarity in order to forget her night even just for a moment. "Yeah, I can see why you two are friends. Stubborn as shit. Okay. I want to go ahead and record a statement from you about tonight first, though, while it's still fresh. Then we'll figure out the rest."

She nodded. As a kid, Kendrick never treated her like she was too young. He was always upfront with her, no matter what.

He got out his phone and hit record. "Okay, whenever you're ready. This is Detective Oscar Kendrick—" He rattled off the day, time, her name, and where they were.

She swallowed. This was going to be hard. Rehashing the events.

"Tonight I finished a shift in the VIP section at the Crescent Club where I work." Emma explained the nature of the club, the corrupt people who frequented it, and the information about the other missing girls being drugged. Kendrick's eyebrows rose when she said they were all connected as employees of the VIP club.

Kendrick nodded. "Which the Phantom informed me during our investigation. Go on."

"Marie and I finished at the same time but she was with…a client. I recognized him as the assistant district attorney. Everything was weird but the Wolf—our boss Wolfgang Meyer—was there. I thought everyone was just on their best behavior for him. But when Marie came out, she…wasn't herself. She was…blank. Like she was possessed. Drugged. She didn't react to anything I said or did. I even slapped her and—"

She choked on the next words. The Phantom's hand settled reassuringly against her back. Kendrick gave her an encouraging nod. "I told her I wouldn't let them hurt her, but I needed to see who it was. So I hid. Heard a man tell her that 'they' were waiting outside. I was just a little too slow and—" God, she couldn't do this. A few tears leaked out.

"We can take a break if you need to," Kendrick said softly. She shivered in the wind. But she shook her head.

The Phantom angled himself so he blocked most of the wind. She shot him a grateful look and press on.

"I'm okay. When I went outside, the assistant district attorney was putting Marie in a car—the one that was wrecked at the warehouse. There were other men with him. One of the men outside the car shot at me, grazing my head. Then they left."

She glanced at the Phantom now. Was she allowed to say that she'd been with him? What should she explain? He couldn't testify in court, could he? He might even be the reason the testimony could be thrown out. She had no idea how a vigilante fit into the justice system.

Both men patiently waited for her to continue. She quickly re-hashed what they went through following the car and entering the warehouse. "When we found her, Marie was still drugged. The assistant district attorney was there. Some other men escaped, and–and then–" She closed her eyes. She had to do this. She couldn't save Marie, but she could make sure the men responsible for her death went to jail. Forever. If she didn't kill them herself first. "The ADA put a gun to her head. The Phantom tried to talk him down. Tried to convince him to testify. But he was frantic. Said he wouldn't make it to jail. Said it all went so much deeper than we realized. He freaked out. And he–he killed her and I–we couldn't stop him, I couldn't stop him–" Hard, hiccupping sobs pushed their way out of her chest but she kept talking. "I wanted to kill him. I tased him even though he was unconscious. I hope he has brain damage, I–"

"That's enough," Kendrick said quietly. He stopped the recording after saying the time again. "Thank you. I'm sorry about your friend. About all of this. Are you sure you want to…go undercover?" Even as a kid, he took her seriously. He never treated her as someone delicate, but rather as someone strong. He was doing the same thing now instead of brushing her off. "I don't know half of what you've been through, but we can find another way if this is too much."

She leveled him with a furious stare through her tears. "I'm positive."

The Phantom couldn't hold his tongue anymore, it seemed. He ground out each word as he said through his teeth, "I *really* don't think–"

Emma whirled on him. "No! You're not the only stubborn one here! You don't get to be the only one doing dangerous things to save people! I am *fully aware* of what doing this could lead to and I don't care!" She was on her toes so she could shout right in his face. Poked him in the chest to punctuate each sentence. She wasn't angry at him, not really. But she couldn't stop hearing the sound of that gunshot. The sound of Marie's body hitting the floor. And the anger was safer, easier, than the guilt.

Kendrick very much looked like he wanted to be somewhere else.

"I have been doing this much longer than you," the Phantom said in that dangerous voice. He didn't back down, but neither did she.

"She was my *friend*." Emma's voice broke on the word. "And I won't let there be any more dead girls. I'm going to do this with or without your help."

"You shouldn't–"

"I just *said* I was doing this with or without you. I don't need your permission," she snarled. She knew she shouldn't be taking it out on him, but the emotions within her were too much. They were too big. She was angry and hurt and scared and goddamn if she didn't want to hit something. And the Phantom might just be that something if he wasn't careful.

His mouth snapped audibly closed. "Fine."

He seemed angry with her for wanting to endanger herself. But she *had* to act. And if she couldn't be like him and put on a mask and cape, she would do the only thing she *could* do.

The Phantom quietly explained that he had some sort of fancy contact lenses and earpieces that recorded audio and visual of everything he did each night.

She was mortified that he had recordings of their sparring sessions. Of each time she stared at him a little too long. But it would be much more helpful than wearing an actual wire, and more discreet, too. Did he have some sort of rich benefactor, she wondered? Or maybe, underneath the mask, he was some sort of genius tech wizard. The more she learned about him, the more her curiosity grew.

Dawn was breaking over the skyline of New Atlas by the time they finished.

Exhaustion settled into Emma's bones.

They told Kendrick goodbye. He promised to do his best to make sure the ADA stayed alive. Promised that her statement would stay in his hands until they had more to go on. He thanked her for her help again. Before he left, he placed one warm, steady hand on her shoulder. That, more than anything else, comforted her.

When the elevator reached the ground, she grabbed her bag out of the car but didn't get in. She continued walking past it.

"Where are you going?" the Phantom asked from behind her.

She stopped. "There's…a subway station near here. It's only one stop away from home."

He was staring at her. "I could–"

She smiled gently. "I don't think I want to explain to James Kane why I'm getting out of *that* at the break of dawn at his security gate." She pointed at the car, which was armored and bulky and not really a car.

He was giving her an odd look.

"Don't worry, I still have my taser." She'd have to get more bullets for her gun. "It's only one stop. Besides, even the criminals are asleep this late. Or early."

"Alright," he said grudgingly.

She didn't want to leave him either. There was a deeper understanding between them now. A bond forged in blood. And he made her feel safe. He *kept* her safe. She remembered the way he angled his body in front of hers as the ADA had waved the gun around. The way he'd roared in fury as he hit the man who'd almost taken her down.

"Goodnight," she said softly. Before she could think better of it, she stood up on her toes and kissed his stubble-roughened cheek. "I'll see you soon."

He was quiet for a long moment. Finally, his voice barely a murmur, he said, "Goodnight, Emma."

When she reached the subway station, she looked back. He was standing at the corner watching her. She lifted her hand in a wave before descending the stairs.

The train was totally empty, which was good because she was still covered in blood. Her own, and–She stopped the thoughts before they reached their end.

When Emma reached Kane Manor, she found Douglas drinking a cup of tea at the kitchen counter. He was reading the newspaper like he did every morning. The sun had fully risen in the short time it took to get from the subway station to home.

She was keenly aware of how she looked in the morning light. The knees of her pants were torn. There was blood all over her shirt and her pants. Her hair was a mess and caked with blood. Her forehead had ugly stitches and to top it all off, she was limping.

Douglas didn't seem surprised to see her, even in her current state, though his forehead did crinkle with concern. She'd expected him to startle or at least leap to his feet, but all he did was stand slowly as he said, "Emma! Are you–"

"I'm okay, Douglas. I promise." She bit her lip and then said, "I just–I'll be fine."

"What on *earth* happened? Are you sure you're alright?" He hovered around her, worry furrowing his brow even more deeply. It made her throat tight. She wished she'd gotten a hug from Kendrick before they parted.

She managed to nod. "A friend of mine was killed." She closed her eyes against the fresh wash of pain.

Douglas settled a hand on her shoulder. "Oh, Emma, I'm so sorry. Is there anything I can do? Would you like breakfast? Should I call Dr. Torres?"

She shook her head. "Maybe later. I just need to shower and sleep. Thank you, though." She swallowed around the lump in her throat. "I just–I just need to sleep."

Douglas nodded and stepped back. He watched her with eyes full of concern. "Please let me know if you need anything. *Anything.*"

She trudged up to her room. She peeled her clothes off and stood naked waiting for the shower to heat up. It seemed like a year had passed since she'd left for her shift. So much had changed in a single night. In just a few hours.

Marie had left for work the night before, and now she wasn't ever going home.

Emma let the hot water beat down on her back. She leaned her forehead against the cold tiles. The water swirled, red first then pink. It burned where it touched the wound on her head and the scrapes on her knees. Her knuckles were swollen and a bruise bloomed on her side.

And she hadn't been able to save Marie.

With a soft sob she slid to the floor. She didn't move, even once the water ran cold.

Only then did she rouse herself and get dressed. She needed sleep. Sleep would make it hurt less. If she was sleeping, she wasn't reliving what happened. Sleep would numb the bright pain she felt with every breath.

She got in bed, but every time she closed her eyes, she heard the gunshot. Saw Marie fall. Felt blood soak into the knees of her pants. Felt it stick to her hands. She couldn't get herself to reach that numbness that sleep promised. It stayed just out of reach. Every time she tried to relax, she jerked awake as she remembered the horror of the night.

The next time she opened her eyes it was late evening. She'd barely slept. She was hungry, though, so she needed to get up and eat. She shuffled downstairs to find James in the kitchen reheating something in the microwave. When he saw her, there was an odd look in his eyes.

Oh, right. The head wound. Plus, the bedhead from tossing and turning. She couldn't find enough energy to be self-conscious. She expected him to be shocked at her state. Not this…calmness.

"How's your head?" he asked softly.

"It's alright," she said, though it hurt pretty badly. She deserved the pain. Deserved its reminder. She was alive. Marie wasn't. And it was her fault. "I was just–getting something to eat."

James's cheeks turned pink. He gestured to the microwave. "This is…for you. I thought you might be hungry." His shoulders hunched.

Something warmed in her chest. She realized why he didn't seem shocked. "Douglas told you then?"

James hesitated. There was an emotion behind his eyes that she couldn't place. "Yes," he finally said.

"I–it was my fault she died," she whispered. She closed her eyes against the emotions. "It was my fault." She opened her eyes again as James reached a hand towards her but drew it back. The microwave beeped.

Who was going to tell Marie's family? Kendrick? Marie left for a normal night of work and now she was never going home again. Her boyfriend would be wondering where she was, waiting on her to get back–

Tears started slipping down Emma's cheeks one after the other. She covered her face with her hands so James didn't have to watch her come apart in front of him *again*. But she forgot about the stitches in her forehead. She hissed as one of her fingers snagged the wound.

James was suddenly right there. He gently grabbed her neck and tilted her face up towards the light.

"You're bleeding," he murmured. He used the sleeve of his shirt to dab at the blood.

"Would you believe that I was shot in the head and that the Phantom stitched me up?" She leaned into his touch. Remembered what it was like to kiss him. A hunger yawned within her. She wanted him to make her forget the night before. Make her present in her body in a way that didn't involve pain.

Her breathing came faster as she stared into his eyes. She traced the shape of his jaw with her eyes. His nose. His lips.

Something stirred in the back of her mind. Some distant bell rang, swiftly dismissed as she closed her eyes.

Please kiss me, she thought. She almost said it out loud.

One of his thumbs gently traced her lower lip. "I am…really sorry about your friend."

Her eyes snapped open.

No. It was crazy. She was crazy. She had a head wound. But–

But James Kane acted and sounded a lot like the Phantom.

She remembered the Phantom stitching her up. *His* thumb tracing her lip. And when she'd been shot, there had been a moment when she thought James had called her name.

No. It couldn't be.

The microwave beeped a reminder.

She took a deliberate step away while her mind spun at a thousand miles an hour.

"I'll let you eat," James said. He stepped away too. He stared at her for another long moment. Then he was gone.

Her mind started piecing things together too fast for her to keep up with. The familiarity she felt when she met James Kane. The long scar on his abdomen, right where she'd put bandages on the Phantom. His odd hours. The blood on him when she almost hit him with a fire poker. His jaw. His voice. His lips.

Another memory resurfaced. Something she'd forgotten. After the Wolf had ordered her to be beaten, she'd woken on the floor of Kane Manor to James standing over her. And she'd seen the oddest thing.

Smudges of black around his eyes.

There was no way James Kane was the Phantom. Right?

CHAPTER SIXTEEN

EMMA

Emma convinced herself that she was imagining things.

Why, of all people, would a *billionaire* become a *vigilante*? He could simply hire people to help in the city. Or fund charities. Or become mayor. Or all of the above. Why would he put on armor and a mask and a cape and fight crime every night? It made more sense for someone like *her*–someone with nothing, someone that New Atlas never did anything good for–to become a vigilante. Someone with nothing to lose. Someone with something to be angry about.

And if he *was* the Phantom, why had James been lying to her? Why not just come out and say it? She spent so much time with *both* of them, had gotten to know them both. Didn't he trust her?

Maybe she just wanted them to be the same person. She couldn't deny that she was drawn to them *both*. James was awkward and sweet and good. She'd made out with him, after all. Definitely had a crush on him.

And the Phantom…they had a bond; there was no denying it. She couldn't exactly call it a crush, but something about him called to her. Drew her in.

Sure, she noticed similarities. But being a nocturnal billionaire who'd been beaten up once or twice did not make him a vigilante. And being a vigilante with all kinds of fancy gadgets didn't mean the Phantom was a billionaire.

The more she thought about it, the less convinced she became. Memory was a tricky thing. It was easy to see things that weren't really there. She was emotionally vulnerable and trying to connect the man who made her feel safe with the cute, shy man she had a crush on.

That afternoon, Dr. Torres came and inspected her head at Douglas's request. He told her she was incredibly lucky, that whoever had done the stitches had done a good job. He promised to come back in a few days to take the stitches out.

James and Douglas gave her the week off, but she worked anyway. She worked until she was so tired she fell into bed each night.

But even exhaustion couldn't keep the nightmares away.

Each night, she got only a handful of hours of sleep before she gasped awake from visions of Marie's body.

"You said they wouldn't hurt me," Marie said to Emma in one such nightmare four nights after her death. Her blonde hair was red with her own blood.

Emma woke with a scream stuck in her throat.

She knew she wouldn't be able to go back to sleep. Not after that. So she dressed quietly and went downstairs to the kitchen for the first of many cups of coffee.

While the coffee machine hummed on the counter, Emma pulled up the news on her phone. She'd been scouring it for anything, *anything*, about the disappearing women, the ADA, or Marie's death.

So far, it had been quiet.

But her heart lurched at a breaking news banner across the top of the Atlas One website.

ASSISTANT DISTRICT ATTORNEY ARRESTED; FOUND DEAD IN CELL

She clicked the news story as fast as she could. Her entire body trembled with trepidation.

> *Elijah Grove, New Atlas's assistant district attorney of the last two years, was found dead late last night. Grove was arrested in what a source inside NAPD is calling a "top-secret sting operation." The details of Grove's arrest have not been made public, nor where he was being held. The details of his death also have not been released, but initial reports suggest suicide. For further updates…*

Emma sat back, stunned, as the coffee maker beeped. *No,* she thought desperately. *Kendrick was supposed to keep him safe.*

But if powerful men *were* in on it, the ADA's murder was no surprise. He'd even said they would kill him. He had warned them.

Emma was lost. What were they supposed to do now? Grove was an important piece of the puzzle–he *knew* what was going on, was going to testify. And now she was the only witness they had.

It was more important than ever that she make herself a target, she realized. There was more riding on it than before.

And she couldn't find it within herself to be too sorry that the bastard had died.

That night, before her shift at the Crescent Club, Emma arrived early and found the Phantom waiting around the corner. He took her up to the same roof as always, but this time from the other side. Her skin was electric where he grabbed her, even though his armor was a thick barrier between them. She glanced up at him as they soared through the air, his face close to her own.

"How are you?" he asked as soon as he set her down. He touched her jaw, inspected her head. Dr. Torres had come by that morning to remove the stitches. Her eyes traced the lines of his chin and mouth, searching for familiarity. But his lips moving quickly distracted her. "Seems to be healing okay."

"I'm okay," she said.

He nodded and took something from his belt.

"Did you see the news?" she asked as he handed her something small.

"Yes."

She took the little piece of plastic from him. "They killed him, just like he said."

"Earpiece," the Phantom explained. "I'll be able to hear you and vice versa. So if you need me, at all, just say the word." She nodded, inserted it into her ear. He handed her the next item, popped it open. "This contact lens is also a camera. I'll be able to see what you see. You won't be able to get too far without me knowing."

She managed to get it into her eye after a few minutes. She blinked until it didn't bother her as much.

"Look at me," he said. She did, tilting her chin up slightly. "Looks good. And I made these this week." He pulled out a small box. It contained two simple black earring studs. "GPS trackers. Even if you lose one, the other will work. If you have to, swallow one or both of them. They'll still work. I tested it."

She almost laughed at the thought of the vigilante swallowing an earring and making sure it still worked after it came out.

"Please tell me that these are a different pair," she teased.

He opened his mouth, then closed it again. "These are–they're new, I swear," he stammered. The laugh escaped her in a burst.

She already felt calmer. Safer. He would be watching and listening. Looking out for her. For the first time in days, she was able to take a deep breath. Knowing she was *doing* something helped settle her, too.

"They killed him," she repeated since he hadn't responded to her the first time. "He can't testify now."

"I know," he said, but he softened the words. His green eyes were shadowed.

"I feel like a spy," she muttered as she put the earrings in. She glanced up at his tall form. "Do I–know you?" she blurted. She hadn't meant to ask. But for a week, thoughts of him and James had been keeping her awake when the nightmares weren't. That one tiny little thought stuck in her head–that maybe they were the same person. For the millionth time, she imagined those two small moments, the thumb against her lower lip.

He went unnaturally still. "Know me?"

"Yeah–I mean, outside of the mask. Have we met before?" She fiddled with the new earrings. "I swear sometimes you're…familiar."

He shook his head. "No. No, you don't know me." His voice was firm, unwavering.

She relaxed. She was probably right that underneath the mask he was someone more like her. Someone who didn't have much. Someone with nothing to lose. Someone who New Atlas had wronged time and again. Not someone like James Kane, who had everything to lose.

"Sorry. I just–" She shrugged. Warmth settled in her cheeks.

"Are you sure you're okay?" His voice softened again.

"I'm okay. Let's just–let's get this over with."

"It might take weeks for anything to happen. They haven't been…taking women as frequently. But don't push too hard." His face was harder to read than usual. A mask within a mask. Was he worried about her?

She grabbed his gloved hand. "I'll be alright. I've got the Phantom watching out for me. Remember?" She smiled, though her chest squeezed. She hated feeling like a burden, like something he had to go out of his way to watch out for.

His grip tightened. "I won't let anything happen to you. I swear it."

She almost reminded him that she had told Marie that exact thing.

It hurt going inside and going downstairs. Everything reminded her of Marie. Of her failure. Had it really only been less than a week? It felt as if an entire lifetime had already passed.

The place was running as usual, though. Like Marie wasn't gone.

She had a short shift that night. Her focus would be laying the groundwork, showing herself as more willing to the patrons. More like Marie. More like the other girls. She wasn't sure what the mysterious "they" were looking for. But she would make sure they were looking for her next.

Lena was her section partner that night. "Did you hear?" she asked in a soft voice while they picked up drink orders from the bar.

"Hear what?" she asked distractedly. So far she'd marked about a dozen likely suspects. Only half of them were in her section. And only half of those were regulars. The assistant district attorney had been a regular. That made her assume that the regulars–maybe all of them–were involved. That, and the atmosphere that night, when Marie was taken. Some of the other patrons had seemed…anticipatory.

"They–found Marie. She's–she's dead." Lena choked out the words. She tried to keep a pleasant expression on her face but failed. Her warm brown eyes filled with tears.

Emma knocked her entire tray of drinks over.

"I'm sorry," Lena whispered. They both bent to clean it up. "I know you two were friends. Hey, what happened to your head?"

Emma held back tears. She took a deep breath to steady herself. "I fell. Do they–is it related to…the others?"

She glanced around as she said it. *Lainey, Becks, Jackie, Heather, Sofia, Marie.* They haunted her. She didn't know any of them other than Marie, but she felt like she did. Like she had failed to protect them all by not protecting Marie.

Lena's expression turned fearful. Terrified. Her eyes darted around the room. She busied herself cleaning up the drinks. "Later," she murmured, so low Emma barely heard it.

"Okay. I get off at midnight."

"Okay," Lena whispered.

Emma's heart squeezed hopefully. Maybe she would get a few more answers.

After they remade her tray of drinks, Emma strode over to the waiting table.

"So sorry for the delay, guys," she smiled pleasantly. "I'm a little clumsy lately." She set the drinks out. Made sure to look each of the men in the eye. "Got a bump on the head to prove it."

One of the regulars who came most weekends grinned up at her with heavy-lidded eyes.

"That's Lionel Maxwell," the Phantom's voice suddenly said in her ear. She almost jumped. "He owns New Atlas National Bank." NANB was a huge bank, really the only one that mattered in New Atlas. Everyone rich and powerful banked with them, and they had seven locations in the city alone.

The man grabbed her arm and yanked her down onto his lap. "You sure are. Look, you fell right over. Good thing I caught you." His arm snaked around her waist. She closed her eyes for the briefest moment. She wanted to throw up. Scream. Strangle him with her bare hands.

Instead, she laughed. "Seems like I did. Thanks for catching me." She leaned in close and gave him a more seductive smile.

JAMES

"Can I reward you with a dance?"

Emma's voice was almost unrecognizable as she said, "I'd love nothing more, baby."

James gripped the edge of the old table so hard it groaned beneath him. He was in a nearby abandoned building, close enough to get to her in case anything happened, far enough away to stay hidden. The table was the only piece of furniture left in the place.

He was watching through Emma's eyes on a laptop, and he hated every second of it. His mouth tasted of ash as he watched other men put hands on her. He had to listen to the disgusting things they promised to do to her.

James's anger became a living, breathing thing.

He likely had to endure weeks of this. He wasn't sure he could. How did she do it, night after night after night?

If it was the last thing he did, he'd make sure no creeps like the one she currently danced with would *ever* touch her again.

Jealousy was an entirely new emotion for him. Something he hadn't known until he met Emma. And now it was almost second nature for him to feel jealous. Every night she worked at the Crescent Club, every night she wasn't under *his* roof where he knew she was safe, every smile she gave someone else, the jealousy threatened to wipe him out. It was an ugly emotion, jealousy. It wasn't familiar, like the anger.

He remembered what it was like to kiss her. It overwhelmed him sometimes. He rarely touched *anyone* unless it was as the Phantom, and that was only ever violence. So the feeling of her skin, hell, the feeling of her simply *near* him consumed his every sense. He had never experienced anything like it before. It was like she'd opened him up and reached inside. Every nerve was a live wire when he was near her.

And the rage–the rage was nothing new.

But with her, it became a wholly different monster. It became more… real. *Alive* in a way it hadn't been in years. His first encounter with it had been shocking, when he'd found his mother dead in their car in the driveway. Strangled. And even at age nine, James knew that stone-cold fury was a strange response to the trauma of it all. Something that only grew and grew and grew after they arrested his father, after his father hung himself in his study.

The rage had never left him. He hadn't felt that kind of pure fury since his parents' deaths, since his first months as the Phantom.

But when Emma was in danger…He could have killed for her. He *would* have killed for her. Something he swore he would never do, a line he would never cross. Yet he would willingly cross it for her.

Watching through Emma's eyes, James caught a glimpse of the Wolf lurking in the background, unnoticed by her. He thought the rage reached a new high when he found out that the Wolf had beaten her.

But that night in the warehouse, hearing her cry of pain, seeing that man standing over her about to hurt her….He acted purely on instinct. Hit the man so many times he was surprised the man *hadn't* died. He only stopped because *she* stopped him. It was like he had become someone else entirely within that rage. Not James. Not the Phantom. Just an animal driven by the basest need to *protect*.

And when the ADA had a gun pointed at her…

He had never purposefully killed anyone before, but that night he would have done it. He would have crossed the one line he had sworn never to cross. For *her*.

He remembered her ferocity that night. Her own rage. The fire within her that he'd only gotten small glimpses of before. It was so like the rage and fire within *him* that it scared him. It scared him to see a mirror image of himself within *her*. There were parts of her–especially now, especially after the death of her friend–that called to the darkest parts of him. But she deserved to have that darkness erased. He wanted to take it from her, take the burden of her shadows upon himself. He could handle shadows and darkness and rage. She wasn't meant for that life. He was.

He still couldn't understand why he felt so…protective towards her. Why he wanted nothing more than to be *closer* to her.

He was worried he might fall in love with her if given the chance.

He didn't know *how* to love. He loved Douglas, sure, but Douglas was…his caretaker. His friend. The only family he had left.

He didn't know if she could love him as he was. He didn't know if he could love her like she deserved.

Emma thought James Kane was good. And she deserved someone *good*. Someone better than him. Someone who didn't put her in danger. He didn't think she could love someone who was barely James. Someone who was the Phantom more than he was normal.

If she ever found out about him, she wouldn't want him.

This darkness in him, this rage, it wasn't made for love. It wasn't made for the light. He was meant for the shadows. To be alone in the darkness.

And she was someone made of light. Even with her own shadows, she was the brightest thing he had ever seen.

She was getting close. Too close. She asked if she knew him, said he was familiar to her. He needed to keep his distance. But he didn't think he could, not anymore. Not when she was in so much danger. The more time he spent with her, the more dangerous it became. And the harder it got to stay away.

James watched as the man, Lionel Maxwell, led Emma off the dance floor.

He was terrified that she would go into one of those rooms with a man. That she might have to in order to get to the bottom of this. Already, because of him, she had been beaten, shot in the head, and forced to watch her friend die. He couldn't bear it if she had to go into one of those rooms, too. She had been through enough.

The table creaked again, threatening to break. His shoulders shook with tension.

He watched as she went back over to the bar. She stared at it for a long minute. He could see her hands on the counter clenched so tightly the knuckles were white.

"Are you okay?" he asked softly.

"I'm fine," she practically growled. She grabbed a drink and went to another table.

She offered another dance.

But James wasn't okay.

He wouldn't be until this was over. Until she was safe. Until he had gotten rid of every monster that could hurt her.

CHAPTER SEVENTEEN

Lena met Emma after her shift. *Later*, she'd told her. It felt like a promise.

"Walk with me to the subway?" Emma asked with a false brightness. She hoped Lena heard her unspoken words. *They're watching.* She had no idea how deep this whole thing went, but she had to assume *anyone* could be a part of it. It made her paranoid, had kept her paranoid all night.

Lena smiled. "Of course. I've been meaning to ask you…"

They chatted idly as they went outside. They talked about nothing for several blocks before Lena unceremoniously yanked Emma around a corner.

"That man," she breathed. "That you were dancing with."

"Lionel," she said with a nod. It wasn't the direction she was expecting Lena to go in, but information was information. And Emma was desperate for more.

"He left with the second girl. I don't–I don't remember her name, she was pretty new, but–hers was the first body they found." Lena trembled with fear. Her eyes darted around like someone might jump from the shadows at any moment. *Becks,* Emma's mind supplied. "Please be careful. That's six now. If there's another–"

Emma held the other girl's hands tightly. "I'm not going to let anything happen. To you or anyone else. Okay?"

But Emma said the same thing to Marie, and she died anyway.

Lena blinked rapidly but nodded. Some of her dark hair blew into her eyes. "I just thought you should know. To be careful. He's part of this. Whatever it is. You shouldn't be alone with him if you can help it."

"Thank you," Emma said, and meant it. "Really."

"I gotta–I gotta get back." Lena's eyes darted around before she hurried back the way they had come.

"Did you hear that?" Emma asked aloud a minute later. "She said Lionel Maxwell is part of this."

"If you don't wan–"

She interrupted before he could finish. "I'm doing this. For–Marie. For Lena, for the other girls. I know you don't like it and I don't either. But I have to. *I have to.*"

The Phantom was silent for so long she started trudging towards the subway station. She'd been nurturing her anger after Marie's death. It was a constant shadow in her heart. Each day that those men were still out there, the shadow grew. But that anger had a direction now. She was acting on it, and she would help the Phantom solve this. And Lionel Maxwell was the next step.

"I don't like it," he admitted. She shivered at the intimacy of having him in her ear. "But I won't let there be another missing girl."

"No," she said. "Neither will I."

Emma didn't mean to put off going into a private room with Maxwell, but every time he offered, fear seized her heart and wouldn't let go. The excuses were wearing thin, and Maxwell was becoming impatient. This was her chance. She needed to act.

For Marie.

"You're driving me crazy," Maxwell said as she let him dance against her. "Please let me take you to a room. I'm not above begging."

She flashed him a quick smile. How could she get him into a room and *not* have sex with him? She knew her limits and knew that she couldn't do it. She simply couldn't. She just needed to get him into a room so he could drug her, take her to the others. Show his hand.

Think, she told herself. But it was hard with his hands on her. He was heavily drunk already. She was practically holding him up as he rubbed against her. Her jaw ached from clenching her teeth so hard. *Think, dammit. Think!* He wasn't going to take many more excuses. For all she knew, he wanted to kidnap her tonight. And that was the goal, right?

But maybe he wasn't going to. Maybe he really did want to–She shut the thought down. She had to keep him thinking she would, but find a way to not let it happen. She wanted to be kidnapped, not raped.

Her thoughts finally cleared enough to think, *Maybe I can get him too drunk to have sex with me but trick him into thinking we did.* Wasn't there a movie where that happened? Marie would have known. Emma's heart ached sharply at the thought.

"Alright," she murmured in his ear. There was a sharp intake of breath in her own ear, but the Phantom said nothing. "But let's get a drink first, yeah?"

Maxwell shuddered. He gave her a predatory grin. "Anything you want, baby."

At the bar, he ordered for both of them. She kept an eye on her drink while they made it and handed it to her. It was the perfect opportunity for him to slip her whatever drug they were using. But he didn't touch it.

The silence in her ear was pointed. Strained. She knew the Phantom was watching. Knew he understood what might be about to happen. She was glad for his silence. If he said anything, she might back down. She knew he was more than willing to jump in and help her, but she needed to do it herself. She relied on him too much already.

Emma took a couple of sips of her drink while Lionel Maxwell guzzled his in one go.

"I'm not finished." She pretended to pout. She leaned in closer and murmured, "I'd hate to waste it…"

He laughed. "I'm done waiting, baby." He grabbed her drink and drank that too.

Emma took his hand and tugged him behind her towards a room with a green light. The drunker he was, the better. The drunker he was, the less able he was to try anything with her. Even if he or an accomplice were going to kidnap her, at least she wouldn't have to suffer through anything else. She wrapped that knowledge around herself like armor.

"I'd love to hear more about your job," she said as she opened the door. "Working at a big bank sounds so…important." She almost winced at how terrible her flirting was.

As soon as the door closed and locked behind them, his hands were all over her. He kissed her neck. Her shoulders. Behind her ear. She forced herself not to tense up. Not to push him away. She gave the fakest sounding giggle she'd ever heard.

There was a noise in her ear like something snapping. She imagined the Phantom clenching his jaw so hard it broke, and the thought made her smile even as it distracted her.

The room was so much smaller with two people in it. She remembered her night with Cohen, who had been sweet, respectful. This was the exact opposite.

"Take a seat," she told Maxwell. She gave him a not-so gentle push. He fell onto the bed, his eyes glazed over with alcohol and desire. "Get comfortable while I make you another drink, yeah?" She ran a finger down his chest, and purred, "Let me take care of you." Her heart was pounding in her throat and she tasted bile. She really didn't want to see this man naked. But she needed to turn her back. Give him an opportunity to drug her, if he was going to. Or give him an opportunity to contact someone who would.

She mixed him a really, really strong drink. "I wish I had a roofie right about now," she muttered. A breath of laughter in her ear.

"What's that, baby?" Maxwell slurred from the bed.

She turned with his drink in her hand and a shy smile on her face.

He was shirtless now, his slacks unbuttoned. She didn't look any closer at his lap.

He stood. Took the drink from her and took a sip. Then he kissed her.

She tensed up. She was going to throw up in his mouth. He tasted of alcohol. He stank of body odor. Every part of him was sweaty where it touched her. His free hand groped for her ass, her chest, anything he could reach. Finally, she relaxed enough to kiss him back a little.

She let her mind drift away, out of her body, to a different night with a different man and a different kiss.

Maxwell pulled away, breathing heavily. "You taste good, baby."

Emma smiled and averted her gaze.

He took another sip of his drink. "Your turn to get more comfortable," he slurred. Her experience with bartending made it easy to tell that he had to be close to his limit. But with each moment that he was still conscious, Emma grew nervous. If he didn't pass out soon…

She pushed him lightly. "Sit," she commanded. "Drink. And I'll let you watch."

"What are you–" came the choked voice in her ear.

"Patience," she said, pretending she was talking to the man she stood over.

She smiled down at him. He stared up at her with a dazed expression. His blinks were slow, like he had to drag his eyes open each time they closed. Close. So close.

She unbuttoned her shorts. "Drink," she said again. "Or no show for you." She gave another fake giggle. Shimmied her hips a little. She imagined what it would be like to wrap her hands around his fat neck and squeeze until he choked.

Maxwell drank. And drank. And drank. He swayed as he did.

He was still conscious.

Emma had to swallow hard to keep from actually puking.

She slid her shorts down with another little wiggle. Turned around and let him see the lacy underwear she wore. She closed her eyes. Fiddled playfully with the straps of her tiny shirt that was really only a bra. She had nothing on underneath it.

There was a soft thunk.

She turned back around.

Maxwell sprawled out on the bed. His mostly empty glass had fallen to the floor.

"Oh thank God," she breathed. She immediately bent and put her shorts back on. Gagged. Went to the minibar and rinsed her mouth with the first bottle of alcohol she could grab. Vodka. She gagged again at the burn of it. Coughed.

"*Fuck*," she said. Her hands were shaking. Her stomach roiled. She smacked a fist into the wall. The pain across her knuckles did nothing to make her feel better, so she did it again. "*Fuck!*" she shouted. She was grateful for the soundproofing in the room.

Emma sank to the floor. She thought she was beyond the fear—thought that she was strong enough to face this. But it choked her, surprising her with its sharp teeth.

"Are you okay?" the Phantom demanded. There was the subtlest shake to his voice. Like he barely held his anger in check.

"I'm okay. I have a plan."

She let her head rest in her hands for a few minutes.

Finally, Emma stood. Got rid of her pants again. Pinched her neck, hard. Then her lips. Shook her hair out and messed up the back.

She stalked over to Lionel Maxwell's prone figure and messed up his hair too. Pulled his pants down a little farther, leaving him in just his underwear.

Then she crawled into the bed next to him with her skin crawling. She straddled him.

Anger rose within her, swift and unexpected. She wanted to hit him. Drag him naked into the streets outside. She reached down and pinched his lower lip as hard as she could.

His eyes flew open.

She giggled again. "That good, huh?" she breathed. Trailed a finger over his chest. Stretched lazily. His hands came to rest on her ass.

"Wha—how long was I out?" He sat up with bleary eyes.

"Just a minute, that's all. Did you forget already?" She gave an exaggerated pout. "Couldn't even get our clothes off all the way." She winked and smirked down at him. Imagined again what it would be like to wrap her hands around his neck and squeeze. She wondered if he had touched Marie. If he had forced any of the other girls into having sex with him, or anything else. She needed him to believe they'd had sex–because then maybe he'd leave her alone. Maybe, if he thought himself satisfied, he'd move on with the kidnapping.

He shook his head and smiled. "Of course not. You're–exquisite. Absolutely amazing."

"I should get back to my shift, yeah?" she said in a whisper. "Maybe I'll see you tomorrow?"

The man smiled wider. "I sure hope so. You've kept me waiting long enough."

When she stood, he stayed on the bed. He fumbled in his pockets and pulled out a hundred dollar bill he tucked into her bra. His hands lingered on her breasts. Pain bit into her palms as she clenched her fists. His eyes were still bleary, confused. Good.

She yanked her shorts back on. "See you later," she murmured. It was a struggle not to run out of the room. From the corner of her eye, she saw the light turn from red to green again.

Emma was shaking by the time she saw her section partner and said she was taking her break.

By the time she was on the elevator, she couldn't breathe.

Air. She needed air. She needed to get *out*.

Upstairs, she grabbed her coat and burst outside.

It was thundering. As the door slammed shut behind her, the first drops of rain started falling. It was a cold rain, but she barely felt it.

She jogged down the alley and around the corner. Then down the very next alley. Found a fire escape and climbed and climbed until she reached a familiar roof.

She scrambled onto the roof and bent over. She gagged and heaved, but nothing came up.

There was a shadow waiting for her.

The rain started pounding down around them.

"Hi," she said. Humiliation spread warm, oily fingers through her. He'd watched all that. Heard all of it. "I didn't realize you watched from up here."

The Phantom stepped closer to her. "It's freezing," he said instead of answering.

She shrugged. The rain washed the feeling of Maxwell's skin and sweat and mouth away. "Do you just sit out here all night with a laptop or something?"

The Phantom shook his head. "No, but I was nearby, just in case."

Something ached in her chest. She watched rivulets of rain trail over the sharp planes of his mask and armor. His hood was down for once. She didn't know why, but she just assumed he watched from far away and would simply track her from there.

It hurt to breathe. She never wanted to go back into one of those rooms again. But she was going to have to if she was going to make herself a target.

Emma was gasping for breath without realizing it.

Everything suddenly felt like a huge mistake.

The Phantom stepped closer and pressed his hands on her shoulders. It grounded her. "You don't have to do this," he said so softly she could barely hear it over the sound of the rain. Water from his mask dripped onto her face as she blinked up at him. "We can find another way."

"Yes, I do," she whispered. For a beat, she studied his masked face. Her heart clenched greedy hands around the concern in his voice and held it tight. He always looked out for her.

Feeling brave, Emma lurched forward and pressed her lips to his. She wanted to forget. Even if only for a moment. She wanted something to hang onto, from someone who cared about her, even if only a little, even if it wasn't in the way she wanted.

The Phantom didn't move.

Face hot, she stepped away. "I'm sorry, I—"

He surged forward and wrapped his arms around her. His kiss was fierce, almost angry.

The harsh corners of his armor bit into her front. She relished the feeling. She wanted to rid herself the taste and feel of that other man. She gasped into his mouth. The barest hint of stubble on his face scratched against her cheeks and chin. She clung desperately to his neck and brushed a feverish hand across his bare jaw.

The Phantom gently pushed away from her and stalked a few paces towards the edge of the roof.

"I'm sorry!" she said desperately. She covered her kiss-swollen lips with her hands.

"Don't be sorry," he said without turning. "I–I don't–" He made a frustrated noise.

"I'm sorry, I wasn't thinking."

He turned around as abruptly as he'd walked away. "Don't you get it?" he said in a guttural voice. "I'm not–You don't even know me, Emma."

She blinked at him. She *didn't* understand. Her mouth opened and closed. She touched her lips again. Closed her eyes. Her memory flashed to another night, another kiss.

When she opened her eyes, she was certain of who she was looking at.

"That's you under there, isn't it, James Kane?" she called to him.

He stopped at the edge of the roof. Barely turned his head towards her. Neon light from below illuminated the line of his jaw and nose. "I don't know what you're talking about." He jumped and disappeared over the edge.

But it *was* James Kane.

She knew it was.

Kissing them both–kissing *him*–made her certain. She couldn't forget a kiss like *that*.

The Phantom and James Kane were one and the same.

And she was pretty sure she might be in love with him.

She texted Lena that she was going home sick. It was close enough to the end of her shift, anyway. She climbed down the fire escape and went back inside to grab her things before she left again. She didn't bother changing and hurried back to Kane Manor.

Her mind skipped around all the similarities she'd noticed and written off. Her memory *hadn't* been playing tricks on her.

The Phantom told her something terrible had happened to him as a kid. And what could be worse than finding both of your parents dead, one accused of murdering the other?

And that rage she'd seen in the Phantom…she'd seen it in James, too. When she'd admitted to being beaten up. When the Phantom saved her in that warehouse. It was the same.

She could see it in the way he moved. The way he walked quietly but powerfully. The gracefulness. The muscles. The sharp jaw. The odd hours. The way he sometimes seemed to already know what was happening with her after she'd talked to the Phantom but not to James. And though he was more confident in the armor and mask, she'd seen hints of that same awkwardness that James possessed within the Phantom.

She touched her lips again.

She'd thought James had been keeping a secret, and she'd been right.

When she got to Kane Manor, she pushed inside and stalked down the first floor hallway. She shoved James's door open. He wasn't there. Of course he wasn't there. He still had on a mask and a cape.

She shed her soggy jacket and sat on the very edge of his bed.

It was him. Of course it was him. Of course she was drawn to both of them—they were the same man. Two sides of the same coin.

She leaned against the post of the bed and let her eyes close. Her mind chose that moment to replay both kisses on a loop. Her hands fisted in the blanket underneath her.

What was she doing? Waiting for him to come into his bedroom in the Phantom armor?

She didn't really have a better plan. There was no way he'd *admit* to having a secret identity, so she just had to catch him herself. The more she sat and thought about it, the surer she was. She lay back across the foot of the bed.

The tangled sheets and blankets smelled like James, fresh detergent and something masculine underneath. She inhaled deeply. Something inside her settled. Calmed.

Before she knew it she was drifting off to sleep.

CHAPTER EIGHTEEN

JAMES

James followed Lionel Maxwell out of the Crescent Club. He watched him get into a chauffeured car that took him to the wealthiest neighborhood in New Atlas. He watched as the man went upstairs to his bedroom. As he made a call that only lasted a couple of minutes. As he undressed and fell into his bed.

James had never wanted to hit someone as badly as he wanted to hit that man.

He had *touched* Emma. Kissed her. He knew she let him–that only her quick thinking kept it from being more.

He hated it. Hated her doing this. Hated that it was their best bet to figure out what happened to those six other women. Hated that he couldn't do anything besides watch and wait. Every time she entered the club, he had to fight with himself not to follow her in there, beat the shit out of everyone, and take her somewhere safe.

James sat outside Maxwell's home for much longer than necessary, simply talking himself out of going inside and beating the man until he felt better.

And God, that *kiss*. She'd kissed him then called him by his name.

How did she know?

But of course she figured it out. She spent so much time with him–both sides of him, James and the Phantom–so of *course* she started to piece it together. She was smart, he knew that. Smart and observant. He didn't really know how much you could tell about a person from a kiss, but he knew he'd be able to recognize her lips anywhere. The shape of her in his arms.

It exhilarated and terrified him all at once.

By the time he finally calmed himself enough to leave Maxwell's house without breaking in, it was almost dawn. He made his slow, winding way through the city to make sure no one followed him to the tunnel entrance. As soon as he entered the tunnel that led underneath his home, he breathed easier. The tunnel was long and winding and covered in hidden cameras and motion sensors he could check from his phone.

The final hangar door slid open, and he drove straight in, stopping just before he toppled a workstation.

He turned off the bike, the sudden silence echoing around him. He slid off, his anger now only an imprint in his tired veins, and started taking the armor off piece by piece. He cleaned and stored it with automatic movements.

When he finished, he ran a shaking hand through his hair.

He glanced at the screen that usually held the video feed from the contact lens Emma wore. It was dark. She must have already taken it out for the night, then. He reached for the controls but hesitated. He wasn't sure he wanted to see her point of view of earlier. But he also wanted to make sure she was home safe.

Solving mysteries, catching criminals, beating the shit out of them…he could do all of that with ease. But he couldn't even talk to Emma without feeling like he was coming undone. Like his every nerve was exposed to the open air.

He knew he could have handled it better when she called him by his name. But it had taken him so off guard, especially after the surprise of her kiss, that he hadn't been able to think. It terrified him to think that she wanted him, both sides of him. He was no good for her. He was violent, and angry, and had a secret that would put them all in danger if anyone found out.

James scrubbed a hand over his tired eyes before taking the elevator upstairs. All he needed was a quick shower and then he could sleep. Things always came easier after he slept for a few hours, something Douglas had been emphasizing for years. Not that James always listened. Nor would he admit that Douglas was right, at least out loud.

The sight of his bedroom door ajar stopped him short. He closed it before he left. He always did.

He immediately shifted to the defensive. He pressed against the wall outside the door and peered into his dark room around the doorframe. Nothing was noticeably amiss. After waiting a full minute and searching the shadows for movement, he realized there was nothing and no one inside. He relaxed and let out a breath. He was always terrified someone would figure out who he was and find him in his own home. Find Douglas. Find *her*.

He shed his sweaty undershirt in an easy movement as he headed towards his bathroom. His bed had never looked so inviting and—it wasn't empty. Emma sprawled out at the foot of his bed, fast asleep. James's heart stuttered. His chest ached. He rubbed it as if there were a new bruise blossoming.

He stood over her and watched her sleep for a long moment.

What was she doing in here? She was still wearing that damned outfit they called a uniform. Her mouth was parted, her breathing deep. Every line of her was softened by sleep. His hands yearned to reach out and brush her dark hair off her forehead. He clenched them to keep them still. She said their first kiss was a mistake, so he avoided touching her. Had already promised himself not to touch her more than absolutely necessary. He failed at that sometimes, he knew that, but then she'd kissed him again. What did *that* mean?

Was she…waiting for him?

The many different implications of that made him dizzy.

Should he wake her?

No. He should let her sleep. It was freezing in his room, he realized. He should—

He glanced around and found a spare blanket. Gingerly, he covered her with it. When she didn't wake, he exhaled slowly.

That's you under there, isn't it, James Kane? The words replayed over and over in his head while he quickly showered off the night. He wasn't sure if he wanted her to be awake when he came out or not.

She couldn't know about him. Not when she was already in danger. Not when her knowing would make the danger *worse*. What if someone found their connection and hurt her to get to him? What if knowing made her hate him? What if she couldn't stand the thought of someone like James having such a terrible darkness within him? She deserved better.

But…he *wanted* her to know. He wanted every part of himself to be revealed to her. Every shadow within him brought into her light.

He dragged his pillow from the bed and found another blanket and curled up on the rug where he could watch her. Where he could see that she was safe. All he needed was a couple of hours of sleep, and then he could figure out a way out of this mess.

You don't even know me, he'd told her. And he meant it. He was no good for her.

EMMA

Emma jerked awake.

Everything around her was unfamiliar. Too dark. Panicked, she tried to untangle herself from the blankets she was under.

Her mind finally woke up enough to remember lying down on James's bed. She must have fallen asleep. She slept surprisingly well, too. No nightmares for once. Probably because her mind had been too busy spinning over James being the Phantom.

She glanced around the dark room.

James was asleep on the rug in front of the dark fireplace. He was curled towards her, a pillow and blanket the only things he'd taken from the bed. He was more relaxed than she'd ever seen him. His hair was still damp from a shower. Should she wake him?

She doubted he ever got much sleep, though. So she decided to let him rest. She could catch him another time.

The embarrassment only came when she was safely in her own shower a few minutes later. What did he think of her, passed out in his bed like that? Did he think she was…waiting for him for a different reason? She didn't know if she wanted him to think that or not.

When she glanced at herself in the mirror while she dried off, she squeaked and turned around.

She still had the contact lens in her eye. He told her he recorded everything to watch back later in case he could find any new details, or in case they needed the videos for evidence later. Cursing, she hoped the Phantom–James–didn't watch that part. She hurried to take it and the earpiece off and store them.

Like a coward, she spent the day avoiding James, afraid of running into him. Afraid of not. Afraid that her traitorous body would give her away and kiss him again.

What had she gotten herself into?

"I'm here," she said to the Phantom through the earpiece as she entered the club later that night.

"I hear you," he murmured, then went silent. Emma could tell something was different the moment she stepped off the elevator.

She could feel the weight of several gazes on her from all around the room. Including that of Lionel Maxwell. He wasn't in her section, but raised his glass and smiled at her. She winked at him even as her heart raced. Even though he had a drink in his hand, she could tell he was sober. His eyes followed her everywhere she went. Like he was sizing her up. Waiting to pounce.

She focused on not spilling her drinks.

Her shift passed slowly, and by the time she was ready for her break, nothing had happened.

Yet her heart stayed in her throat.

It was going to happen tonight. Lionel Maxwell hadn't taken his eyes off her for even a second. Every time she met his gaze, he smiled at her like he knew something she didn't. She pretended she didn't notice, smiled back at him like she was flirting.

The drink in his hand got no emptier.

There was something in the air. Something frightening. More men besides Lionel Maxwell were watching her. She knew they were. She thought back to the night Marie–she forced herself to think the word *died*–and remembered that something had been different then, too. She remembered seeing a flash of a hungry gaze on the assistant district attorney's face. Maxwell looked hungry like that, she thought. A different hunger than what she saw the night before.

Emma just needed air. Needed to think.

As she pushed outside into the cold air of the alley and jogged around the corner, she realized the bouncer at the door was missing. Fear swooped through her stomach as her breath fogged in the air. Autumn was descending on the city earlier than usual, likely because it had been such a wet summer.

"Is everything okay?" the Phantom asked her. His voice was…too loud. She whirled, and there he was, in person.

"I–" The words stuck in her throat. "There's something different about tonight."

His gaze sharpened. "Different how?"

"They're all watching me. There's…I don't know, I felt it when Marie–I felt it that night, too, when they took her. I think they're going to do it now. Maxwell is here again but he's a lot more sober now–"

"You don't have to do this," he said urgently. His gloved hands wrapped around her upper arms. "I'll figure out something else. Just say the word."

Emma closed her eyes. Let the fear in for a minute. Let it take hold.

Then she recalled Marie's blank stare. Her body crumpling to the ground. The feeling of her friend's blood soaking into her pants. Blazing anger replaced the icy fear. Burned it away until there was no trace.

She opened her eyes. "I have to." *Lainey, Becks, Jackie, Heather, Sofia, Marie.* Their names bolstered her, gave her courage.

The other women hadn't had someone to look out for them. But *she* did.

"I'll be okay," she said. If she said it enough, she would believe it.

He stared down at her with an intensity that dried her mouth. "I'll be right behind you, wherever they take you." His grip tightened painfully. "I won't let them hurt you," he said in a deep voice. "I swear to you, I won't let them hurt you."

"I have to–get back." She took a step away. Turned back. Made up her mind.

Emma crushed her mouth to his. The kiss was savage, desperate. Afraid.

She let her kiss say what she couldn't. In case she didn't come back. In case his promise to her was a lie, like hers had been for Marie.

Emma didn't know how she'd gone so long without kissing him, didn't know how she could continue without it.

She pulled away with a wild gasp. "See you soon."

She ran inside before she could talk herself out of it.

Downstairs again, she didn't miss that Lionel Maxwell was now sitting in her section.

She took the order from another man at another table. She somehow kept her hands from shaking as she handed him his drink.

She couldn't put it off any longer. She caught a glimpse of the Wolf heading back upstairs. The lights flashing threw the scars on his face into sharp relief as his head turned. Unnervingly, his eyes met hers from all the way across the club.

Emma's stomach dropped, and then the Wolf disappeared again.

"Hi there," she said pleasantly as she stopped in front of Lionel Maxwell. She made herself take a seat. "I'm glad to see you here tonight," she said in a low voice, just for him. There was a gleam in his eyes. Different from when he wanted to sleep with her. Definitely different. Goosebumps rose on her skin.

"Emma," he practically purred. "Care to join me again tonight?"

"Of course."

Don't fight it, she told herself. She wouldn't think about what might or might not happen. The Phantom had her back and that would be enough. He was watching everything. And if he saw something like that happening, he would intervene.

For Marie, she thought, and it settled her nerves.

Maxwell stood and took her hand to lead her to one of the rooms. He let her go in first. A soft *snick* sounded as he locked the door behind her.

"Do you–" She turned to ask if he wanted a drink.

He sprayed something right in her face.

Emma coughed at the biting chemical smell. "What the f–"

Something cold slid through her veins. The more she breathed, the harder it got to move. She could feel her consciousness being shoved roughly into the farthest reaches of her mind. She tried to reach out a hand. Tried to speak. All she could do was twitch her fingers and lips.

"Not much longer now," Maxwell murmured. He paced around her slowly, as if inspecting something he was going to buy. Or eat.

"Now," he said. "Can you hear me?"

She beat mental fists against whatever prison this drug had shoved her into. She could hear, see, smell, taste. But she couldn't *move*. Her mind and her body weren't connected anymore. Whatever cord that linked the two had been snapped. An out of body experience except she was trapped inside, not out.

Maxwell chuckled. "I'm sure you can." He hauled back and punched her in the stomach. Had she had control of herself, she would have doubled over in pain. Or lost her breath. Cried out. But she merely stood there. The pain was sharp yet she couldn't move to soothe it. Was this what it was like for Marie? The thought caused a different sort of agony. Had Marie watched everything that happened to her, heard everything, and been able to do nothing?

Had she heard Emma's promise and watched as it turned into a lie?

"Perfect," he said. "Not even a spark."

"I'm here, Emma," the Phantom said into her ear. Relief alleviated some of the fear in her bones. "Don't worry. I'll be here every step of the way."

Maxwell was still talking. "–have you myself first, of course. He doesn't care so much who we pick, as long as the opportunity presents itself. But since you caused trouble already…He has big plans. And as it turns out, you might be the key."

He stopped circling her. "Touch your toes."

Of its own accord, her body bent forward and her fingers skimmed her feet. It was bizarre and frightening to feel her muscles stretch without having told them to do so. Like a part of her was missing. Like she was possessed.

"Stand up." She straightened. "Better response time than the last one," he murmured to himself. His phone chirped. He quickly typed something, then returned his focus to her.

"Go upstairs and wait for me by the employee elevator. Talk to no one. Don't move. Just stand there and wait until I come and tell you what to do next." As soon as he finished speaking, her feet were moving.

Lights flashed from blue to purple and back again. She saw Lena from the corner of her eye, but the other girl wasn't paying attention. *Help me!* she wanted to scream.

The elevator doors closed.

"Does it work if I tell you something?" the Phantom said in her ear. "Raise your right hand."

Nothing happened. He cursed.

How was it that Maxwell could give her orders and the Phantom couldn't? Was there something about proximity? Her mind spun even as her feet carried her out of the elevator. She stepped off and stood beside it. She had no idea how long had passed. Had no way to tell. She couldn't even so much as shift her gaze.

She fought and fought to move, almost on instinct. This was so much worse than she'd expected. She had no control over her body and she was aware of *every single second* of it. She wanted to cry. Scream. Fight. But all she could do was stare blankly at the wall of lockers in front of her and wait.

It was worse knowing that six others had come before her. That they had been forced to watch their own deaths coming for them, unable to do anything to stop it.

The elevator dinged behind her. Its doors clanged open.

"Alright, baby, follow me," Maxwell said. He breezed past her like it was no big deal that he had somehow taken her fucking free will away.

She followed him. She had no choice.

There was a car waiting.

Maxwell unceremoniously commanded her to get in and shoved her into the backseat before getting into the passenger side. The driver turned just slightly. Emma wanted to gasp when she saw who it was.

It was the Wolf.

Emma's fear crescendoed, even knowing the Phantom would be right behind her.

The Wolf had been in on it the whole time. She should have known. How could she have been so stupid? So naïve. Of course he was at the center of it. He knew everything that went on in his club.

"Emma," the Wolf said pleasantly. "I always knew you were trouble."

There was another curse in her ear as the Phantom realized who spoke.

Don't kill me, she wanted to tell them. Not before they got what they needed.

The Wolf reached out and struck her hard across her face.

She saw cracks in her vision.

The contact lens.

The next time she blinked, the cracks cleared a bit.

Another curse in her ear. "I'm still here, but I can't see," the Phantom said softly.

"That was for fucking things up for us," the Wolf said, still a picture of perfect calm. "Not to worry, though. It turns out that you'll be able to help us more than we could have ever imagined. Along with the added bonus that you no longer get to be a thorn in my side."

What was it, exactly, that they were stealing and drugging women for? Killing them for?

Now that she knew the drug took away her free will, that it made her susceptible to suggestion, she knew it wouldn't be good. Not in a place like New Atlas. Being able to make anyone do exactly what you wanted...

The car pulled away.

"Think he'll come?" Maxwell asked from the front seat.

"Oh, he'll come. They get together almost every night she works," the Wolf said. "Don't know where they disappear to, though. Cameras are only in the alley."

Emma's heart gave a painful lurch.

They're talking about you! she wanted to scream at the Phantom. The Wolf had been spying on her. He saw her get picked up after every shift.

"Who knew the mess Grove made would actually work in our favor?" the Wolf continued. "Two birds with one stone."

No, she thought with desperation.

It was a trap.

CHAPTER NINETEEN

Emma had never felt such all-encompassing fear. It rose and rose within her, blocking every coherent thought, as she sat trapped in a car with the Wolf and one of the wealthiest men in New Atlas.

But she didn't fear for herself.

She feared for the Phantom. For James, if he was James—and she almost started hoping she was wrong. So that at least one of them would be safe.

He stayed silent in her ear which only made it so much worse.

Did he hear that it was a trap? Or had the Wolf's slap messed up the earpiece too? The Phantom said he couldn't see anymore, but maybe the sound shorted out after that. And with the earrings still in place on her ears, he was *going* to find her. There was no way for her to lose them, to keep him from coming after her.

She wanted to close her eyes. To curl into herself. To clench her fists to relieve some of the tension the fear created. The fear was a living, breathing thing. It pierced her heart, her lungs, twisted her organs.

If they used the same drug on the Phantom—the possibilities horrified her.

I really hope you heard that, she thought to him even though he couldn't hear her. *Please have heard that. Please be prepared. Or just leave me. Don't rescue me.*

If she had to die to keep him safe…she didn't think she would mind that.

New Atlas needed him more than she did. He needed to stop this–to take the things she'd recorded to Kendrick and get the sons of bitches responsible. Even though the lens in her eye was cracked, she was positive she looked at the Wolf long enough for them to identify him on the recording.

The car stopped. She couldn't move her head or eyes to see where they were.

"Get out and walk down the alley," the Wolf said. Her body obeyed. "Wait at the first door."

So she could obey commands from him *and* Maxwell, but not from the Phantom in her ear. And they were semi-complex orders. She stopped at the indicated door and stared at it. Goosebumps spread over her skin in the freezing air. All she had on was her work uniform.

She could hear the men talking somewhere behind her but couldn't make out the words. She strained to hear more, see more, find out more. There had to be a way out of this.

"Follow me," Maxwell said from her side several minutes later. From the corner of her eye, she saw two men with guns. Where were they? How many men were lying in wait?

Maxwell unlocked the door before them. They descended a staircase. She glimpsed plush carpet and then–

"Close your eyes," he said before she could see anything more. "Step forward. Sit."

She sat without being able to tell if there was a chair there. She had the sensation of a brief free fall before she felt the seat beneath her.

"Tie her up," the Wolf said.

"Why?" said Maxwell, voice almost petulant. Emma concurred. Why tie her up if they already had her free will?

"The drug wears off, unfortunately, so we can't be too careful. She only got a small dose, much smaller than normal. But it's mostly for show. We're pretty sure her friend the Phantom will follow us. Having her tied up is part of the act."

Her hands were quickly bound behind her, her ankles tied to the chair. The restraints bit into her bare skin.

She wished she could do something. Anything.

"This drug is quite a wonder," Maxwell said. There was a noise like him stepping back. Another rustle from somewhere behind her. And—was that the sound of a door closing? "Think of all we can accomplish with the suggestibility without the side effects of a date rape drug. And the counteragent? Genius."

"That one was the hardest to perfect," the Wolf mused. Emma's heart sped up as they talked. They were revealing things in front of her as if they didn't care that she heard. Like they didn't expect her to live to tell their secrets. "We had to figure out a way to render ourselves immune while also being able to make suggestions."

"And they only respond to orders from someone using it?" Maxwell asked with an impressed sound in the back of his throat. "It's a miracle drug, really."

Was she alone with the Wolf and Maxwell, or were there guards? Was her earpiece still working? She struggled to do *anything,* but her body wouldn't cooperate. Whatever they tied her up with was too tight, anyway. She could tell that simply from the pain it caused. Already her fingers had started to lose feeling.

Please, she silently begged. Her body couldn't even respond to her own fear. She should have been shaking, trembling, crying. But all she did was sit quietly with her eyes closed and listen.

"Good thing you have an endless supply of girls like *her*," Maxwell spat in her direction. She imagined the sneer on his face with perfect clarity. "…who take money from guys like me. To perfect the drug. Easy to get rid of when we're done."

The Wolf sighed. "Her little friend was going to be our final test subject, but…well, things didn't go as planned. We're close enough now that it doesn't matter. She only got a small dose. But when *he* arrives to save her…he's getting much, much more. And then when he's under our control…" He trailed off. She could hear the smile in his voice. She imagined it stretching the scars all over his face taut. "They walked right into our trap without even realizing it."

It was so much worse hearing them talk about her like she wasn't there. Like she was a piece of meat and nothing else. Bait in the trap left to die for their grand plans.

"You must know by now we're going to kill you, sweetheart," the Wolf's voice said from somewhere behind her. "We have bigger plans after the Phantom is under our control, but you won't be here to see it. He won't be able to save you. Just like he couldn't save your friend." He chuckled quietly, as if to himself. "And I'll have taken something else James Kane cares about away from him."

James? What did he mean about James? Surely he didn't know—no, he couldn't know his identity. She barely did.

And what he was saying he would do to the Phantom…A mist of rage descended over her like a cloud. She was going to kill all of these bastards. She tried with all of her might to wiggle her toes, open her eyes, move her tongue–*anything*. But the drug still held her in a vise grip. She had to warn the Phantom. Had to save him. Had to convey to him that he needed to leave her there so that he could live. She wouldn't let them get to him. She would do whatever it took to keep him safe.

"Open your eyes," Maxwell said. "I want you to watch your friend lose himself. I want you to watch him kill you."

Her eyes burned. She poured all her hatred and fury into her stare. She hoped he could see it beyond the hold the drug had over her. She was going to kill him if it was her last act on earth.

Two birds with one stone, the Wolf said. Kill her to get rid of a witness, take control of the Phantom for…any number of incomprehensibly terrible things.

Gunshots echoed outside.

No, she thought. Maxwell stood and walked behind her. She kept staring at a wood-paneled wall. From what she could tell, there was lush carpet beneath her.

Emma blinked. Then blinked again.

The drug was wearing off, but barely. Too slow. It was too slow. She was running out of time. She estimated it had already been about an hour since she was first dosed. What was it they'd said? She only received a small amount. She remembered briefly how, at the end, Marie still hadn't been able to move.

Emma shoved those thoughts aside and focused all of her energy on moving. *Come on!* she shouted at herself, at her useless body. *Move!*

A small explosion preceded more gunshots and shouting.

Please don't let them get to him, she begged God, the universe, anyone out there that might listen. *Please don't let them get to him.*

Her left wrist jerked in its restraints.

A click, a thump, and another small explosion. Thick white smoke poured into the room. Emma's lungs burned, but she was forced to keep breathing evenly. Maxwell cursed, though, then coughed.

Her other wrist jerked.

Something thumped behind her.

A black shadow appeared within the smoke.

The Phantom wore a gas mask.

Emma could have cried with relief. He heard. He knew to prepare for the aerosolized drug.

"I've got you," the Phantom said. The mask distorted his voice. He pulled a blade from a strap across his chest. He deftly cut her free and scooped her into his arms with a soft grunt. She tried to say something. Anything. Nothing would come. She jerked her arm frantically. She hoped he could see the warning in her eyes.

Instead of taking her up the stairs she used on the way in, he shouldered through a door into another room. There were more stairs in there. The whole place looked like a recently abandoned home.

As the Phantom climbed the stairs there were more gunshots.

His breath huffed out of him. He tucked her more solidly into his arms. Protected her with his body. Each shot thumped against his back. She had never been so glad for his armor.

Emma managed a groan. She could lift her head now, but barely.

More gunshots. He slowed down. *She* was slowing him down.

He couldn't fight if he was carrying her. And if he couldn't fight, it would be so much easier for them to drug him.

"Le–" she tried to say. Her tongue loosened all at once. "*Let me go.*"

"No," he growled. He pressed a button on one gauntlet then pointed his fist over his shoulder. Something flew out and exploded behind them.

"You have to let me go," she sobbed.

"No!" It came out as a distorted snarl behind the gas mask. "I'm getting you out of here!"

He switched her weight to one arm and whirled. His fist connected with a man's face. He divested him of his gun. Punched him again. The man fell limply to the floor.

The Phantom kept going.

"Please," Emma begged. "You have to save yourself. They want to drug you, they—"

"I heard what they want from me," he said. "I'm not leaving you."

More gunshots. She heard each one strike him. She was afraid that his armor wouldn't hold. But he curled himself around her and kept going. They went up another flight of stairs.

He gave a sudden guttural grunt of pain. She twisted her head to see as he yanked a knife from his side. Maxwell grinned at them. The Phantom tossed the knife away.

Maxwell held a syringe in his other hand. Emma cried out in fear.

A much stronger dose, Maxwell had said. Not aerosolized.

"Watch out!" she cried.

The Phantom blocked the blow. His arm shook as Maxwell pressed the needle towards his neck.

"Let me go!" The words tore from her lips with desperation. If that needle went in, all was lost. It would be over. She was still in his arms, hindering his ability to fight back, endangering him. Her arm twitched as she fought to help block the blow. If she could just move her legs, she could make him drop her.

With a roar, the Phantom shoved Maxwell back. He hit him on the wrist so that he dropped the syringe. Then his fist connected with Maxwell's face four times in quick succession. He fell to the ground, unconscious.

The Phantom staggered forward. Emma tried to reach for him. Her arm only twitched pathetically and stayed put. She screamed through her teeth in frustration.

There was blood. A lot of blood. "*Please*," she said. "You're not going to make it carrying me. It's okay, I'll be okay, please go, *please*." Tears leaked from her eyes. She was utterly helpless. She couldn't control her body. Couldn't help him. Couldn't save him. If anyone else came after them with more of the drug, he wouldn't make it. He was too injured and too weighed down by *her*.

His eyes met hers. Anger lit them from within, turned them into green fire. "*No.*"

He pushed open a door. Frigid wind assaulted them. A soft click made the Phantom abruptly turn back. He used the closed door to half shield her and half hold her up as he blocked more gunshots with his body. He tossed something over his shoulder and the street in front of the building exploded. Her rings rang from all the noise.

He picked her back up and ran. She heard his grunts of pain every other step, but he didn't slow. All she could do was watch and pray that they made it. Everything was quiet. Too quiet. Despite all the commotion, there were no cops. No witnesses. Nothing.

They made it around a few turns and a couple of blocks away before turning down an alley. The Phantom hid behind a dumpster. He gently set her against the brick wall behind it. She still could barely use her arms and legs, but she could at least sit up.

The Phantom swayed and caught himself against the wall with one hand. He slid to a seated position. With his free hand he ripped the gas mask off.

"You're hurt," Emma said. "I can't–*fuck*! I still can't really move." Every muscle strained towards him. Her breath came in panicked heaves. *Please*, she silently begged. *Please save him. I don't care what happens to me, just get him out of this somehow.*

"I'm fine," he said, but his eyes closed. His face was drawn tight with pain.

"Look at me!" He opened his eyes at her sharp words. "Where's your car?"

"Not far," he said. "I just need a second." His breaths came in heavy pants. She could see the wetness spreading on his armor where the knife had slid between two of the plates. That couldn't be good. He was bleeding too much. She lurched forward and nearly toppled over. Managed to get one arm to cooperate and catch her even though it shook violently. "This alley connects to a series of alleys," he said in a too-quiet voice. "We can…make it through here."

She slid forward further, got her other hand to hold her up too. "Please don't make me watch you die," she said to him. She managed to scoot slightly closer. The asphalt scraped against her palms and knees. The sharp pain helped her focus. Every muscle trembled with the effort of the fight between her will and the drug still in her system. The Phantom pressed one gloved hand to his side. Too much blood. There was too much blood. "You're an idiot," she added. "You should have left me."

That got his attention. He gave her a ghost of a smile. "You're welcome," he murmured. Of course he was joking. He barely cracked jokes at any other time, but now that he was bleeding to death in front of her he wanted to be funny.

Her heart ached. More tears fell. *Please, please, please.*

His eyes slid closed again. He grimaced.

"Look at me!" she demanded. It wouldn't be long before they were discovered. They weren't out of the woods yet. She needed to get him help. With sheer determination, she straightened onto her knees. She took his shoulders and shook him roughly. She had to sort of support herself against him as she still fought for control of her own body.

His green eyes focused on her again.

"Come on. Get up. We'll have to help each other."

He groaned in pain as he forced himself onto his feet. He pulled her up with one hand. They wrapped their arms around each other and stumbled down the alleyway like a couple of drunks. Her legs trembled with the effort. She had to focus on moving them, on getting them to respond to her commands. Their steps were halting at first. Slow. The Phantom tried to pull her along but his breath wheezed out of him with pain. From a distance, she heard shouts and pounding footsteps. At least their pursuers were on foot. Hopefully they re-mained that way. If they made it to his car, they could get away.

The farther they walked, the more the drug left her system. Each step grew easier. But with each step she gained, the heavier the Phantom's body leaned against her. He mumbled directions to the car.

By the time Emma saw it, she was practically dragging him. Her muscles shook in earnest now.

"Almost there," she said. They could make it. She was going to make sure they made it. "If you die before I can say I told you so, I'm going to kill you."

His eyes fluttered back open. "You told me so?"

"Yes," she said. "But you have to *stay alive* for me to explain, you bastard."

He saw the car and seemed to get a second wind. He aimed for the driver's side but she ran around the front of the car to get there first. He stumbled towards the passenger side instead, and half-fell inside.

Emma frantically ripped at the plates of armor that covered his side. Oh God, there was so much blood. She pressed her hands against it. Tried to stop it. He passed her the key.

"I—where do I take you? I can't take you to the hospital like this." Her voice rose in panic.

"Underpass outside of the city," he mumbled. "There's a place. I'll show you."

She turned the key in the ignition. The car gave a loud growl that echoed the urgency within her. It was in drive before she even had the seat scooted forward for her shorter legs. The car took off like a rocket. She felt its power underneath her hands. It would go fast, and willingly. At any other time, it might have thrilled her.

Right then, all she felt was terror.

She couldn't help her startled scream as gunfire erupted around them. The window closest to her cracked and she could just make out several men on foot running after them. She pressed the accelerator as hard as she could and took several turns to lose their pursuers. After a minute, she loosed a breath.

"Fuck," she muttered as she glanced around for anyone else following them. They were running out of time.

She focused on dodging traffic, including several illegal maneuvers one after the other. She used the shoulders and sidewalks and medians to speed around other vehicles. Her heart pounded a frantic rhythm in her chest, telling her to hurry, *hurry*.

While she drove, the Phantom braced himself with one hand and put pressure on his wound with the other. He gave her the rest of the instructions on how to get where they were going and then fell abruptly quiet.

"I swear, if you fucking passed out on me–" She didn't know what to do. How to keep him alive. She was already pushing a hundred miles per hour and taking turns far more quickly than she should. His body went suddenly limp beside her.

She did the only thing she could think of and reached over and pressed her finger into his wound.

He woke with a deep shout of pain.

"I'm sorry! You passed out!" That noise–it echoed in her mind. Ripped her apart. If he died–*No*. She would not let him die.

He shook himself and cursed under his breath. He grabbed at his belt until he had a phone in his hands. Blood smeared across the screen as he dialed. He was shaking.

"Who are you calling?" she asked. "Kendrick?"

He either didn't hear her or ignored her.

"We have a problem," he grunted to the person on the other end of the phone. "Call Dr. Torres and meet me downstairs. I–I'll need blood. It's…not good."

The phone dropped from his hands.

Emma cursed. She pressed his side again to try to wake him up. Nothing. God, there was so much fucking *blood*.

She almost missed the turn. She didn't care that she was throwing his unconscious body around as she twisted the wheel as hard as she could to turn. She had to save him. There was no other thought in her mind.

She sped into a tunnel. It curved gently and seemed to go on forever. Finally, a door at the end rose as she approached. She accelerated through it before it was all the way open. The tires squealed.

An immense space spread out before her.

It looked like it used to be some sort of underground warehouse. There were computers, worktables. Extra pieces of the Phantom's armor here and there and a dummy to hold the complete set. A motorcycle. A raised platform, presumably for the car. Even an elevator.

And Douglas.

Emma threw the car into park and leapt out.

Douglas stumbled a step back in surprise.

"I know it's Jamie!" she shouted at him. "*Help me!*" Her desperate cry echoed around them. She ran around to the passenger side and yanked the door open.

Douglas wasted no time hurrying over. He glanced at her with something akin to amazement. Then his focus shifted wholly to James. Douglas was efficient in his movements. He produced a wad of bandages from somewhere and shoved them against the wound, quickly bound it and wrapped a longer bandage around James's waist.

"He's lost a lot of blood. Someone stabbed him. He–I–"

"Help me get him upstairs. We have to get him out of this armor before Dr. Torres arrives in a few minutes."

Douglas smacked James's face. When that didn't work, he opened a pocket on the Phantom's belt. He took out a glass vial and stuck it into the uninjured side of James's stomach.

"It's just adrenaline. Stand back," he warned her. Liquid emptied out of the vial.

James surged away with an animalistic snarl. He was on his feet, panting, glaring around with clenched fists. It lasted only a moment before he swayed. He caught himself with one hand on the nearest table with a curse.

"It's just me," Douglas said. "Let's get you out of this armor and upstairs. Emma, help me please."

Douglas acted like he'd done this a thousand times. And maybe he had. How often did James come home so close to death? She didn't want to think about it. She started unclipping and unstrapping the armor with shaking hands. Piece by piece thunked to the ground.

She pulled his hood down, surprised to see it was only attached with magnets, then reached for the mask. James grabbed her wrists with surprising speed and strength. His knuckles were bloody.

He stared at her with fear in his eyes. His grip tightened painfully. His lips formed a word, but no sound came out. She gave him a stony look and yanked herself free.

She pulled the mask off.

"I told you so," she said to him. His breathing hitched. He studied her face with an intensity that made her skin heat. She smirked at him with a confidence she didn't feel. "I knew it was you, James Kane." Now she just had to make sure he didn't die.

CHAPTER TWENTY

When James was down to just a dark thermal shirt and his underwear, Douglas wrapped his arm around his waist and helped him to the elevator. Emma wrapped her arm around him from the other side. Douglas gave her a grateful look as James started to sag again. She held him tightly. One of his arms settled over her shoulders. Her heart pounded with urgency.

"Almost there," she said as the elevator doors opened. She had no idea where "there" was though. They were in a long room that looked like a basement of some sort. There was a door with a panel next to it. Douglas put in a code. James grunted as they took each step achingly slowly. She tightened her grip on him. Vividly, she remembered the night that they met, tucking herself essentially into his armpit in much the same way.

The door opened to reveal the first floor hallway of Kane Manor.

James's secret lair was in the basement.

She couldn't help it. "I *knew* you were hiding a secret lair down there," she said.

He huffed a breath that might have been a laugh right before his eyes rolled back into his head and he went limp between them.

Douglas and Emma both cursed as they struggled to hold him up. He was massive, made of thick, heavy muscles.

They somehow got him propped back up.

"Jamie?" Emma said, lightly pinching his arm. No response. Her entire body went cold. If she hadn't been able to feel his heart beating where she held him, she would have feared the worst.

Between the two of them, they got James onto his bed. He continued to bleed too much. Douglas disappeared into the bathroom and came back with a pack of makeup wipes. She gave a small, slightly hysterical laugh when she saw them.

Douglas gave her a funny look. "These are the same brand I use," she choked out. Hysteria crowded the words in her throat. She took the wipes. She sobered as she looked down at James's slack face. He had dark makeup or paint smeared around his eyes to blend them in with the mask when he was wearing it.

"I'm going to go get Dr. Torres," Douglas said. "Try to get him awake. Please get all of that off before the doctor gets here." Somehow, he was calm, though she could see the fear drawing his features taut. She wanted to scream, to freak out, but knew that getting the doctor in there quickly was the best course of action.

Swallowing her own fear, Emma nodded. Got on her knees at the edge of the bed to better reach James's face. With one hand she wiped at the black under his eyes, and with her other she pressed urgently into the wound on his side. He flinched. His eyes opened. They were extra green within the black that framed them.

She let out a stifled sob at the sight. "You're awake."

"Was I asleep?" he asked, voice muffled like he really had been asleep.

"You passed out on the way up here," she said softly. "Douglas went to get the doctor."

"You don't have to stay," he said in a raspy whisper as his eyes drifted closed again. "It's okay."

"I'm not getting you this far for you to die," she said as she finished one eye and started on the other. "Besides, it was my turn to help patch you up anyway."

A smile ghosted his lips. One of his hands came to rest on her leg.

"I'm not kidding, Jamie," she said. She shook his shoulder a little with the hand that held the wipe. He blinked at her. "If you die, I'm going to be so pissed off. You have no idea how many questions I have."

"You are…" he trailed off for a moment. Inhaled sharply. "An extraordinary creature."

"I hope that's a compliment and not you calling me a freak."

His smile grew more defined even as his eyes closed again. "At least you don't run around in a cape and a mask."

She finished wiping the black from his eyes but let her hands linger on his face. "You've got me there," she murmured. "You're definitely more of a freak. I can't believe you wait until you almost die to crack a fucking joke, you asshole." She realized there was still something in her eye. The contact lens. She fished it out.

Dr. Torres and Douglas burst into the room. "Step back, please," the doctor said. "You said he lost consciousness?"

"Only for a minute or two." She stepped back and dropped the contact lens onto the nightstand. Something within her loosened now that the doctor was here.

He inspected the wound. "I have no way of knowing how severe it is unless…" He gave Douglas a sharp look. "If you expect me to do surgery *here*–"

Douglas yanked out a checkbook and a pen and held both out. "Name your price." He quickly signed the top check. "Any price."

Dr. Torres stared blankly. "I could write a million dollars on there."

"I would pay it," Douglas said. There was no waver in his voice. His eyes remained steady on the doctor. There was a steely resolve in his gaze that she had never seen before. "I'm sorry for the trouble, but you can understand how Mr. Kane would prefer to stay away from anywhere public after getting into such a…brawl."

"How about a hundred grand?" Dr. Torres glanced from Douglas to James and back again, one eyebrow raised. "I think that's fair, if I have to do surgery."

Douglas quickly wrote the figure and handed the check to Dr. Torres, who muttered a curse before tucking it away. Emma felt faint.

A hundred thousand dollars gone, just like that. More money than she could ever imagine.

"I'm going to need a sterile environment," Dr. Torres said.

"We have whatever you need," Douglas interrupted. "Mr. Kane's grandfather was on dialysis for a long time and wanted all of his healthcare to be at home. We've kept it updated even since his passing."

Dr. Torres quickly inspected the wound again. James was still awake, thankfully, watching him through slitted eyes. Dr. Torres pulled a few bandages out of his bag and quickly re-wrapped the wound.

"We need to move him. I need a closer look to see what the damage is."

The minutes it took them to drag James down the hall to the medical wing–thankfully on the first floor–were as long as hours. Halfway down, James passed out again, which added an urgency to Dr. Torres that Emma didn't like.

"Is he going to die?" The words slipped from her mouth unbidden as she opened the door Douglas indicated. The inside looked like an operating room.

Kane Manor did, indeed, have an extraordinary stockpile of medical equipment.

Dr. Torres didn't answer. "I'm going to need an assistant," he said instead as they arranged James's limp body on the waiting table.

"I can do it," Douglas said. Emma blinked in surprise.

"Perfect," Dr. Torres said. He turned to Emma. "I'm sorry, I don't remember your name. Miss…?"

"Warner," she said automatically. Her eyes stayed glued to James. Was he going to die? Had she gotten him killed? This was her fault, after all. *She* wanted to become the next target. *She* needed rescuing. *She* kept James from being able to fight back. She was a burden and it had cost him dearly.

"I'm sorry, Miss Warner, I'm going to need you to wait outside."

She was on autopilot, her feet taking her outside the door. It shut behind her with a note of finality. This couldn't be happening. It couldn't.

The door didn't have a window, no way for her to know what was happening inside.

She paced back and forth for a moment before leaning against the wall. She had no idea what time it was. But she didn't want to leave. Just in case. So she slowly slid to the floor and waited.

She had no idea how long her vigil lasted until Douglas stepped through the door.

Her bones creaked in protest as she clambered to her feet. Nothing came out when she opened her mouth to ask a question, any question.

"He's okay," Douglas said. "Getting stitched up and a blood transfusion right now. He has a concussion, too. Dr. Torres said you could come in."

"Why…do you have all of this?" she asked Douglas as they both watched the doctor stitch James up. Blood still covered her, but she barely noticed. "I know you said his grandfather was treated here, but why keep it?"

"For this very reason," Douglas murmured. "Even if he were…not who he was, I think he would have all this stuff just in case. James is the sort of man who expects the worst of every situation. And he likes to avoid being in public whenever necessary. Especially in instances like this. What would the world think if one of the very few times James Kane was seen was at a hospital?"

While she watched Dr. Torres, Emma fit the two pieces of James together in her mind. Now that she knew the Phantom and James were one and the same–knew for *sure*–she didn't know what to think. All she knew was that it hurt to see him incapacitated like he was.

Finally, Dr. Torres stepped back. "He's going to be fine. Nothing vital was hit. He is *extraordinarily* lucky. Though I really should recommend–"

"Thank you, doctor," Douglas said. "If you would please stop by during the week to check on him at your convenience, we'd appreciate it. You'll be compensated for each visit, of course."

Dr. Torres hesitated. Nodded.

"Let me walk you out, then," Douglas said. The two disappeared through the open door. She heard the doctor giving Douglas care instructions as they went.

She shuffled over to the bed. James was sleeping, or drugged, or passed out again. It was hard to tell. But Dr. Torres said he'd be fine.

James's eyelids were almost translucent.

Emma took his hand, the one not hooked to an IV. It was easier to be brave with him when he wasn't awake. "You should have let me die," she whispered. A sob shuddered through her chest as the night caught up with her. "You should have let me die back there. If you died, or if they had–" She inhaled sharply. "You fucking *idiot*." She wasn't sure if she was saying it to herself or to the man on the bed. With her free hand, she wiped her eyes. She made a noise when she realized his blood still covered it.

Her attention shifted to the room around her then quickly away. It was too…antiseptic. Too much like a hospital. It reminded her of finding out her mom was sick, and the memory *hurt*.

James's fingers tightened around hers.

"Hey," she said when he opened his eyes a minute later. "You're not dead."

"Thanks to you," he murmured.

"Really it's thanks to your checkbook." She joked to cover up her tears. "Pretty sure Douglas almost gave him a million dollars." Even the hundred grand they settled on was an ungodly amount of money to her, but barely a drop in the bucket for him. Emma remembered Marie's tears over not being able to pay rent. Something inside her ached.

James made a noise in his throat. He was still holding her hand. Her hands were sticky with his blood but she didn't want to let go. Not yet.

"I'm sorry," he said, the words barely a whisper.

"For what?" she asked, frowning. "I should be apologizing."

"I–screwed things up." His eyes fluttered and he seemed to drift off.

"What? No."

He made a humming noise. She wasn't sure he was awake anymore.

"I'll let you sleep," she said quietly. But he was already out. She watched him for another moment, noting each rise and fall of his chest.

When had her center of gravity shifted to the man before her? When had he become the center of her orbit? Of her every thought? Both pieces of him, the man and the mask, had always captivated her. Now that she held all the pieces of him within her hands, she knew him. Really knew him. And it made all the difference.

She bent and brushed her lips over his forehead.

She was in love with James Kane and the Phantom both.

The feeling scared her. She had never loved someone like she loved him. The good and the bad—she'd seen every side of him and still wanted more. She was willing to die for him, and that alone shook her to her core. She wasn't sure what to do with the emotion. It was vast and frightening.

In the safety of her own room, Emma finally let the emotions free. Her clothes were covered in his blood, and even though he was *alive*, even though he'd be fine, it was somehow almost worse than Marie's death. Her hands shook so violently she could barely pull off her clothes. When she removed the GPS earrings, one clattered to the floor.

She struggled to get the shower turned on. Her vision blurred with tears. She had to bite her lip to hold back bone-wracking sobs.

She stepped into the spray of water with her eyes closed. She didn't want to see the blood. But it covered her. She suddenly, overwhelmingly, needed to get it *off*.

She scrubbed at the blood with a ferocity that rubbed her skin raw. Memories mixed together, James and Marie, their blood coating her, drowning her.

"Fuck," she whispered. For a second, she imagined she couldn't move. She strained and strained until her hand finally jerked towards the soap. "Fuck!" she said a little louder. She sank onto her haunches and let the water pour over her.

The fear was back. Less insistent now, but still present. It sat perched within her and waited to pounce. Waiting to drag her all the way under. She knew that the moment she let her guard down, it would drag her down and not let go.

And there she had been, so confident that being taken would be—not easy, but *easier*. Her cockiness led them down this path. She never considered that they were being watched, night after night, that the connection between them was being drawn. She should have been more careful. She *knew* to be more careful. They were always watching. She learned that lesson the hard way and had forgotten it. And it almost cost her everything. Her ignorance had almost gotten James killed.

The thought hit her so hard that she couldn't breathe.

James almost died. Because of *her*.

Her mind suddenly tried to convince her that something was wrong. That he hadn't actually made it out alive. That he was fighting for breath at that exact moment. The water ran cold over her. She wasn't sure when the hot water had run out. Wasn't sure how long she'd been sitting crouched there.

She yanked the knob to turn it off.

God, what if Dr. Torres had fucked it up somehow? What if he had lied, or gotten it wrong, or–she didn't know what. But she was certain James was in trouble.

She dressed quickly and hurried back downstairs.

Her breath came in panting gasps like she had just run a mile.

James leaned against the doorway of the hospital-like room. He was wearing clean sweatpants now but still no shirt. He'd taken out his IV, too.

There was blood on the new bandages.

"You–What–" she stammered. She reached for him as he tipped forward. "What are you *doing*? Did you already forget that you were *stabbed*?"

With her arms around him, he was so close she could see every detail of his bloodshot eyes. She could see the pain in them. His muscles couldn't even properly distract her because her heart was squeezing nervously in her chest.

Well, at least she hadn't exactly been wrong about him being in trouble.

"I wanted–my own bed," he ground out. "I'm fine."

"If you waited five more minutes I could have–I don't know, I'm sure you have a wheelchair around here somewhere." She shifted so he could lean on her. But instead he stepped away. He gave her a withering stare. He swayed again and caught himself on the doorframe. "Let me help you, you big stubborn asshole." He glared down at her. She glared back. A muscle ticked in his jaw. But he eventually stood very still. She took that as permission and tucked herself under his arm. He was warm against her. She savored the feeling. *Alive*, she reminded herself. *He's alive. He's okay.* Even if he was an idiot. Already her breathing came easier, the weight on her chest lighter.

He grunted as they walked. The muscles in his back were tense. His room wasn't far, but she was sure, to him, it felt like miles. She couldn't blame him for wanting his own bed. When her mother died, she had only stayed in the hospital one night at her sickest before signing herself out so she could die in her own bed.

James practically collapsed onto the mattress when they reached it. She didn't miss how he bit back a noise of pain.

She reached out automatically to stack pillows behind him so he could sit propped up. It was something she'd done for her mother thousands of times.

He caught her wrist in his hand.

"What are you doing?" he asked. He was closed off for some reason. She didn't know why. He'd been in a much better mood when he was at death's door.

"What does it look like?" she snapped. She was suddenly angry too. Angry at him for risking himself for her. For almost dying for her. He should have left her. Her life didn't matter like his did. "I'm taking care of you. You know, you were much nicer when you were almost dead."

He grit his teeth so hard she was surprised she couldn't hear a crack. But he let her fix the pillows behind him. Relaxed into them even though he was still way too tense. She climbed onto the bed and sat cross-legged at his feet.

He watched her warily. "You were much nicer when you didn't know I was the Phantom," he grumbled.

A surprised grin spread across her lips. "Ah, so he's *not* as grumpy as he seems," she teased. He glanced away from her. "I'm going to sit here and make sure you don't hurt yourself," she told him. "And ask you questions."

He very much looked like he was trying to disappear into the pillows. His eyes darted around the room as if trying to find the nearest escape.

It was almost like he was scared of her, now that she knew who he really was.

"Why did you…choose to become a vigilante? And when?" It wasn't the most pressing question, but it was something she wanted to understand better.

"You know my father was accused of killing my mother. What happened after. Nobody listened to me when I said he didn't do it, that he *wouldn't*," he said. "And I saw what this city really was. The injustice in it. I didn't want anyone to go through what I went through when the cops wouldn't listen." He paused and took a deep, careful breath with the barest flinch. "The first person I saved was by accident. I was wandering around late one night, years ago, when I couldn't sleep. A woman was getting mugged. I'd learned how to fight from Douglas among other places, so I beat the mugger up." James inhaled sharply and repositioned against the pillows. "I realized that doing *that*, actively saving people, would make more of a difference than my money ever could. And…I'm angry. I'm angry at how this city is. How it treats people. I've always been angry."

Emma couldn't argue with that. She let the words sink in, then asked, "What were you doing in the club?"

He kept staring a hole in the wall somewhere to her right. "Which time?"

"As James," she said. "I already know what you were doing there as the Phantom."

His fingers strangled the blankets. "The same thing both times. Investigating. As James Kane, I could buy my way in. Get information like I was one of them. The first time I wasn't surprised because I remembered your resume. I didn't–I had no idea you had been transferred downstairs."

A slow curl of relief furled through her. She'd known he was good, but it helped to hear it all the same. The silence stretched between them, expanded, filled the room.

"Why were you asleep in my bed?" he asked after a moment.

Emma flushed and laughed nervously. "Um. I was trying to catch you. In the armor."

James stared at her for a minute, and then smiled. A real smile. Her heart flipped even as she returned it. She laughed again. "I realize now that you don't–you know, you don't go roaming around the house in it. But it was the best way I could think of to catch you. But I fell asleep…obviously. Sorry about that, by the way."

James's smile faded. "Wh–" he started. Stopped. Tried again. His voice dropped lower, grew rougher. "Why did you tell me to leave you tonight?"

It was her turn to avoid looking at him. The pain was still too fresh, too sharp. She shook her head. "It doesn't matter." How could she explain it to him, this feeling that utterly devastated her? That had laid waste to her heart and left her bare and bleeding? How could she explain the intense *need* she'd felt to save him, even at her own expense?

He let it drop.

She let herself take in his room. The sun had risen fully, and his curtains weren't all the way closed. The room was messy. There were clothes strewn on the floor like he'd hurried to step out of them. A desk with papers, blueprints, tools, and schematics all over it. And bookshelves. Tons of bookshelves, even though there was a library upstairs.

"I need Douglas to take some of your blood," James said as she inspected his room. She flushed as if she'd been caught going through his underwear drawer instead of simply looking around.

"My blood?" she asked stupidly.

"For traces of the drug. He'll run some tests and the rest will go to Kendrick. In fact–" James huffed out a harsh breath as he tried to sit up more. "I need to meet with him and tell him what we found out tonight."

"Like hell you're going anywhere," she said. "I can go."

"It's not–"

"I swear, if you say it isn't safe, I'm going to stab you again. I was *kidnapped* tonight. Doesn't get much more dangerous than that. Besides, you trust Kendrick, right?" She crossed her arms. Silently, she dared him to challenge her. "Because *I* do. And I've known him much longer than you."

His jaw worked, but he finally jerked a nod.

"Don't make me send Douglas in here to sit on you so you don't leave," she threatened with a finger pointed at him in warning.

"I thought I might find you in here," Douglas's amused voice said from the doorway. Emma was so startled she almost fell off the bed. "And she's right. I'm not above sitting on you like I did when you were younger and wouldn't let anyone come near you with a needle."

Emma snorted at the mental image.

"Will you take a few vials of her blood, Douglas?" James said as if the man hadn't spoken. "Run some tests for me? We need to get samples before the drug completely leaves her system."

Douglas nodded and left the room again. Emma learned during one of their conversations that Douglas was in college on a premed track when he dropped out to become James's guardian.

"You know…what to look for?" she asked skeptically. "In my blood."

James shrugged. "I have…a few degrees. Kane Industries does a lot with pharmaceuticals."

"How many is a few?" Emma raised an eyebrow. "And your gadgets? You buy those?"

He looked almost embarrassed. "I make them myself. Experiment. For the most part."

How smart *was* he, she wondered? She made a mental note to look up his degrees later. Here she had barely one degree and he had *a few*.

An idea came to her. She sat up straighter. James's eyes tracked the movement but he waited while she teased the thought out.

"How hard do you think it'd be for Kendrick to get his hands on the ADA's body?" she finally asked.

A spark in his eyes. "Of course," he murmured. "The counteragent."

She nodded. Leaned forward enthusiastically. "If his body has any trace of it left–"

"–we might be able to have it replicated," he finished. His expression blazed. "Especially with the traces of the drug in your bloodstream."

She leaned back on her hands and stretched her legs out. "*Exactly*. I feel like I'm on an episode of *CSI* right now or something. Does it ever feel like that? Being the Phantom?"

James laced his hands together and rested them on his bare chest. Now that he wasn't half-dead or trying to kill himself by ripping his stitches open, she let herself enjoy the view. Just a little.

"No," he said. He didn't elaborate.

"Do you even know what *CSI* is?" she asked with a raised eyebrow. He gave her a look. "What? You didn't know about *The Incredibles*!"

Douglas came back in with a small kit.

James mumbled something that sounded an awful lot like a petulant, "I watch TV."

She scooted to the edge of the bed and dutifully stuck out her arm. Douglas tied a tourniquet and tapped for a vein. James carefully avoided his eyes and she remembered Douglas's comment about James as a child. All of her mom's treatments had thoroughly desensitized her to blood and needles.

"What about the recordings from tonight?" she asked. She winced as the needle pierced her skin. "We need to get those to Kendrick. Maybe it'll be enough."

Douglas looked between the pair of them with an indecipherable expression. He filled one small vial with blood and promptly started on the next.

"I'll work on putting it together," James said.

"Can you do that from up here?" she asked skeptically.

"No, he can't," Douglas said at the exact moment James said, "Yes."

Douglas shook his head and gave a long sigh. "I'll put it on a thumb drive for you and bring up your laptop."

Emma smirked at James over her shoulder. He ignored her.

"Ask Kendrick when he can meet," she told him. "Sooner is better."

James didn't move for a minute. Douglas started on a third vial of blood. Then James heaved a sigh and pulled out a cell phone.

"I knew the Phantom had a cellphone," she muttered to herself.

"He actually has two," Douglas said conspiratorially. "One is for James. The other is for the Phantom."

Emma pressed her lips together so she didn't laugh. "It sounds like he's a drug dealer," she noted. She couldn't help it, a small laugh crept through. James's eyes darted to her and away again.

Douglas finished a fourth vial of blood and pressed a bandage to the crook of her arm. "Sometimes I wish that he was," Douglas mused. He glanced over at James, who was talking in a low voice, presumably to Kendrick.

"How do you do it?" *How do you love him and watch him destroy himself every night?*

Douglas didn't have to ask what she meant. He packed up his supplies, separated two vials each. "It's hard, I'll admit," he murmured. "But I think it would be just as hard if he were, say, a police officer or firefighter. Throwing himself into danger in order to do good."

Emma hummed. Yes, she could see that. But Douglas was lying to himself a little with that assessment. What James was doing was...*more*. More dangerous. More taxing. More intense.

"He said he can be at the tower in an hour," James interrupted. She wondered if he heard her conversation with Douglas.

Emma stood and collected two of the four vials of her blood as James gave her the elevator code for the tower.

It was time to figure out what the hell was going on in New Atlas.

CHAPTER TWENTY-ONE

The wind at the top of the abandoned tower was brutal. Emma shivered as she waited next to the elevator. Her hands reached automatically for her phone. But her bag and cell phone were still at the Crescent Club. She had no idea how she was going to get it all back— she had no idea who she could trust there. And by all rights she shouldn't be alive. She couldn't just waltz back in and get her stuff. The Wolf would probably just have them grab her again. Or kill her on sight.

The elevator rattled to a stop. With an abundance of caution, Emma stepped into the shadows behind one of the thick metal supports. She peered around it and only relaxed when she saw Kendrick.

As a concession to James, she'd put in the earpiece so he could hear everything. The contact lens remained broken, but he refused to let her go alone without some direct line of communication. He threatened to follow her if she didn't use the earpiece at the very least.

"Hi," she called out in a soft voice. Kendrick's hand drifted to his gun holster but he dropped it when she stepped into the light.

"Emma," he said warmly. He hugged her briefly. "Our friend said you had something for me?"

She passed over the vials of her blood. "That's my blood. I was drugged last night with the same stuff you found in the bodies that were recovered."

Kendrick's expression morphed into vague shock. "Drugged?" he repeated. "How? Where? By who?" His hand unconsciously touched his gun again.

"Lionel Maxwell drugged me," she said. "And then I was kidnapped by him and the Wolf. The drug somehow takes away free will–" Her throat closed up. She coughed to cover up her hesitation. "There's a type of counteragent they have–I don't know if they wear it or inject it or what–but it allows them to make suggestions. It renders them immune to the drug, too. And this drug makes you *highly* suggestible."

Kendrick frowned. She could sense the gears whirring in his mind as he started piecing things together. "Are you okay?"

"Yes," she said. "I recorded enough of it. He's getting all of that ready for you as we speak."

"Are you sure you're okay? Is the drug still in your system?"

"I don't think so but I'm not sure. That isn't all, though. They're planning something big. They wanted to use the drug to influence the Phantom, but we managed to escape." She averted her gaze. She focused on the skyline of New Atlas, illuminated before them in the weak morning light. "But they kept alluding to perfecting the drug and using it on a large scale. We can't–we can't let them do it. This drug–it's bad. Really bad. Under its influence they can make *anyone* do *anything*." She wanted to grab him and shake him until he felt the same urgency she did.

"I'm glad you're okay, Em. I'll look into it and let you know what I find out. If we could get that counteragent…" He trailed off and seemed to lose himself deep in thought.

"About that," she said. She crossed her arms and paced in a tight circle. "How hard would it be for you to access the assistant district attorney's body? Or if not his body, any blood or tissue samples from the autopsy?"

Kendrick's eyes snapped to hers. "It wouldn't be easy."

"You could always steal it." She shrugged and half smiled.

"I can't just steal a body," Kendrick said. But she could see him considering it. His lips pursed. A cold wind suddenly shook the tower and made them both shudder and hunch their shoulders. "If it hasn't been buried yet, that is. Or cremated."

"I know for a fact he had that counteragent that night because he was influencing my friend, Marie. The one he killed. If you can get enough of it to make a difference, to replicate it…"

"That could take weeks–"

Frustration rose within her, hot in her veins. She spread her hands in a sharp motion. "It's worth a shot, isn't it? We have to figure out a way to counteract the drug *and* the counteragent if there's any hope of stopping whatever they have planned."

Kendrick laughed softly. He paced a few steps one way and then the other. "Yeah, I can see why you're friends with him. You're both persistent as hell. And stubborn. You always were."

She flashed him a smile then let it fade. "I can't stress enough how bad this could be. Imagine being able to make *anyone* be able to do *anything* you want. The possibilities are…too endless. And with it being aerosolized…they can use it on a large scale, if they wanted."

"I'll do what I can," Kendrick said. "Let me know when you have those recordings. It's going to take some time to get everything prepared so I can start making arrests when the time comes. It's…been hard to find people to trust."

"I understand," she said. "But we might not have time. If you could…maybe find a way for the Phantom to get a sample from the ADA's body…" She didn't finish the sentence.

Kendrick's expression closed off. "I'll see what I can do. Is there any way you might be able to get more information on what they might have planned? Anyone at the club you could get in contact with?"

"Don't even think about it," James said in her ear.

She ground her teeth and ignored him. "I really don't know. I don't know who I can trust either. With the Wolf's involvement…"

Kendrick dipped his chin in a curt nod. "Alright. I'll be in touch. Let me know if you find anything else." He grabbed her in another quick hug. "I'm glad you're okay, kid."

As Kendrick stepped onto the elevator, Emma mused to James, "How hard do you think it'd be to steal a body?" She turned and watched the sun try to peer out from between the clouds over the city. The day was warm already, summer's last gasp before autumn came to stay.

"You wouldn't even have to steal the whole body," James pointed out. She had no idea how she hadn't figured out the similarities in his voice sooner. There was no mistaking it. "Just some samples of skin, hair, maybe some organ tissue."

He rattled off information about the decay rate of dead bodies and autopsy procedure and she smiled as she looked out over the city. After a minute, he trailed off.

"Are you still there?" he asked.

"I was just listening," she said. "I'm coming back now." She called the elevator back up with the press of a button. "If I find you anywhere but in your bed, I *will* tie you down."

He breathed a laugh. "I never knew you were so bossy. You're as bad as Douglas."

"My mother would have told you in a *second* how bossy I am. I was the same way with her when she was sick. She started calling me Sarge because I was always giving her orders." While Emma laughed, she still felt a tightening in her throat. Talking about her mom never seemed to get easier. But she never wanted to forget her, so she worked through it. She relished sharing a memory with someone who understood her grief, understood the need to share the memories despite the pain.

He laughed again. She wanted to bottle the sound. She could count on one hand how many times she'd witnessed him laugh or smile. And half of that had been the night before, while he was almost dead. Why was it so much easier to get him to open up when she couldn't see his face? He was so much more…himself with the mask on. And now, too, when he was nothing but a voice in her ear.

"You do sound a bit like a drill sergeant," he said. "You can be quite intimidating when you want to be."

Her cheeks hurt from smiling. "And don't you forget it."

He disconnected from the earpiece while she rode the subway back. It was quiet, empty, everyone already wherever they needed to be for the day.

When she got back to Kane Manor, James was still in bed as promised. She wasn't so sure he hadn't tried to get up and been stopped by Douglas, who sat pointedly by the fireplace reading a newspaper.

A laptop sat propped on a pillow besides James, the screen blank for the moment.

"Anybody want lunch?" she asked. She wasn't sure what to do with herself. She wanted to be useful but didn't know how, now that talking to Kendrick was out of the way. Keeping everyone fed seemed like a simple enough task.

Douglas almost leapt to his feet. "I'll take care of it, Emma, don't worry." He was gone before she could so much as open her mouth.

She and James shared a frown. She perched on the edge of the mattress.

"Is that…for the footage from last night?" She gestured to the laptop.

He nodded, jaw tight. "I haven't watched it yet."

She didn't want to watch it. To relive it. Once was bad enough. And watching things through the lens…it would be just like when being trapped in her own body again. Able to see and hear but do nothing.

She changed the subject. "How do we find out where the ADA's body is? Can't be that hard to find a grave, right?"

"It depends."

One of her eyebrows lifted when he didn't outright dismiss her line of thought. "On?"

"Things don't ever go like they're supposed to in New Atlas," James said with a note of bitterness in his voice. "Especially with powerful people behind everything. He could have been cremated. Someone could have purposefully botched the autopsy. And if there's no body, any samples they might have kept might conveniently disappear, if they were collected at all. There's not really a way to know until we look into it."

Emma pointed a stern finger in his face. "*You're* staying here until you recover from being stabbed." He only stared stonily at her. "Let's see what Kendrick comes up with first."

They lapsed into silence. She reached for her phone out of habit but frowned when she remembered again that it was still in her locker at the club.

"What?" James asked when he noticed her expression.

"My phone–my bag–is still at the Crescent Club." She shrugged. She wasn't sure how much a new one cost, but she had a little money saved up. Maybe she could set up a payment plan.

"I'll get your bag back," James said without hesitation. When she opened her mouth he cut his eyes at her and continued, "There are lots of things Douglas is good at."

"Douglas is a petty thief?" she asked with a raised brow. "Why isn't *he* a vigilante?"

"Because I'm too old to get beaten up like he does," Douglas said as he came into the room with a tray.

She jumped up. "I could have helped you with that!"

"Not to worry," Douglas said with a kind smile. "It's nothing I'm not used to."

She still helped him clear a space at the foot of the bed for the tray and divide up the sandwiches. She noticed Douglas didn't bring enough for himself. "I'll be in the kitchen if you need me," Douglas said. He caught her eye when James wasn't looking and winked. Embarrassment bloomed in her stomach and made its way into her chest, up her neck, and into her cheeks. Douglas must know how she felt about James. Emma supposed it wasn't all that hard to figure out, especially for someone as observant as he was.

The panic and fear she'd experienced while James had bled on her, when he'd passed out–

There was no way she could have hidden it.

James looked as lost in thought as she was. "Have you slept?" he asked. He waited until she took a bite of her sandwich before starting on his own.

"No," she said. "But neither have you."

"I slept," he said with a defensive set to his shoulders.

"No, you were drugged so the doctor could dig around inside your abdomen then stitch you up. You've been awake as long as I have." She arched an eyebrow and silently dared him to argue. Besides, she wasn't the least bit tired. She didn't want to sleep. Didn't want to know what waited for her behind closed eyelids. She was practically as nocturnal as he was these days, anyway. So staying up like this was nothing new.

A muscle feathered in James's jaw. Finally, he half-growled, "I'll sleep if you do."

"*I'll* sleep if *you* do," she countered.

They glared at each other.

James gave up first. "You're *impossible*."

"I believe the actual term you used was '*extraordinary creature*.'" Emma grinned when he blushed. One of his fists bunched in the sheets. She softened toward him. "Look, I know—I know you hate sitting around and doing nothing. But the more you rest, the faster you'll get better." She'd used a similar speech on her mom once, and the memory of it formed a lump in her throat.

James nodded without looking at her.

"I'll let you sleep," Emma said after a beat of silence. She gathered their now-empty plates and stood to go. A warm hand caught hers. She looked down at him in surprise.

He seemed to have to force the words out. "You can…stay."

Her whole body went warm. She knew it wasn't an invitation to *bed*, just to sleep but…She couldn't say her mind didn't go there, even if only for a split second. But wouldn't she sleep better with him next to her? Wouldn't it be easier to only have to open her eyes and see him breathing beside her? She could still feel that fear within her, waiting to pounce.

"Alright," she said.

"I just—" He swallowed hard. He still wasn't looking her in the eyes but hadn't let her hand go either. His grip was just shy of too tight. "I don't want to let you out of my sight."

His green eyes swept up to hers. He watched her from under impossibly long and dark eyelashes.

Why was it suddenly so hard to breathe?

"Alright," she said again. He released her and she put their plates and tray on the nightstand. She walked slowly to the other side of the bed. She probably wouldn't even be able to tell he was there, the bed was so big. And thankfully she was already clean, already dressed comfortably.

She slid onto the bed over the covers. James clicked off the lamp.

Don't make it weird, she told herself. She forced herself to relax. To breathe.

She rolled onto her side to face James. He was on his back, staring up at the sweeping arches of the ceiling above them. She saw him dart a glance at her from the corners of his eyes and away again. One hand fisted tightly atop his chest. The other continued to strangle the sheets that covered him up to his waist.

She closed her eyes and breathed in the masculine scent of him that clung to the bed. She imagined she could hear his heart beating steadily beside her. *Alive, alive, alive,* it told her. She relaxed a little more. Inhale. Exhale.

She opened her eyes to find him watching. His cheeks pinkened in the dimness, but he didn't look away.

"Thank you for saving me," she whispered. Every line of him was taut as a bowstring. "And for not dying."

The barest hint of a smile. "You're welcome," he murmured. His eyes closed. Bit by bit, his body relaxed. She watched his slow, careful descent into sleep. Watched the fist on his chest loosen. Watched his breathing deepen. She matched her breaths to his.

Earlier emotions rose unexpectedly.

He had almost *died for her*. She remembered him bracing her against the door of that building, his back to the men shooting at them. The intensity of his gaze. The determination in those green eyes. How he hadn't let her go, not for a moment, not even when he had been *stabbed*. He hadn't faltered, not once.

A tear slipped from the corner of her eye. Then another.

He had been looking out for her all this time—for all of New Atlas—but who was looking out for *him*? What if she hadn't been there? She realized that if she *hadn't* been there, his injuries would not be as severe. It was her fault. He had been forced to save her at his own expense. It terrified her that it would be so easy to lose him, that she almost had because of her own actions.

Just look at what happened to Marie. She'd been here one moment and gone the next.

Emma was going to solve this case if it killed her. Anything to help him.

Anything to save him.

CHAPTER TWENTY-TWO

Emma's impression upon waking was that of pure heat. She was much too warm, her entire body cocooned in it. She blinked in the darkness, tried to bring the world into focus.

She was in James Kane's bed.

Correction, she was *in James Kane's arms*. She forgot how to breathe for a moment. She was on her side facing him. One of his arms was pinned beneath her neck and the other rested lightly around her middle. They curved towards each other in sleep, almost sharing a pillow. Their legs tangled together. He was on his back but still pressed tightly against her.

He was still asleep. She studied him for a minute. The soft lines of his lips. The sharp angles of his jaw and nose. His long, dark eyelashes. His dark hair, rumpled from sleep. He was bare-chested, the bandage on his abdomen starkly white in the darkness. Her heart squeezed painfully.

She very carefully scooted backwards, though she ached to stay in his arms for longer. For him to hold her. For him to keep the nightmares at bay.

But he wasn't hers. It would never work between them: her, a poor girl with nothing to lose, and him, a rich CEO with everything to lose. Her, the reason he almost got killed. Him, with an entire city to protect. Not to mention the tiny fact that he was still her boss.

He wasn't hers, but he was alive. And that would have to be enough. Outside the circle of his arms, Emma was suddenly too cold. She shivered, and he opened his eyes. He seemed confused for a moment. He tensed then relaxed all at once.

"Hi," she whispered.

"Hi," he whispered back.

"This is weird, isn't it?" she asked. She bit her lip.

"A little," he said quietly as he shifted positions. His hand went to his side as he stretched with a wince.

"Are you alright?" she asked, more awake as she zeroes in on the movement. She sat up and leaned towards him to check the bandage for blood.

"Yes," he said. He took one deep breath then another. She climbed out of the bed and went around to his side.

"There's some blood on the bandage—Dr. Torres said we should change it and keep it dry."

James carefully sat up. She tried not to watch the way his abs clenched as he moved. "I can do it."

"Let me," she said. She prepared for him to argue, but it seemed like he was too tired. Everything she needed was on the nightstand beside the bed. She braced one hand on his stomach and unceremoniously ripped the bandage off with the other. He huffed out a breath. "Sorry," she said. "Didn't want you to tense up."

Emma became very aware of his abs beneath her hand. Her brain emptied for a second. Her entire body grew hot. She was lying to herself if she pretended not to fantasize about kissing him, just for a moment. She mentally shook herself and quickly put the new bandage on.

"Thank you," he murmured when she was done.

Douglas gently knocked on the door a second later. "Ah, you're up. Breakfast?"

Emma had no clue what time it was. The room was still dark. Douglas acted like this was totally normal and simply turned on a dim lamp beside the bed after he set a tray in James's lap. James squinted in the light.

"Thank you," James said.

"I'll–I'm going to make coffee," Emma said. "Anyone want any?"

Both men shook their heads. Right. Tea drinkers.

She made her escape to the kitchen. Douglas hadn't seen them sleeping in the same bed, had he? Her face heated at the thought. She realized that their plates from lunch hadn't been on the nightstand, that the first aid kit had been laid out neatly. The heat in her cheeks deepened. Douglas *definitely* saw them sleeping in the same bed.

The comforting smell of coffee wrapped around her. The clock on the microwave informed her it was after one in the morning. They slept almost twelve hours.

As Emma drank her coffee, the quiet slowly overwhelmed her mind. Too much had happened. Too much had changed. Her mind needed to focus somewhere else, somewhere other than her feelings for James, somewhere other than the fear she still felt for his life. Somewhere other than the immense pressure to figure out what was going on in New Atlas.

The stakes were higher than ever. If they didn't find out exactly what was planned for that drug–and who exactly would benefit from it–all of New Atlas could be in trouble.

And *James* was in trouble. She had no idea if they would keep trying to capture him and drug him for their nefarious purposes. She needed more answers. Lionel Maxwell and the Wolf gave her a couple more pieces of the puzzle, but she couldn't see the complete picture yet.

Emma glanced at the clock again. After two in the morning.

An idea struck. Kendrick asked if anyone at the Crescent Club could give her more information. Well, she wouldn't know if they could until she tried. She would start with Lena–they'd formed a tentative bond. Lena warned her about Lionel Maxwell, after all.

She went upstairs and changed into darker, more practical clothes before she could change her mind. It wouldn't take long, and she'd hopefully be back before James even noticed she was gone.

As if her thoughts had summoned him, she bumped into Douglas back in the kitchen.

"Oh, hi," she said a bit breathlessly. "I need to…run to the store." She winced internally. She probably didn't even need to lie. "I'll be right back."

Douglas raised his eyebrows. "Alright…Be careful."

Emma flashed a quick smile and darted outside before he could question her. She rode the subway but got off a stop early in case someone recognized her. It was better to be cautious in case the Wolf came after her. She walked the last two blocks to the club before she ducked into an alley. She pressed herself into the shadows behind a recently emptied, but still rank, dumpster and waited.

Within half an hour, Lena went rushing past. Emma had a pretty good idea of the other girl's schedule since working with her, and she'd been right about her shift that night.

"Lena!" she called out. The other girl hurried down the sidewalk with her head down.

Her head whipped up. She screamed.

"Shh!" Emma covered her mouth and quickly pulled her into the shadows in the alley. "It's just me!"

"Oh my *God*, you're not dead!" Lena's mouth hung open in shock. "God, I thought you were dead too!"

"I'm not! I'm just…in some trouble."

"Here, wait–I've got your stuff from your locker. I was–" She dug around in a huge tote bag and pulled out Emma's smaller backpack. "–I was going to stop by Kane Manor and see…I don't know. If you were dead for sure. Or if they knew who to call. Where have you *been*? You just disappeared and–"

"I'm fine, I promise." She grit her teeth. Struggled to find the words. "That guy–Lionel Maxwell. Was he in tonight?"

Lena said, after a pause, "No, he wasn't. It was actually pretty empty. It was weird."

"Listen to me, Lena. Stay away from him. You were right about him." Emma's hands shook. She would never forget the feeling of having control of her own body taken away from her. "Actually–you should quit this job, okay?"

Lena bit her lip and looked away. "Look, I know you've already got that nice job working for James Kane or whatever it is you do in that fancy mansion…but the rest of us don't have any other way to pay off our debts. I've got a family, you know? A son. I can't just quit."

Emma clenched her fists. "I know, I just–it's not *safe*."

"It's New Atlas. Nowhere is safe." Lena scoffed. "I am glad you're not dead, though. What happened to you?"

"I–" She stopped. She forced the words out. "They took me, Lena. They drugged me and took me just like they did Marie. Just like those other girls before her. But the Phantom saved me. Promise me you'll be careful, okay? Some very powerful men are behind this and–" Lena wasn't looking her in the eyes. Was looking everywhere *but* at Emma. "You know something." It wasn't a question.

Lena glanced around fearfully. "I don't–I don't know what you're talking about." She clenched her tote bag more tightly to her chest.

Emma was suddenly irrationally angry. She shoved Lena a little too hard. "You do know something! You have to tell me! Lena, *they killed Marie right in front of me.* They almost killed *me*! They almost–" The words choked off. *They almost killed the man I love.*

Lena's whole body was shaking. "I don't, I swear!"

"*Tell me.*" Emma grabbed the girl by the shoulders. Dug her fingers in so she couldn't escape. She knew, in a distant sort of way, that she shouldn't be taking her anger out on Lena. But she was desperate.

"I don't–I heard some guys talking, that was all! I think they're planning something for this charity gala. They mentioned the Phantom–"

Emma cursed. That was only three weeks away.

"I swear I don't know anything other than that!" Lena trembled before her.

Emma softened. "I'm sorry." She took a purposeful step back and held out her hands. "Thank you. Really. Please be careful, okay?"

Lena nodded hastily. Tears dripped from her chin.

"Please text me if you hear anything, okay? If you can find out *anything*." Emma took a deep breath and set one hand gently on Lena's shoulder. "I might be able to stop this. Whatever it is. And if you can quit this job, please do. For your own good."

"Okay," Lena whispered. "Yeah, okay. I'll let you know if I hear anything. I didn't…I didn't know about Marie. I'm sorry."

Lena sniffled. Emma hesitated, then grabbed her hand and squeezed gently. "I'm going to stop this," she swore.

Emma said goodbye and hurried back to Kane Manor. Originally her intent was to get Lena to spy for her, but the girl had thankfully already heard something useful. She hoped. And with Lena having a son…Emma didn't want to endanger her any further. *Lainey, Becks, Jackie, Heather, Sofia, Marie*. She didn't want to add another name to the list.

If whoever was behind everything planned to use the drug on a large scale, what better place than a charity gala with the rich and powerful of New Atlas all in the same room? She needed to look up the guest list.

When she burst back into the kitchen at the manor, Douglas was there making a cup of tea. She slung her bag onto the kitchen island. It was closing in on four in the morning. The subways didn't run as frequently so late at night, so it took her longer than expected to get back.

They only had three weeks. It wasn't enough time.

Douglas watched Emma with keen eyes as she hurried past him to James's room, but said nothing. As she approached, she slowed to a stop at the sound of her own voice.

"You have to let me go."

"No!" James's voice this time. "I'm getting you out of here!"

The footage from the night before, she realized. There was a soft noise. A click. And then her voice again, repeating, *"You have to let me go."*

She leaned against the hallway wall and closed her eyes. There was another series of taps within James's bedroom. Her voice echoed out and down the hallway.

"Please. You're not going to make it carrying me. It's okay, I'll be okay, please go, *please."*

It was hard to hear her own desperation. She squeezed her eyes shut. At that moment she thought he was going to die. That he would die trying to save her. And he very nearly had. She took a deep breath, then pushed the door open.

James sat propped up in his bed with the laptop on a pillow in his lap. An expression blazed on his face that she couldn't decipher.

"I found something out," she said, ignoring how quickly James snapped shut the laptop. She wanted to move on, forget all the horrible things they had just been through. And now she had something to focus on. "They're planning something for that huge charity gala coming up. That's in three weeks."

James sat up straighter. He still wasn't wearing a shirt and she wanted to curse him. Kiss him. Press her fingers into his skin so she could feel the reassuring warmth of his aliveness. Touch him until he saw just how much she loved him and how much she hated that he had almost died for her.

"What–where did you hear that?" His dark brows furrowed.

"I went and saw a girl I worked with at the Crescent Club." She shrugged. "I–"

"You went *to the Crescent Club*?" There was no mistaking the anger in his voice. "They could have–"

"I didn't go *to* it, just waited a block away. I know her schedule and that she uses that subway stop. She also happened to give me my phone back." She waved said phone triumphantly.

James dragged a hand through his hair. The strands stood up for a moment before slowly falling flat again. "That was–"

"Dangerous, stupid, yeah yeah, I get it. You've given me the speech. Did you hear what I said? Three weeks." Why was he so bothered with her getting information? She'd found out something *important*. Something to work towards. Another piece of the puzzle. "Besides, it's statistically unlikely I'll get kidnapped again, just because it already happened once."

James gave her a withering stare. "It's *more* likely because you escaped and pissed them off. You should let me check your phone for tracking software too."

She sighed. Opened her mouth to argue. Let it go. He was right. "I'm sorry. But I had a hunch, and I was right. We have to tell Kendrick."

"I'll tell him."

He stared at his hands. She saw bruises on his knuckles that she hadn't noticed before.

"You shouldn't go back to the Crescent Club," he said in a much softer tone. "It's too dangerous. They took you once, and…" He trailed off while his long fingers tugged at a loose thread on the quilt. "I'll write you a check for the Wolf," he said without looking up. "That way he doesn't have anything to hold over you anymore."

"Jamie–"

He held up a hand. "It's my fault you're in this mess. Let me do this for you."

She bit her lip. Him paying off her debts…her mind spun. It wasn't insignificant. Wasn't something that someone would do simply to be nice. But they had a bond now–that was undeniable. She might be in love with him, but love or no, there was a bond. It had been forged in blood and fear and rage.

Yet she couldn't bring herself to be beholden to anyone else. She knew, logically, that James was nothing like the Wolf. That the money would be a gift. But something within her still rejected it. She didn't want to be a burden to him, to anyone. She didn't want another thing in a long list of imbalances between them.

Maybe it would be better to find a different job, a voice inside her whispered. She pushed the thought away. She could worry about that later.

"I need to think about it, okay?" she said. James seemed to visibly relax. He nodded. "I really–" She swallowed hard and tried again. "It really means a lot that you'd do that for me. I…I just need to think about it." She didn't know what to do with the emotions fighting for dominance inside her. So she made a joke. "I really hope you aren't offering this just because I saved your life." Her laugh came out nervous.

He didn't smile. "Of course not."

Though he *wouldn't* own her, her mind wouldn't stop poking at the thought like a sore tooth. She knew he was doing it free of any strings but she couldn't just accept.

They fell into silence.

"I told you to leave me because I wanted you to save yourself." She didn't know why she said it. Why she reopened that still-raw wound inside herself. But she owed him at least this one truth. "My life isn't worth as much as yours. You should have let me die."

She turned and left before he could answer.

CHAPTER TWENTY-THREE

JAMES

You should have let me die.

The words haunted James as he sifted through the video footage for Kendrick.

Every time he thought of those words—*you should have let me die*—his heart began to pound painfully in his chest.

Those words colored the footage in a new way when he restarted it again as the sun began rising behind his curtains. The light was a soft shade of orange like the creamsicles he and his father used to sneak at midnight.

The fear she must have felt, not being in control of her own body. Hearing those men say what they planned to do and not being able to do anything about it. Having to watch and wait and do nothing.

But why would she want to save *him*? His brain couldn't process it. It wasn't logical. It didn't make any sense. Why did she think she was worth *less*? *My life isn't worth as much as yours.* James rejected the notion outright.

He watched himself with critical eyes as he shielded her with his body. Her eyes stayed trained on his face, covered by the gas mask. The earpiece caught the heavy, panicked sound of her breathing.

James absently rubbed a spot on his chest.

He could have done it better. But he had been so frantic to reach her in time that he hadn't be as careful as he should have been. He knew to expect a trap, to expect them to try to drug him. But his entire focus was on getting *her* out alive. Everything and everyone else be damned.

Even now, the rage threatened to overwhelm him. His jaw ached from clenching it so tightly.

He saw the flash of the knife in the video footage, but hadn't noticed it at the time. Everything in him had been solely focused on Emma's safety. He watched himself yank the knife out and grapple with Maxwell with a critical eye. He could have done better. He *should* have done better. It was too close a call.

Because that's what it meant, wasn't it? That she didn't have faith in him? Since he hadn't done better? *You should have let me die.* Because she knew he couldn't handle that many men on his own. She didn't think he could save her and save himself both. She didn't know that he would die for her, a thousand times over, and gladly.

James rewound the footage to earlier in the night. To her coming outside, frantic, afraid. To their kiss. He wanted to kiss her again. That alone terrified him.

It terrified him that he would kill for her. That he would die for her. He had never felt this way before, and it was like a great black chasm yawning open before him, ready to swallow him whole. It had *already* swallowed him whole. Everything was about her. His every thought, his every dream, his every breath. He could barely focus on saving New Atlas because he was so worried about saving *her*.

James watched the footage continue to play.

He pulled it up to look for clues, for anything he might have missed during the fight.

But then Emma and her insistence that he leave her behind captivated him instead. He started watching for his own mistakes, things he could have done differently to save them both without injuries.

"You have to let me go." He wouldn't. Not ever.

He gently pressed a hand to the wound in his side, testing it out. It still hurt. He remained exhausted from blood loss, despite having had probably the best night of sleep in his life. He'd opened his eyes that night and found Emma mere inches from him. Her breath had stirred his hair. Her body had been warm where it touched his. It was blissfully easy to fall back into a deep, dreamless sleep, knowing she was safe next to him.

He tried to understand why she didn't simply let him pay off her debts. She seemed to be considering it, but she hadn't jumped at the chance like he thought she would. He wanted to make sure she wouldn't ever have to go back to that shithole again. That she wouldn't ever have to put up with a man touching her when she didn't want him to. The money was no object, surely she knew that.

Maybe that was the issue, he realized. With vivid clarity, he recalled her tiny one bedroom apartment the night they met. She was from an utterly different world in him. Even during the worst times in his life, James had never, not once, had to worry about money.

He frowned at this realization as he rewound the footage even further and let it play while he idly changed the bandage on his stomach. Poking it made it bleed a little, and he didn't want Emma to see and worry. His mind flashed to the feeling of her hand flat on his stomach. He pushed the thoughts away. There was no use daydreaming about her. She wasn't his.

When he looked up at the screen again, Emma was taking off her clothes.

With a curse, James fumbled for the controls as his face heated. He heard her squeak of surprise and her eyes shut, effectively blacking out the screen. All he caught was a glimpse of her bare skin and nothing else.

James cursed again and snapped the laptop shut.

She somehow forgot the lens and had *showered.*

His face burned. He glanced around, guilty, making sure Douglas wasn't lurking somewhere. Or, worse, that Emma hadn't walked into his room without him realizing it.

He closed his eyes as he leaned back against the pillows with a groan.

Emma was going to drive him utterly mad. She already had. Every time she touched him, it set his skin on fire. Every time she kissed him was seared into his memory. The feeling of her soft, warm curves underneath his hands haunted him.

He wanted her, all of her, and didn't know what to do with those emotions.

He thought she was going to die that night. And then, when he saved her, when he was bleeding and the world was fading at the edges, all he could think about was not getting to kiss her again. Not getting to hear her voice again. Not getting to take care of her like she deserved.

But it was his fault she was in danger in the first place. He had already played those words over and over, where *he* was the big missing piece in the Wolf's plans. The reason they took Emma in the first place: to place a trap for the Phantom.

And James wasn't so selfish that he would ever put her in that position again.

Being the Phantom meant he couldn't have the kind of love he craved, and he was okay with that.

Even if it meant letting Emma go. As long as she was safe, even if it was safe from *him*, he could rest easy.

EMMA

Blood filled Emma's mouth. It slid into her eyes.

When she opened them, she saw the Phantom hanging from his cape above her, bleeding from dozens of wounds. Pieces of bloody flesh showed through torn armor. His blood dripped steadily. It covered every inch of her. His eyes stared blankly ahead.

Dead.

It was her fault.

Emma woke with a muffled scream.

Dead. He was dead, and it was her fault. He died trying to save her, he–

No. James was alive. He was downstairs.

But every time she closed her eyes, she saw his lifeless body.

She couldn't move. Her body wouldn't cooperate.

The drug–

No, she was in her bed. She wasn't drugged.

But she couldn't move–panic rose and tangled with the fear within her.

Finally, her arms moved. She rolled over. It wasn't real. None of it was real. She wasn't drugged, and James wasn't dead.

Great, heaving breaths shuddered out of her.

She had to check. She had to be sure he was okay. She needed to know, without a shadow of doubt, that he was *alive*.

She grabbed a pillow and her quilt and quietly walked downstairs. She gently pushed open his door. She put the pillow down on the rug by the fireplace and curled up where she could see him. The easy movements of his breathing soothed her. In. Out. In again, and out. She matched her breathing to his. Watched his hand twitch in his sleep.

Emma was back in her room before he woke.

The next night, she did the same thing. The dreams were so vivid that each time she woke, it became harder to convince herself that they weren't real. That James wasn't actually dead because of her. She couldn't stop seeing his limp body before her, his blood on her hands and clothes. And when she didn't dream about his death, she dreamt about Marie's.

The only thing that made it better to watch him breathe. To hear him stir slightly as he dreamt. To inhale the scent of him that permeated his room. She knew it was crazy to sneak into his room just to watch him sleep. But it was the only thing that worked. It was the only thing that settled her panic and fear. She wouldn't bother him with her fears. So she would watch instead. That was all.

The third night, she woke to a dull pain in her side and a muffled curse.

"Emma?" James's voice was rough with sleep. He squatted before her. "Wh–"

He must have tripped over her. She furiously rubbed her eyes and hurriedly gathered her pillow and blanket. A touch on her arm made her pause.

"What are you doing on the floor?" His voice was the gentlest she'd ever heard it.

"I'm sorry," she whispered, ashamed. "I keep–I keep having these nightmares and I can't sleep and–" She looked away from him.

"What are they about?" he asked softly. He seemed content to crouch there on the floor beside her as long as necessary.

She didn't want to admit to it. The latest one was still fresh in her mind. She hadn't been in his room that long, but she must have fallen asleep again quickly. It had been the worst and most realistic nightmare yet. She cried for half an hour before she could get it together enough to go to his room and check, the fear so thick it choked her, paralyzed her.

"You," she said. Hurt and then confusion flashed across his face. "I keep–I keep seeing you die. And it's always my fault." Her voice dropped to less than a whisper. "It was almost my fault. Just like Marie was my fault." She closed her eyes against the wave of pain. Tears slipped out before she could stop them. "I can only sleep if–if I know you're okay." Her voice cracked. "I'm sorry."

James took her hand. Placed it on his chest over his heart. She could feel it beating steadily under her palm as he covered her hand with his. "I'm alive. I'm okay."

"I'll go back to my room now," she said. "I'm really sorry."

He was still holding her hand. "Stay," he said. "Sleep in the bed."

She shook her head. "I don't want–"

"It's alright. There's plenty of room."

He pulled her to her feet. Grabbed her pillow and blanket out of her arms. Walked with her over to the bed and waited until she was lying down before he did, too.

They stared at each other in the dark.

"I'm okay," he said again. Her eyes closed of their own accord. She was exhausted. Sleeping on the floor wasn't restful. But neither were the constant nightmares. His voice soothed her. It eased the panic and fear that laid in wait. "It wasn't your fault."

She hummed. Warmth spread through her limbs. She listened to his quiet breathing. He was alive. He was okay. He was with her.

When she jolted awake a little later, he was still watching her. She was crying before she'd fully woken. Still half asleep, he reached over and placed her hand over his heart. Felt it beating. Felt his warmth. He was alive. He was okay. He was with her. His hand covered hers. His thumb ghosted over her knuckles.

She drifted back to sleep.

An alarm was going off.

Emma groggily fumbled for her phone to hit snooze.

"Get up." James's voice was urgent in her ear. Where—Oh. Right. She was in his bed. Her tired eyes focused blearily on his face. The quiet alarm stopped. His phone, not hers. "There's someone breaking into the house."

She shot up, adrenaline pouring through her veins more effectively than any caffeine. "Wha—Douglas?"

James knew what she meant. "He'll have heard the same alarm. Don't worry about him." His voice was low. Every muscle in his body was tense, alert. She had the strangest sensation of deja vu. Here was the Phantom before her, but in James's body. She had never seen it so clearly.

The light from his phone briefly illuminated his face before he grabbed a fire poker from the fireplace. She almost laughed.

"Stay here." He darted into the dark hallway before she could protest. She ground her teeth together. Like hell she was staying there. It hadn't even been a *week* since he got stabbed. Her taser was upstairs in her room and she hadn't bought new bullets yet.

Emma frantically searched for something else she could use as a weapon. He'd stolen her idea.

There was a screwdriver on the messy desk. It would have to do. Better than nothing, she thought.

On quiet feet, she peered into the hallway. She listened carefully. The house was *too* quiet. Did James go downstairs to his secret lair? No, that'd be stupid. It would be too obvious for him to come into James Kane's house as the Phantom. The Phantom had no reason to care about James Kane as far as everyone else knew.

She quickly reviewed what she knew of the house's layout. The kitchen door and front door were the only ways in, besides the many windows. And the basement, but she was pretty sure no one would be able to accidentally find that. James probably had all sorts of extra security for it.

Whoever was in the house would probably use the kitchen door or a window then, not the front door. The front was too obvious. Then they would probably work their way upward to clear each floor. So they were either in the kitchen, or in one of the rooms that faced the front or side of the manor. Unless they split up, some in the front door, some coming from another way.

She couldn't just sit and wait to find out. She made sure the hallway was empty before hurrying up the stairs. She could at least make sure Douglas was okay, and maybe get her taser.

As soon as she reached the top, strong arms grabbed her tight. A hand covered her mouth. She let out an involuntary gasp as she struggled against her captor. She raised the screwdriver and tried to angle it to stab the attacker in the arm to let her go.

"*I told you to stay there*," James breathed into her ear.

She relaxed. Did he realize she had almost stabbed him with a screwdriver for grabbing her like that?

He was in nothing but a pair of sweatpants. She was keenly aware that he was not wearing the Phantom's armor, that he was vulnerable. In one easy move, he pulled her deeper into the shadows of the hallway and through a doorway. Her feet barely skimmed the floor. God, he was strong.

Douglas waited behind the door with a shotgun. His phone screen lit his face as he studied a video feed. He pocketed it after a second and turned to James. He wore the same old fashioned pajamas she'd seen him in before.

He held up one hand, fingers splayed. Then three fingers. Eight men in the house? James nodded. Douglas held up one finger. First floor, maybe?

James pointed to Douglas then pointed down. Then, he pointed to himself and then up. Douglas nodded and stepped through the doorway. He disappeared towards the back stairs.

Eight men in the house on the first floor, Emma thought. Douglas was going at them from below while James hit them from above. The pair moved with practiced ease.

James went to step out of the room, but she stopped him by gripping his wrist as hard as she could. Her eyes blazed with fear. James stared down at her for a long moment. *Be careful*, she silently ordered him. He tilted his chin in a nod. He pressed his hands against both of her shoulders, hard. *Stay put.* He stepped outside without any noise whatsoever and melted into the shadows as if made of them.

Emma pressed her ear to the door once they were gone, but couldn't hear anything. She opened it a crack to peer out. Not knowing what was happening was unbearable. She would stay put–but only for as long as she wasn't needed. The second it seemed like James needed help, she would act. Even injured, she knew he was the better fighter, but she was *not* going to let him get himself killed.

Through the tiny crack in the door, she saw the first man come up the stairs. He wore a bulletproof vest and held a gun in his hands. Another, stockier man was right behind him, dressed similarly.

There was a booming gunshot from downstairs. Douglas's shotgun, she guessed.

When the two men turned towards the noise, James erupted from the shadows.

Seeing James in action without the armor was a marvel. Every movement was powerful. Purposeful.

The fire poker smashed into the first man's wrist. He dropped his gun with a curse. He swung a fist, but James ducked under his guard and hit him in the side. James twisted his body as the man's punch connected with his hip, angling his bandaged side away. In the same moment, James brought the fire poker down against the man's outstretched arm. Even from down the hallway, Emma heard the bone crack. The metal connected with the man's head next. He went tumbling down the steps, unconscious.

The second man fumbled with his gun. James hit him in the head with the fire poker and the man went down. As he fell, James knocked the gun from his hand for good measure. There was another blast from downstairs and several staccato shots in answer. An unfamiliar voice shouted something unintelligible.

James came alive in the fight in a way Emma couldn't see whenever he wore the armor.

He took a step down and exchanged blows with a third man. This man lost his gun quickly, but seemed to be a better fighter, or at least more prepared for resistance. His fist hit James in the thigh, then the shoulder. James dropped the fire poker in the process with a resounding clatter. Even without the armor, she could see him absorb the hits that connected as if they didn't bother him. His face was a mask of calm, cold anger.

She had to admit that it did strange things to her heart to watch him. She was afraid for him first and foremost, especially seeing him shirtless up against men in body armor. Not to mention with a stab wound.

But she was also strangely fascinated. Captivated.

She bit her lip as she watched the pair of them descend several steps as they fought furiously. The light outside the front door poured through the stained glass windows, lighting the fight in blue and green and yellow.

Finally, James smashed his fist into the other man's face. Once. Twice. The next hit was to the gut. The man doubled over with a grunt of pain and James used the opportunity to smash his knee into his face. The man fell. A fourth man stepped out of the way of his fallen comrade and raised his weapon. James disarmed him almost easily, completely unphased as the gun went off right next to his ear.

Emma flinched backwards, afraid the bullet would hit her as it went wide.

When she looked out a again she saw James catch a punch with his forearm and press downwards. The muscles in his back and arms flexed. The man was forced to concede a step.

Downstairs, all was silent. Too silent.

She couldn't stand by and watch. James had it handled there, but Douglas–

She hadn't heard anything after those last shots.

Emma hurried out of the room and down the back stairway. She clenched the screwdriver tightly in her sweaty hand.

She pressed herself against the wall at the bottom of the stairs and strained to listen. James had taken care of three, probably four, of the men. Douglas had indicated there were eight. There were two shotgun blasts. If Douglas was a good shot–and she somehow knew that he was–that meant there were only two men left.

Then why was it so quiet now? There were no sounds of fighting from the kitchen, no sign of struggle happening around the corner.

She inched forward to peer around the corner into the kitchen.

There were two bodies on the floor. Emma glanced away quickly, bile rising in her throat at the sight of the blood and open wounds of the dead men.

Her focus shifted to Douglas, on his knees in the center of the kitchen, face bloodied. One man pointed a handgun at his head. The other man pointed his gun at the kitchen doorway. Towards James. The shotgun lay discarded on the floor between the two armed men.

A cold sort of rage settled into her bones.

This was her *home*.

James stepped into the weak yellow light coming from above the oven then stopped short. His mouth twitched angrily, but he said nothing.

"Mr. Kane," said the man closest to Douglas. He was taller than James, but much skinnier and bald. "We don't want any trouble. We just want the girl."

"The girl?" James repeated. Emma could hear the strain in his voice. The barely contained fury. His eyes didn't leave Douglas for a second. A dark stain marred his bandage, yet he was barely winded. There was no sign that he'd just fought four men hand to hand and won. She could see the hard lines of the Phantom in the way he held himself. Feet planted. Fists clenched. Shoulders tight. For a split second, she blinked and could see the ghost of a cape and mask in how he stood.

"Don't play dumb. Your little assistant. Housekeeper. Bed warmer. Whatever you call her."

James's eyes flicked up to the bald man's face, then back to Douglas. "What do you want with her?" His face gave nothing away. His tone was utterly casual.

"She's created some...trouble for my employers. We just want to take her to them and make it right, is all. Then we'll leave you and your cousin here alone. Like we were never here. Even forgive you for what you had to do to defend your home." The man shrugged. His hands remained steady on his weapon.

Emma started inching out of the shadows. Both men focused solely on Douglas and James. She knew this house. Knew where the floors creaked. Knew where the shadows were deepest.

She knew James saw her, but his eyes never wavered from Douglas to give her away. She raised the screwdriver. Held up three fingers with her free hand.

Two.

One.

She struck.

The screwdriver didn't go in easily—she had to shove it hard before there was a soft pop as it punched through the skinny man's side. She didn't hesitate and left the screwdriver where it was as the man shouted. She smashed her hand into the wrist that held the gun. A shot went off, but it went wide. Her fist connected with his face next. Pain danced across her knuckles.

The moment she stepped forward, James had jumped into action. He hit the other man in the stomach several times in quick succession. He wrestled the gun away from him and knocked him in the temple.

Pain lashed through Emma's head as the bald man recovered enough to hit her. He raised his fist again. There was a loud thunk, then he fell to the ground. Douglas stood over him with the shotgun in his hands. He smacked the butt of it into the man's head again for good measure.

James was there in an instant. "Are you hurt?" he asked. His voice was a deep rasp. He grabbed her chin and tilted her face towards the meager light.

"I'm okay," she said. "Douglas—" She turned to the other man, whose head was bleeding.

"I'm alright," he said wearily. "Just a bump. Shouldn't need stitches. I believe we have some zip ties somewhere."

He ran off, presumably for zip ties.

"I have to call Kendrick—" James said. His body was still tense with adrenaline. She touched her fingertips to the back of one of his clenched fists.

"I'll do it. It makes more sense for me to call him."

He paused and looked down at her with an unknown emotion blazing in his eyes. He nodded once. "I'll make sure there are no more surprises waiting."

Emma hurried back to James's room for her phone. She didn't know what time it was. Only that it was the middle of the night. Only hours ago, she had fallen asleep with her hand pressed to his heart while its beating lulled her to sleep.

Now there were eight men scattered across the house, either wounded or dead. She had no idea if the screwdriver hit anything vital in that last man. If they were dead, then good riddance. They came into her home to take her, to kill her, and could have killed James and Douglas in the process. But she still tasted bile at the back of her throat.

She fumbled for her phone in the darkness. It was four in the morning. The darkest part of the night.

She dialed Kendrick's number.

He answered after three short rings. "Hello?" he said, voice groggy with sleep. "Detective Kendrick."

"Hi, It's Emma."

"Emma?" he said. He instantly seemed more alert. "Everything alright?

"Eight men just broke into Kane Manor trying to kidnap me," she said carefully. "I told Ja–Mr. Kane that we could trust you."

"I'll be there in ten minutes," he said. "Are they still in the house? Get somewhere safe–"

"No, I mean yes, they're still in the house. But we…took care of them. You might need to send an ambulance too. For them. We're fine."

Kendrick let out a long breath. "You sure seem to get in a disproportionate amount of trouble, Em."

"Trust me. You have no idea."

CHAPTER TWENTY-FOUR

"–what were you *thinking*!" James's angry voice reached Emma from the hallway. She slowed before she reached the kitchen, curious. She ignored the four men tied together at the base of the stairs even as they stared at her, their mouths gagged. Her eyes trailed to the beautiful stained glass around the front door. There was one perfect bullet hole in one pane. She couldn't imagine how expensive it would be to replace.

"I was *thinking* that this is my home and that I almost lost you once already," Douglas said back, voice scathing. "I have no qualms about killing. That's *your* thing."

Emma blinked. They were arguing about the two dead men.

"Douglas–"

"No more of this, James. I will not be made to feel bad for protecting my *home* and the people I *love*." It was the angriest she'd ever heard Douglas. She didn't think she'd *ever* heard him be anything other than calm. It unsettled her. She realized a beat later that Douglas included her as *people he loved*. Her heart warmed almost unbearably.

To keep them from arguing further, she hurriedly stepped into the kitchen.

"Detective Kendrick said he'll be here in ten minutes," Emma informed them when she stepped through the doorway. They were making quick work of tying up the intruders. She swallowed hard and averted her gaze from the two men they *weren't* tying up. There was a splash of blood on one cabinet, and her mind flashed back to another night, to the feeling of liquid on her knees. She pushed the memories away.

Emma didn't miss the pointed way James currently ignored Douglas. His arms crossed tightly across his bare chest.

"Anything?" Douglas asked as James checked the security footage on his phone one more time for any stragglers. James shook his head.

"No movement at the gate either," he murmured. Emma didn't want to think about what that meant for the nice night guard.

"Are Mr. and Mrs. Banks okay?" she asked, suddenly worried about the elderly couple. She imagined them dead in their beds, none the wiser of what happened at the manor.

"I didn't see anyone go past the house, but I'll make sure Kendrick checks," James said softly. He walked towards his bedroom and she trailed after him.

"I think you ripped your stitches," she said. She couldn't get the image of him fighting out of her head. He was powerful, graceful, like an apex predator. She never realized how...*attractive* she found it until she saw him in action. A memory flashed through her mind of the Phantom jumping from the metal walkway in that warehouse, cape blown wide like wings.

"I'm fine," he said curtly. He yanked a t-shirt out of a drawer.

She squeezed herself between him and the dresser, stopping him with a hand to his chest. "Need I remind you how aggravated I'll be if you die after all the hard work I did to save you?" She raised an eyebrow. He didn't smile, but he paused. One hand fisted around his shirt. Every tendon on the back of that hand stood out. She could see pain in the tightness of his jaw, in the corners of his lips and eyes. "Let me see," she said softly. They were so close their breaths mingled in the small space between their bodies.

He said nothing but remained utterly still. Unnaturally still. She assumed that was his way of giving her permission and gently peeled back the bandage. He kept his gaze fixed somewhere over her shoulder.

"We should call Dr. Torres–" she started. She brushed one finger over the skin about an inch below the sharp line of stitches.

James's hand grabbed hers so fast she jumped, startled. "Douglas can stitch it," he almost growled.

"Did I hurt you?" she asked. She hadn't meant to touch him—it had sort of happened subconsciously. Her hands simply sought out his warmth. It saw automatic. A reflex.

"No." His voice was strained.

She carefully stepped away. He inhaled deeply. Exhaled. Shrugged the shirt on. She followed him back to the kitchen where Douglas had out a first aid kit.

"Let me do that," James said. He grabbed the kit and set to work cleaning the cut on Douglas's head and carefully placing two butterfly stitches on it.

"James popped a few of his stitches. He said you could stitch him back up, Douglas," Emma said when James was done. James gave her a withering look of betrayal. She stared defiantly back. She resisted the urge to stick her tongue out at him.

"Of course. Here, sit. Shouldn't take long." Douglas gave her a small smile. James was glaring at her around Douglas. She gave in and stuck her tongue out. His lips twitched like he wanted to smile but he resisted.

"Get some ice for your head, and Douglas's," James said softly as Douglas had him lift his shirt. She did as he said, having already forgotten about her own pain. Her focus had been on that bloodied bandage, on the blood on Douglas's head. Her head and knuckles throbbed now that they were brought to her attention.

Ping. Douglas's phone chimed from his hand. There was someone at the gate. They watched the feed on James's phone as Detective Kendrick got out of his car, went inside the guardhouse, then came back out and made a quick phone call. Then he got back in his car and continued up the long drive.

"All finished," Douglas said, tying off the new stitches right as there was a knock at the front door. That too was on the feeds on their phones. Emma hadn't realized just how many cameras there were.

She remembered dancing stupidly the last time she made dinner and flushed. Hopefully, that wasn't on camera.

"I'll see him in," Douglas said. "Emma, would you mind putting a bandage on that? It's still bleeding a bit."

James was sprawled in the chair, knees wide, and she moved into the space between. From this position, her standing and him seated, she was taller, forcing him to stare up at her from underneath his long eyelashes. Her heart fluttered.

"Feels like we've been here before," she murmured with a small smile. "A few times now."

She traced the thin line of a scar on his abdomen with one finger. The one from when they'd first met. She'd had no idea then how deeply her life would become intertwined with the Phantom's.

James shuddered under her touch. "Don't–don't do that." He ground out each word like it pained him.

Emma yanked her hand back. Her face grew hot. "Sorry. I was just–remembering."

She quickly opened a bandage and carefully smoothed it over his skin. She pulled his shirt back down to cover it. As she started to step away, James looped his long fingers around her wrist. His thumb slid up the inside, right over her pulse. She wondered if he could feel it jump at his touch.

"Just–whenever you touch me–" He inhaled shakily. "It's–"

There was a different sort of intensity in his eyes. She recalled vividly what it was like to kiss him. Their kiss in the very same room they were currently in. His hands on her ass, lifting her onto the kitchen island. Her gaze flickered to his lips.

Did she imagine it, or was he watching her lips too? Their breathing sped up in tandem.

One of the men on the floor groaned.

"Right this way, detective," Douglas's voice said from the hall. His tone was light, pleasant. Like the detective was merely dropping by for a visit.

"Your man at the gate was killed." Kendrick's voice preceded him into the room. "I'll need to clear the house–"

"I can assure you we've done that already."

James let his hand drop as Douglas and Kendrick's voices moved closer. She moved back as he stood.

James held one hand out to Kendrick. "You must be Detective Kendrick. Emma speaks highly of you." Emma watched the exchange, impressed with how well James played it off.

The two men shook hands. "Nice to meet you, Mr. Kane." Kendrick looked around and gave a low whistle. "This all of them? Is—is that a screwdriver?"

The man with said screwdriver in his side was waking up. "It was all I could find," Emma said, a bit embarrassed. She tried to ignore all the blood on the floor. She felt as Douglas did—she wouldn't feel bad about protecting her home and those she loved. Even if it was with a screwdriver.

Kendrick lifted an eyebrow and gave her a strange look.

"There are eight of them. Two are dead." Douglas showed the detective where the others were tied together at the bottom of the stairs.

"Alright," Kendrick said after a moment of silence. "I'll need to get statements from all three of you. I have backup on the way. Including…ambulances. Were any of you hurt?"

"Minor injuries, that's all," James said in a voice barely more than a mumble. Every trace of the Phantom had disappeared. His shoulders curled in like he was uncomfortable with the attention. "Detective, I shouldn't have to say that if a single word of this leaks to the press, I'll be suing the department."

Kendrick paused. Nodded. "Of course." Emma could tell he was just as uncomfortable. She wanted to smile at the awkwardness between them. Kendrick had no idea that James was someone he already knew and trusted.

"I'll have the lawyers draw up some NDAs," Douglas said. He dialed a number on his phone. Emma watched, a bit awed. It was like the routine was practiced. Maybe it was. Plus, who had a lawyer they could call at the crack of dawn for a nondisclosure agreement?

Sometimes she forgot James was…wealthy.

"I'll start with you, Em. You two wait here, please."

Kendrick gestured for her to follow and led her into the formal living room. She blinked when he turned on a lamp, having forgotten that it was the middle of the night.

He pulled out a small notepad and settled into an armchair.

She sat on the stiff couch across from him.

"You said they were trying to kidnap you?" Kendrick wasted no time in getting to the point.

"That's what they said. They told Ja–Mr. Kane that they would leave him and Douglas alone if they handed me over. Said I caused their employers a lot of trouble already. I'm assuming it has to do with…our mutual friend." She knotted her fingers together in her lap. "Did you ever–"

Kendrick shushed her. "If you're asking what I think you're asking, yes. I was able to…get something. I brought you a sample to take to…your friend. I was going to call tomorrow, get it to one of you then, but since I was already on my way…" He pulled out a small cooler bag. Presumably the samples from the ADA's body. "I have someone I trust working on analyzing it, too."

"Thank you. We only have two weeks before–"

"I know, I know. It's not much time."

"It's not *enough* time." Especially if people were being sent after her. She wondered if they wanted *her* or wanted to use her to get to the Phantom again. They probably had gotten a good idea of his capabilities when they escaped the first time. A memory of James passed out in the seat of the car flashed through her mind. She knew which idea scared her more.

"I really do need to get your statement," the detective said after a moment. "Your boss really takes his privacy seriously, huh?"

"You have no idea," she muttered. She bit the inside of her cheek.

"How much does he know about…what we're working on?" Kendrick asked. He peered at her over the rim of his glasses.

Emma hesitated. Her mind raced to figure out exactly what to say. "Enough," she said. "He knows that my friend was killed. That the Phantom helped me. That kind of stuff. That we can trust you."

Kendrick made a noise in the back of his throat. "So what happened exactly?" He lifted his pen above the notepad and looked at her expectantly.

"James woke me and said someone was in the house, and we went upstairs to make sure Douglas was okay. I guess James and Douglas saw on their security cameras that there were eight men, and decided to defend their home."

"You were downstairs, then went upstairs to Douglas's room? Is your room on the first level?" Kendrick asked as his pen darted across the paper with gentle scratches.

Emma realized her mistake. She flushed. The need to explain that her relationship with James wasn't inappropriate rose within her. She already had to force herself to call him *James* every time and not *Jamie*. "Um…no. I was–James's room is on the first floor. Mine and Douglas's are on the second floor. It's not–it isn't like that between us–"

Kendrick didn't look up. "It isn't my business whether it's like that or not. I just need to know exactly what happened. Keep going."

Emma told the detective everything she could remember without giving too much away about James's extracurricular activities. The embarrassment lingered, but at least she knew Kendrick was good, that he was trustworthy. Everyone already assumed she and James Kane had a…different sort of business arrangement, anyway. The last thing she needed was the press getting wind of that rumor. The last thing *James* needed was the press getting wind of that rumor.

As she finished her story, she worried about every word she said, worried that Kendrick still knew how to tell when she was lying. She made sure to note that James and Douglas both had a lot of self-defense training. "One man had a gun to Douglas's head. Another had a gun pointed at James. I knew I had to do something, so I stabbed the bald guy. It was enough of a distraction."

"With the screwdriver?"

She flushed again. "Yes. It was the only thing I could find on short notice." She fell quiet and listened to the scratching of Kendrick's pen while he finished writing her statement.

When he looked up, he said, "Should you…call our friend and tell him about this? If it really is related to the trouble you caused…"

"I–" Her mind went blank. She had no idea how James juggled two lives. But she guessed the Phantom and James had never intertwined so directly before. Not like this. "Yeah, that's a good idea. Maybe he can look into it too. And I can pass this to him." She held up the small cooler bag.

Kendrick nodded towards it. "You didn't get that from me, by the way."

"Got it."

"Send James Kane in next, please," he said. She stood to go. "And…I'm glad you're okay. You've been through a lot lately. Plus, I think our friend has a soft spot for you. So you should definitely bring him into the loop." He winked.

She paused in the doorway. "I'm glad you're on our team."

In the kitchen, Douglas was still on the phone. James sat at the island with a watchful eye on the men tied up on the floor.

"Your turn," she said to James. He sighed and stood, shuffling towards the formal living room like a man headed to the gallows. She really wanted to eavesdrop, but then there were cops and paramedics coming through the front door at that moment, a storm of noise and activity.

Kane Manor suddenly swarmed with people. She and Douglas were sequestered in James's room by another detective, nearby but out of the way. James came back after a long while, then Douglas went to give his statement.

Emma pulled out the bag after Douglas went for his interview. "From Kendrick. Officially, it's not from him and it's not samples from the ADA's body."

James's fingers brushed hers as he took the bag. Douglas had opened the curtains. The sun was just beginning to rise.

"We only have two weeks," she said. "And we have no idea what they're planning. Just where it'll probably happen."

"I'll figure it out," he said.

"We," she said with a smile. "*We'll* figure it out. Haven't you learned that you can't leave me behind?"

He gave her a half-smile in return. "Hm. It's–aggravating."

Emma snorted a laugh. "Yeah, well, so is your terrible concept of self-preservation." She nudged him with her shoulder. "You know,

Kendrick said he thinks the Phantom has a soft spot for me." She meant it to be teasing, but James's face went abruptly serious. His dark hair was deliciously rumpled, his green eyes bright.

"He does," he said in a low voice. He took a deliberate step closer to her. His scent assailed her nostrils. She almost asked what deodorant he used or what detergent because it always smelled heavenly.

Her heart started pounding. What was he saying? His eyes darted down to her lips. She wet them with the tip of her tongue. He tracked the movement, so close to her that his breath stirred the hairs on her forehead.

"I've been given permission to get some breakfast going, as long as I don't get in the way," Douglas's voice said as he pushed the door open.

They sprang apart as if caught doing something they shouldn't be. Douglas glanced between them and smiled almost knowingly.

"Let me help you," Emma said hurriedly. She didn't think it was technically allowed since part of the kitchen was a crime scene, but breakfast sounded good. It sounded like a distraction, too.

"There's *no* need–"

"It's okay, I don't mind." She turned to James. "*You* should relax. It's barely been a week since you were stabbed." When he opened his mouth to argue, she said, "I will go steal handcuffs from a cop right now. Don't make me steal from a cop."

She didn't miss how he tried to hide his smile. He held his hands up in surrender and sat in one of the armchairs by the fireplace.

Face still flushed, Emma followed Douglas into the kitchen. They made quick work of breakfast, enough for a small army–which was about how many people were currently in the house. Emma made coffee for anyone who wanted it.

"*Why* do you have so much food in the house when only three of us live here?" she asked Douglas as she passed a mug of coffee to a grateful-looking cop.

Douglas shrugged. "I suppose I'm like James in that way–always prepared for the worst."

"The worst being a house full of starving cops?" She and Douglas both laughed.

Her skin prickled, and she glanced up to see James beside her. "I came to see what was taking so long," he said a bit sheepishly.

"Everyone loves free food," she said. "And it doesn't even count as a bribe. Here, take this to Kendrick." She passed him a mug of coffee. James stared down at the cup as if it were foreign to him. "Coffee. Kendrick." She gently pushed him.

"Why?" he asked.

"Because we *like* Kendrick. And sometimes a cup of coffee goes a long way." She nudged him again, and he went, skirting the other investigators as he did.

"Here," James said gruffly to Kendrick, who was in the hallway talking to another detective. Kendrick turned with a bemused expression. "Coffee," James said. She wanted to laugh at the way James avoided looking Kendrick in the eyes as he held out the mug like a sullen child getting in trouble. Was he worried Kendrick would recognize him? Or did he just really hate interacting with others that much?

"Uh…thanks, man," Kendrick said, accepting the mug. James visibly relaxed when Kendrick had the mug and he could escape back into the kitchen.

She couldn't hold it back anymore. She laughed into her hands.

"What?" James asked with a frown. He wordlessly accepted a cup of tea from Douglas for himself.

"*Here. Coffee*," Emma said, deepening her voice in an imitation of him and making it sound like a caveman. She laughed again.

James's cheeks turned pink. She bumped her hip against his so he would know she was kidding. He smiled down at her, but there was a tightness in his eyes.

As she watched Kendrick hold his coffee without sipping it, Emma thought of a day years before. The day her mom and Kendrick broke up. She was only thirteen at the time. Kendrick had picked her up from school and taken her for a rare treat—coffee. She'd felt like an adult getting her own drink, even more so when Kendrick told her the bad news like she was an equal. And then, when she cried, he held her and gently reassured her that he would always be in her life. He kept that promise too, always checking in on her at least a couple of times a year, sending her birthday and Christmas cards. When she needed him most, at her mom's funeral, he'd been there.

She never forgot that moment at the coffee shop.

"They want us out of the way again," James said softly, pulling her from her memories.

Inside James's room once more, Emma and Douglas sat in the armchairs while James paced restlessly.

"At least they didn't try to drug us," Emma said helpfully when she grew tired of watching him pace.

He didn't stop. "We're extremely lucky they didn't," he said darkly.

"And at least we know we're on the right track," she added.

He gave her a withering look.

"I mean it," she said a bit defensively. "They're going through an awful lot of trouble to get rid of me."

James made a noise in his throat and continued pacing.

"They were in my *home*," James said. "They–"

He opened his mouth to say something else, but Emma held up a hand.

"I'm not trying to downplay it. It's called being *optimistic*." She rolled her eyes. Douglas coughed to hide a laugh.

James's pacing was driving her crazy, so she stood.

"I know your fancy lawyers are on it," Emma said. "But I'm going to go contact the PR team and draft a statement just in case."

"Good idea," Douglas said softly. James nodded silently and kept pacing.

After getting permission from an officer, Emma closed herself in her office upstairs and took a deep breath in the quiet. She knew there was a lot of work piling up, so she grabbed her laptop to take back to James's room.

Somehow she knocked a box over, one of many she hadn't unpacked. Sorting and scanning documents had fallen to the wayside lately, and she knew it'd be a long while before she could get back to it.

She cursed and bent to shove the papers back into the box.

It was all…newspaper clippings and journals.

A word caught Emma's eye. She grabbed the topmost paper. The headline glared up at her. *Local Nightclub Owner Denies Mafia Ties.*

The article was about the Crescent Club.

And the author's name was Katherine Kane.

James's mother had written about the Wolf?

She grabbed another paper, and it was the same thing: an article about the Wolf by James's mother. This time it was about the Wolf being acquitted of embezzlement and racketeering twenty-five years ago.

James's mom had been…obsessed with the Wolf, it seemed. There were at least five more articles about him, all about how he'd been accused of something and acquitted or something regarding the club that was never proven.

Emma grabbed a journal but hesitated. Was she allowed to read Katherine Kane's journals? They *had* been in her office among the stacks of things to organize and scan into digital files.

She studied it for a moment, knees protesting from crouching on the floor for so long. As she studied the cover, she realized it was stamped with the year the Kanes died.

She flipped it open. Dust collected on her fingers from the cover and the pages.

The more she read, the more Emma's heart sank. On top of everything she'd researched for the articles Emma found, Katherine Kane had information on shell accounts that tied back to the Wolf. All of it was detailed in a neat hand, beginning to end.

Emma froze as she neared the final pages, then jumped, startled, as her office door opened.

"There you are," Douglas said. "What are you doing on the floor?"

"Douglas," she said quietly, unsure how to broach the subject. She knew she had something big, something important, in her hands but she wasn't sure what.

"That's–That's Kate's handwriting." Douglas sank to the floor next to her. "Where did you…?" He trailed off as his finger traced over the page.

"She was looking into the Wolf when she–died." Emma pointed to the thing that had stopped her cold. "Remember years ago, there was that drug where you put drops on your tongue? It killed like fifty people? She tied it to the Wolf, look." She showed him the flowchart in Katherine Kane's handwriting.

"I knew she was investigating him," Douglas said almost reverently as he traced the letters on the page. "I…That was all a long time ago." He gently shut the journal. He seemed to shake himself. "The cops are leaving."

Emma wanted to press the issue, to dig further into what she'd found. But he was right–it was a long time ago, and she didn't want to hurt him or James by dredging up a painful past.

By the time they emerged downstairs, Kendrick was the only one left. He promised Douglas to get everyone on the scene to sign the NDAs the Kane lawyer sent to the station. He promised, too, to let them know how the investigation went, though Emma wasn't holding her breath on that one.

As he left, he caught Emma's eye and nodded once.

She nodded back.

At least there was someone else in New Atlas they could count on when the time came.

Emma, Douglas, and James stood in the kitchen for a moment, each of them lost in their own thoughts.

"We don't have a lot of time," she said eventually. "If something is happening at that charity gala…."

James ran a hand through his hair. "I'm going to run some tests on the samples Kendrick gave us. Maybe I can replicate it or find a cure based on the samples of your blood, Em."

Em. The short nickname sent a thrill through her. Only her mother–and Kendrick–ever called her Em.

She enjoyed hearing him say it probably a little too much.

"Do you think they'll use the drug at the gala?" she asked to cover up her heated cheeks.

"Possibly. They either have specific targets they'll be after, or they'll use it on everyone to cause chaos while they do something else. We still don't have enough information." James made a frustrated noise. Emma imagined fog coming out of vents in a ballroom, filling New Atlas with the mind control drug.

"I don't know how we can get more," she said, equally frustrated. "Lena was my last source. Unless I go back to the Crescent Club."

James's response was immediate. "*Absolutely not*," he snarled.

"No, I wasn't seriously considering it," she said hurriedly. "Calm down. I just–it's about the only option we have left."

"No."

"I *know*, Jamie, I'm just–I don't want to just sit around and wait for something to happen."

He sighed. "I don't either," he said, voice softening. "But right now it's all we have. We'll work on those samples of the drug and counteragent first. I'll start right away."

He hurried off, likely to his secret lair, and Douglas left the room soon after.

Emma bit her lip and stared into the empty kitchen. They were running out of time. She could feel it pressing down on them. Six dead girls, and for what? To take over New Atlas at some party? There was more to it, more they were missing, but Emma didn't know how to figure it out.

But there was one thing she could do. First and foremost, they had to get into that gala.

Good thing she knew a billionaire who could get them in.

CHAPTER TWENTY-FIVE

"Hi, my name is Emma Warner. I'm calling on behalf of Mr. James Kane. He wanted me to see about an invitation to the gala you're hosting for pediatric cancer research…He'd very much like to attend." Emma chewed her lip as she waited for a response. "I apologize that it's so last minute…"

There were several quick footsteps, and James burst into the kitchen. She had no idea how he heard her. She smiled blandly at him and pointedly turned her back.

"Wow, thank you for calling. Yes, I can put Mr. Kane down on the list, no problem. Will he…have a plus one?" The secretary on the other end of the line sounded breathless.

"Yes, please."

A stunned silence. "Okay, yes, Mr. Kane and a–a plus one. I see here that Mr. Ramos is also attending, but there's a donation required for each guest–"

"Of course, no problem. Could you send the details to my email? The donation will be sent as soon as we get the information." She wondered how long it would be until word spread that James Kane would be attending. She knew he was uncomfortable with the attention, but she didn't know how to keep his attendance under wraps. Douglas had given his permission for the donation in James's name and said he would handle it, but maybe she should have asked James first. Oops.

James stepped in front of her. His eyes were wild. Bewildered. He started shaking his head vehemently.

"What is that email?"

"Of course," Emma said, then gave her official Kane Industries email.

"Thank Mr. Kane for his contribution. We look forward to seeing him at the gala." The secretary hung up, but not before Emma heard her say distantly, "Oh my *God,* you'll never—" Apparently, word would spread *very* quickly.

"*What* are you doing?" James demanded.

"Getting us invited to the gala," she said. She set her phone down on the counter and went back to her coffee. In roughly the day since Kane Manor was broken into, James had already gone crazy setting up more security. She didn't even know he was even in the house when making the call. He and Douglas and the new security guards they'd hired had been going over every inch of the grounds, gates, and outbuildings. He even had an outdoor camera installed on the Banks's cottage just in case. Emma was glad they were unscathed from the encounter. "Douglas was already going, but we needed to be on the guest list too."

He was still staring at her like she'd grown a third eye, or maybe a second head.

"It's for *kids*. With *cancer*. Douglas said it was fine. Want a coffee?"

James didn't answer.

"What?" she asked innocently. "How did you think we were going to get into that party?"

He blinked. There was an echo of the Phantom in his eyes. "*You* weren't going to. And neither was James Kane." He rubbed his face. She wasn't entirely sure he'd slept between installing the new security measures and whatever experiments he was conducting on her blood in the basement. "I don't go to stuff like this. I don't…like being the center of attention like that, like a piece of meat."

Emma softened. "The Phantom can't just break into a huge party like that. Not with the most important people in the city. Besides, you need backup. Douglas is already going. We might need some bribe money, though." The joke fell flat. To cover the awkwardness, she carefully sipped her coffee. James's expression was a mixture of bewilderment and frustration, his mouth slightly parted. It was hard not to laugh. "We have to do some reconnaissance. Thus, the invitations."

"We still don't have any idea what they're going to do. We still haven't figured out an antidote or even how to replicate the counter-agent. Why–"

She spun around on the stool to face him fully. "Jamie, you don't have to do this alone. They killed my friend, drugged and kidnapped me, stabbed you, broke into your house–I'm not going to just sit here. Douglas isn't either! Not this time. You need all the help you can get." She crossed her arms and stared him down.

He made a frustrated noise and ran a hand through his already messy hair. "You've known about me for all of a week and you're already–already–*meddling*." He threw his hands up in the air. She'd never seen him so flustered. It was…endearing. "Why are you smiling?" He punctuated the question with a frown.

"Because I'm aggravating you, and it's funny." She shrugged and finally gave in to the urge to laugh. "Get over it."

He stared at her while she washed out her coffee cup. She grabbed her bag and keys from the counter and pocketed her phone.

"Where are you going?" he asked.

"To get a dress. I'll forward you the donation details. And make sure you have a tux."

"Of course I have a tux." He stepped in front of her. His body blocked her way out.

"Listen, you're not going to stop–" She began, but stopped when he handed her something. A credit card. A thick, black credit card.

"I don't think I pay you enough for the kind of dress you're going to need," he said quietly. His eyes dipped to her lips and then back up. She swallowed. "Spend whatever you want. I mean that."

Emma couldn't think of a single thing to say. Her instinct was to brush it off with a joke about him not paying her enough, period, but he was so close that she could feel his warmth. She'd snuck into his bed again the night before, and both of them pretended she hadn't.

And now he was handing her his credit card and telling her to get whatever she wanted.

She hadn't accepted his offer to pay her debt to the Wolf. But maybe she could start by accepting this. It went against all of her instincts and made her feel vaguely sick. But she really, really didn't have enough money in her account to get a nice enough dress. Her plan had been to hit as many thrift stores as possible hoping for a unicorn of a dress to appear.

The moment stretched before she finally took the card.

"Thank you," she finally choked out. "I...Thank you. I'll be back later."

As the door shut behind her, she heard him quietly say, "Be careful."

Since the gala was so close, Emma's options were limited. It was hard to find the right size, and then from there to find a dress that she liked. Add to that the fact that she'd spent almost an hour researching *where* to get formal dresses. But she finally had a breakthrough and found the perfect dress, shoes, and earrings in one fell swoop. She secretly compromised with James and only let him pay for the dress, the cost of the accessories coming out of her own account.

Then she decided to get a coffee and do something she hadn't done in a long time.

It was a sunny day, rare for New Atlas in the fall, and the sun warmed her wind-chilled skin as it set behind brilliantly orange and pink clouds.

"Hi, Mom," she said when she reached the tombstone. She took a seat in the grass beside it. Let her fingers trail through the dry stalks. "I've missed you a lot lately. Sorry it's been so long." She reached out and brushed some dirt from the tombstone. "I met someone. Two someones, really, but it turned out to be the same guy, if you can believe it. You have no idea how much I want to hear what you have to say about all of this."

She trailed off, sipped her coffee. She studied her mom's name, the dates underneath. *Margaret Warner.* Remembered picking the tombstone out. Remembered lowering her mother's casket into the earth where she now sat.

"You always told me you wanted more for me. And I don't know if–Let's just say, I'm trying. I'm trying to save New Atlas and after that…I don't know. It's a mess, really. See, I'm in love with this guy, but I don't see how it can work. He's really rich. I know, I know. A dream guy. But I've always been under someone's thumb, especially since you got sick. I don't see how it can work with the world he's from and the world I'm from. I think it might be time to move on. Because I don't know if I can do this." She'd been thinking about it a lot lately. She hated the thought of leaving Kane Manor, not knowing what else to do in the after…if there was an after to all this. Her throat tightened. "I have no idea what you'd say, but I really wish–" She swallowed hard. "I really wish I could hear it."

She leaned against the tombstone in the row in front of her mother's. Pulled her knees up. "I miss you," she said. "More than ever. It's been–so hard without you, Mom. I just want you to be here. It's so…lonely without you."

She brushed the tears from her cheeks. "I just really need some guidance right now. I don't know what to do. I don't know what's next. Literally. This whole thing–this mess I've found myself in, I don't know how to fix it. I really, really wish I could get your advice."

She closed her eyes. The sun dipped below the line of trees bordering the cemetery. The shadows lengthened. "Anyway, I just had some time and needed to talk. I have to go see a man about a fancy party. I swear, you'd really get a kick out of this."

Emma stood and brushed off her pants. The headstone was cold when she gently touched it with two fingers. She should get back home before it got too late. She wasn't afraid of the dark. Far from it. But she didn't want James and Douglas to worry.

It was fully dark by the time she let herself in the back door of Kane Manor. Douglas was in the kitchen cooking something that smelled amazing.

"Hey, Douglas." She smiled fondly at him. Visiting her mother's grave always made her extra sentimental. "Where's Jamie?"

"You just missed him by a few minutes," Douglas said as he kneaded dough and adjusted the oven temperature. "He went downstairs."

"By downstairs do you mean the secret lair?" She wiggled her eyebrows.

He laughed. "Yes, that's what I mean. I think…maybe he wouldn't be too angry if I gave you the code. Don't you think? This has to rise anyway." He gestured to the dough.

Emma gave him a brilliant smile. "Yes!"

Douglas laughed again. "I have to admit, it's nice to share this with someone. Here, let me show you." He moved the now-covered dough to one side and wiped his hands on a towel.

As they walked down the hallway, she asked, "How do you do it alone? Watch him do what he does every night? Especially when–when things happen to him." She swallowed, glad he wasn't looking at her.

They stopped at the basement door. "It really isn't easy. It's an argument he and I have had thousands of times by now. But he refuses to see reason on this one thing, despite how much he's always looking for things to make sense." Douglas looked at her with a sharpness in his gaze that had her fidgeting. "You two are a lot alike, you know."

Emma scoffed. "I don't think so. We're both stubborn, maybe, but that's about it."

Douglas raised his eyebrows and crossed his arms. "Oh? How about your ferocity in protecting those you love? Or your desire to see justice brought to those who have done wrong? Your need to protect others, even if it gets you hurt? I could go on, you know."

Heat rose settled in her cheeks. She winced. "Well, when you put it like that," she said lightly. She chewed the inside of her lip.

"And another thing you both share–the inability to talk about your feelings."

She couldn't help her surprised laugh. "You've got me there."

Douglas winked. "I think it would do you both good to be honest with each other. Now, as for the code…" He entered it and explained the security system to her as they stepped into the elevator.

Relief washed through Emma when Douglas let the subject drop. He was right, she didn't like talking about her feelings. It scared her. It always led to her getting hurt, or hurting others. The thought of telling James how she felt was much more terrifying than facing men with guns. Besides, she was used to not getting a happy ending. Her dreams were as dead as her mother. Her life had never gone according to plan. She made a friend for the first time in years and had to watch her die in front of her. That meant the most likely scenario was that the man she was in love with didn't love her back. Especially since that man was from an entirely different world. He was rich, a CEO, a genius with apparently a bunch of degrees. She was in debt to the Wolf, had come from nothing, barely had one degree. It would never work. Even if he *did* share her feelings, she felt certain it would all end horribly when they realized just how different they truly were.

"I'll be up here if you need me," Douglas said as the doors closed behind her.

Emma took a deep breath and put the conversation out of her mind.

The elevator jerked to a stop a minute later. She eagerly pushed the doors open and stepped into the Phantom's secret lair. The first time she saw it, she'd been too focused on keeping Jamie alive to take it all in.

It was a huge, open space made entirely of concrete and filled with tables and workstations, what looked like a wrestling ring, a bunch of weightlifting equipment, interesting gadgets, and all kinds of other things. There were various racks of weapons, backups for gauntlets and other pieces of suit armor, and the armored car. Her eyes darted around, greedily trying to take in everything at once.

"Jamie?" she called softly. Her own voice echoed. She inhaled the cold, damp scent of the space around her. "Jamie?" she called a little louder.

No answer.

She walked over to the tables and computers clustered in the center. There were sticky notes everywhere, too, filled with James's familiar, hurried handwriting. Only one table had a chair. Atop that table an open notebook showed the same scrawl and several sketches. One whole side of the paper was a sketch of the city's skyline, a streetlight in the foreground. Yet it was almost too clean, a dreamer's version of the city. James was a good artist, she noted with surprise.

When she finally tore her eyes from the sketch, she noticed the computer screen moving. She could hear a vague roar from the speakers, like an engine or heavy wind.

It took her a minute to realize what she was looking at.

James wore one of the contact lenses, and here was the video feed for it. From what she could tell, it was live. He currently wove in and out of traffic. She studied the screen to try to figure out what she was seeing.

Oh, right. A motorcycle.

She frowned at the computer. "Jamie?" she asked. "Can you hear me?"

Nothing.

She noticed a small microphone with a switch next to it.

She flipped the switch and then said again, "Jamie?"

On the screen, the motorcycle swerved slightly.

"Emma?" came James's voice from the screen. "What–"

"What the fuck are you doing?" she asked impatiently. "And yes, Douglas let me into your secret lair."

"What–" He dodged a truck. It looked like he was on the highway. "What are *you* doing?"

"I haven't been *stabbed recently*. You stupid, stubborn–"

"I had something I had to do," he growled. She could tell from his tone of voice that he was angry.

"What do you mean, you had something to do?" She crossed her arms even though he couldn't see her.

"I'm trying to get some information," was all he said. He took an exit from the highway without slowing down. "Now please, just go back upstairs. I won't be long."

"Fine," she said. But all she did was flip the switch off to watch while muttering a string of curses that he couldn't hear.

He was in the nicer suburbs outside the city. Where the most important people in New Atlas lived and the houses were more like mansions. On the screen Emma saw that they were spaced so far apart that every home was very private.

James hid the bike at the end of one street before he darted into the shadows and over a fence.

An alarm wailed. She heard him curse through the feed.

Several dark figures emerged from the darkness. Motion sensors flipped on and bathed the vigilante in bright light.

Emma echoed his curses. He was in trouble. She heard the sharp intake of breath he took before he vaulted back over the fence. The loud, staccato sound of multiple gunshots. Obviously, he hadn't expected so much company…wherever he was.

Her eyes landed on the armored car. She'd seen the exact route he'd taken, the exit on the highway familiar to her. It was maybe ten minutes away. Five, if she took *that*.

Luckily, the keys were on the table next to her. She grabbed them then ran over to a rack of weapons to snatch the first thing she touched. A crossbow. She jumped into the car without a second thought.

Emma wouldn't be quite as worried if James wasn't healing from a stab wound. But one good hit—even with the armor on—and he would be down for the count. Dr. Torres called him extraordinarily lucky, and James was really pushing that luck. His stitches already popped once.

The car roared to life. She answered it with a feral smile. A shiver of anticipation raced up her spine. She quickly adjusted the seat to fit her shorter frame.

With a single press of the accelerator, she had the car spinning around and facing the tunnel outside. It lurched forward with another press. The giant door opened as the car got close and immediately closed once she was through.

Faster. Faster. She made it to the highway and floored it.

She gave a wild gasp as she was pressed back into the seat.

Traffic was heavy, but there was enough room for her to weave around everyone.

Within a couple of minutes, she was taking the same exit as James. She gunned it down the empty road and the car purred in answer. She *loved* this thing. She understood it in that moment—it was *exhilarating* driving it. Last time she'd been more concerned with keeping James alive than with paying attention to the car itself. Now she could enjoy it a little bit.

The house at the end of the street was lit with bright white floodlights. Gunfire echoed down through the quiet suburb.

Emma really hadn't thought this through.

The car plowed through the wrought-iron gate in front of the house. The metal was no match for the armored plates on the front bumper. She sped across the gravel driveway. With a twist of the wheel, the car spun around. A spray of gravel caught several of the armed men around her. Good. She had their attention.

Within minutes, bullets smashed into the windows. Thankfully, the bulletproof glass had all been replaced since their escape from the Wolf and nothing made it through. She flinched at the noise and shoved her foot against the accelerator. Several men jumped out of the way.

Where was James?

It didn't matter. She grabbed the crossbow from the floorboard on the passenger side and spent a harrowing minute figuring out how to load it. She probably should have watched an instructional video first. Or grabbed something else.

"*Fuck*." She gave up and simply threw the car into reverse. There was a heavy thunk, and then another, as two of the armed men bounced off the rear bumper in indirect hits. She winced, then shoved the gearshift into drive.

When Emma looked up, she saw Lionel Maxwell standing on the front steps.

She remembered the feel of his hands on her. His smiles, his touches. The feel of his tongue in her mouth. She saw his blade sink into James's side. Rage rose within her, choked her, made her hands shake where they rested on the wheel.

The car went careening towards him. She relished the look of shock and fear on his face before he dove out of the way. She slammed on the brakes to avoid hitting the stairs then reversed and aimed the car at him again. More bullets peppered the windows. The rear window looked like it was finally going to shatter at any moment. *Where was James?*

She had to give up her pursuit of Maxwell as a couple armed men got too close. She sped past them and yanked the car around again in a wild circle. Another thunk and a shadow careened over the hood. She was forced to stop. The man rolled to the ground. *Oops*, she thought a bit distantly, still too worried about James to focus on much else.

A gloved hand smacked against the passenger window. She shrieked in surprise but fumbled to unlock the car when she saw who it was.

James shoved a now unconscious Lionel Maxwell into the car and climbed in after him.

"Drive!"

She obeyed and took off back down the driveway.

"Why did we just kidnap Lionel Maxwell?" she asked breathlessly as the car galloped down the empty streets.

"What are you *doing* here?" James didn't shout, but she heard the strain in his voice. What she could see of his face beneath the mask was tight with anger. She almost laughed at the sight of him, scrunched up against the passenger side door with an unconscious man in his lap.

"You clearly needed help," she snapped back. She flexed her fingers around the steering wheel. "Where are we going?"

"The tower," he said. She made a quick turn.

The tower was dark when she parked underneath it a few minutes later. She could feel the anger emanating from James but chose to ignore it. He hefted Maxwell over an armored shoulder. "Go home," he said, but she followed him into the elevator.

He gave a small snarl of frustration at her but punched in the code anyway.

"Are you going to tell me why you kidnapped Lionel Maxwell?"

She could see him debating whether or not to answer her. "We need more information. I figured he could give it to us. He was the easiest to get to."

"Are you going to torture him then?" She crossed her arms. She really wasn't against the idea, but– "Why don't we just call Kendrick, have Maxwell arrested? We have the recordings from that night."

"This is faster," James said. "We're running out of time."

Emma couldn't argue with that.

Plus she might have wanted to hit Maxwell a few times herself. Not for information. Just because he deserved it. She watched as James produced a zip tie from his belt and secured Maxwell's hands. When they reached the top of the tower, he unceremoniously dumped Maxwell on the floor and whirled on her.

"*Go home.*"

"No." She widened her stance and crossed her arms more tightly. She grit her teeth so hard it hurt.

"Do you have *any* idea how dangerous–"

"You needed help!" she shouted. She stepped forward until their chests brushed. A single finger poked him hard in the armor even though he couldn't feel it. "You were stabbed a week ago! And he *clearly* was expecting you."

"I had it handled!" He took a breath then lowered his voice. "You could have been hurt. It's dangerous! Do you understand that? If you get hurt–"

She poked him again, in the cheek this time so he could feel it. He grabbed her hand with his gloved one. "You idiot, I've already been hurt! I'm in this now, and there's no going back. You needed help and I couldn't just sit back and watch!" Her breath heaved out of her. She wasn't going to let him shut her out. Not now. Not when they were so close.

He made another noise that was almost a growl and stalked away from her. His cape rippled in the wind.

"I couldn't live with myself if I was the cause of you getting hurt!" he half-shouted, still facing away from her.

"And I couldn't live with myself if your stupid lack of self-preservation got you killed!" she shouted back.

Emma didn't care if she got hurt helping him. And she had already watched him get much too close to death. She never wanted that to happen again. She couldn't bear it. She still couldn't sleep at night without watching to make sure he kept breathing. Whether he liked it or not, she was helping him finish this.

"You keep getting in the way! I can't do this if I keep worrying about you, if I keep having to save you!" he said. The words punched her in the chest like a physical blow. She sucked in a sharp breath at the pain of them. *Oh.*

"No need to feel *guilty*, I'll be out of your hair sooner rather than later," she said scathingly to cover up the sudden tears in her eyes. "I won't be a burden much longer."

She watched his shoulders rise and fall quickly for several beats. She told herself the tears in her eyes were from the wind. God, she really didn't want to cry in front of him over something so stupid. But it was her worst fears realized out loud: she was a liability.

James frowned at her. "That's *not–*"

"Why do I feel like I've interrupted a lover's quarrel?" Lionel Maxwell croaked from behind her. He didn't seem very concerned about his current predicament. Emma's mouth curled in disgust.

James was on him in an instant. He hauled him up by his shirt and smashed him against one of the supports.

"You're going to tell me what you have planned," James said in a low, dangerous voice that sent a chill over her skin. Maxwell let his head loll back and turned a smile towards Emma. James hit him in the face. "Don't look at her. Look at me. What do you have planned?"

"It doesn't matter," Maxwell said. He seemed almost…gleeful. "There's no stopping it now."

James hit him again. Then again. Blood exploded from Maxwell's nose as it broke with a sharp crack. It ran over his lips and covered his teeth. Maxwell smiled at her again, teeth coated in red.

"*Look at me,*" James snarled at Maxwell. Every line of him was taut with rage.

Emma watched impassively. She couldn't lie to herself–she had imagined variations of this scenario. After Maxwell's hands and lips had been on her, after he'd *drugged* her and stabbed James, she had imagined all the ways she would like to see him suffer.

"How did you know he was coming?" she asked in a cold voice she barely recognized.

Maxwell stared at her with an expression that made her skin crawl.

"We've all upped security," he said, shrugging as much as he could with James's unrelenting grip. "We knew you would target us. It almost worked, having–"

The elevator started descending. Maxwell immediately shut up at the noise.

She and James both went very still. "Someone's coming," she said needlessly.

"Get behind one of those," James said, pointing at the support. He hit Maxwell until he went limp, unconscious again. The man was going to have some serious brain damage, she thought as she hid. She wasn't so sure she minded the thought.

James tied Maxwell up and dragged him behind the support next to hers. Had some of Maxwell's men followed them? Sure, there was a code, but the elevator honestly didn't seem that secure. She'd left the crossbow in the car, even though she didn't know how to use it. But it would be better than nothing. She could stab someone with an arrow, at the very least. From the corner of her eye, she saw James pull out his phone and open an app.

He relaxed at whatever he saw right as the elevator slid to a halt. The doors screeched open.

"Hello?" Kendrick's voice called out. "I texted you to meet then saw you were already here."

James stepped out of the shadows. "Detective," he said curtly.

"Car looks a little beat up," Kendrick noted drily. His long coat whipped around in the wind. "Everything okay?"

Emma came out of her hiding place. "Hi, Kendrick."

He nodded at her. "Why am I not surprised to see you here too?" he muttered. "I was coming to tell you we found out some information about that counteragent. Looks like it stays in the blood. I thought at first it might be like…pheromones or something, but the lab tech analyzing it for me said that wasn't it. It's almost like it's antibodies, he said. Like it sticks around in the blood after each use. He thinks he might be close to reproducing it. There was a lot of stuff I didn't understand, but…is that Lionel Maxwell?"

James said nothing, so Emma said nothing.

"I—what is he doing here?" Kendrick looked stunned. His mouth opened then closed almost comically.

"I needed information," James said in his deep, gravelly voice. She was starting to notice that the Phantom's voice was always a shade deeper and more intense than James's.

"He's one of the ones who kidnapped me," Emma added. She clenched her fists to hide their trembling. "In fact, *he's* the one who drugged me and ordered me around."

"He's too high-profile. He probably has fantastic lawyers, too." Kendrick pinched the bridge of his nose. "You have to let him go until we have enough evidence to arrest him. Including those recordings you've been promising me. I'm going to pretend I didn't see this."

Emma's mouth fell open. "He *kidnapped me*. I'll testify. Isn't that enough? We still don't know what they're going to do at that gala–"

"I'm sorry, Em," Kendrick said. His voice was tired. "I can't let you just beat information out of him. That's not the right way to go about it, and you know it." This he said with a look leveled at James, whose expression was indecipherable behind the mask.

"Ugh!" Emma aimed a vicious kick at Maxwell's side. His eyes fluttered open with a groan.

"Hey!" Kendrick said. He stepped forward to grab her or stop her, she didn't know what. But in the same breath, James stepped in front of her and placed a hand on Kendrick's chest. He stared down at him until Kendrick backed up with his hands in the air.

"What else did your guy find out?" James asked as if nothing had happened.

"That's pretty much it. It's in the blood and acts like antibodies. He said it a lot more scientifically than me, but that's the gist of it. He's working with Emma's samples to see about an antidote, but reproducing the counteragent seems a lot more likely. But I thought you might want to know what I found out sooner rather than later." Kendrick shrugged.

Maxwell groaned again and seemed to come to.

Kendrick leveled a disapproving stare at her and James. "I mean it, you have to let him go. We'll get him for everything, I promise, but this isn't the way to do it."

Emma stared down at Maxwell for a long moment. She briefly wondered what Kendrick would do if she shoved Maxwell over the side of the building. "Let's go," she said to James.

He grabbed Maxwell and quietly said they'd dump him on the side of the road somewhere so Kendrick wouldn't be implicated in anything.

Emma swore to herself that Maxwell would get what was coming to him one day soon.

CHAPTER TWENTY-SIX

EMMA

James ripped off his mask as soon as they were back in the secret lair and let it fall onto one of the desks. The screen before him multiplied as he stared at it. He carefully removed the contact lens to put it away. The screen went black.

He started yanking off the armor piece by piece. Emma knew he was angry, but she didn't care. She was angry, too, but for wildly different reasons.

"Let me," she said. She pushed herself between him and the table he was taking his anger out on. She started unhooking each piece of armor, having watched him do it enough to figure it out. His hair was mussed and his eyes were ringed with black. He stared at her almost blankly. Like he wasn't James yet. Like he was still only the Phantom. There was still an intensity in the way he held himself, in the set of his jaw, in his bloodshot eyes.

As soon as she had the last piece of armor off, he immediately scooped them up and began cleaning them and placing them on the dummy.

"Once this is all over," she said softly to his back, "I'll find a new job and an apartment."

James stopped moving but didn't turn around.

"You won't *ever* have to worry about me telling anyone," she continued. She fiddled with a piece of his armor. Held it out to him. "I would die before I told anyone about you."

She didn't want to have to leave, but he so obviously hated having her in his Phantom business. And he was worried about her getting hurt. So worried that he would get *himself* hurt by being distracted. She was a burden to him. *You keep getting in the way.* He didn't like her meddling, didn't want her help. She was the reason he got stabbed, after all. Everything was so…unequal between them. She couldn't take it.

"You can–" James started. He paused for a long moment. "You can work here for as long as you'd like."

She deflated a bit. *Ask me to stay*, she thought to his back. *Ask me to stay with you.*

But of course he didn't.

The elevator began descending as the silence spread between them.

"Are your stitches okay?" Emma asked James as Douglas came out of the elevator with a tray of food. James gave a terse nod. She wasn't sure she believed him. She almost reached out and pulled his shirt up to check the bandage, but didn't want to cross a line.

"Thought you might like some dinner," Douglas said with a small smile. He paused when he saw the makeup on James's face. But he said nothing, just put the tray on the table closest to James. Emma wondered exactly how much Douglas enabled James's lack of self-preservation.

"Thank you, Douglas," Emma said, bitterness lacing the words. "Jamie here just got back from kidnapping a very prominent banker in New Atlas and trying to beat information out of him while still recovering from a stab wound. Oh, and there were a bunch of armed men waiting for him."

Both men looked at her. Douglas with confusion, James with something akin to angry betrayal.

"Oh?" was all Douglas said.

Emma groaned and threw up her hands. "These two," she muttered to herself as she inspected the food Douglas made. Some sort of bread and stew that smelled amazing in the cold, damp air.

"Don't worry," she said louder where they could hear her. "I kept him from killing himself."

James still glared at her. She glared back. She was angry. At him for trying to get himself killed. At Douglas for letting him. At herself, for being so stupidly in love that she didn't realize what a liability she was. If she was unsure about leaving before, she wasn't any longer. *You keep getting in the way*. The memory of the words took her breath away. Things between them were already too imbalanced . That gap was only becoming clearer and clearer.

"Maybe after I leave you won't get into so much trouble," she muttered, for James's benefit. His expression closed off, and he went back to messing with the armor.

"After you leave?" Douglas echoed. He rested his hands on the back of the lone chair.

"Once this is all over," she said. "Once we save New Atlas. I guess this is my two-week notice." Something twisted in her gut, but she ignored it.

Douglas gave James a sharp look that was ignored.

"Maybe you should wait until things…settle, to decide," Douglas said carefully. She couldn't read his expression.

She shook her head. "No, I've been thinking about it already. I think it'd be better for everyone. I don't—" She bit back the words before they could escape, before she could give away how much James had hurt her. *I don't want to be a burden*. Besides, she needed to do things on her own, solve her own problems. She didn't want to rely on anyone else's generosity. Not anymore.

She didn't notice how tense James's shoulders were or the second look Douglas tried to give him.

"I'll be out of your hair sooner rather than later," she repeated quietly. No matter how much she loved James, it was better this way. It was better *because* she loved him. What was the saying? If you love something, let it go?

"Jamie?" Emma called into the darkness. She couldn't see anything, but somehow she knew he was there.

She inched forward. Her bare feet slipped on something wet. When she looked down, a spotlight flickered on, and revealed James lying in a pool of blood. His green eyes stared sightlessly upwards. His skin was pale, his body stiff. Cold.

The dream shifted and rewound before her eyes. She watched James leap in front of a bullet to protect *her*, killing himself in the process.

Emma started shaking as the dream played out again.

Once more, James was dead at her feet. Cold. Still. Stiff.

"No," she said. "No."

She fell to her knees. The blood was still warm where it soaked into the knees of her pants. She pressed frantic hands to the wound on his chest to staunch the bleeding.

Emma woke with a scream.

Her body was frozen atop the bed. She couldn't move. Could barely breathe.

Panic settled into her bones. She was drugged again. She was drugged and James was dead and it was all her fault.

She strained against her own body as hard as she could. She had to move. To get help. James was in trouble. James was–

Her arm twitched.

Her face was wet with tears.

With a shuddering sob, she was finally curled onto her side. She couldn't breathe.

It wasn't real. It was a dream.

She closed her eyes and inhaled deeply.

Except the feeling of his body underneath her hands had been so *real*. The feeling of her own body being outside of her control. The blood on her hands. The scent of death. It was all so terrifyingly real.

She really didn't know why she bothered trying to sleep in her own bed. She couldn't. Her mind wouldn't let her. As soon as her eyes closed and the darkness settled in, that fear came and ripped her to shreds. He kept dying in her dreams for *her*. To protect *her*.

He was right. She got in the way, and it had almost cost him his life.

Emma struggled to get her breathing under control.

A few days had passed since the disaster with Lionel Maxwell. She and James had barely spoken. Which meant that, since then, she had barely slept. She didn't want to bother James just because she was so pathetic she couldn't sleep alone.

It was catching up with her. Making her crazy. The less she slept, the worse the nightmares seemed to get. Nothing worked. She tried melatonin, cold medicine, a shot of whisky from a bottle she found in the pantry. She tried meditation, incense, scented lotions. Nothing worked.

Emma sighed up at her ceiling, her face still wet with tears. One thing would work, she knew that, and she was finally desperate enough to try it.

She grabbed her pillow and quilt and crept downstairs.

She hovered in the doorway of his room for a moment. Her eyes tried to adjust to the darkness, but the shadows in James's room were much deeper than in the rest of the house because of his blackout curtains.

She took a small breath and tiptoed forward. Felt for the edge of the bed, familiar to her now, and around to the other side.

The moment she laid down, his eyes were on her.

She trembled at the sight. Remembered the deadness in them within her dream. She couldn't stop the tears that leaked out. She hoped it was too dark for him to see.

All he did was stare at her for a long moment, and then roll on his side to face away from her.

What did he think of her? She was a pathetic mess. The only thing that helped her sleep was the warmth of his body next to her, the steady sound of his breathing, reassuring her that he was alive. She was already enough of a burden to him, and now this.

Maybe I should start seeing a therapist, she mused as she watched the space between his shoulder blades rise and fall. Maybe then she could have some peace. Or be medicated. Surely this wasn't normal, this kind of response to a trauma.

Her eyelids grew heavy as she matched her breathing to James's.

She was doomed to a life of sleepless nights if she left.

It would be a relief for him, probably. She hated how the embarrassment twisted in her gut as she thought about him seeing her in his bed. Crying. Shaking with fear. Unable to sleep alone.

Pathetic. She was utterly pathetic.

The next night she found James in the basement.

She'd already done laundry, dusted shelves, and pretty much every other household chore she could think of. She'd sorted through emails, taken messages, and forwarded everything that James needed to see or sign off on. She'd even texted Kendrick to see if there was any sort of update. There wasn't.

She needed to *do* something. She couldn't stand sitting around and waiting.

James may have been an idiot with how he did it, but he'd been right–they desperately needed more information. But she was at a loss as to how to get it.

He didn't glance up as she stepped off the elevator. He tinkered with something on the car's engine, wearing sweatpants already stained with grease and an oversized shirt with a giant hole in the armpit.

"So you make all this stuff?" she asked. She sat in the lone desk chair and gave it a twirl.

"Yes."

"*All* of it? Even the armor? The car?"

"Some of it I have custom made, but for the most part I make it." He grunted a little as he twisted a wrench. Emma watched his forearm flex. She looked around at the cluttered table and started cleaning as she talked. She gathered several dirty dishes into a separate pile, stacked up blueprints, and sorted crumpled papers into their own pile to ask if she could throw them away. She saw the same sketch of the city from before and traced it with a finger, briefly distracted. Next to it was a printed picture of a yacht with nothing written on it except a question mark.

There was a lone hair tie, separate from the clutter. With a frown, she reached for it.

"Don't touch that," James said from behind her. Guilty, she tucked her hands behind her back.

"I'm honestly surprised you're not already running around New Atlas with a death wish," she said to change the subject. James turned back to the car, his back muscles bunching underneath his shirt. "I thought I might have to tie you down, or something."

James sighed.

She bit back a smile. "Sorry," she said. "I'm tired of sitting around, so I'm sure you are, too."

"I have noticed the house becoming rather sparkly," James said drily. "And the number of emails is getting concerning."

She gave a surprised laugh. "Wow, was that a joke when you aren't half-dead?"

He glanced at her over his shoulder. She caught the edge of his smile.

"We could spar," he said after a moment.

Emma blinked. "Spar?"

James turned and gave her a full smile that stole her breath. *That thing is dangerous*, she thought dazedly. "Feels like we've been here before," he teased. Because she'd had the exact same dumbfounded response the first time he suggested sparring as the Phantom.

She was a goner. Her chest ached just looking at him. The smile, the messy hair, the baggy shirt. She loved him so much she couldn't breathe.

"You were stabbed," she said to cover up the blush settling in her cheeks. "I don't think it's a good idea to–"

"I'll prove to you that I'm alright," he said. "Or are you afraid you can't win without using the cape to cheat?"

She scoffed. She'd never seen him like this. So…light. So teasing. She wanted to live in it. Wanted to bottle this memory for the future.

"All I'm afraid of is your organs coming out of your stab wound," she said.

"I didn't know you had a medical degree," James said in a low voice. He wiped the grease from his hands.

"What, is a medical degree part of the many you have?"

He chuckled, a low, sensual sound. "Not yet." She watched his forearms flex again, a bit faint. She couldn't even manage a smile at his teasing. "Come on. Show me what you remember. You're out of practice."

She sighed. "Fine."

He led her to a section of the room that looked vaguely like a wrestling ring. The floor was covered in soft mats.

"Douglas is the one who taught you to fight, isn't he?" she said.

James nodded. "That's where I started learning, yes. We still spar, sometimes, to keep him in shape. He did all sorts of martial arts and other stuff as a kid and kept going as an adult. He knows a lot."

She laughed. "Oh, I would *love* to see that." She had a feeling that Douglas was very capable in a fight. It seemed that ambition ran in the family, too: not only did Douglas know how to fight, he was also COO of a major company, and apparently still knew enough from his premed days to be able to draw blood without it hurting.

"Are you stalling?" James asked. One dark eyebrow rose. There was a hint of a smile at the corners of his mouth.

Instead of answering, Emma lunged. James smiled fully as he caught her punch in the palm of his hand like it was nothing. But she expected it–she'd seen how he fought, both in and out of the suit. He was always absorbing the punches.

So she swept out one of her legs, caught him by the ankles, and sent him sprawling onto the mat. Except he grabbed her wrist on the way down and used his momentum to roll so he was on top of her. Her breath left in a *whoosh*. One of his hands caught her so she didn't knock her head on the floor on the way down.

"Damn, I really thought that was going to work," she said, the words half-gasped. His hands splayed on the mat on either side of her head. He hovered over her, easily holding up his weight. As she stared into his eyes, she wished his arms would give out so their bodies would be flush together. She went hot all at once. Some of his dark hair fell over his forehead, and she had to fight the urge to brush it back.

"Almost," he said with a small smile. He got to his feet and held out a hand. She let him help her up. "It was a smart move."

They circled each other.

He pounced in the span of a blink. She dodged his fists, but barely. She managed to get behind him and kick him in the back. To avoid hurting him, she pulled back a little, though. He stumbled forward and whirled and caught her by the ankle before she could lower her leg. He yanked so she had to hop on one foot closer to him.

She growled in frustration but got free.

He kept smiling.

Emma had never seen him smile so much. In the suit, when they sparred, he always remained serious.

But here, in his own home, he was relaxed in an entirely new way. His green eyes were bright and alive in a way she'd only gotten brief glimpses of before. She reveled in it. If it were even possible, it made her fall a little more in love.

It also made it a bit harder to concentrate.

They exchanged a flurry of blows that was mostly him blocking her. Her frustration grew. He was *injured* and was still easily kicking her ass.

She tried to hit him again—*really* hit this time, because she was getting pissed off—but he grabbed her wrist and twisted it behind her. Her back bumped against his chest. He captured her other hand and held both wrists in one strong, calloused hand.

"Fuck," she huffed.

"Believe me now?" he asked. His breath ghosted across the shell of her ear. She shuddered and went still. A different sort of heat built within her. Her heart galloped in her chest. Could he feel it, pressed together as they were?

"Believe what?" Emma asked stupidly, because she couldn't think past the feeling of him pressed against her. She had a very sudden, very vivid image of them in the same position except with her against the wall and his lips on her neck. She could feel every rise and fall of his chest.

"I told you that I'd prove I was alright," he practically purred. Her eyes closed of their own accord, and she pressed back against him. His breathing hitched. Her head tilted back just a bit as she felt him breathe against her neck. His grip on her wrists loosened. He inhaled shakily, and she suddenly *wanted* him. All of him. Every secret, every shadow, every smile and laugh and kiss. She wanted him to pull her closer and kiss her until she saw stars. Until she couldn't breathe.

You keep getting in the way.

The memory of the words was a bucket of cold water. She blinked and came back to herself.

"Fine, you win," she said a bit breathlessly. She stepped away, and he let her. "I should–"

Emma couldn't finish a coherent sentence. She cleared her throat and walked back over to the desk chair. She'd left her phone on the table and pretended to check it so she didn't have to look at him. She needed to get control of herself.

"Are you angry with me?" he asked softly, echoing another night, another conversation.

She frowned and faced him. "No, of course not."

James rubbed the back of his neck. "Then why–" He swallowed. He seemed to gather his thoughts. Then he shook his head. There was a flash of frustration on his face.

"Why what?" she asked. His eyes flickered to her and then away.

"I thought maybe you were mad about Lionel Maxwell." He shrugged.

"Why would I be mad at that? If anything, I'm mad at Kendrick for keeping you from beating the shit out of him." She scoffed. She didn't tell him she'd given some serious, albeit brief, consideration to pushing Maxwell off the top of the tower.

James gave a wry, humorless smile. He hummed, then went back to whatever he'd been doing under the hood of the armored car. She hadn't realized how much she enjoyed seeing how capable he was. Fighting, fixing things, figuring things out. She'd never met anyone like him before.

"Why did you think I was mad?" she asked, unable to help herself. "I–I thought maybe you were mad at me for following you."

James was shaking his head. "I'm not mad," he said softly without turning around. But he didn't elaborate.

Something ached in her chest. She rubbed at it absentmindedly. He was so…immovable sometimes. She wanted to pry his head open and peer in. See what made him tick. She wanted to see every piece of him laid out before her in some sort of logical order so she could make sense of him.

Emma stared at his back as he fiddled with the engine.

Without knowing exactly why, she suddenly felt like crying.

Maybe because he kept shutting her out. Maybe because he'd said, in not so many words, that she was a burden. Maybe because things would never work between them. She wasn't sure, but she couldn't breathe anymore, couldn't stop the tears pricking her eyes.

"I'm—I'll make dinner," she said and left without another word.

She didn't see him watching her go.

JAMES

It was the middle of the night, and James watched Emma while she slept in his bed.

His eyes traced the familiar lines of her face, softened by sleep. The light dusting of freckles across her nose and cheeks. The long, dark lashes. The slope of her shoulders. The curve of her hip underneath the blanket. His hands ached to follow the path of his gaze. He listened to her breathing, the exhales heavier than the inhales as she dreamed.

His mind was a jumble. That was new for him. He thought he'd been confused before, but now…now he had no idea what to think. It was difficult to think, actually, with her so near. And their sparring earlier didn't help matters in the slightest.

He couldn't *think* around Emma, and it frustrated him to no end. That's why he always said stupid things to her. His mind simply stopped working. He tried to convey his fear for her on the tower, but it came out all wrong because she short-circuited every wire in his brain.

And her actions were so damn *confusing*.

Her kindness and ferocity enraptured him from the first moment they met. She helped him when so many other would have turned their backs. She *kept* helping him. She saved his life, convinced he should have left her to save himself.

Emma had taken his mask off, taken one look at him and his darkest secret, and simply said "I told you so." One look, then she continued on as if she hadn't turned his world upside down and given it a shake for good measure.

James thought back to that night when she told him he should have let her die. She told him she kept having nightmares where he died, and seeing him alive was the only way to make it better. She spent every night now in his bed, at some point or another, sometimes waking with a cry, sometimes crying while she slept. Sometimes, when she was asleep, she reached for him.

But she also said she was leaving, and he couldn't lie to himself about it anymore

It broke his heart.

He had driven her away. He knew it was too good to be true. He knew *she* was too good to be true. Had expected it.

And still, it fucking hurt.

The want and the need for her mixed the impending loss of her all got so tangled up that he couldn't breathe. He *ached* to reach out and hold her. To ease whatever shadows created the furrow between her brows.

But she wasn't his.

He wished he knew what he'd done to drive her away so suddenly. Was it because she saw the truth of him? The darkness? The shadows? He thought back to how satisfying it was to watch Maxwell's nose break under his fist. Maybe that was the moment. Or maybe it was when those men broke in, and she'd seen the truth of his violent nature, without the mask to hide behind.

And still, he gave in to the desire to be near her. To tease her. Touch her. He used sparring as an excuse—it had always been an excuse, even before she'd known the truth—and tonight was no different. He remembered her sprawled beneath him, cheeks flushed, irritated that he'd won so quickly. The feeling of her back pressed against his chest.

James finally gave up on sleep entirely and headed on silent feet to the kitchen. Though he preferred tea, he'd taken to drinking coffee, just to feel nearer to her.

It was pathetic.

As he pressed the button on the coffee machine, Douglas appeared in the doorway.

"Little early for you to be up, isn't it?" Douglas asked softly. Douglas's eyes jumped to the coffee machine and back to James, an all-too-knowing glint in his eyes. James didn't answer. He didn't think he could speak around the lump in his throat.

"What's wrong?" Douglas asked. *Damn his perceptiveness.* James shook his head. "Doesn't have anything to do with the girl in your bed, does it?"

James whirled, suddenly angry. "It's not like that and you know it!" he snapped.

Douglas held his hands up in surrender. "I only said she was in your bed. It's a fact, James, not a judgment."

James clenched his fists and took a deep breath to steady himself. "She has nightmares," James explained softly. "She said–It doesn't matter." Frustration rose within him again, swift and acrid.

Douglas merely looked at him.

James sighed. Sometimes he hated the older man, even as much as he cared for him. "She said she keeps having nightmares where I…die. That seeing me alive is the only thing that helps…" He trailed off. He had to swallow hard. "The bed's plenty big enough," he finished in a barely audible mumble.

Douglas made a noise in his throat. "I see. And are the two of you ever going to talk about your feelings for each other?"

James gave him a sharp look. "She's leaving. It doesn't matter anymore."

"I think it matters more than you'd think."

"I can't stop her, can I?" James inhaled sharply around the pain in his chest and turned back to the coffee machine. "It's my fault, anyway. She doesn't–there's no way she can–" Frustrated, he knocked a fist on the counter. This was why he avoided talking about feelings. Nothing ever came out right. Even that night at the tower, he'd fucked it up. *You keep getting in the way.* It made her angry, he knew that now, but he hadn't had a chance to explain. And besides, he wasn't really sure what he'd been trying to say. How could he explain in words that he would die for her? That he would give up New Atlas to save her? How could he express how thoroughly he worshiped her, how fearful he was that she would die, how much he craved to know her every thought? It wasn't that she kept getting in the way. It was that he was always, *always* going to care more about her safety than anything else. And *that* got in the way. He'd been so panicked seeing her show up in his armored car that his feelings had exploded from him without thought. But it had come out all *wrong*.

"I think you at least owe her the truth about how you feel about her." Of course Douglas knew. He'd always been able to read James like an open book. So although James had never once spoken his feelings out loud, Douglas knew.

"I—"

"Just think about it. She's leaving, right? What could it hurt?"

With that, Douglas left him alone.

It could hurt a lot, James thought bitterly. It already did. He didn't think he could stand a more explicit rejection than the one she'd already given him. He didn't want to hear what it was about him that had driven her away. He didn't want to hear how she was afraid of the darkness and violence within him. How she thought they were too different, too unsuitable.

It could hurt so much fucking more.

CHAPTER TWENTY-SEVEN

It was the night before the gala, and they didn't have enough to go on. Emma knew it, James knew it, Douglas knew it. They were rushing headfirst into danger with a drug that could make them do anything, armed with nothing but the knowledge of some of the key players, a location, and some gas masks. They were running out of time. Close would have to be close enough.

Emma headed down to the basement underneath the manor. She slept in James's bed again, which is how she knew exactly where to find him.

Wordlessly, he made space for her in his small lab area. It was the most well-lit part of the place, and she had to squint at the brightness.

"Feel like helping me with these?" he asked softly, and her heart gave a small squeeze. She loved how in sync they had grown, how he was starting to accept her help. Neither of them much liked sitting still for long, especially with the gala hanging over their heads like the blade of a guillotine.

"Sure. What are you making?" She stepped up next to him, the warmth of his body a balm in the permanently chilly air of the underground space.

"Smoke bombs." James cut his eyes at her and smiled mischievously. One dark eyebrow quirked upwards. Emma was suddenly, vividly able to imagine him as a teenager who got into trouble and did science experiments in his basement. He'd once mentioned a propensity for pranking Douglas when he was a teen, interested as he was in things like, well, smoke bombs. She wished she had known him then, younger and more carefree, before he'd become CEO of Kane Industries, before he'd become the Phantom.

"Smoke bombs," she repeated with a shake of her head. She laughed. "Are you sure it's safe?"

"Yes, perfectly. It's all chemistry. I mixed the paste already, we just need to fill these—" He gestured to a few dozen half-spheres, each about the size of a baseball that was cut in half, "—and weigh them to make sure they're all the same. Then we add a small fuse to the top." He picked up one of the half-spheres to their left and clicked something on it that made it spark. "When I put the halves together and press it, the spark catches the fuse, which burns the paste, and creates smoke that comes out of the holes all around it."

Emma took one half and pressed it to make it spark too, impressed. "You made these?"

He shrugged. "Yes. Took me a while to get the mix right and figure out a way to make it spark. I made some small explosive ones earlier, but those are more dangerous. It involves a lot more chemistry and careful handling."

She stared up at his tall form. His dark hair fell across his forehead, and his green eyes were clearer and more open than ever. He seemed excited to share this with her, to show off his knowledge and skill to someone new. Every little thing she learned about him made her fall deeper in love. The emotion rose within her on a tidal wave, choking her, pulling her under. She took a shaky breath to steady herself.

They worked in relative silence for several minutes. James only interrupted to check her measurements or gently correct how she did something. It was an easy kind of quiet, comfortable. Neither of them mentioned her sleeping in his bed. Neither of them mentioned the gale. They simply *were.* Their shoulders brushed every once in a while. He was so warm, she thought, resisting the urge to lean all the way against him as they worked.

After the last smoke bomb was done, James thanked her quietly. Their gazes snagged and held. He absently rubbed a hand against his chest, smearing a glob of the paste across his shirt without noticing.

Emma wanted to kiss him so badly it hurt.

She pulled her eyes away first. "I'll go make us something to eat, yeah?"

He smiled, and the urge to kiss him only worsened. "Yeah. Thanks."

Mostly she needed a break from his presence, from her overwhelming emotions, from the easiness with which they worked together. She knew it was all going to end. The gala was going to be the end of how things, one way or the other.

Emma took her time upstairs making dinner. She let herself sink into the easy familiarity of the kitchen, of preparing food, and her mind went blissfully blank.

Back downstairs, James was still at the lab area.

"I think I found something," he said as soon as he heard her step off the elevator. He hadn't even turned around when he'd said the words, focused as he was on what he was doing.

"Found what?" she asked as she brought over a covered tray that held a new recipe for chicken and dumplings she decided to try. Something to help settle their nerves before the gala, something warm and comforting in contrast to the cold basement air.

"I think I replicated the counteragent," he said from where he bent over a microscope. He was comparing two samples of something, back and forth and back again. He was wearing the armored pants of the Phantom suit now, and nothing else. Getting ready to head out, maybe?

She tore her eyes from his muscled back. "Really?" The hope in her voice was obvious. She was scared, and she hated that she was scared. She'd been drugged once before and still woke up paralyzed with the fear of it happening again. She feared for herself, for Douglas, and most of all for James. She feared for more girls meeting the same fate as Marie and the five others. She feared for New Atlas. So if he found a way to help them out of this…

"It's as close as I can get in time." He straightened and stared down at her from his full height. Her stomach turned over. "Actually, I should have said I have good news and bad news." He smiled and her stomach flipped again. She would never get used to him.

"Please tell me that was the bad news," she said.

He rubbed at his neck. "No, that was the good news. The bad news…is that I can't make any more by tomorrow night."

Her heart sank. "And how much did you manage to make?"

"One dose. For one person. I don't think it'll work if it isn't as potent, based on what was in those samples from Kendrick. So I can't split the dose either." He shrugged, almost…self conscious.

"You're amazing," she said, the words bursting from her lips unbidden. He flushed. She wanted to devour the sight. "You—I mean, are you fucking kidding me? What *can't* you do? You're a genius, you can fight, you're a billionaire."

"I'm not—" He shrugged again as if embarrassed.

She wanted to kiss him.

Fuck it, she thought. They had less than twenty-four hours before all hell broke loose. The future was uncertain. But her desire wasn't.

Emma stepped forward until she could feel the warmth from James's body. She tilted her head up to look at him. His breathing turned ragged, and her heart raced with anticipation.

"Emma," he said so softly it was almost a whisper.

She slid one hand up his chest and around to hold his neck. "I don't know what's going to happen tomorrow," she murmured, eyes on his jugular as he swallowed hard. "I just know that I really, really want to kiss you right now."

And in the span of a breath, they were. Emma couldn't tell who moved first, but the feeling of his lips on hers was an instantaneous relief so profound that she groaned.

His hands pressed flat against her back. She melted into him, his bare chest blazing hot against her. He made a soft noise in her mouth as his tongue traced her lower lip.

Their first kiss had been overwhelming, but she'd been drunk and confused. Their next kiss had been quick, desperate.

This kiss….this kiss was scorching. It was desperate, too, but in a completely different way. Emma couldn't get close enough, couldn't kiss him hard enough, couldn't feel enough of his skin against her.

His hands moved over her sides to her hips, his bare fingers tracing patterns on her skin underneath her shirt. His hardness pressed into her stomach. She ached with want, with a *need* for him, so intense it left her dizzy.

One of his hands gripped her ass and she groaned again.

"Please," she said against his lips, but she didn't know what she was begging for. Please, keep touching her. Please, touch her more. Please, make her forget everything looming over them.

As his lips traced over her jaw to the pounding pulse in her neck, Emma realized that, even though he was kissing her, even though he was obviously attracted to her…

It would never work between them.

She wanted him anyway.

The sound of the descending elevator broke through the fog of lust in her mind.

"Jamie," she said, his name half a moan in her mouth. He hummed against her skin, and her thoughts scattered.

"Douglas," she said.

James froze. He straightened as soon as he heard the elevator thud to a stop.

He cursed and strode away.

Emma touched a trembling hand to her lips.

When James came back, he had a shirt on. She heard Douglas's voice, but her brain was still too scattered to think clearly.

"–oh, hi Emma," Douglas said, interrupting whatever he was saying to James.

Emma tried very, very hard to keep the blush from her cheeks, but she had a feeling Douglas knew exactly what he had interrupted.

"I was telling Douglas about the counteragent," James said, as if everything were still utterly normal between them. Except he wasn't looking her in the eyes.

"I think you should take the dose," she told him. "They're after you, we know that much."

His eyes flickered to hers. "No," he said, and went back to the microscopes.

"What do you mean, *no*?" she said. She and Douglas shared a look.

"You're taking it," he said.

"No, I'm not." All the lust in her veins evaporated in the wake of her annoyance. "Besides, what if having been drugged before fucks it up somehow? We can't waste it like that. And, as I *just* said, they're after *you*."

James turned to Douglas as if for help. The older man held up his hands. "I'm with her on this."

James looked like he was about to roll his eyes but merely turned away, back to his work. "We'll discuss this later," he muttered to the microscope, as if it personally offended him.

Douglas raised his eyebrows. He and Emma shared a look. "I'm…going to bed. Goodnight."

Emma flushed all over again as her thoughts turned to *going to bed* with James.

As soon as Douglas was gone, James faced her and opened his mouth.

"I know what you're going to say," she interrupted. "And I'm still going tomorrow. There's too much at stake. I can't just *give up*. I can't sit by and watch when I might make a difference."

She was doing it for him. For herself. For Lainey, Becks, Jackie, Heather, Sofia, and Marie. She would see it through to the bitter end, no matter what it took.

James must have seen it on her face. He closed his mouth. "If there is anything I can do to talk you out of it," he said quietly. "I'll do it. Anything."

She smiled softly at him. "There isn't, and you know it. You know what happens when you tell me to stay put."

A ghost of a laugh. "Unfortunately, I do."

"We'll just have to hope for a bit of a miracle tomorrow, right?" she said.

Because she was starting to think that a miracle would be the only thing that could get them out of this alive.

The morning of the gala dawned early. Emma barely slept for a handful of hours, and she wasn't sure James had slept at all. She'd gone to bed and didn't remember him ever coming into the room.

Their paths crossed mid-morning in the kitchen, where he wordlessly handed her a cup of coffee exactly how she liked it, and disappeared. She had a sneaking suspicion that he was working until the last possible second to make more of the counteragent.

As time crept closer to the event, Emma carefully styled her hair and applied her makeup. She wished for a hidden weapon, but her dress didn't really allow for one. She didn't want to be helpless while James did all the work.

She studied her face in the mirror. She debated covering the scar on her head, but decided against it. She idly traced one finger over it. She would remember Marie. Would honor her by saving New Atlas. Would honor the other five girls, too. *Lainey, Becks, Jackie, Heather, Sofia.*

Her gown was a simple thing, made of black silk with a slit up one side–perfect in case of a fight–and a low back. It had a cowl neck that showed just enough cleavage and delicate crystal straps that were stronger than they looked. She matched drop earrings to the straps with teardrop pearls on the ends. A black silk wrap draped over her arms since the night was going to be cold. Her shoes were black with thick, sturdy heels. Thankfully, she had a lot of practice being in heels at the Crescent Club, so it wouldn't be a problem to fight or run in them. She never thought she'd be thankful for *anything* to do with the place, but there it was.

James warned her that there would be paparazzi. That they would take pictures of them together. That there would be articles, rumors, gossip columns. People talking about her on the internet, digging into her life. Whenever James Kane stepped into the outside world, it was a big deal. Especially since he'd never brought a woman along before. All these years, he avoided the press and the public like a plague, so him attending *any* event meant it was going to be a huge deal.

Emma didn't care about any of that. All she cared about was whether *James* was comfortable with it. She offered to make his condolences and go alone, with him joining later as the Phantom. But he refused and said he needed to get a good look at the place first in case their plans needed to change. She had a feeling, too, that he didn't want her in there alone until it was absolutely necessary.

They both had the same goal that night–to save New Atlas before it was too late. Before any innocents died. And try not to get killed in the process.

She had another goal, though, that he didn't know about.

She wanted to dance with James Kane, just once. Just one dance before shit hit the fan. Before she left Kane Manor behind. Their dance at the Crescent Club didn't count. It was performative, really, and the memory was tinged with all the awfulness she associated with the club. She wanted a *real* dance with James, with the two of them dressed up, as if on a date, not caring what anyone else around them thought.

It was time to go before she knew it. She took one last look in the mirror, satisfied. Her outfit was her own armor that night, flimsy as it was. And she had to admit, she thought she looked good. She finished the outfit off with the contact lens and earpiece that would connect the three of them for the night.

She went down the back stairs and into the kitchen. Douglas was already gone, and James was struggling to put on cufflinks.

"Here, let me help with those," she said with a soft smile.

James faced her and stopped dead.

His eyes roved over her, head to toes and back up again. His mouth parted. No sound came out as his lips formed her name. Her entire body flushed. She stared at him with the same intensity he was staring at her.

He looked good. Better than good. He was in a carefully tailored tuxedo that hinted at the muscles underneath. His hair was clean and slicked back. Still slightly messy. Still James. The black of his jacket made the green of his eyes pop. He looked, to put it simply, good enough to eat.

"You look…great," she said, mouth dry. It was an understatement. An image flashed in her mind of slowly undoing his bowtie and letting it fall to the floor. Unbuttoning his shirt. She mentally shook herself and stepped forward to help with the cufflinks.

He still hadn't said anything. His fingers grazed the inside of her wrist as she secured the first cufflink. She had to bite her lip to keep from visibly shivering as goosebumps erupted over her skin. She had never wanted to touch him so badly. Trying to focus, she moved to the other sleeve.

"I–" James started to say. Her eyes met his. Every thought disappeared from her head. He was so incredibly mouthwatering that she wanted to say fuck New Atlas and skip the gala entirely. He wet his lips and tried again. She tracked the movement with heated cheeks. "I have something for you." He presented her with a long, slightly dusty, dark blue velvet box. "This was my mother's." He opened the box, revealing a delicate pearl necklace. "She always said…every woman needs a set of pearls."

She gently traced it with one finger. She pulled her hand back quickly and gazed up at him with uncertainty. "I can't take your mother's necklace, Jamie."

He ignored her and lifted the necklace from the box. He gently brushed her hair off her neck. She couldn't hold back the shiver this time. She closed her eyes and imagined his lips touching the same place.

The cold necklace settled into the hollow of her throat.

It was all part of the show they were putting on that night, she told herself. He wasn't really giving her his mother's necklace. She was only borrowing it while they attended a gala with New Atlas's rich and powerful. He was helping her look the part. That was all.

But she could still feel the weight of the moment. The weight of his trust in her, enough to let her borrow something of his mother's. Something she knew he treasured.

James's fingers lingered for a beat longer at the back of her neck.

"We should go," he said after a moment. As he walked away, she took a split second to collect herself. Her breath shook.

He led her to the garage, trailing slightly ahead of her. She hadn't paid much attention to it before. The only other time she'd been in it was the night she'd been drunk. The night they first kissed. She shook off the memory. There were six cars inside, ranging from an official-looking SUV to a small but expensive sports car. Which was of course the one he aimed for. She knew little about cars, but could tell it was older, a classic. It was black and well-taken care of.

"How are you going to fit in that?" she asked with a raised eyebrow.

He gave her a half-smile as he climbed in. Her heart stuttered. The interior of the car was roomier than she would have expected.

She had to take a deep breath as he pulled out of the garage and down the driveway. James was literally taking her breath away, and all he'd done was put on a tuxedo and give her a necklace to wear.

"Are you nervous?" he asked softly.

Yes, she was. But not because they headed straight into danger without a clue how they were going to stop the bad guys. And not because the bad guys had a drug that took away free will.

She was nervous because James Kane looked so good it hurt. Because this was one of the last times she would be around him before she moved on. Because how could he ever love a girl like her, a girl with nothing and no one to her name?

"Yes," she said. "But not about…you know. The bad guys."

He raised a dark eyebrow. "Not about the bad guys?" He sounded skeptical.

The half-truth came easily to her tongue. "I'm nervous because I'm not a good dancer."

He flashed her a real, full smile that was gone so fast she swore she imagined it. Her heart gave another painful squeeze in her chest. "I'm not a good dancer either."

"Wow," she said with a laugh. "Finally something James Kane *can't* do."

"I can't sing either." He smiled again and her heart almost exploded. She loved him so much she couldn't think straight. "Or cook. Definitely not like you can." She warmed at the compliment.

"How are you not freaking out right now?" she asked. Really what she meant was, *why are you in such a good mood when we're headed into unknown danger in formal clothes?*

He shrugged and sobered a little. "Because at this point, we'll either stop it or we won't. I can't change anything that's led to this point. We can only do our best from this point forward."

She didn't miss the way he said *we* and not *I*.

She glanced out of the window and smiled at her own reflection.

The moment he stepped out of the car at the venue, the gathered paparazzi and crowd went absolutely crazy. She heard his name repeated thousands of times in only a handful of seconds.

James rounded the front of the car, handed the keys and a tip to the valet, and reached for her door. Her heart started beating itself against her ribcage. *Here we go*, she thought. No going back now.

James opened her door and offered her a hand. It didn't seem possible, but the crowd got even louder. They screamed his name. Flashes of bright light went off so frequently it was as if someone had turned on a flickering spotlight. She gripped his hand tightly and smiled at him. He smiled back. His touch was an anchor in the storm of the noisy crowd.

They ignored their surroundings as they headed inside, where it was much quieter. They gave their names and passed through the security checkpoint and metal detectors.

Emma released a small breath. Her hand sweat nervously in James's.

"That was nuts," she said. He made a small noise in the affirmative. She saw the shift within him as he began taking everything in. Noting every exit. Every shadow. Every security guard, and probably some who blended in with the crowd. The mantle of the Phantom settled on his shoulders. Tonight, he was only pretending to be James.

The glass skylight above them held huge gold drapes that swept down to the entryway. Flowers in unseasonably bright colors burst from pots and small arrangements on every surface. Directly in front of them, propped open double doors led inside to a ballroom.. A staircase curved upwards on either side of the doors.

"This is the fanciest thing I've ever been to," she told James in a whisper as they headed inside the ballroom. The pair of them were earning lots of double-takes as they went. She couldn't find it in herself to care about the attention, not so long as his hand remained warm and steady in hers.

"Me too," he murmured back. His fingers tightened around hers. Unconsciously, she let her thumb rub the back of his hand and knuckles. She wasn't sure if he was kidding about the event or not, but she appreciated his comment all the same.

More gold drapes and thousands of flowers dripped from the ballroom ceiling. For a moment, it took her breath away. The lights were dim, but not so much that she couldn't see. Everything glowed in the golden light. The flowers perfumed the air, mingling with the scent of food. New Atlas's rich and powerful mingled around artful centerpieces and a thousand candles at crowded tables. It felt like something out of a dream, the opulence, the gold light, the man holding her hand.

To the left were tables for a silent auction, already being perused by several men in sharp tuxes and women in sparkling gowns. To the right was a wall of several sets of glass doors leading into a courtyard. More of the gold drapery, dancing in a slight breeze, covered the open doorways. Outside were more floral arrangements, tall tables with candles, and upright heaters. There were deep shadows along the outside wall, allowing for hidden pockets filled with outdoor couches.

Between the doors leading outside were tables laden with food. The bar was right next to where they stood, covered in guests taking advantage of the endless free alcohol. A dance floor spanned the opposite end of the room with a DJ next to it and a stage set up for a live band.

Emma let herself take it all in. Let herself imagine, just for a moment, that she belonged there. That she belonged with the man at her side, who still hadn't let go of her hand. She tensed as she caught sight of Douglas across the room holding a glass of champagne and mingling.

"Hi, Douglas," she said softly into her earpiece. The gold drapes by the doors fluttered gently.

"Glad you two made it," Douglas murmured back. He caught her eye and winked. "You are causing *quite* a stir. I knew the moment you arrived from the absolutely frantic screams from outside. I thought maybe someone famous had shown up."

She snorted and hid her smile behind her free hand. Even James smiled a little.

"Let's eat first," she said eagerly. She tugged James along behind her and effectively dodged the people trying to engage them in conversation. She knew it would come off as rude, but she didn't care. And she would bet that James didn't care either.

They let go of each other to get plates and drinks. He seemed distracted and only put two strawberries on his plate as he kept peering around the room. There was a slight pinkness to his cheeks. A nervous set to his shoulders. He trailed behind her outside to a high table in the darkest shadows of the courtyard. A heater scraped loudly over the ground as she dragged it closer. It was freezing outside, summer a swiftly fading memory already. Soon there would be frost on the ground.

James seemed to relax slightly now that there wasn't anyone around them. Soft light from the candles in the center of the table illuminated his face with a golden glow. She lost her breath again for a second. Her lips parted to tell him how absurdly beautiful he looked, but he interrupted before she could.

"Are you really going to eat all of that?" he asked with a glance at the array of plates she set on the table.

"I might," she said teasingly, though half of it was for him. "You should eat, too. Did you have lunch?"

He just looked at her.

"Of course you didn't. Well, just think about how embarrassing it'd be if you passed out in the middle of dancing with me," she said with a grin. "Or if you passed out–later." Fighting, she meant. As the Phantom.

He reluctantly picked at some of the fruit.

"Douglas?" he asked as he chewed. "Is everything set?"

"Yes. I've heard nothing yet."

"Have you seen the Wolf or Maxwell?" Emma asked.

"I have not."

James's eyes tracked Douglas around the edge of the dance floor. Douglas threw a glance their way as he passed by.

"Either they won't make a move until they're here," she said, "Or we're fucked because they're trying to stay out of whatever they have planned."

James grunted. Another piece of fruit disappeared behind his lips. She almost fainted when he absently licked a bit of juice off one long finger.

What was *wrong* with her? Nothing like impending danger to make one incredibly horny, apparently.

They all three lapsed into silence. Emma hright. The party food for rich people was *excellent*. She let out a soft sigh of pleasure as she ate.

James gave her a sharp look.

She flushed. "Sorry—It's just good." She laughed, a bit embarrassed. She was certain there was etiquette for these kinds of events, etiquette she had never learned.

The song inside shifted to something slower. She watched as several couples made their way onto the dance floor. The song was familiar, something she'd heard on the radio a few times over the years.

"Dance with me?" James suddenly murmured. Her eyes snapped to him in surprise. He was...*so* handsome. A swarm of butterflies took off in her stomach as she nodded. The flames from the candles softened the angles of his jaw and cheekbones.

Emma started to walk back inside, but he gently caught her wrist in one callused hand. The simple touch sent another shiver down her spine. The music drifted through the open doors and filled the courtyard.

"No," James said. There was the faintest tinge of pink to his cheeks when she looked at him, even though it was hard to tell in the dim light. "Here. Just us this time. If—if you want." Was it her imagination, or was he nervous? Nervous to dance with *her*? There was the faintest tremble to his fingers. "Just us."

She nodded. "Yeah. Okay." She smiled in hopes of helping him relax a little.

James pulled her close. The hand holding her wrist slipped to her palm while the other settled on her lower back. She shivered again at the feeling of his touch on her bare skin where the dress dipped low. Her free hand settled on his shoulder. Even in heels, he was much taller than her. They started slowly spinning to the music.

"We should talk," James murmured. "Later. After. We should talk."

A flash of panic jolted down her spine. Those words never preceded anything good. She swallowed hard as they continued swaying.

Emma couldn't look him in the eye anymore. "Okay," she said, mouth dry for an entirely new reason now.

His grip on her tightened. "I–I'm not–" He made a frustrated noise and looked over her shoulder. The piano in the song swelled. "I'm not good at saying…things," James finally said. His thumb idly brushed against her spine, and she had to bite her lip to keep from reacting.

Just that simple touch, and she was a goner. She wanted to kiss him. Maybe push him over to one of those half-hidden couches she'd seen. *Focus,* she told herself.

"I don't want you to leave."

The words dropped into her, one by one. Her lips parted in surprise.

She stared dumbly at him while they danced, pressed together and hidden in the shadows.

"Jamie…" she said.

"We'll talk more later," he said. His hands trembled again, ever so slightly. She became very keenly aware of Douglas being able to hear every word. But he remained almost pointedly silent in her ear.

Her mind rushed through all the possible meanings of what he was saying. Of what their talk might look like, after.

"And…I wanted to say–the other night, it came out all wrong. What I said." He tightened his hold on her, inadvertently causing her to stumble even closer. Their chests brushed. She caught herself gripping his neck tightly in order to stay upright.

"What you said?" she asked with a frown. "You haven't–" But he had. *You keep getting in the way.* She closed her eyes briefly at the memory of the words. But he didn't know that they hurt her the way they did.

It was hard to breathe. *Tell him how you feel*, she silently urged herself. What could it hurt? He said they would talk *after*, but what would after look like? They still had no antidote, no idea what was going to happen. She had a terrible feeling that their luck had run out long ago, and that tonight might end badly. Or maybe that was simply the nerves.

"I–I didn't realize I was a burden to you and–" she finally whispered. They had stopped spinning and were simply swaying now. She blinked rapidly, embarrassed at the sudden sting of tears. "I know I'm not as good as you at any of this stuff, and it makes me a liability."

"I'm sorry," James said again, voice low and gruff with an unknown emotion. He crushed her to his chest in one abrupt movement that stole what was left of her breath. Both of his hands slid up her bare back. She shuddered at the touch. Trails of fire blazed up her spine where he touched her. "No," he said into her hair. "That's not– I didn't–" He made the same frustrated noise again. "It came out wrong. You're not a burden."

"It's okay," she said. "Don't feel guilty. I know I came in and messed up your whole life and–"

James's arms tightened around her even more. She barely noticed that the song had ended. "*No*," he said again. "I didn't mean it like that. At all. I fucked up saying that. I'm sorry."

Emma remembered again that Douglas was listening. Her heart was too full, her mind too muddled. What was James saying? What was he implying? He didn't want her to leave, and he didn't see her as a burden. But what did that mean?

She let herself lean into the embrace. Her forehead brushed against his jaw where there was the barest hint of stubble. "What *did* you–"

"Mr. Kane, I'm sorry to interrupt–" said an unfamiliar voice.

James took his time pulling away from her. "We'll talk more later," he said firmly. Some unknown emotion blazed in his green eyes. "When there aren't any interruptions."

Emma turned to face the interruption with irritation. "I'm sorry," she said coldly to the man, "My date and I were just headed to the silent auction. Excuse us."

She grabbed James's hand and marched away without making sure he was following. She was proud of herself for the smooth delivery of the line when her insides were an absolute fucking mess. Her heart pounded with the simple knowledge that maybe there was more to all of this than she thought. She shut the thoughts down. No use speculating. They had a mission to accomplish first. "Who was that?" she asked James in a mumble as she stopped at the first table for the silent auction. Her eyes stared uncomprehendingly at the information in front of her. She couldn't afford to bid on any of it, anyway.

From her periphery, she saw James shrug. "No idea. But thanks for saving me." She felt James's arm come around her and settle gently on her waist. If she didn't want to jump him before, now…Now it was so much worse. *I don't want you to leave*, he said. *I didn't mean it like that*. Then what? What *had* he meant? She was more confused than ever.

She wished the Wolf and his ilk would get on with it, because she needed James to finish this conversation. And *without* Douglas listening in. "Any sign of them, Douglas?" she asked in a mumble as they slowly shuffled down the table, ignoring everyone else. James still held her tightly. He seemed almost…possessive.

"Nothing yet. Not even a hint," Douglas said, acting for all the world like he hadn't heard anything the past few minutes. Maybe she had gotten lucky, and he'd taken the earpiece out until he saw them reenter the ballroom. But she doubted it.

"Best to get ready, I think, just in case," Douglas continued. His tone was almost…regretful. Douglas somehow hid their gas masks and extra weapons in the building, along with the Phantom armor for James to change into.

"I guess we should mingle," Emma said with a sigh. The plan was to make sure James was seen publicly, and frequently. When the subject came up in the planning, she joked about gaslighting a crowd of people into thinking that James never left the party. James and Douglas had both stared at her like she was crazy, but then Douglas turned thoughtful. It could work, he said. That way, if the Phantom showed up, they could pretend James and the Phantom were in the same room together, at the same time. James simply wanted to disappear, but she pointed out how impossible that would be for someone so recognizable. It made a lot more sense to make it as public as possible. Everyone would be so busy talking about him that no one would think to tie James to the Phantom. Not like they might if James simply disappeared, and the vigilante reappeared in his place.

"Another dance?" James murmured in her ear. She let her eyes close at his proximity. Goosebumps formed on her skin at the brush of his breath against her neck. *No*, she wanted to say. *Let's go home. Let's forget New Atlas and go home.*

As if the DJ could read their thoughts, another slow song started right on cue. James confidently led her onto the dance floor. He ignored the way several mouths opened in shock at the sight of them together. Ignored the other couples. Ignored everything but her.

James gently took one of her hands in his. He pressed the other flat against her bare lower back and drew her close. Closer than they had been earlier. She put her free hand on his shoulder as they began to sway to the music. She gave in to the urge to curl her fingers into the hair at the base of his neck. He tensed against her.

"You look really beautiful," he said softly. His cheeks flushed all over again. "I meant to say so earlier."

"You aren't so bad yourself," she said with a newfound confidence. She couldn't help looking up at him flirtatiously from underneath her lashes.

James smiled even as he glanced around the room. She knew he was on high alert, searching for any danger.

Leaning in close, she nuzzled against his ear. Her lips brushed against the spot just below his earlobe. "You think the Phantom might save a dance for me later?"

Both of his hands spasmed and tightened against her. They were pressed flush together. She really, really hated that they had to save New Atlas. She imagined dragging him to a private corner and–

"He might," James murmured. He opened his mouth to say something else but the song finally ended. The attention on them waned as they melted into the crowd around the edges of the room.

"Do you think we've drawn enough attention?" Emma asked with a little sigh. She didn't want the night to end. But the longer it went without anything happening, the more her nerves grew.

Without waiting for an answer, she smiled coyly at James and pulled him out of the ballroom and down a hallway towards the restrooms.

"Time for phase two," she said fake, deep voice, which earned a soft laugh from Douglas in her earpiece.

"We aren't spies," James said, but when she looked over her shoulder, he was smiling. They ducked down another, quieter hallway without letting go of each other's hands.

"I mean, we kind of are. The outfits, the gadgets, saving the city…?" Emma gestured around them. "And now I'm going to pretend I 'just saw you right over there' for as long as I can. Operation Gaslight is a go."

James hesitated, staring down at her with an intensity that made her bones tremble. "Please be careful," he said in a low voice.

"You first," she said with a stubborn jut of her chin.

With a single knuckle, James reached out and traced her cheekbone. "See you later."

"See you later," she said back. It was a promise, she hoped, that no matter what was about to happen, they would be together later. That everything would be fine.

Yet Emma still felt sick with worry.

With one last lingering look, James walked away–towards the rooftop and his hidden armor, towards whatever was going to happen.

When Emma walked back down the hallway, an older man stopped her. The same one from the courtyard.

"Ah!" he said jovially, face red. "Mr. Kane's assistant, yes?"

Emma smiled sweetly. "Yes, sir, I am."

"Where has Mr. Kane run off to?" he asked, peering around curiously. He eyeballed her as if wondering if they were in the middle of a secret tryst and James would come out in his underwear or something. "I'd like a quick word."

"Oh, he was in the ballroom talking to Mr. Smith last I saw. I was just headed to the restroom." She smiled wider and tilted her head to the ladies' room, which was right beside them.

"Leon Smith?" the man said with a frown. "Yes, yes. I'll just go catch them both." He hurried away with a glance over his shoulder. A shiver of disgust ran through her stomach. She wondered if the man had ever been to the Crescent Club. He seemed the type.

Inside the posh bathroom, Emma locked herself in a stall. It was completely empty for the moment. She needed to collect herself anyway. It was probably for the best that James had to go, because another moment in close proximity and she wouldn't need the aid of alcohol to make stupid decisions.

"Operation Wild Goose Chase is in full swing," she said into the earpiece.

"I thought it was Operation Gaslight? Either way, it was *very* convincing," Douglas said. She could hear the laughter in his voice. "And I'll direct him outside next if he comes asking."

Emma laughed softly.

"Be careful," James interrupted. "Both of you."

"Spoilsport," Emma said petulantly.

The door banged open. "*–James Kane?*" an unfamiliar voice said. Emma's ears perked up.

"Unbelievable. This has already been the best party of the year. Think I could catch him at the valet and get a ride home?" The sound of tipsy laughter echoed through the room.

Emma kicked open the stall a bit angrily. Jealousy burned hotly in her chest.

The two young women at the sink went quiet.

She ignored them while she washed her hands. She was jealous even though she *knew* James wouldn't take anyone else home. But part of her hated that other people noticed how good he looked. She forced herself to take a steadying breath.

"Hi," the shorter of the two women said. Her dress was brilliant purple.

"Hi," Emma said with a bland smile. She didn't want to add to any rumors and hurriedly dried her hands. She left with a little wave as both women stared at her, barely holding their delight in check.

"Oh my *God*," one woman whispered and giggled as the door closed. "Sleeping with his assistant?"

Emma flushed as she entered the ballroom once more. Douglas caught her eye from the other side as she approached the silent auction tables and pretended to look at each listing with extreme interest.

She spotted the same man from the hallway just as he noticed her. He made a beeline for her.

She sighed and barely stopped herself from rolling her eyes. "This man is determined to–"

From outside, there was a massive explosion.

The floors shook. There were several screams, the sound of shattering glass, then silence as the music abruptly stopped.

Every light winked out at once. The only light came from the candles on the tables and from the flames of the heaters outside. More screams cut through the sudden quiet. Emma ran over to one of the doors outside in time to see a ball of flame erupt somewhere nearby.

This could not be good. The bad feeling was back and worse than ever.

"Everyone please stay calm!" A voice called from the stage. Every eye turned to see who it was. A few people turned on the flashlights on their phones and pointed them at the stage in a makeshift spotlight.

It was the Wolf. Her blood went cold, then hot.

"I'm going to ask that we lock this room down until we figure out what that was, and until we get the backup generators going. There's no need for alarm." He smiled and stepped down from the stage. He was walking right toward her. The crowd parted around him. Everyone thanked him, asking him questions. It was as if were the mayor; his influence spread far and wide before her.

"I'm going to go check it out," James said in her ear.

Emma turned and tried to hurry away but ran right into someone. The apology died on her lips.

Lionel Maxwell stared at her with a black eye and broken nose. He sneered as soon as he recognized her. *Fuck.*

She sucked in a breath and whirled away from him, only to come face to face with the Wolf and two members of his security detail instead.

The Wolf stopped in his tracks. "*You,*" he said with no small amount of surprise when he saw her.

"Me," she said, and then she punched him in the face.

CHAPTER TWENTY-EIGHT

JAMES

James watched as a fireball bloomed over the city, the brightness of it rising above the nearby rooftops. It couldn't be more than a block or two away. He flipped through the mental maps of New Atlas to try to figure out where it was, how many casualties there might be, what the best escape routes were. He'd just finished putting the armor on, conveniently hidden for easy access.

"I'm going to go check it out," he said even though he was already on his way there. What were they planning? Maybe the information about the gala had been no good. A way to get them searching in the wrong place.

"Me," he heard Emma say. He opened his mouth to ask what was happening, but then she started shouting. "Let me go! Let me *go*, you bastard! Fuck you!"

"Emma?" he asked as he rounded a corner and came face to face with the flames. It seemed to be an abandoned building, still under construction, but he couldn't be sure. His heart pounded a frantic beat in his chest. By the time first responders arrived, it would be too late for anyone stuck inside. "Douglas? What's going on?"

"She punched the Wolf," Douglas said softly, a hint of awe in his voice. "And he's having security remove her from the premises."

James cursed. "Can you go after her? I–"

Out of the corner of his eye, he saw someone step out of the shadows beside the burning building. He whirled, his guard up, ready to fight, but worrying about Emma rendered him distracted.

It was one of the Wolf's men, vaguely familiar. Murray, maybe? He struck out with one arm which James barely had time to block. Before he could make another move, the man's other hand went low.

There was a sharp pain in his leg. James glanced down, almost dazed. There was a now-empty syringe sticking out between the pieces of padded armor on his thigh. A lucky hit. One that shouldn't have been possible if he had only paid more attention.

Sudden panic overwhelmed every other sense.

He hadn't had time to dose himself. Or to give it to Emma or Douglas. It was still in his belt, unused.

No, James thought desperately. It wasn't supposed to happen like this. Already he could barely twitch his fingers. His muscles weren't responding to his mind's commands.

"Douglas–" he said urgently. "*Get her out–*"

His words choked off.

Bit by bit, his body stilled.

His consciousness receded into the deepest reaches of his mind. No matter how hard he fought, his body wouldn't move. Wouldn't obey. There was noise in his ear, Douglas and Emma's voices blending together in an indistinguishable clamor.

Mentally, he thrashed against the drug's constraints on his body. But physically, nothing happened. There was no outward sign of his fight to regain control. For a moment, there was no fear, only determination to wrangle his body back under his will.

The man in front of him stood wreathed in light from the flames. James recognized him from the night Emma was drugged.

The rage built within him, a hurricane of sensation. If only he could *move* so he could hit the man, wrap his hands around his throat and squeeze–

But his body wouldn't cooperate. He couldn't so much as twitch. Is this what it was like? What Emma had endured?

Shit. The fear started to take over the anger. The counteragent. *Emma*.

"Hello, Phantom," the man said with a sinister smile. "I have to admit, I thought it would be harder to draw you out. Who knew that all it took was a little explosion? Maybe we could have been done much sooner."

James screamed against the bonds of his own body. Thrashed. But his body didn't move. He barely breathed. Barely blinked.

He hoped Douglas got Emma out.

"Now, follow me. We're going for a ride."

EMMA

Emma struggled against the two security guys as the Wolf ordered her to be hauled off.

"Emma? Douglas? What's going on?" James asked in her ear.

"She punched the Wolf," Douglas said softly. "And he's having security remove her from the premises."

James cursed. "Can you go after her? I–"

He stopped. Gave a small grunt. She wanted to ask what was going on, but she didn't want to give away that she was recording everything and communicating with someone else. Just in case.

"Douglas–" he said. "*Get her out–*"

His words choked off.

Probably busy fighting whatever bad guy had blown up part of New Atlas. She should be out there *helping* him, not being dragged away like some fucking party crasher.

They tossed Emma into a small conference room. The Wolf and Lionel Maxwell stepped through the door behind her. There was noise in her ear from both James and Douglas, but it all blended together until she couldn't make anything out.

She was on high alert. Her whole body trembled with the surge of adrenaline in her veins.

A signal from the Wolf and the men holding her arms let her go. She launched herself at Maxwell with a snarl. Barely got her fingers on his suit jacket before she was being pulled backwards again. She should have killed him when she had the chance. She should have thrown his fucking body off the tower. She should have run him over with the armored car until he was nothing but a smear on the tires.

The Wolf sighed. "Hold her. It won't be long now."

"What won't be long now?" she demanded. She tried to wrench her arms out of the guards' grip, but they were too strong. She hadn't even had a chance to go after their hidden stash of weapons. "What did you blow up?"

"It was just an empty building. Probably," Maxwell said with a sneer. "Just a distraction."

"A distraction for what?" She needed to keep them talking. First, so James and Douglas knew what was going on. Second, so she could use this as evidence against them later. The recordings were being sent back to the basement underneath the manor, as well as to each of their phones. Just in case. So even if she somehow didn't make it, if none of them made it, there was proof of what happened.

"For the main event, baby." Maxwell walked up to her. He leered down the front of her dress and ran a finger along the strand of pearls at her neck. "I admit, you clean up nice. If I didn't know you were a prostitute, I'd think you belonged here."

She craned her neck and tried to bite his finger. He just laughed.

"You know we never slept together, right?" she taunted him with a sneer of her own. "You were so drunk you passed out. All I had to do was mess my hair up a little and tell you how *amazing* you were. And you believed it. As if a dick that small could ever make a girl come."

Maxwell gave a wordless sound of rage and hit her in the face. Blood poured into her mouth as her lip split. She gave him a bloody smile.

"Might as well tell me what you're planning," she said. "Or rather, what the Wolf here has planned. Sorry, Lionel, I just don't think you're smart enough to come up with any kind of evil plan. A small dick *and* a small brain."

Maxwell made another noise of disgust and stalked away.

"Enough," the Wolf said in an authoritative tone. He checked his watch. Leveled an icy stare at Emma. "You're right," he said. "I'll tell you what we have planned, but only because you won't make it out of here this time. Your masked friend won't be able to save you. We won't even need to drug you this time." He stepped closer and studied her as if she were a bug beneath his shoe. His eyes were flat and dead like a shark's, the scars around them emphasizing the lack of emotion. She struggled against her captors again, desperate to wrap her hands around his throat. "First, we're going to turn New Atlas inside out. Take out the competition…and then we're going to step in. Fill the void left behind. Take care of the problem ourselves. Become kings among men." The Wolf smiled a smile that chilled her to the bone. "Tonight is only the beginning. But tonight is all you're going to see. I've gotten tired of how meddlesome you've been."

She spit blood in his face. He merely sighed and pulled out an actual handkerchief to wipe it away.

His phone rang in his pocket.

"Is it done?" he asked when he answered. "Good. We're waiting. Start the next step."

He hung up and took a seat on one of the many chairs around the room.

Emma heard a small explosion from the direction of the ballroom. She realized too late that Douglas and James had both been silent for too long.

The sound of screaming reached them a beat later. She could hear it directly in her ear and from behind the closed door.

Emma struggled against the men holding her. "What have you done?" she demanded, but the Wolf and Maxwell both ignored her.

"*No*." Douglas's voice in her ear was anguished. "*No*. What have they–" His voice abruptly cut off, though the screams in the background continued. Douglas grunted in pain.

Emma was truly afraid for the first time all evening.

"*What have you done?*" she screamed. Her shoulders wrenched and her feet came off the floor as she struggled with every ounce of her strength against the men holding her.

She smashed one thick heel into the instep of one of the guards. In the same movement, she head-butted the other in the nose. Both of them let her go at the same time. She darted away. One of them caught her by the silk wrap she still had over her arms. She whirled and used the momentum to wrap the cloth around the man's hands. She kicked him in the chest and then ran.

She wrenched the door to the room open and made it into the entryway before they caught her again.

Emma glimpsed the chaos in the dark ballroom through the open doors as someone inside pulled them closed.

A shadow in their midst. Douglas on the ground, blood on his leg, fear and desperation in his eyes.

"No!" her scream of agony was drowned out by the cacophony of fear before her. Not Douglas–

They dragged her back into the conference room. The door shut with a soft snick and cut off the worst of the screams, except for what she could hear in her ear. The guard she head-butted cursed quietly at her, calling her all kinds of nasty names while his broken nose bled freely. She bared her teeth at him and tried to rear her head back for another hit.

"Not falling for that again, bitch," he spat. He twisted her arms painfully behind her back until one of her shoulders wrenched.

Douglas was hurt–he was bleeding and she didn't know how bad it was, and she had no way to get to him. She had to help him, had to help the guests out there, had to find James.

There was a knock at the door. "Come in," the Wolf said.

In stepped a bouncer from the Crescent Club, a guy named Murray that was the Wolf's right hand man. The noise outside rose to a crescendo, then cut off again as he closed the door behind him.

"Well?" asked Maxwell. He crossed his arms.

Murray winked at Emma. He was the one who had called her a cunt all those weeks ago when the Wolf had them beat her. "Fancy seeing you here, sweetheart."

"Is it done?" Maxwell said. Each word was short, impatient.

Murray looked back at the Wolf as he said, "It's done. It's all going perfectly."

Where was James? The question pounded through her in time with her racing heart. *Where is he where is he where is he where is he where is he?*

The Wolf lounged in his seat as if he had all the time in the world. Emma stilled.

"You see, there's one thing New Atlas has in our way," the Wolf said softly. Emma couldn't breathe. Her body knew what was happening before her mind did. The panic tasted metallic on her tongue. Or maybe that was her own blood. *A shadow in their midst.* "And what New Atlas has is the most powerful thing of all."

He looked up and stared into her eyes. "A symbol is more powerful than anything else. So, in order to get true power, we need to take New Atlas's symbol away from it. But we can't create a martyr. No. That'd be too easy. We need to turn it into something to fear. Then we step in as heroes ourselves when we stop him. *That's* how we get the power. And if we use that symbol to take care of the competition against us? Even better. Bring him in."

The last words were directed at Murray. He stepped out of the room. The screaming had stopped. There was still noise, but it had shifted. Yet there were no sirens. There should have been sirens. Emma needed her phone, needed to call Kendrick. He could help them.

"What have you done?" Emma asked for a third time. But the words had lost all of their strength.

"Let her go," the Wolf said. The two men let go and stepped away. "See for yourself."

Emma turned as the door opened again. Her heart stopped beating altogether.

The Phantom stepped through the door. He was dragging someone unconscious behind him. It was—fuck, it was the *mayor. Take care of the competition.* The words echoed in her mind.

"Let him go," the Wolf said. The mayor dropped to the ground with a thud. Murray stepped back into the room.

"Wh—What?" She choked on the word. James's eyes didn't meet hers. His face, what she could see of it, was blank. The world fell away from her. This couldn't be happening. *Not him*, she silently begged. *Not Jamie.* They were going to use James to *take care of the competition.* He never killed, she thought in almost a daze. He had never purposefully taken a life. Not ever.

But the counteragent—

"Kill her," said the Wolf as if he were ordering wine at dinner. "Slowly. Make her suffer."

James lunged for her and wrapped his hands around her throat.

Emma's cry of anguish cut off as James started slowly tightening his hands. Black spots danced in her vision. There wasn't even a spark of recognition in his green eyes. Tears leaked out of her own eyes as she tried to silently communicate with him. Her fingers pulled at his. She couldn't breathe. The pearls he had given her earlier that evening dug into her throat.

She managed to get her knee up and hit him in the groin. He didn't react, but his hold loosened. She tried to kick one of his legs away, but he was too strong.

"I said *slowly*," the Wolf growled, emotion finally bleeding into his tone. "Don't *strangle* her yet. Make her *suffer*! Make it hurt!"

James let go. She darted away, but he grabbed her by the elbow and dragged her back. His gloved fist connected with her face. She was able to block the next hit. She shoved him away. She kicked at his knee to try to knock his feet out from under him.

"*No,*" she sobbed. "No, this isn't you, it isn't–"

He hit her again, this time in the ribs. Something cracked, and she cried out. That pain was nothing compared to her anguish at seeing him so…blank. And knowing he was aware, that he was *in there*, watching himself hurt her, being unable to stop it…She knew exactly what it felt like, knew he would remember every detail, and that was the worst part of it all.

Had the counteragent not worked?

"It's okay," she said desperately. She dodged another flurry of blows. He snagged one strap of her dress. It popped in an explosion of crystals as she scrambled away. "It's okay, I know you can't help it. It's okay, you're okay." She could barely see through her tears. Could barely breathe through the pain in her ribs and her heart. Her heel connected firmly with his knee this time, and he went down. But only for a second. He was back up again in the blink of an eye.

James hit her again. Again. Something else cracked. Another rib, she thought. Blood poured into her eyes from a cut on her forehead. She stumbled over a chair onto her ass.

James straddled her. He held her down with one hand and hit her again.

"It's okay, it's okay," she said through her sobs, even as she fought. Even as she thrashed against him. She started to crawl away. He caught her by the train of her dress and dragged her back. The carpet scraped against her elbows.

Think, she told herself through the pain. She had to save him. Had to save him from himself. She sobbed again as she realized what this would do to him. Killing someone. Killing *her*. He would never recover from it. He would hate himself until the day he died. *Think!* she commanded her feeble mind. But the pain and fear made it so hard to think.

James hit her in the face again. Somehow, he was only hitting her on the side of the face that didn't have the camera contact lens. At least Kendrick could see what had happened, after.

Her vision fuzzed. Everything went out of focus for a second.

Maybe it wasn't that the counteragent hadn't worked.

"Stop," said Maxwell. James went utterly still, a statue sitting on her chest. Maxwell circled the pair of them, his expression gleeful. "What if I want her to myself? I'm sure I could purchase enough of the drug from our suppliers to last me a good long while."

She touched her fingers to James's jaw. Did she imagine it, or were his lips shaking? Were his eyes watering? He was still sitting on her. She was stuck beneath him. The sharp points of his armor dug into her legs and hips but she barely felt it underneath the pain blaring from her ribs.

Maybe he hadn't taken the counteragent at all, she thought through the haze of pain.

"It's okay," she whispered, just for him to hear. She brushed one thumb across his cheek. She stared into his eyes so he could see that she wasn't afraid. He was so utterly, terrifyingly blank as he looked down at her.

The Wolf gave a long sigh. "Lionel, we talked about this. There are other girls. Ones you don't have to drug."

Maxwell shrugged and smiled a little sheepishly. "But I like the fight in her. I like knowing what it would do to her to know she couldn't do anything about it. I like the thought of breaking her."

No. She would kill him before she let that happen. Would rather die. She would burn this whole fucking city to the ground first.

The counteragent, she thought distantly, trying hard to refocus. James must have kept it with him. He was always prepared, always thinking the worst would happen. And he had been insistent that she take it, not him. So he probably hadn't taken it yet.

An idea began to form. She just needed to–

"Not this time," the Wolf said. His voice was almost bored. "Kill her."

James pulled out a blade from a hilt at his belt. But he didn't bring it down. His lips *were* shaking. She saw a flash of something in his eyes. Knew he was in there fighting. Knew it was a fight he would lose. Knew there was still too much of the drug in his system.

They were out of time.

"I love you," she whispered. She swallowed a mouthful of her own blood as her hands fumbled at his belt. There was one pouch that clinked like glass, and she carefully slipped the small vial out. "I'm not going to die without telling you that I love you. It's okay. It's okay if you kill me. Don't hate yourself for it. Please. It's not your fault. Do you hear me? It's not your fault." She choked on her words and pressed her hand to his face again. She was shaking. She closed her eyes.

The least she could do was keep him from seeing the life leave her.

The Wolf made a noise of disgust. "What would your date think?" he scoffed. "Though I'm sure he'll be glad not to have to see you die. You know, I can see why he liked you. You're so much like his mother…sticking your nose where it doesn't belong."

Emma's eyes crashed to James's. *No*. There was a flash of something in their green depths. Another, older pain.

"I'm sorry," she whispered to him. "I love you."

"Kill her," the Wolf repeated.

The blade bit into her abdomen. She choked on a scream. Sharp pain spread from where sliced through her. She wouldn't open her eyes, wouldn't let him see. She felt every inch of the blade as it slid in and tore her apart from the inside. God, the *pain–*

Emma went limp with the blade still in her.

James stood, his mission done.

"Satisfied?" Maxwell asked the Wolf. "Can we move on now?"

"Yes, for now. Bring me that list of targets for him in the ballroom." Emma cracked open her eyes and saw the Wolf hold out an impatient hand. One of the security guards passed him a phone.

Their attention was away from her as if nothing had happened. Maxwell was standing next to her like she was another piece of furniture. Like she wasn't bleeding beneath him. James stood staring at the Wolf, awaiting his next orders. Did she imagine it, or did one of his fingers twitch?

Emma opened her eyes all the way. Her entire body hurt. There was a fire in her belly. Her fingertips felt cold, almost numb. She looked up at James. The blood pooled around her, warm and thick.

It came back to her in a snap of thought. *The counteragent.*

She gripped the blade in one hand and yanked it out with a cry. In the same moment, she downed the contents of the vial. With the counteragent in her system, she could give James orders. Maybe she could override everyone else. She had to try, for him.

"God*damn* it," said the Wolf on a sigh as she rose unsteadily to her feet.

Maxwell lunged for her. On instinct, she brought the blade up between them. It sank into the soft flesh of his stomach. His eyes went wide with shock. His hands scrambled for purchase, tried to shove her off, tried to get the knife from her.

"*Kill her!*" the Wolf shouted at James.

Emma whirled so Maxwell was a shield between her and James. She pulled the knife out. Stabbed him again. Twisted. Then she yanked the blade out and stared into his eyes as his blood poured over her hands.

"I promised I would kill you," she said to him.

Hands yanked her backwards. Threw her to the ground. Wrestled the knife from her grip.

She pressed bloody hands to James's chest. Was the counteragent working within her? "Come back to me," she said. "Stop. Don't kill me. *Come back to me.*" She hoped it would work. It was all she had. Maybe it would work. It had to work. There was no other way.

He held the knife above her. It started to lower. "*Stop!*" she shouted. His knee pressed into her side where the blade had gone in. The pain turned her vision black. She blinked it away. No. She would do this. She would save him. She caught his raised arm in her hand, tried to slow its descent, but she was too weak. "*Stop.*"

James stopped. He was trembling now. His entire body shook. She almost sobbed in relief. *It was working.*

"Don't listen to the others," she said, hoping with every fiber of her being that it would be enough. "Only me. Only listen to me, okay? Listen to my voice. Don't listen to *anyone* except me. Come back to me."

James's eyes didn't waver from hers. A single tear slipped from underneath the mask.

"I love you," she said firmly. She took a deep, shuddering breath. It hurt. All of it hurt. "None of this is your fault. Put the knife down."

It hit the ground with a clatter.

The door burst open to reveal Douglas, framed in the doorway with a shotgun. He was limping, one leg bloodied with his tie as a makeshift bandage. He shot one of the security guards without any hesitation. There was a cut on his chin. There were men behind him, trying to stop him. The guards within the room drew guns.

"Help him!" she commanded James. He sprang into action. He disarmed one guard and knocked out another with two precise blows. The Wolf darted outside, away from the fight.

"Stop!" the Wolf shouted. "Stop, kill him, kill the girl!"

Behind Douglas, there was a noise. Shouting, brief gunfire, and—sirens. Finally, sirens.

Kendrick came bursting into the room next, gun drawn, badge flashing. He had on a vest with NAPD emblazoned across it.

"Oh thank God you're here," the Wolf said. "The Phantom's gone on a rampage, he's—"

"Mr. Meyer, you're under arrest," Kendrick said. His eyes darted around the room, taking stock of the blood and violence.

"Stop," Emma said weakly to James. She managed a few fumbling steps forward. Her own blood covered her hand as she pressed it to her side. It probably shouldn't be gushing that much, she thought dazedly. She shivered with cold. Was there a window open somewhere? She was freezing.

She had done it. She'd stopped them. She had saved James.

But she was still dying.

"Go with Douglas and don't look back until you're home," she told James where no one else could here. She pressed her forehead to his as her strength flagged. "I love you," she whispered again. "Never forget that I love you." He stepped away and followed Douglas.

"Take him home," she murmured to Douglas. He took a tentative step towards her on his good leg.

"Emma," he said worriedly. "You're hurt."

"*Go*," she said with every bit of strength she had left. "Get him out of here, now! I'll be okay. Kendrick's here. I'll be okay."

Suddenly, there were cops everywhere. Shouting–there was so much shouting.

Douglas hesitated a minute longer before running out, limping heavily.

James went after him. She caught a glimpse of something in his eyes and then he was gone.

Emma's knees hit the floor.

"Fuck, that hurts," she mumbled. The edges of her vision were going dark. She had to reach out and catch herself with one hand. The other hand pressed against her side. Her fingers were slick with blood.

Kendrick had the Wolf in handcuffs. There were people everywhere. Cops. Others. She couldn't see, couldn't think. Kendrick hurried to her side. His hands pressed into her wound. She went limp in his arms. He had her now. She didn't have to fight so hard. Kendrick had made it.

"Hey, hey, stay with me," he said to her as he scooped her into his arms. "Paramedics are right outside. They're coming. You did good, kid. You got them."

James was okay. He was going home. Douglas would make sure he was okay.

"The phone," she said to Kendrick. He needed that last piece of the puzzle. "The Wolf's phone."

"We got it, don't worry. Save your strength." Kendrick grunted as he pushed through a door. Blue and red flashed across her vision.

"Make sure—" she said, but coughed. It didn't even hurt any-more. "Make sure he doesn't blame himself, Kendrick. He'll hate himself for killing me."

"You're not dead yet, Em," Kendrick said. Emotion coated his words. "Don't give up on me, kid. Stay with me. Come on. Almost there."

She smiled softly.

It was over. She had saved him.

She could rest now.

CHAPTER TWENTY-NINE

JAMES

James came back to himself slowly. He watched it happen as if from far away, inching haltingly closer to controlling his own body again. He watched as he followed Douglas outside through the chaos. As they got into a car and sped towards home. As they reached the abandoned basement. As they went up the elevator and into the medical room. The drug forced him to follow Douglas without turning back.

"I'm sorry," Douglas said. He was crying. "I'm so sorry."

James felt a small pinch in his neck before blackness took over.

When he woke, he was disoriented. He wasn't in his own bed. He was half out of the armor.

"What–" he asked. The word scraped from his throat like it was made of sandpaper.

Douglas jerked awake in the chair beside the bed. James blinked in the brightness. He was hooked up to an IV. The needle disappeared into the crook of his arm. He tried to find a clock, his phone, anything to tell him how long it had been.

Douglas wasn't wearing pants. James blinked again. His leg was crudely stitched.

A blade in his hand, screams of terror, Douglas's anguish–

James shuddered.

There'd been an explosion.

"Where is she?" he said in a low rasp.

A jolt as he realized Douglas was crying.

Panicked now, James tried to sit up. Pulled the IV out. Yanked at the sheet covering his legs.

"Stay down, you still have morphi–" Douglas was saying, but James pushed past him. Swayed as he got to his feet. The entire world spun unpleasantly. Bile rose in his throat.

"*Where is she*?"

Wetness on his face. He already knew. He already knew, but it couldn't be true. It couldn't.

"James–"

James kept going. Aimed himself towards the basement. Made it all the way to the elevator before Douglas, limping heavily, caught up with him. He tried to stop him, but James smacked the button.

"James, please," Douglas begged as he followed James into the elevator. His eyes were wet and bloodshot, and dried blood covered his chin. "It's been hours–" Douglas grabbed James's arm but James shrugged it off. "Jamie, *please*, listen to me."

He never called him Jamie, not ever.

Only his parents had called him that. His parents…and *her*.

James reached for the keys on the worktable.

He saw the blood on his hands.

His hands were red. Covered almost to the elbow in blood.

His resolve crumbled.

He collapsed to his knees. Barely caught himself before he hit the concrete floor face-first. His arms shook. His whole body shook.

Her blood.

His hands.

His blade.

An anguished cry tore free.

"*No,*" he begged anyone who could hear him. It couldn't be true. No. He couldn't have–

Douglas wrapped him in his arms. Rocked him like he was a child. "She was alive when we left, but–"

But there had been so much blood.

James cried out again. It ripped him in two, this pain. He couldn't see, he couldn't breathe, he couldn't do *anything*.

He killed her.

He loved her, and he had killed her.

"*No*," he sobbed. Tore at his hair. "No. I–I–"

Douglas smoothed his hand over the back of James's head. He tried to hide his sobs but didn't succeed.

James scrambled for his phone. No messages, no missed calls. "Kendrick hasn't called, so–she might not–she might be–"

He couldn't see through the blur of tears.

There had been so much blood. His hands were still red and sticky with it. *Her* blood. His hands had done it. *He* had killed her.

He fell forward onto one hand. Clawed at his chest with the other. The pain–he had to smother the pain, it was suffocating him. It hurt, God, it *hurt*.

Tremors wracked his body. He couldn't breathe. Tried to suck air in but nothing came. He gasped. Black filled his vision. His ribs were crushing his lungs. His heart.

Douglas was in front of him. "Breathe. Breathe, Jamie. *Breathe*."

He obeyed the authoritative command and breathed. The tightness in his chest loosened. But the pain was still there. He was breathing, but he was still suffocating.

"It wasn't your fault," Douglas said. But it was. A tear slipped down Douglas's cheek. "You were drugged. Don't blame yourself, please."

But he did. He did blame himself.

She said the same thing. He couldn't even think her name. It hurt too much. She told him that it was okay, that it wasn't his fault. Told him not to blame himself. But *his* hands pushed the blade into the softest part of her. *His* hands had hit her, strangled her, torn at her skin. *He* did that. There was no taking it back. Drug or no drug, his hands had destroyed her body and taken her from this earth.

And he remembered every second of it.

He remembered every awful fucking second.

James screamed. Shoved the table closest to him. The computer went crashing to the ground. He swept his arms across the next workstation, and the next, and the next. Kicked over the motorcycle *she* helped him retrieve just a few nights ago.

Douglas wiped at his face but made no move to intervene.

The man who had been his father these past two decades in every way that had counted. What did he think of James now? Now that James had killed the only person he had truly loved? Someone Douglas loved too?

Another scream. Rage. Pain. Regret. Guilt. He poured it all into the sound and screamed until his voice broke. Until the noise choked off, his throat straining to continue the sound.

He crouched and covered his head with his arms. His fingers ripped at his hair. Anything to help with this pain.

He was dying.

No. He had already died. Her last breath had been his. James Kane and the Phantom were both dead now. They both died with her. His world did not exist without her in it. It couldn't.

"James," Douglas said, but his voice broke.

The sound of it was another arrow of anguish shot directly into James's heart. He tried to scream again but the sound was gone.

A phone rang.

James didn't move. His breath heaved from him. Each inhale was a shard of glass in his chest. Each exhale was a trail of fire. It hurt. It hurt too much. There was no way he could survive it.

He would stay down here until he withered and died. If he moved, he would see reminders of her. She was everywhere. There wasn't a single place in his life that she hadn't touched.

He didn't want to live anymore.

Not without her.

The ringing stopped. Started again.

Douglas's low voice. James didn't listen. He merely shifted until he was curled on the damp earth. This was it. This was the phone call.

"James," Douglas said. Shook him gently. "James, it was Detective Kendrick." James closed his eyes, expecting to hear the worst.

"She's in surgery."

EMMA

The world came back to Emma slowly.

One blink, and there was light.

Another, and shapes formed.

Another blink. Sounds slowly trickled into her mind. A soft beeping. A rustle. A breath.

She blinked again and again until her eyes focused. It took a long time, but the world around her finally sharpened.

James sat next to her.

Rather, he slumped headfirst onto the bed she was on. Limp with sleep, her hand in his. Even in sleep, his grip was strong.

She was alive. She was in a hospital room, and she was alive.

And James was here. Her eyes roved over him greedily for any sign of injury, but, miraculously, he seemed fine. Several days of stubble covered the side of his jaw that she could see. The beginnings of a beard. Even asleep, there were dark circles under his eyes. But he wasn't injured. He was whole. He was here.

She let herself relax back into the pillows.

He was okay. Somehow she hadn't died, and James was okay.

And they saved New Atlas.

Huh, she thought with no small amount of surprise. This was unexpected.

Her eyes opened again, and she saw a TV screen. The sound was muted, but she was just able to make out the headline across the bottom.

BREAKING NEWS: FIFTEEN ARRESTED IN NAPD STING OPERATION

They had done it. They had really done it.

She sighed with relief.

James jerked awake.

His green eyes met hers.

His whole body shuddered. He pressed her knuckles to his cheek with a soft moan. He turned his head away as a tear slipped from one eye and then the next.

"Hi," she whispered. Her throat was dry. But she was alive. There was a slight pain in her side, but everything was…fuzzy. Drugs. She was on drugs. She sighed again. "Some party, huh?"

But James didn't laugh or look at her. Emma squeezed his hand like a lifeline.

There was a counter and a sink across from her with a mirror above it. She caught sight of her reflection and winced. Her face was brilliantly purple on one side. There were bruises around her neck. Oh. *That looks pretty bad*, she thought a bit distantly. But none of it hurt. That was good, right? That it didn't hurt?

Douglas stepped into the room with two cups in his hand. She smiled to see him. He was fine, too. Good.

"*You're awake*," Douglas said. He rushed to her side, coffee spilling, and took her other hand, careful to avoid the IV that was stuck in the back of it. "Oh, thank God. Thank God." She didn't miss the emotion in his expression, the tears in his eyes.

Wait, Douglas was limping. She frowned.

James released her hand and wordlessly went to clean up the coffee. Her hand reached automatically for him, then fell, limp, back to the bed. She watched him with confusion and hurt. She looked up at Douglas who only smiled sadly. He gently patted her shoulder.

"How are you feeling?" Douglas asked.

"Fuzzy," she said truthfully. "Did you just pour my coffee on the floor?"

Douglas laughed. James stopped. He tilted his head towards them but didn't turn. He looked kind of nice with an almost-beard, she thought. "Oh, she's going to be fine for sure," Douglas said with another laugh. "More worried about the coffee than the stab wound." She smiled weakly and closed her eyes. She was so tired. Getting stabbed was hard work. How did James manage it? How many times had he been stabbed, anyway? Every thought in her head slipped like water through her fingers. It was hard to focus.

She opened her eyes to ask James how many times he'd been stabbed, but he was gone.

Douglas stared sadly after him. "He's going to get the doctor," he said. "Now that you're awake."

"Why?" she asked.

Douglas knew what she meant. He took a seat next to her bed. He released her hand and patted her arm again. "He thought he killed you. He was…inconsolable. I've…never seen him like that." His expression was haunted. She didn't want to think about it, what it had been like…after.

Emma opened her mouth, closed it again. Finally, "I told him not to blame himself."

"Don't you know that goes against everything he stands for?" Douglas sighed. "He's harder on himself than anyone. And even though it *wasn't* his fault…He will still think it is. He blames himself for his parents' deaths, you know, though he was just a boy."

Her heart squeezed. No. She wouldn't let him brood on it. He couldn't blame himself. Really, it was her own fault. She should have fought harder. Should have stabbed Maxwell sooner. Shouldn't have even let the Wolf's security grab her in the first place. And, though she might not admit this part, she probably should have listened to James and taken the counteragent in the first place.

Another thought came to her, slow and fuzzy. "Douglas, are you okay? You were limping."

Douglas grimaced, as if he hoped she wouldn't notice. "I'm fine. I was just hurt in the fighting, but it's nothing serious."

"I'm not sure I believe you," she said skeptically.

Douglas smiled softly. "I promise it's fine. It only needed stitches. My leg was injured. I patched it up rather poorly to get James home and…Well, then we came here in a rush to be with you and…" He trailed off, gaze hooded. He was leaving details out.

"Are you okay?" she asked, reaching for him. To hug him or grab him or shake more answers out of him, she didn't know.

"I'm fine, don't worry." He smiled down at her. He took her hand in his. "Don't worry about me."

Something else came back to her. She groaned.

Alarmed, Douglas asked, "Are you alright? Should I–"

Mortified, she whispered, "I told him I loved him!"

Douglas stared at her with an open mouth. Then he laughed. A full-bellied laugh. She couldn't help her answering smile, though she was still humiliated. "Oh, you two are…perfect for each other. The *worst* timing." He chuckled again. Before she could ask what he meant, they were interrupted.

"Ah, good to see you're in high spirits," said an unfamiliar Black woman as she stepped into the room. She wore a white coat over blue scrubs and a brilliant smile. *The doctor,* Emma thought hazily. "That's always good to see. I'm Dr. Wright. It's nice to finally see you awake, Emma."

Dr. Wright came over and lifted her gown to inspect her wounds. "Everything's looking good so far. You went through quite a lot, huh?" She smiled kindly as she replaced the gown and tucked Emma back in. "You've got a broken rib and severe bruising on top of this nasty stab wound. You lost a lot of blood in surgery but I think you'll heal fine." Emma's fuzzy mind could barely latch onto the words. It was enough that she had survived.

"How long…?" she asked, unsure how to phrase it. How long since the gala? How long had she been unconscious?

"Two days. We kept you sedated for a while to make sure everything was okay."

Two days.

With a jolt, Emma remembered something she really should have considered sooner. "Um–the man I sta–his blood–" She flushed with embarrassment, unsure how much the doctor knew, how much she was allowed to tell. Her mind flashed with a memory of a blade. She pushed it away. She could think about all of that later.

Douglas understood. "Don't worry, we had them run a full panel of tests for STDs and everything else."

The doctor nodded. "Yes, your friends were…quite insistent." Something flashed in her eyes. "Don't worry, you're all clear on that front."

Emma relaxed again. All of his blood near the huge open wound in her gut…She was lucky on all fronts. She wasn't sure how a creep like Maxwell *didn't* have some sort of venereal disease, but at least she'd finally had a stroke of luck.

The doctor left with a smile and a promise to send a nurse in later with more pain medicine.

James hovered in the doorway.

She met Douglas's eyes. They exchanged a silent conversation, then Douglas stood and said, "I'm going to get more coffee."

"I'll go," James said. He was staring at the ground.

"No," Douglas said firmly. "Stay here." It was an order, that much was clear.

James stayed in the doorway for a full minute after Douglas left.

"Jamie," she said. He finally looked at her. The anguish in his expression wrecked her. She started crying without quite knowing why.

He hurried over to her side. "Are you in pain?" he asked in a hoarse whisper. His voice sounded like he'd been sick recently. Used up. Scratchy. "Should I get the doctor back?"

"I'm sorry," she cried. "I'm sorry, I'm sorry." She wiped her eyes. Somehow she got tangled in her own IV. Frustrated, she yanked at it.

"Let me," James said. He gently took her hand and untangled her. He leaned over her. His breath mingled with her own. She clutched desperately at his fingers. He stared at her for a long moment and then drew away. He was closing himself off to her.

"No," she said firmly. She pointed an unsteady finger at him. "I won't let you do that. This isn't your fault. Stop beating yourself up over it."

He said nothing. A muscle jumped in his jaw. She continued to stare him down. He sighed. "Emma…"

"No!" she said. She struggled to sit up. He pushed her down by the shoulders with a glare. She glared back. "I'm not going to let you do this. I'm *alive*. I'm *okay*. We both are. And that asshole is going to jail forever." She pointed behind him to the TV screen, where a picture of the Wolf popped up. James's hands were still on her shoulders. "I know it's going to be awkward after I confessed my love for you right before I almost died, but I won't let you feel guilty."

He went completely still. Slowly, so slowly she could have stopped him, he let her go and sat back.

Her face was hot. "It's better if we just pretend it didn't happen. In fact, how about we pretend that the night went swimmingly well and catching the bad guys was actually very easy? That way–"

She sighed and squeezed her eyes shut. This was more humiliating than she had expected. He was upset that he had almost killed her. *She* was upset because she had admitted her feelings for him but didn't have the luxury of dying to avoid the consequences. Now she had to own up to what she said.

"I almost killed you." His voice was broken. A tear slipped down his cheek. It followed the sharp line of his jaw before it dripped from his chin. The sight of that lone tear almost broke her heart in two. "*I almost killed you.*"

She reached for him. Her heart hurt for him. If she could just touch him, let him have the proof that she was alive, it would be better. Like the night she had woken from a nightmare and pressed her hand to his chest. If he could feel her heartbeat, the proof it gave him, maybe it would be better.

"You didn't," she said tremulously. "I'm right here, Jamie."

He took her hand and pressed it to his cheek again. There was a cool wetness on her hand. He was still crying.

"Jamie," she said in a mournful whisper. She pressed her palm fully against his scratchy cheek. She tried to sit up again. She needed to be closer. If he could just have proof that she was *alive*, that she was fine, he wouldn't be as upset.

"*Stop doing that,*" he said sharply. He half-stood to push her gently but firmly down by the shoulders again. His eyes flickered to her lips.

His head lowered slightly and frowned at their sudden proximity, like he hadn't realized they were leaning closer.

Emma wanted him close. She wanted to kiss him, to hold him and never let go, to revel in the fact that they were both *alive*.

A small sound escaped her as one of his hands tangled in her hair. Her entire body flushed with delicious heat. She could feel his breath on her lips as she struggled to lean upwards without the use of her abdominal muscles.

He yanked back.

"Jamie," she whispered, hands stretching out for him again. "I–"

But he pushed away from the chair, knocking it over, and brushed past Douglas in the doorway.

Emma shoved her head back into the pillows with a groan of frustration.

"I don't know how to fix this," she told Douglas. "I don't–I don't know what to do."

Douglas set the two fresh coffees on the tray next to her bed. "He's…I think he's unsure what to feel at this moment. He'll come around." He righted the chair that James knocked over.

She eyed one of the cups. "I don't think I'm allowed to have that yet, but I *really* want it." She fake pouted. One thing about the drugs they had her on, she realized, that it made staying upset very hard.

Douglas pointedly covered his eyes with his hands and laughed. She snuck a sip of the coffee and sighed. Even shitty hospital coffee was better than nothing.

She ached to go after James. To make him *see*.

She almost died to save him. Now he needed saving from himself.

It took a few days, but Emma was healing nicely and was finally set to be released from the hospital. While Douglas kept her entertained with stories about James as a child and angry teenager, and with his competitiveness when they played card games together, James was withdrawn and barely visited. Instead, he lurked. He stayed close, but rarely let himself be alone with her. Usually she would wake up just in time to see him leave the room.

The day before they discharged her, Kendrick came to visit. The first thing he did after giving Emma a long, careful hug was take her statement. He raised an eyebrow at James Kane hovering in the hallway, but said nothing.

Kendrick's presence made Emma miss her mother. She had never missed her more. She wanted a hug, company, advice. And her mother had plenty of experience in making the most out of hospital stays, something Emma desperately needed. Douglas did his best, but sometimes a woman just needed her mother.

She was glad to see Kendrick, even if it was on police business. He was a friendly face, a link to her past and her mother both, despite the grief aching in her chest.

When they finished her statement, Kendrick said, "Make sure our friend is alright?" There was a note of something behind his eyes that she couldn't figure out. Almost mischievous. "If you see him around, that is. I'm hoping *your* vigilante days are over now."

"I saw him," she said without thinking. "He's–" She didn't know what to say. "He's upset, I think. With what happened with…me. But I'll make sure he's okay."

Kendrick nodded. "You did good, kid. Really. You're going to help put a lot of people in jail where they belong."

Each time someone brought it up, it was a blow to the chest. She had done it. She'd actually done it. She avenged the six dead women, and prevented more murders. There was a constant mix of pride and guilt whenever she thought about it. She was proud she had done it, but the cost had been so steep. The loss of six women. Of Marie.

And James was taking everything hard, she knew, even though she hardly saw him. But they had somehow pulled it off.

"Mr. Kane?" Kendrick called a moment later. "Can you come in here?"

Almost a full minute passed before James came through the doorway. His eyes roved over Emma quickly, as if to assure himself she was alright, before he looked away again. He didn't look back.

"Yes, detective?" he said in a flat, polite voice.

"I…went by your house, but Douglas said you were here. I wanted you to be the first to know." Emma had never seen Kendrick so…uneasy. The sudden shift in his mood was dizzying.

James zeroed in on Kendrick, shoulders straightening. "First to know what?"

"When we arrested the Wolf, it was his first arrest," Kendrick said. A fact that made the big headlines even bigger–a local business-man long thought to be tied to the mob, finally arrested. "There were several hits on his prints." Kendrick looked even *more* uneasy, if that were even possible.

Emma suddenly had a very bad feeling.

"As you know, there was only one print found at your mother's crime scene."

"What are you saying, detective?" James's words were sharp enough to cut. Several things clicked into place in Emma's mind right before Kendrick spoke his next words. The journals. The Wolf's obsession with James and the Kanes, his comments about Katherine Kane. The fervor with which James believed his father wasn't responsible for her death.

"The print was the Wolf's. He killed your mother."

All the air suddenly seemed to flee the room at once.

"Wh–" He didn't seem able to get the words out.

"The Wolf killed her?" Emma said. She unthinkingly reached her hand out to James and he took it as if on autopilot. He trembled violently.

"Yes. He confessed in a ploy to get a lesser prison sentence, though it didn't work." He paused again and took a deep breath. "There's more."

Emma wanted to close her eyes and hide. She wanted to wrap James in her arms and hide *him* from what Kendrick was going to say next.

"They never released this information, but a print was found at…the scene of your father's death as well. That was a match, too."

James made a noise of pain that pierced straight through Emma's chest.

Kendrick stood and put a hand on James's shoulder. "I'm sorry, man. After all this time…at least you know."

"His mom–" Emma said, straightening. "Katherine Kane was researching the Wolf. I have all of her old notes." James and Kendrick both stared at her. "I'll figure out a way to show you."

Kendrick nodded, leaned down, and gave Emma a quick hug, murmuring, "I'll leave you two alone. Call me if you need anything."

She barely noticed him go. She tightened her hold on James and tugged him closer.

"Jamie," she said softly. Tears threatened to spill from her eyes. She felt his pain as acutely as if it were her own and she wanted nothing more than to shield him from it.

James slid to the floor. He clung to her hand like it was a lifeline, even as his body folded forward. His head rested on the mattress. His shoulders shook.

"Jamie, I'm sorry," she said. She choked on the words. With her free hand—IV be damned—she reached out and gently stroked his hair.

Breaths heaved in and out of him. Her fingers ached from his hold on them.

After a long while, James lifted his head. His eyes were blood-shot. "I'm going to kill him." His voice was a rasp. Lethal. The deadness in his eyes made her shiver.

"You can't," she said. He opened his mouth, but she hurried to say, "He's in police custody already. And—you don't kill people."

There was nothing in his eyes, just that same cold deadness. "He killed my parents. I thought I'd—moved past this, but—"

"I know." She stroked her thumb across his knuckles.

His eyes closed at her touch. She untangled their fingers with a wince and gently reached out to touch his face. "I'm not saying he doesn't deserve it. God—I would kill him myself. But it won't change anything. It won't make you feel better."

A tremor rocked his frame. He stood abruptly and stalked away. "I have to go."

"Jamie, wait!" she called.

But he was gone.

CHAPTER THIRTY

JAMES

James watched Emma sleeping in her hospital bed and wondered at what he was about to do. What would she say, if she knew? What would she think? His first instinct was rejection. She would reject it outright, condemn him for it. But after a moment, he realized it might not be true. His mind flashed back to all the times he'd seen her angry, truly angry. He still marveled at her strength.

Maybe she would have beaten him to it if she wasn't in the hospital.

But no—she wouldn't do it unless she *had* to.

He softened as he watched her stir slightly despite the storm of rage churning in his gut.

No, she wasn't like him at all. Everything she had done, she had done out of necessity. Even Maxwell. Especially Maxwell.

James forced himself away before he could change his mind.

He had twenty years of anger to resolve.

At first he planned for the Phantom to slip into the prison where the Wolf was being held. But it would be hard to disable all the cameras and security he needed to without someone to help him do it.

Normally he would have Douglas help him, but tonight he didn't want Douglas to know. And bribing anyone as the Phantom would create more questions about his identity than he wanted asked. Not to mention, if he got caught…there would be no escape for him then.

Instead, he decided to use what had been given to him—an ungodly amount of power and wealth as James Kane.

No one would question James Kane bribing his way into the prison cell of the man responsible for his parents' deaths. No one would question why he bribed them to turn off the security cameras.

No one would dare question why the Wolf committed suicide right around the time of James Kane's visit, either.

It was incredibly easy, all things considered.

"Well, look who it is." The Wolf sat back in the hard metal seat, handcuffs clinking, as if he were the one who had set up the meeting. James requested the private interview room typically used for inmates and their lawyers. "The son." He enunciated the words carefully. The scars on his face sharpened as he smiled.

James kept quiet, though he couldn't stop how his breathing quickened.

His whole life changed because of the man before him. For twenty years, he questioned *why*. For twenty years, he questioned *how*. His father's reputation, ruined. Two lives ended, too short. James's quest for justice started the day they accused his father of his mother's murder. His rage had simmered and flared every single day since.

And it all culminated in that moment as James stared down at the man they called the Wolf.

Without the Wolf, there would be no Phantom.

Without the Wolf, James would still have his parents.

"Why?" he asked, his voice slipping unconsciously lower as the anger within him reached a fever pitch. He knew he was too close to the Phantom at that moment, but he didn't care. Not anymore. Not when he was counting every breath the Wolf took as each one brought him closer and closer to his last.

The Wolf cocked his head. "Why what?"

"Don't play dumb with me!" James half-growled. His fist smacked the table with a loud bang. The Wolf merely blinked.

"Because your mother kept stirring up trouble." He uncrossed his legs and recrossed them like he had all the time in the world.

James couldn't breathe.

Twenty years, and that was it. *Because your mother kept stirring up trouble.* That was the reason both his parents were dead.

"She was getting too close to some very, very important things that I didn't want out in the open." The Wolf shrugged and picked at a fingernail.

James saw red, but forced out the next question before he moved a single muscle. "And my father?"

"I needed a scapegoat. He was the easiest. The most believable."

The words rang in his ears.

Static crackled through his mind. His fist snapped out without him even considering it. Pain flared across his knuckles as they connected with the Wolf's face. The Wolf chuckled darkly and spat a wad of blood to the side.

Twenty years and his parents were dead for *nothing*. Because his mother was too smart, too good of a reporter, and his father was the easiest one to blame for it. All because of the man in front of him.

James shook out his fist and paced away, struggling to regain his control.

"And yet you ended up in jail anyway." His words were hollow, a way for him to try to catch his breath. His heart was breaking all over again and every single crack was being filled with that all-consuming *rage*. This man killed his parents, had tried and almost succeeded in killing *Emma*, and still he continued to breathe.

"She's a smart one, your Emma," the Wolf said.

Emma. For a moment, James felt her blood covering his hands again, hot and sticky and too much of it. *Your Emma.* He hated the way the Wolf said her name, but loved the way the words sounded.

In a blink James was in front of the other man, hand fisted in his jumpsuit, yanking him halfway out of the chair. "Don't you say her name." He snarled the words, the rage blinding him for a moment before he came back to himself and let the Wolf go.

The Wolf's eyes flashed with the first hint of emotion. James met the other man's gaze and saw himself reflected back. It was as if they held a mirror between them, reflecting their respective anger back times infinity. "I've had my eye on her for years, but I didn't expect her to…survive." A small twitch under one eye betrayed growing rage. James's own hands shook. The Wolf casually licked a spot of blood in the corner of his lip.

"And will you?" James asked. His breath came heavier as he imagined sinking a blade into the Wolf's flesh. *That* would erase the memories of Emma, of her blood, of her almost-death. "Survive?"

The Wolf spread his hands. "You tell me. I can only imagine the reason for our meeting, for the absence of the guards and the cameras switching off." He leaned forward suddenly and grinned almost manically. "The question is, will you do it yourself? Here, and now? Or will someone else? Or will it be a suicide in my cell when you're spotted somewhere far away from here?" He sat back again, once more the very picture of ease.

Instead of answering, James paced away and said to the wall, "Emma thinks I'm a good man." He expected to be plagued by images of the man's death for their entire meeting, but Emma's face kept haunting him. Her smile. Her laugh.

Her blood on his hands.

"And are you? A good man, James?"

That was the question, wasn't it? Was he the man Emma thought he was? The one who had never, not once in two years of his time as the Phantom, purposefully killed someone?

Would he change that for the man cuffed behind him? For the man who had taken his parents from him, who had come so very close to taking *Emma* from him?

Earlier in the night, he had been so certain of his decision. Had made a plan. Had put everything in place.

And yet now he was hesitating.

"If you ask me, I think you are," the Wolf said in a dangerously quiet voice. "After all, you've spent two years fighting back the tide of crime in this city. Two years behind a mask."

James, half turned away, fought against every instinct to freeze. His heart leapt in his chest and took off at a gallop.

The Wolf chuckled again.

He knows, James thought in a haze of panic. If his identity leaked, everything would end. Emma would be in danger. Douglas would be in danger. Everything James worked so hard to build, to *change*, would be undone if the Wolf told the correct person what he knew.

James would have to ensure his death, then. Wouldn't he? Not to protect himself, but to protect the ones he loved.

But maybe the Wolf *didn't* know. Maybe he was just guessing.

All of this went through James's head in an instant.

"I don't know what you're talking about," he said coolly, barely a beat passing since the Wolf had spoken. "I've been donating to charities for years, but I've always done so openly." He shrugged, letting his face betray nothing.

"You're a good liar, James Kane, but it takes one to know one. What would happen if I let slip that I knew the identity of the infamous *Phantom*?" He said the name tauntingly, like it was a joke. "What kind of deal do you think I could get, then, hmm?"

And suddenly, James saw the man before him for what he really was. A coward, trying desperately to hold on to his power. A clever coward, yes, but a coward nonetheless. James knew without a shadow of a doubt that the Wolf was afraid of prison. That he would rather die than lose his power. That he was doing all of this to manipulate James into killing him—one final act of control.

James pictured Emma's face. He traced the freckles dotting her nose, the crinkle of her brow as she frowned at him, her warm brown eyes. Everything within him settled.

He was angry, but he was still the man Emma thought he was. He knew it with a bone-deep certainty.

He laughed softly as his mind cleared. "No one would believe a desperate man pointing fingers, especially without proof," James said quietly, calmly, the world around him crystal clear for the first time in days. "But feel free to tell whoever you like. It won't change anything. I won't have you killed. I will, however, ensure that your time in prison is miserable. I'll put money in the right hands so that you never have an ounce of power in this place, no special treatment, *nothing*. And then I will forget you ever exist, except for the rare moments where I make sure you continue without any ounce of power."

James didn't wait for the Wolf to speak. He left him there, coward that he was, to rot for the rest of his days.

James was dying.

Every time he closed his eyes, his blade entered Emma's stomach. Her blood coated his hands. The life left her eyes.

And he woke alone, covered in sweat, with his heart in his throat.

He thought, naively, that confronting the Wolf would solve everything. That the clarity he felt in those final moments of their meeting would stick with him.

But then he saw Emma in the hospital bed again and everything else faded. The rage had cooled, yes, but in its place settled self-loathing.

He was barely sleeping as it was. He spent his nights in Emma's hospital room watching her sleep, watching the reassuring rise and fall of her chest. When he slept at all, it was on accident, when the world was quiet and she was already asleep.

As soon as she woke, he left.

He avoided her even as much as he craved being near her.

He couldn't stop watching her die.

And when *those* nightmares didn't find him, old ones resurfaced. Ones where he found his parents' bodies, over and over again, always too late to save them.

The news had…broken him. All the years he'd spent grieving and moving on were gone now and it was as fresh as it had been in the beginning. His decision not to kill the Wolf was the right one, he knew, but he still ached for it in his darker moments.

Not just for his parents, but for Emma.

James would never stop hearing the Wolf's order to kill her ringing in his ears as his hands were forced to obey. Nothing made it easier. It was his fault.

Everything he touched withered and died.

Even her. He took the light within her that he fell so deeply in love with and dragged it into the shadows with him. She loved him. She told him she loved him, and he'd almost killed her for it.

Being around her was too dangerous. He couldn't trust himself. If he could hurt her once, it was only a matter of time before it happened again.

Even as much as he craved her life and her warmth, he kept away. Broke his own heart as he heard her beg him not to shut him out and then shut her out anyway.

He loved her so much it hurt. But she was better off without him.

But every time he saw her or heard her voice or even smelled that telltale scent that was all *her*, it got harder.

He didn't *want* to stay away from her.

I love you.

Those words were the worst part of his dreams, because every time he had the joy of hearing them, his blade punched into her and her blood poured out and her love died with her.

"You can't keep doing this to yourself," Douglas said that morning when he caught James slipping out of Emma's hospital room.

James jerked in surprise. He hadn't heard Douglas approach. He actually couldn't be sure he hadn't dozed off where he leaned against the wall. More than twenty-four hours had passed since he was last home. He couldn't even remember the last time he'd slept.

"I'm not doing anything," James said automatically.

"You and I both know you're punishing yourself for what you did to her," Douglas said firmly in the same voice he'd used when James stayed up too late on a school night. James flinched. "Have you realized that you're punishing her, too? She did nothing wrong, and yet you're acting like *she* stabbed *you*."

"I'm *not*–" James started, but Douglas interrupted.

"You can't keep doing this to yourself. I know you love her. And *she loves you*. She has forgiven you for everything. She–"

"*Stop*," James begged, because he couldn't take another word. His gut twisted and churned. He didn't know what the two of them talked about every night when they stayed up late watching movies on Emma's laptop or when they played card games on her hospital bed. "Douglas, please. I–I can't. Not yet."

Douglas put a gentle hand on James's shoulder. "It's okay to feel guilty," he said softly. "But you have to try to forgive yourself. I know I–I know I don't say these things often, and frankly I'm not very good at them, but you deserve love, James. You deserve someone like her. You *are* good enough for her."

James stilled and didn't turn. Kept his eyes trained on the floor in front of him. His vision blurred.

After a long minute, Douglas sighed. "Please, just think about what I said. She loves you, and you love her. That's as simple as it should be. I'm tired of pretending it isn't."

James heard the door to Emma's room close.

The first tear fell.

You deserve someone like her.

CHAPTER THIRTY-ONE

EMMA

Emma was finally being released from the hospital. She spent most of her free time during her stay watching the news coverage. Shaky videos leaked of the Phantom in the ballroom that night, beating the shit out of people and kidnapping the mayor, creating chaos as he strode through the crowd.

Since there was no footage from inside the room with Emma and the Wolf, it caused a *lot* of speculation. Kendrick, bless him, kept her out of the media coverage as much as possible, but her information still leaked. People were calling her a hero.

But on top of that, he'd released an official statement from the NAPD saying that the Phantom had been under the influence of the drug, and had actually helped the NAPD.

Some still thought the vigilante was in on the whole thing. They called for his arrest, for his head, for his identity. But…most people were on his side.

Fifteen men were arrested in all, including the Wolf.

And Lionel Maxwell was dead. The media didn't release the details of his death. All they said was that, had he been alive, he would have been the sixteenth arrest. She knew Kendrick was behind this, too, protecting her.

While she was glad she had done it, glad she had saved James, sometimes she woke at night remembering the way Maxwell's flesh had given way beneath the blade. The way the light leaked slowly from his eyes.

But it saved James, and that's all she let herself focus on.

Whenever Douglas visited, he shut the news off.

Douglas was great company, but she missed James. She wanted his company so badly it hurt almost as much as her healing wounds did.

Dr. Wright gave her strict instructions while she was being discharged. No heavy lifting, no straining her abdominal muscles, a careful easing back into her regular diet because of the surgery she'd undergone. "And absolutely no sex until after your six-week follow-up." A glimmer of something in her eyes. All the nurses and other hospital staff were rabidly curious about her relationship with James Kane. She didn't comment on any of it.

Emma's face grew hot. Of *course* the doctor said that in front of Douglas. She wanted to melt into the floor.

"Um, no worries on that front," she stammered. Even if she'd wanted to–and who was she kidding, she had always wanted him that way–James was avoiding her like the plague.

The doctor forced her to sit in a wheelchair to be taken out front by a friendly nurse. Emma was secretly glad about it. If she had been standing, she probably would have fallen over when she saw James waiting for her by his car.

"Hi," he said. He rubbed the back of his neck with one hand. Douglas had, thankfully, brought her some comfortable clothes from her closet to change into. So at least her bare ass wasn't hanging out of a hospital gown. As if she needed to be any more embarrassed in front of James Kane.

"They need me to go over some of your paperwork, Emma," said Douglas from behind her. He patted her shoulder. "I'll take a taxi when I'm finished."

She *strongly* suspected he was lying. And based on his face, James did too.

The nurse helped her up, bid her good luck and kissed her cheek, and ogled James on her way inside. Emma knew for a fact that James was about to be the subject of discussion inside the hospital. Every time he visited–or rather, lurked–the nurses whispered and giggled about him. They asked Emma point blank if she and James were dating. She hadn't needed to lie. The answer was no.

James opened the car door for her. She crouched to get in and grunted when the movement pulled at her stitches and her ribs. He took her arm and helped her gently lower herself into the seat. She wanted, more than anything, to lean into his warmth.

As he pulled away from the hospital, she said, "How the fuck did you fight a bunch of people after getting stabbed?" She grumbled a bit to herself as she looked out of the window.

"I didn't have major surgery. Or broken ribs," James pointed out. "You were–" He gripped the steering wheel so hard it creaked. She heard the unspoken words. *Almost dead*. She'd heard that quite a bit over the last ten days. *A miracle*, they said. *A fighter*, they called her. *Lucky*, they murmured every time they looked at her chart.

She desperately wanted to change the subject. "Hey, did I ever tell you that you were trending on social media after the gala?" James stayed silent, so she pressed on. "James you, that is. Not just...the Phantom. Apparently you're the city's most eligible bachelor." She wiggled her eyebrows.

Still nothing. But the tension in the car lightened. God, what she wouldn't give to make him laugh. Smile. *Anything*. Something other than this...this forced stoicism.

As the gate of Kane Manor opened before them, she said, "So, Douglas was full of shit, right? I know you already paid the bill." She had asked one of the nurses that morning if they needed her insurance card. She planned to have Douglas bring it with her stuff when he picked her up. But they promptly informed her that Mr. Kane had already put a credit card on file and taken care of everything. The thought of it made her stomach clench painfully, but she really didn't have the money to pay for extensive surgery and an extended hospital stay, so she told herself to be grateful and move on.

James gave a humorless laugh. "Yeah, he was. Meddlesome old man."

She twisted her mouth to hide her smile. "He's not so bad."

James flashed a smile at her, so quick it was practically a trick of the light. She was suddenly dizzy. She couldn't remember the last time he smiled at her.

Actually, yes, she could. When they were dancing at the gala.

She desperately wanted him to do it again.

He pulled into the garage and was at her door before she could get herself out of the seat. She gratefully took his arm. Maybe leaned into him a little longer than necessary. He kept a hand on her elbow as she carefully climbed the few steps to the door and into the kitchen.

She hurried over to the coffeemaker as quickly as she could. "Oh, I missed you," she cooed to the machine. She immediately set about fixing herself a cup of coffee. The machine purred as it percolated, as if happy to see her. Or so she imagined. Even the to-go cups Douglas brought her from places outside the hospital couldn't compare to her own coffee.

When she turned around, she caught James smiling at her. Her heart jumped in her chest. She imagined taking a snapshot with her mind and tucked the memory away for later.

Her smile faded. *Now or never*, she thought. Douglas made sure they had this opportunity to talk.

"I missed you too, you know," she said. "Kind of rude not to visit me in the hospital."

James rubbed the back of his neck again. "I did visit," he said defensively.

She rolled her eyes. "You lurked. *Douglas* visited."

He had no excuse, and he knew it. The machine behind her beeped. She was too excited for her coffee to continue the conversation until she'd had at least a sip.

A couple of minutes later, Emma faltered at the bottom step of the stairs. She'd never realized how much she used her ab muscles when climbing steps. Or how much getting stabbed sucked. She cradled her coffee in both hands and took another sip to cover her hesitation.

The first step wasn't too bad. Neither was the second. But by the fourth step, her stitches were pulling uncomfortably.

James's hand found her waist. "Are you okay?" he asked softly. She turned and looked down at him, two steps below her. She studied the angles of his cheekbones, the soft fall of his hair, the curl of his long lashes. She wanted to kiss him. Kiss him until he saw how much she loved him. Until he saw that she didn't mind dying, not if it was to save him. Until he saw that she didn't care that it was his hands that hurt her. Until he saw that she had forgiven him before it even happened.

"Yes," she lied. "Almost spilled my coffee." She took another hurried sip, so he didn't realize she was actually taking a break.

James scooped her into his arms with ease. She squeaked in surprise and really did almost spill her coffee.

"Hey!" she said indignantly.

She couldn't think this close to him. He was so warm. So alive. His heart was beating almost in her ear. She gave in to the urge to rest her head on him. He tensed but didn't stop walking. The masculine scent of him was intoxicating. Her nose rubbed against the smooth skin of his neck. He'd shaved in the days since she'd woken up. She wanted to cry so suddenly that her breath shook a little. James glanced down at her, probably assuming she was in pain.

Even in the hospital, the nightmares had found her.

But she hadn't been able to just go downstairs and make sure James was okay. While she was still on a heart monitor, the night nurse had repeatedly checked on her. Told her that PTSD was normal after traumatizing situations.

It wasn't herself she was worried about. It was always James.

She bit her lip to keep the tears at bay.

He made her feel safe. Even now, even after everything. She wished she could convey that to him.

James set her down on her bed and made sure her coffee was secure as he did so. She set it on the nightstand and snatched his hand before he could leave.

"Please don't shut me out," she whispered. Her eyes closed briefly against the sting of tears.

"I'm not," he said, but it was a lie. His face was already closed off to her.

"That night, you said–you said we could talk later. This is late enough, right?" She hated the pleading note in her voice.

"I–It wasn't anything important," James said, but that was a lie too. He didn't look her in the eyes when he said it.

"Jamie, wait–" she said, but he was gone.

She cursed into the empty room.

That night she woke near dawn with a scream in her throat from the same nightmare she'd had most frequently since the night of the gala. She was straddling James in that conference room. It was *her* hands pushing the blade into *his* stomach. Watching him die. Watching him choke on his own blood. Her subconscious remembered exactly how it felt to be under the influence of that drug, and it never hesitated to remind her that it did.

Sometimes he was the Phantom underneath her blade. Usually, he was just James. She watched the light go out in his eyes, again and again. Watched as blood spread across his tuxedo or his armor.

It was worse because she was feeling the same pain he experienced. He had actually *done* that to her. She didn't know how to fix that pain for him. Didn't know how to save him from it. Every night, her heart broke for him.

She tried to go back to sleep, but the pain in her side kept her awake. Finally, she drifted off again.

The dream shifted.

In this dream, James took her home after their slow dance as if it were a date and nothing more. He pressed her against his bedroom door and let his hands explore her skin through the slit of her dress while he kissed her. She had gotten her wish, and let his bowtie float to the floor and watched as her hands slowly undid the buttons of his shirt.

She woke covered in sweat with her legs pressed together, and angrier than she'd been in a long time.

Cursing, she somehow fumbled her way out of bed despite the pain in her side, her anger fueling her.

James wasn't in his bed when she finally emerged downstairs. She frowned at the empty room as if it itself had offended her.

She turned to the door across the hall and punched in the code.

James was standing shirtless before a workstation in his armored pants and boots. The mask was next to the computer. The screen showed a gloved fist hitting a man over and over. James was scribbling something on a paper as he watched.

The table he was at was the only one left. Every other table had been…smashed. Several computers, too. The weapons rack. The motorcycle was on one side, a side mirror and its taillight broken. She gaped at the destruction for a minute before her anger refocused.

The set of his shoulders said he'd heard her and was ignoring her.

God, she was so *pissed off* that he was shirtless. It only made matters worse. Her dream flashed in her mind, and she wanted to snarl her rage at his bare back.

"James," she said. Not *Jamie*. He continued writing. The video played on. "If you don't talk to me I'm going to–I don't know, put itching powder in your armor. Paint your mask pink. I don't know! Look at me."

She was angry and didn't quite know why. But it had been building and building beneath her skin.

She stalked over to him and pushed him, hard. He didn't even budge, which further pissed her off. She tried again.

He turned abruptly and caught her wrist. "What are you doing?" he demanded. "You shouldn't be out of bed."

"Oh, *now* I get a response?"

The look in his eyes was all Phantom. All predator.

"If you don't stop brooding, so help me–" She couldn't think of another threat. Not when he was looking at her like that. Like he was…so detached. Like he wasn't even James anymore. There was a sharp pain in her chest at that look.

She pressed her hand flat against his sternum. He grabbed her other wrist but didn't move her hand away.

"You could rip your stitches," he said, finally softening, if only slightly.

"He speaks!" she said triumphantly. He gave a small smile that quickly vanished into a frown.

"Let's go back–"

"If you tell me to go back to bed I'm going to punch you." She balled her fist up threateningly even though he still held both of her wrists. "I'm not going anywhere until you stop being so–so–I don't know, *broody.*"

"I'm not brooding," he said. "I'm working."

"You're brooding, and it's because you almost killed me."

He flinched as if she had hit him.

"Go ahead," she said. "Feel bad about it. It sucked. Is that what you want? Me to never forgive you? Me to hate you? To call you a bad man? A murderer?" His breaths turned to short gasps. Something flickered in his eyes. Pain. Guilt. Something else. She kept pressing. Poked a finger into his chest. "Fine. You're an asshole, I hate you, and I wish you would die."

His eyes narrowed. He was trembling. His chest heaved.

"Oh, is that *not* what you wanted to hear?" she continued scathingly. Her voice pitched higher than normal, and she was breathing as heavily as he was. The anger rose within her. Her mind swirled between memories of his face above her as he stabbed her, and his dreamed face as she stabbed him. "Fine, how about the truth? It wasn't your fault. There's nothing to forgive. There never will be. I don't hate you, so you can't hate yourself. In fact, you big, dumb, stubborn asshole, *I still love you.*"

She glared at him. They were matching each other breath for breath. He opened his mouth. She jabbed her finger into his chest again.

"No! I'm not done. Since you're finally *listening.* I don't care if you–if you feel differently. If you see me as a friend. Or as just an employee. The Phantom's partner. I don't care! Even if it's–fucking crazy! Because I'm in love with you, and I want you to know that you are still worth being loved. I don't care what you've done. You're a good man. Nothing will change that in my eyes. Do you get that? *Nothing.* You fucking stabbed me and I *still fucking love you!*" To her horror, a tear slipped out. She wiped an angry hand across her face and stared at James.

He shoved away from her and ran shaking hands through his already mussed hair. He paced over to where the motorcycle rested on its side. He picked it up and set it upright.

"I almost *killed you*." His voice was anguished, broken. It was an echo of what he'd said that first day at the hospital.

She walked over to him. Again, she stood in front of him, forcing him to look at her. She put her hands on either side of his face. "I don't care," she said. "It wasn't your fault. It wasn't you."

"I'm not a good man, Emma," he whispered. He pulled away from her. A tear traced a track through the blackness of the makeup. A pang went through her chest at the sight of him crying. "I went to the jail to kill the Wolf. While you were in the hospital."

The words caught her by surprise. "But you didn't," she said with conviction. "You *are* a good man. In your heart, you're a good man. Even good men do bad things sometimes."

"You don't get it. I'm no good for you. You deserve someone who is *good*. Not someone…*angry* like I am. Someone who won't put you in–"

"Stop it!" she said sharply. She grabbed his face again. "Look at me." Reluctantly, he did. "I have seen the darkest parts of you, James Kane. And I am not afraid. I have seen the worst parts of you and I am still *right here*. I'm angry too. I have been just as complicit as you have in all of this. I killed Lionel Maxwell."

He shook his head vehemently. Closed his eyes. "No," he said. "You're not like me at all, Emma. You're too good."

"I love you," she said. "I don't care if you don't feel the same way about me, I want you to know that. You make me feel *safe*."

The words shuddered through him like a ripple through still water. "You shouldn't."

"When have I ever listened to you?" she asked with a small smile. Her heart squeezed for him. His mouth twisted in a humorless smile. "I love you, even though you're impossible. And stubborn. You have to stop blaming yourself. I'm *alive*."

"Don't you get it?" he said. His voice broke. "Don't you see? I love you and I *almost killed you*." His hands pressed flat against her back. He was shaking against her. "All these people I've been trying to save, and I would have let all of them die to save you."

Her breath caught in her throat.

She kissed him. Hungrily, like it was her last act on earth.

He kissed her back. Pressed her against the table and splayed his fingers against her back. She tasted salt on her lips.

James groaned and pulled away. "I can't," he whispered. "Every time I look at you, I see your blood on my hands. I can't do this."

He loved her. He loved her, and he had almost killed her, and that knowledge was killing him. Things suddenly became so much clearer to her. She closed her eyes and touched her lips. He loved her. *He loved her.*

"Jamie," she said. He pointedly turned away from her. "Jamie, you can't just–" The words caught in her throat. *You can't just turn my whole world upside down and act like you didn't.*

"Please," he said in a broken voice. "I can't do this. Not now."

She would not let him shut her out. She walked to him and pressed a hand to his bare back. Traced one of the scars there with her thumb. "I don't care. Please look at me."

It took a long, long moment, but he did. She rested her hand on his chest. His heart beat steadily underneath her palm. "Emma," he murmured, her name a prayer on his lips. He closed his eyes.

"Look at me," she said. "I'm alive. There's no blood on your hands. There's nothing I need to forgive you for." His green eyes met hers. "I can't believe you almost killed me and didn't tell me all of this sooner, you fucking jerk."

He let out a soft noise but didn't smile.

"Jamie, I killed a man." It washed over her. She'd been pushing it down and down and down, not letting the thought rise to haunt her. Not when she had so much else to worry about. But she had killed Lionel Maxwell to save herself, to save James. "I killed a man," she said again. "And here you are, beating yourself up over almost killing me when it wasn't even your fault. If anything, *I'm* no good for *you.*"

He pulled her closer, achingly gentle so as not to cause her pain. He inhaled shakily. "I don't care," he said. "I should care, but I don't. Not when it's–not when it's you."

"Don't you get it, then?" she said softly. She poured all of her love into her gaze as she looked at him. "That's what I feel about you. *I don't care about any of it.*"

His breath left him in a rush. She could see it in his eyes, the moment he realized what she was saying, the moment it sank in for him. He pressed his forehead to hers. "I'm sorry," he whispered. He was staring at her with something like wonder.

"You have nothing to be sorry for. Except for maybe not telling me that you loved me sooner." She brushed her lips across his. She closed her eyes. "Do you mean it? Because I'm going to be so pissed off if you don't."

He huffed a laugh and then groaned. "*Yes.*"

Emma kissed him.

He made a desperate noise against her mouth before releasing her.

She growled. He laughed. "You're not cleared for physical activity, remember?"

She made a face and then tugged his lips back down to hers. She kissed him hungrily, desperately. He clutched her hips tightly, still being so careful not to hurt her.

He pulled away with his eyes still closed. He rested his forehead on hers. "Every time you touch me, it's like–like I'm on fire," he breathed. "It's too much. It's not enough."

She pressed her hands firmly against his back. "I thought you didn't want me, all those times you didn't want me to touch you," she said. "But I couldn't make myself stop wanting you."

"I never said I didn't want you," he said. He kissed her again. Hard and desperate. "That night you first kissed me–" He groaned as her hands slid up over his ribs and around his neck. Tangled in his hair. "–I wanted it to be your choice, wholly your choice. Not because you were upset at work, or because you were drunk. I have *never* stopped wanting you."

He carefully stepped away from her. "I'm sorry," he said softly. "I want you. Trust me, I do. But you just got out of the hospital, Em."

Em. A completely different sensation swooped through her insides. Her mother and Kendrick were the only ones who ever called her that.

She loved hearing it from James Kane's lips.

"I'm so mad at you," she said instead of anything else on her mind. He went very immediately still. "I'm so *mad* we could have already been doing this. And now I had stupid surgery and have to *wait.*"

He laughed softly and tugged her closer to him. "I'm sorry," he said into her hair.

"I'm serious, I hate you," she mumbled against him.

"You're going to hate me more because you really should go back to bed," he said. And then he scooped her into his arms again without warning.

"Asshole," she said, reminiscing about the first time he'd taken her to the roof outside the club as the Phantom. "You get off on that, don't you?"

He gave her a wide smile as he maneuvered them into the elevator but didn't answer.

"You totally do," she muttered, but she was smiling too.

They fell into an easy silence as the elevator made its way upstairs. Before she knew it, James was gently putting her in *his* bed, his lips brushing her forehead, his hand squeezing hers comfortingly.

When he straightened, she grabbed his hand. "Will you stay with me?" she asked quietly.

"Let me just shower," he said softly. "I'll be right back." She nodded, and he leaned down to kiss her. "I promise."

True to his word, James was back in less than ten minutes, but Emma was already asleep.

CHAPTER THIRTY-TWO

JAMES

James watched Emma sleeping peacefully next to him and wondered how he had gotten so lucky.

He never expected Emma to return his feelings. That someone so *good* would, or even could, love him back. That she would love him so deeply she didn't even care that he had almost killed her.

They'd found an easy rhythm with each other over the past several weeks. She fully moved in to his bedroom with her stuff in the dresser and her quilt on his bed. She'd become more nocturnal, too, both of them staying up late and sleeping through the day. She stayed up and waited for him to get back each night from being the Phantom.

And she told him she loved him every single day.

Her warm brown eyes slowly blinked open. She smiled at him, a secret, sleepy smile that made his chest ache with affection.

"I'm sorry," he whispered. "I couldn't fall asleep. I didn't mean to wake you."

"What are you thinking about?" she murmured. She was naked in his bed, the pair of them tangled together like they had been every night so far. Memories from the night before came back to him in a rush.

James blushed. "What are you thinking about?" he countered. There was a glint of something in her eyes.

"I–Nothing," she said, too quickly. It wasn't too dark for her to see the quirk of his brow as it raised. She sighed. "I was remembering the night those men broke in."

James's heart stuttered. Oh. He flushed for an entirely different reason. "I don't–we never talked about that. I'm sorry if I scared you. I know it's–It's one thing to see the Phantom do that, but me?" He trailed off, uncertain. He closed his eyes. Because really, how could she be okay with the violence within him? The darkness? The insecurity washed over him, cold and painful. How could she be okay with it after what he'd done to *her*?

When he opened his eyes again, he frowned.

Was Emma…blushing?

"What?" he asked. Every time he saw her thinking something and couldn't decipher it, it drove him mad. And it happened often. Too often.

Emma coughed delicately. "You didn't scare me," she said. She wouldn't look him in the eye.

"Then what?" he asked, trying his hardest to keep the impatience and vague panic from his voice. *Why* was she thinking about *that* night?

"I…God, this is embarrassing. I was just thinking about how…hot…it was." She grimaced and covered her face with her hands. She rolled onto her back with an embarrassed groan.

James's mind was utterly blank. She found it…hot? "Hot?" he said aloud, unsure that he'd heard right.

"Um. Yes. I know, I'm a freak, but seeing you fight–" She stopped. Swallowed. Kept her face covered. "It was–hot. Alright? Sue me."

Emotion swelled in his chest. He reached over and tugged her hands off of her face so he could look at her.

She wasn't shying away from his violence like he'd feared.

The exact opposite, in fact. It was hard to breathe. Hard to think. She was *attracted* to it?

He had to admit, there was a certain allure to seeing her fight, too, as much as he was always simultaneously terrified for her safety. When they sparred, there was something about her that drew his eye. Her focus. Her intensity. And seeing her in a real fight had been no different. She was purposeful in her movements, powerful. The fear always mixed with a certain appreciation for the way she moved and the ferocity with which she fought.

He wanted to tell her he thought she was hot too. That, that night, he had gotten so close to killing those men, all to protect her. That he would do it for her, and do it gladly.

That hearing her say she was *attracted* to it was the best news he'd ever heard.

He had to try. He was bad at speaking his feelings aloud, but for her he wanted to try. "I'd do anything for you," he said. There. The simplest way he could put it. Nothing to fuck up with something that simple. "I bought you a coffee maker because you love coffee. I follow you *everywhere* to make sure you're safe. I–I would kill for you. I have gotten so close to–" He stopped. Swallowed. "I've always been crazy about you."

"The coffee maker really should have been the clue," she teased as she rolled out of bed. His eyes greedily traced the lines of her bare skin as she wandered over to their dresser.

"You let me drive your superhero car," she pointed out. "That's a big clue too."

"*Let* you?" He raised an eyebrow. "As I recall, I was passed out the first time. The second time you stole it."

Emma grinned. "Okay, fair point." She dug around until she found a faded Nirvana t-shirt. She laughed when she saw it, then put it on.

"Make yourself at home," James muttered sarcastically. But he smiled.

Her voice was casual as she pulled on a pair of shorts next. "I've been meaning to ask…What happened downstairs? It's been wrecked for weeks."

James's blood went abruptly cold. He stared up at the ceiling.

He remembered that night clearly. Too clearly. The blood on his hands. The rage. The pain. The guilt.

"I–" He couldn't form the words. "It's nothing."

She made a noise that told him she knew he was full of shit. "Didn't look like nothing."

James sighed. "When I thought you were–" He still couldn't say it. *Dead.* The word stuck in his throat. He grunted in frustration and fisted his hands in the sheets.

"Oh," she said with so much love and understanding in her gaze that he suddenly wanted to cry. "You freaked out."

He made a small noise of affirmation but said nothing else.

She sat on the edge of the bed and scooted closer to him. She grabbed one of his hands and placed it over her chest, where he could feel her heart beating steadily beneath his palm.

"I'm right here," she whispered. "And I'm not going anywhere."

Did she know how much he needed those words? How terrified he still was of losing her? How glad he was that somehow, by some miracle, she was here next to him, loving him, her heart beating?

Slowly, very slowly, he relaxed. He let out a long breath.

God, he loved her. He wanted to take her on a date. He wanted to do everything right, everything she deserved. He wanted to–

The thought hit him so hard it was like a physical blow. He couldn't help the hitch in his breathing.

He wanted to marry her.

It was too soon for that, he knew. But…maybe one day. Maybe, soon, they could talk about all of that. And if she didn't want it–that was fine. He just wanted to be with her. Always.

He would start with a date first, see how that went.

"You know," she said thoughtfully. His heart stuttered like she could hear his thoughts. "Douglas knew all along. How you felt."

James laughed, slightly relieved she *hadn't* heard his thoughts. "Yeah. He's known for a while."

Her expression was still pensive. "He dropped a lot of hints, didn't he? Because he knew how I felt too. Ever since–" She stopped and looked away.

The curiosity was going to eat him alive. "Since what?" he finally asked, unable to stand it.

"I don't know when *exactly* I, um, fell in love with you but…Douglas definitely knew I had a crush on you since at least…after the Wolf beat me." The last words fell flat.

Familiar anger rose within him. Sometimes, in moments like these, he regretted walking away from that prison.

Emma watched all the emotions play across his face. She gently touched jaw, grounding him.

Her words sank into his mind. "Since then?" he asked, surprised. She had liked him for that long. That was *ages* ago. His limbs warmed all over again, affection flowing through him like warm sunlight after a cold rain.

"Well. Yeah. I mean–I've had a crush on you basically since I met you. And…" She was embarrassed again. His eyes searched her face greedily for what she was embarrassed about. She didn't let him suffer long. "I used to always watch videos of the Phantom. Before we met." She shrugged.

He smiled. "I think it goes without saying that I've *always* had a crush on you," he murmured.

But it was true. It had taken him all of ten minutes of knowing her to fall hard and fast.

That night, the night they'd first met, she'd said *let me help you.*
And he was a goner.

EMMA

The sharp edges of her nightmare were already beginning to fade when Emma woke with a start. She was getting used to them. Too used to them. She rarely went without them, but had learned to manage it.

Her cheek was stuck to James's bare chest, his arm curled around her protectively.

They had fallen asleep again after talking for a while. She was still in the soft Nirvana shirt, but had lost her shorts. Her sleep schedule was a lost cause at this point, she mused as she watched James sleep for a moment.

His brow furrowed.

Unable to help herself, she reached out and gently smoothed away the line.

His eyes fluttered open. He blinked and seemed to finally focus on her.

"Sorry," she whispered. "I didn't mean to wake you."

He looked away from her, tense and breathing heavily.

She frowned and reached for him again. He flinched away from her. "Jamie?" He still wouldn't look at her.

"Did you have a nightmare?" she asked. He glanced at her from the corners of his eyes and nodded. "You can tell me about it if you want."

He didn't move. So she simply waited. She might prefer physical comfort after her nightmares, but he usually didn't. She'd learned that in the weeks they had spent together after her release from the hospital, and she felt a little thrill at the fact that she got to know something like that about him.

After several minutes, he relaxed slightly. "I'm okay," he finally murmured. He reached for her and rubbed a hand down her arm before lacing their fingers together. His other hand went flat against her bare stomach. His fingers gently traced the line of her scar.

His breath shuddered against her neck. She could feel his heart thundering against her back.

His shaky inhale gave him away.

She grabbed his hand and guided it to her chest. Let him feel her heart beating there.

"I'm okay," she murmured to him. "I'm alive. I'm here."

His hand pressed against her chest. There was the slightest tremble to it.

"I love you," she whispered, in case he had forgotten. She would spend every night reminding him of that. She would ease every nightmare he had with the words. She would make sure he always knew she felt safe with him.

His hand pressed against the scar on her abdomen. Emma frowned down at it and traced it with a finger. "We match," she said. She reached over and touched the scar from where Lionel Maxwell had stabbed him. It was in almost the same exact spot as her own scar. Though hers was longer and more puckered, uglier. The doctor had chastised her for yanking the blade out, but she didn't care about an ugly scar. Or almost dying. All she cared about was the fact that she had saved James.

She watched as his expression shuttered closed.

"No," she said. She poked his stomach until he opened his eyes again. "Don't do that. Don't feel guilty. Our scars show that we survived." To prove her point, she touched the scar on her forehead. The scar on the other side of his abdomen, from when they'd first met. "I wouldn't trade them for anything," she told him firmly. Poked him again until his lips twitched upwards, just slightly.

"I'm trying," he finally said. His green eyes still held a hint of sadness. "It's–It's hard. I think of all the things I could have done differently–"

"Don't," she said. "You can't change anything. And everything we did, every mistake we made, brought us here. Granted, we probably could have been doing *this* a lot sooner, but…" She grinned. "At least we get to do it. And I really do mean *do it*."

He laughed softly. *Mission accomplished*, she thought. "I wish we had started sooner, too," he said. He scooted closer and wrapped an arm around her middle. "Though we were a bit busy solving murders and saving New Atlas."

"And repeatedly getting injured. I can't believe neither of us are dead, actually," she said.

James tensed and then relaxed. "You're too stubborn to let either of us die."

She grinned. "Probably," she said with a shrug. "Though you're just as stubborn as I am. Kidnapping people after getting stabbed, etcetera."

"You're the one who fought off armed men after getting shot in the head." There was a tightness in his eyes, but she appreciated his effort to joke about the hard things with her. How else were they going to cope?

"I was amazing, wasn't I?"

James laughed again. "You scared me shitless, driving through that door. I told myself you were safe, but–"

"But I never listen to you, do I?" she finished for him. She smirked, then added, "Unless it's in the bedroom. I can be a *very* good listener in the bedroom."

James pulled her closer to him. She curled into his chest. "Are you really so insatiable?" he asked.

Emma hummed happily. "Yes," she said. "I think my feelings for you have always been *very* clear, actually. I've wanted you very badly since–well, really since the first time I saw you shirtless. You drove me *crazy*. Probably before that, though, if I'm being honest."

"I'm yours," he said. "I've always been yours."

"I lied earlier," she said into the warmth of his chest. The room around them was cold, but she was perfectly content where she was. "I think I was in love with you when you fell out of the sky."

James gave a surprised laugh. "I was pushed off of a roof, actually," he said. "A burglary suspect caught me off guard."

Emma let out a peal of laughter. She laughed so hard her still-healing abdomen hurt. "Are you–" She had to stop and laugh again. "Are you fucking kidding me? You were pushed off the roof?"

James tightened his grip on her. "*Yes*, I was pushed off of a roof," he sighed. "In my defense, I did have the knife wound at that point already. I'd been hit in the head with a bat, too."

She laughed some more and had to wriggle to fit her arms between them so she could wipe the tears from her eyes. "Oh man, I can't fucking believe it. Pushed off a roof." She laughed harder.

James chuckled, the sound rumbling in his chest against her ear. "I *never* should have admitted to that."

"Nope," she said cheerfully. "I promise I'll bring it up often. Though I would like to find that guy and thank him, though, since he introduced us."

Emma had never been so happy. She had no idea what time it was, and she didn't care. It could have been the middle of the night, or it could have been noon. But she had nowhere to be other than James Kane's arms.

Eventually, hunger drove her from the bed. James followed her lead as they both dressed and headed for the kitchen.

Her phone informed her that it was actually one in the afternoon, not breakfast time. She was already halfway nocturnal because of him.

"How about omelets?" she asked. She was feeling nostalgic after hearing the story behind their first meeting, and omelets were the first thing she had made for him.

"You don't have to cook anything."

"I want to," she said, slowing her steps until they were side by side. She took his hand and smiled up at him. "I like cooking for you."

He squeezed her hand and gave her a soft smile in return. His eyes were bright, the bags under them much less pronounced than usual. "Fine. But only because I know it's useless to argue with you."

"He learns fast!" Emma joked. She pulled him along into the kitchen, where Douglas was sitting at the island with a newspaper and the remnants of his lunch. James tugged his hand out of hers as if embarrassed. Emma raised a brow at him disbelievingly and took his hand again, kissing him right there in front of Douglas.

When she pulled away, James's cheeks were pink.

"Douglas's been meddling, remember?" she asked. "Also, we've been living in the same room for *weeks*."

"You're not very sneaky, James. Never have been," Douglas said without looking up from his newspaper. She glimpsed the edge of his bright smile behind the pages. "Besides, you two dancing around each other forever was about to make me resort to drastic measures."

Emma choked on a laugh as she went to the fridge for the ingredients she'd need.

"What kind of drastic measures?" she asked with genuine curiosity as she got out a bowl, whisk, and pan.

"I had decided to conveniently lock you two in a room together somehow," Douglas said. He snapped the newspaper shut. There was a glint of mischief in his eyes. "I have an extra master key that I was going to break off in the lock, since I know James can pick them."

James looked like he wanted to sink through the floor.

A surprised laugh burst from Emma's lips. *"Really?"*

Douglas shrugged. "Desperate times. Like I said, you two circling each other was getting tiresome, even for me. I thought I would die of old age first."

Emma glanced at James and couldn't help but grin. She mixed the ingredients for the omelets and said, "I think James would rather jump out of a window naked than have to talk about his feelings." Douglas laughed while James gave her a withering stare.

James sighed and muttered something about being ganged up on.

Emma was so happy her chest hurt. Douglas patted her shoulder on his way by. From the corner of her eye, she saw him stop beside James and whisper something. She couldn't hear what he said, but James's cheeks turned pink again and he reached out and squeezed Douglas's arm with a nod.

"What did he say to you?" she asked James a few minutes later as they sat at the kitchen island to eat. "Sorry, you don't have to tell me if you don't want to."

James took a bite first. She started eating, too, accepting that he wasn't going to answer. It wasn't her business anyway. Then, "He said to remember what he told me in the hospital."

"Oh?" she said. She didn't want to pry in case he didn't want to tell her, even though she burned with curiosity.

"He'd told me…that I deserved someone like you. That I was worth your love. That I was good enough for you."

Emma's heart warmed further, if that was even possible. She reached over and put a hand on his shoulder. "You are," she told him, voice thick with emotion. "You're so worth it."

He gave her a small smile. They lapsed into a companionable silence. Every few minutes, she would catch James looking at her or vice versa.

"I want to take you on a date," he said later. "A real date."

"Okay," she said a bit skeptically. "Where? When?"

"We can go tonight," he said. "Or whatever you want to do." He went to rub the back of his neck.

"I don't care what we do, as long as I'm with you."

"I just–our only real date wasn't a date," he said. "The gala."

"And it also ended with me almost dying," she said. She nudged him in the side with her elbow so he knew she was making light of it. "Okay then. So let's go on a date."

He smiled then, a real, full smile. She couldn't help it. She grabbed his shirt and kissed him.

So that evening, Emma put on a nice dress and heels and did her makeup and hair. When she came into the kitchen at ten minutes until eight, she found James already waiting for her.

"I changed my mind," she said when she saw him. Her mouth was dry. He was wearing black slacks, a light gray button-up that brought out the color in his eyes, and a black suit jacket. The shirt had a couple of buttons unbuttoned. He looked good. Better than good. She had to admit, she loved when James dressed like the rich man he was. She'd been ready to tear into him the night of the gala, and now was no different. Especially now that she knew what having him was like.

James frowned. "You don't want to go?"

She moved closer to him and tugged him against her by his jacket. "I would much rather stay home," she said in a husky voice.

James swallowed. There was naked desire in his eyes.

She stood on her toes to kiss him but he stepped back. She frowned an exaggerated pout.

"I want to take you on a date," he said firmly.

She sighed. "Okay, fine. But as long as you promise to take me back to your place after."

He grinned. "I promise." He bent and kissed her, giving her a taste of what he was promising. "Let's go. I made reservations."

"You look beautiful, by the way," he said as they got into the car. He held the door for her like a gentleman.

"Careful, James Kane," she told him, an echo of her words to him from months before. "Or I might think you're flirting with me."

He smiled again as they pulled out of the garage. "Oh, I am."

He flashed her another smile, though he blushed. One of his hands came to rest on her bare knee.

He took her to a fancy restaurant that apparently Douglas liked to frequent.

"I don't get out much." He said as they pulled up to the valet. He said it like an apology. "Douglas told me where we should go."

"I don't either," she said. "Like I said, I don't care where we go."

"I want to do this right," he said. "I don't want all of our dates to end with one of us bleeding."

"That's fair." She smirked, but it faded quickly as another thought struck her. "You do realize that we'll end up on social media, right? And paparazzi might show up? If you're not okay with that, it's okay. Don't be uncomfortable just because you want to take me on a date."

"I don't care," he said. He turned to look her fully in the eyes. "I want to show you off." She shivered at the words.

Inside, they were led to a small, private table with a bottle of wine already waiting.

The restaurant was beautiful. It was a few floors up, with a brilliant view of New Atlas spread before them. There was a fake trellis on the ceiling, complete with honest-to-God vines and low, golden lighting. It was, she admitted to herself, pretty magical.

The dinner was exceptionally good, though she didn't care about the food as much as she would have thought. She hadn't had many opportunities to taste things made by professional chefs at starred restaurants—and hoped to have more experiences—but she couldn't help but be distracted by her date.

She reached under the table and squeezed his thigh. She was rewarded by him spilling his water as his eyes flicked to hers. She smiled serenely at him.

They talked idly about various things—Douglas and his meddling, the inevitable trial that would come from everything, the research Katherine Kane had done on the Wolf adding to several more criminal charges. Emma had also heard through the grapevine that an anonymous person had recently bought the Crescent Club. James said nothing, simply shrugged and moved on.

Finally, Emma worked up the courage to say what had been weighing on her mind all night. "I want to be your partner," she blurted before she could think better of it.

"I thought we were partners." James set his fork down and furrowed his dark brows. "With the…date and everything."

She couldn't help but laugh. "Yes we're partners, but I mean…like Kendrick is your partner."

James's head snapped up, and his eyes met hers. She stood her ground and said, "I don't want you to answer right now, because I know it'll be no. But just think about it. You can–you can teach me to fight more, get me kevlar, a suit of my own…I don't know. I want to help. Even if I just sit and watch the live feed from the lens in case you need help, or go over files. You can't do everything by yourself." The words left her in a rush.

James was still frowning. She knew how he was thinking–that she'd been in danger enough already, that he could handle himself just fine, that the idea wasn't worth considering.

"Please just think about it," she said, tone softer now. She fiddled with the cloth napkin on her lap. "Because I know you don't want to stop helping the city, and I would never ask you to. I want to *help*."

Several minutes later, he said, "Alright. I'll think about it."

She had to resist the urge to pump her fist in the air and instead smiled. "Maybe we could…start sparring again regularly either way? Just so I can stay in shape."

Emma didn't want to be helpless again, and she swore to herself she wouldn't be. She wanted to be strong, capable. Someone James didn't have to worry over. Someone who could always hold her own, just in case.

"Okay," he said, and smiled a genuine smile that had her heart flipping in her chest.

They spent the rest of their date talking and laughing. She had never seen James smile so much in one night. Out of curiosity, Emma stole the bill when it came and blanched at the amount.

"I have to say, sometimes I forget how *rich* you are." She tried to laugh it off. They'd talked at length about her insecurities, about how imbalanced she felt with him, but he'd soothed her fears. Sometimes, though, they reared their heads.

"I'm not that rich," he mumbled.

She snorted. "I'm pretty sure every year you're listed as the *wealthiest* and most eligible bachelor in New Atlas."

"Not anymore," he said, suddenly no longer shy. *His* hand found *her* thigh under the table. Was he trying to distract her? Because it was working. "What's mine is yours."

Her face heated. "If you don't take me home right now, I don't think we'll get invited back to this restaurant again."

She would never get tired of the look in James's eyes.

He paid the check and they were headed home within minutes. He held her hand as he sped through traffic.

She couldn't help but laugh. At his questioning look, she said, "You're driving like the Phantom."

He grinned and accelerated to punctuate the thought.

They were kissing the moment they were out of the car. She kicked off her heels in the kitchen and grabbed James by the lapels of his jacket. He backed her against the kitchen island and hoisted her up onto it with ease. Her dress bunched around her waist.

"I remember this," she said breathlessly. His hands explored her thighs underneath her dress. She unbuttoned his shirt and yanked at it. "But if you stop this time, I'm going to scream."

He laughed against her neck.

"Anything you want," he swore, and lifted her into his arms. He carried her back to his bedroom and did as she'd asked.

They stayed wrapped together until the middle of the night.

It was the best date she'd ever had.

EPILOGUE

The newspaper headline glared up at Emma as she tugged on her mask.

JAMES KANE TO WED

She smiled at the words as she tucked the ring in question safely under her shirt from its place on a long chain.

It had been his mother's. The second piece of jewelry he had given her. The pearls had been carefully cleaned of her blood and returned to her at the hospital after the gala. Despite the events of said gala, she treasured them.

The ring had been a surprise. It was a simple band with a decently big diamond. Simple, understated. Perfect, like James.

Her heart squeezed happily as she remembered the moment he presented it to her.

He had woken from a nightmare. Kissed her senseless. Told her he loved her with his words and with his touch. Let his tears coat her skin as they moved together in the dark. It happened like that, sometimes, one of them waking in fear and needing touch in order to be reassured.

She made breakfast while he showered. Brought it into the bedroom–*their* bedroom. He had been in a pair of sweatpants and nothing else, water dripping from his hair, when he went to the dresser and turned around and got on one knee, the shock of it so intense she had almost fallen over.

"I wanted to do this better," he had said. He'd stuttered adorably as he continued, "I–I'm no good with saying how I feel. So all I'm going to say is that I love you and want to spend my life with you. Will you marry me?"

She said the words "Are you serious?" about six times before he gently reminded her that he'd asked a question.

The answer was yes, of course.

That was a couple of months ago. She wasn't really sure how the media learned of their engagement, but she didn't really care. She strongly suspected that Douglas told them. He'd beamed like a proud father and immediately gone for their most expensive bottle of champagne and cried when James asked him to be the best man.

Now, the ring was nestled safely near her heart while she got into the armored car and put the key in the ignition.

Emma sighed contentedly as it roared to life.

"Please don't tell me that's what I think it is," James said in her ear. He promised to keep her in the loop these days when he went out as the Phantom. Just in case.

Sometimes she went to help him if he needed it. Sometimes she followed cases of her own, like she was doing now as she sped down the tunnel and out into the streets of New Atlas. They had an agreement now: he trained her whenever he had time, brought her in when he needed help on cases, and had even gotten her a vest and mask to wear, both bulletproof. He made her promise to stay disguised at all times. She'd also had a condition of her own: no capes for her gear.

"I just got a text from that girl Kendra," she said by way of explanation. She met Kendra in a bar about a week before as the girl begged the manager to let her see the security videos from another night. Kendra had been looking for solid evidence that a man had drugged her.

Because she'd been raped.

"Let me–"

"I can handle it," she said firmly. "I'll let you know if I need your help."

The man Emma was after had been doing bad things for months, and *she* wanted to be the one to stop him. Not the Phantom. Sometimes she needed to take matters into her own hands.

Like now.

She had paid the manager at the bar handsomely for the videos that first night, watched them, and then followed Kendra home. She got Kendra's story as they watched the security footage together and then promised to help.

The man she was following was the one who drugged and raped Kendra.

And the more she looked into it, the more managers of bars she had bribed, the more women she found.

Kendra was the fifth.

Kendra would be the last.

Emma and James worked together for months. The arrest of the Wolf and the other men had created a power vacuum. All sorts of terrible criminals started appearing and making grabs for power and territory. Drugs and violent crime were worse than ever. It had been a taxing seven months for New Atlas and for the Phantom, too.

She'd gotten much better at fighting. Had learned which of his weapons she liked best. Had learned she had a deep, deep love of the armored car, while he seemed to prefer the ease of the motorcycle. Her disguise had started simple, just a hood pinned to her hair and a cloth covering the lower half of her face. Sometimes, when she wanted to be funny, she stole James's eye makeup and wore that, too. It always earned her a smile or a rolling of his eyes. Working together gave her the confidence to pursue her own cases, like Kendra.

Plus, the trial was set to start by the end of the year. She would be Mrs. Kane by then. The trial loomed over her like a dark cloud most days, but getting married was the silver lining.

She was finally pursuing a case that mattered to her—because she knew what it was like to be drugged, to have her free will taken away. Not to be raped, but the rest was bad enough.

And it made her angry.

Emma parked behind the bar Kendra sent her the address for. They'd been splitting time staking out the five bars where the man found his victims in an effort to catch him in the act. That night, however, he had done nothing. He'd simply had drinks with friends.

But Emma was going to figure something else out. She was tired of waiting. She didn't want to be too late, like she was with Marie.

The man in question was stumbling drunkenly down the alleyway, singing a pop song she'd heard on the radio just that afternoon.

As he slowly made his way to the neighboring street, Emma closed the gap between them. She raised her crossbow, which was more of an intimidation tactic than an actual weapon, and pounced.

It was too easy to send the man sprawling. To stand on his hand as he scrambled to reach for his phone.

She pointed the crossbow at his face. Then she thought better of it and pointed it at his crotch instead.

"Hello," she said pleasantly. "Enjoying a night out?"

"Who the fuck are you?" the man spat, trying to wriggle away. She stepped on his hand, harder, satisfied at the crack of bones beneath her heavy-duty boots. He shouted and cursed at her, called her a cunt. Nothing new to her.

"I'm someone who does not take kindly to men drugging women." For emphasis, she pressed the point of the arrow down. He went very, very still.

"I mean it," she said, leaning over him, letting the point of the arrow underscore each word. "I do not tolerate men who drug women and rape them." A familiar rage washed over her. She was lucky, extremely lucky, that she'd only been drugged before, not raped. Or murdered. The piece of shit in front of her became the focus of months of anger. Even now, she was haunted by nightmares of everything she'd been through.

She would not let anyone else be a victim.

Emma crouched. Leaving the crossbow aimed where it was, she fumbled around in his pockets. "Don't get excited," she told him, finally freeing his wallet from his front pocket.

She flipped it open, held it so it caught the light of a distant streetlight.

Her breath fogged out before her as she read, "Derrick Smalls. 104 Ridge Court. Ah, the East Side. What are you doing so far from home?" She raised an eyebrow at the man lying on the concrete beneath her. He blinked furiously at her, wiping at the rain on his face with his good hand. "I'm really trying not to make a joke about men with small dicks thinking they need to rape women. Get it? Smalls?"

"What the fuck do you want from me?" the man snarled. He was at least smart enough not to try to get away while there was an arrow threatening his favorite body part.

"I want you to stop drugging and raping women, you asshole!" Emma snapped. "You're really lucky it's me, and not the Phantom, by the way. He'd have already beaten the shit out of you and had one of his cop buddies throw you in jail."

The man glared at her. "You have no proof I did anything! Otherwise you would've tossed me in jail yourself, you cunt!"

Emma leaned down and smiled right in his face. Then she yanked out a tuft of his hair. He shouted. She pressed the point of the arrow into his shoulder this time and kept leaning over him as she said, "I don't have as many hold-ups as our vigilante friend about killing people, you know." She didn't really mean it. The death of Lionel Maxwell still haunted her sometimes. She didn't think she could do it again unless she was under extreme duress, like she had been that night. And even then—now that she knew what it was like to take a life, to truly take a life, she wasn't so sure she could face it again.

Derrick Smalls went still again. "What do you want?" he asked in a more defeated tone.

"All I want is for you to stop drugging and raping women! I've got your DNA now, asshole, and your information. One of the girls remembers you. Hell, maybe they all do, but at least one of them does. If you don't stop, I know where you live. And I might just decide to finish the job myself."

"I'm sorry!" he said, suddenly crying out. "I didn't—I didn't do it!"

Emma sighed. "Now you're trying to play innocent?" She smashed one fist into his face then held him up by his shirt. "Shut up. Stop drugging and raping girls, and this will be the last time you see someone like me. Don't stop….And I might come visit you. Depends on how generous I'm feeling at the time."

There was suddenly a loud burst of laughter at the end of the alley behind her. Emma turned to look, cursing her mistake immediately when Derrick Smalls scrambled away and took off in a dead sprint away from her. All it had taken was a brief distraction, and he was gone.

She sighed. The Phantom wouldn't have made that mistake.

Well, at least she had his DNA now.

She pulled a small plastic bag out of her belt–not as many fun bits and gadgets as James's had, but it served her well–and put the wet chunk of his hair in it.

Once that was safely tucked away, she turned and headed in the opposite direction.

She easily climbed the fire escape of an apartment building several blocks away and knocked on one of the third-floor windows.

Kendra opened it almost immediately. She had tan skin, wildly curly hair, and freckles over every inch of her body.

"Did you get him?" she demanded the second she saw who it was.

"I got his DNA. I'm taking it to my cop friend first thing tomorrow. Lieutenant Kendrick. You can trust him. I'll let him know you're coming and give him the tapes so it's all set up, okay?" Emma reached out with a gloved hand and squeezed Kendra's arm. "If you have second thoughts at all, let me know. Whatever you need. I gave you my number already, so just text or call anytime. Kendrick will make sure this asshole goes to jail. We've got all the evidence we need."

She'd taken another idea of James's and gotten herself a "work" phone for instances like this.

Kendra bit her lip and nodded while looking away. "I–I can't thank you enough. People like you…looking out for people like me…you have no idea how much it means to me."

Emma felt tears prick her eyes. "Trust me," she said thickly. "I used to be in your position. I'm going to do everything I can to stop this kind of stuff."

Kendra nodded. A single tear slipped down her freckled cheek. "Seriously. Thanks. You, um, want coffee or anything? Sorry, I should've invited you in–it's pouring and–"

Emma gave her a genuine smile. "No, that's okay. I gotta–I gotta get home."

"Someone waiting on you?" Kendra asked, but Emma was already slipping back down the fire escape and back into the rainy streets of New Atlas, just another shadow in the night.

"I'm about to meet with Kendrick about another case if you want to bring that by," James said into her ear as the roar of the armored car filled the night air.

"See you there."

Minutes later, she turned towards the dark tower–still only half built. It was close to the old Crescent Club, which was now a halfway house for battered women that was owned by her old coworker Lena.

Emma herself had gotten the charity bug and built a place she named the Atlas Project. It was her pride and joy, and she even hired women from the old club who needed jobs or girls that Lena sent her way from the halfway house. It was an amalgamation of the things she loved: cooking, and helping New Atlas. She also hired newly released (and carefully vetted by Kane Industries' finest private investigators) convicts as waiters, chefs, and hosts. People paid to come eat, or they paid it forward for someone less fortunate to enjoy a good meal. She provided supplies for the needy, too, helped by generous donations, including a *very* generous one from her fiancé.

It was long past the middle of the night when Emma entered the elevator that would take her to the top of the tower, where James and Kendrick were already waiting.

"Are you two partners now?" Kendrick asked with raised eyebrows when she emerged from the elevator together.

"Something like that," Emma said. She had to be very, very careful not to touch James or look at him too lovingly while near Kendrick. He was a detective, after all, and he knew that she was in love with James Kane. If they weren't careful, it wouldn't be hard for him to fit the pieces together that she was in love with the Phantom, too.

"Congratulations on the engagement, by the way," Kendrick said with a flash of a smile. He glanced at James. "Looks like you were too slow, buddy."

Emma couldn't help it. She snorted.

"We're just friends, detective," James said. She could hear the amusement in his voice.

"Lieutenant," Emma corrected him. "Kendrick got a big, fat promotion for all the work he did to root out the corruption in New Atlas."

Kendrick looked…embarrassed. "Yeah, well, I still have lots of work to do, alright? They're sending me over to Meridian City to investigate all that stuff with Christian Reeves and his wife. What did you need me for, Em?"

She grabbed the hair sample from her belt and quickly explained the situation with Derrick Smalls. She also handed him a paper with Kendra's contact information written on it. Kendrick's face clouded over.

"I'll look into it and let you know what I find," he said when she was finished.

"Thank you. Keep your eye out for a wedding invitation, by the way," Emma said with a smile. "We picked a date." She had asked him to walk her down the aisle right after they'd gotten engaged. He'd accepted, of course.

Kendrick winked at her as he got on the elevator. "Good luck with the wedding planning, you two." The elevator doors closed.

James tugged her closer. "Kendrick's invited to our wedding, huh?" he joked.

She smiled. She finally gave in and kissed him, now that Kendrick was gone. "Of course he is. It's a *very* exclusive event, only a select few of our closest friends get to come."

James laughed. She held the sound close to her heart and basked in his joy. She had never loved anything as fiercely as she had loved him. As she loved *all* of him.

"A few?" he asked skeptically.

"Well, a few others from the club wanted to come too. *Not* because you're famous, I might add. Mostly because they're my friends." They had started meeting up after the mysterious benefactor had bought the club–a benefactor who had turned out to be the man she was engaged to. He'd sold it to Lena for five dollars. "And Bryn and Ollie, of course." Bryn, a former employee of the Crescent Club, was the project manager at the Atlas Project and Ollie was her head chef. They had both wiggled their way very thoroughly into Emma's heart in a short amount of time.

James sighed. Kissed her temple. "Invite as many friends as you want."

Emma smiled and hummed thoughtfully. "I wish my mom could come," she said around a sudden lump in her throat.

"Me too," he murmured. "My parents would love you."

"My mom would have figured out faster than me that you were the Phantom," Emma said. James laughed again. She let him pull her close against his side. "Have you seen the paper, by the way?"

James stilled. "No, why?"

"The engagement is public now," she said.

James was quiet for a long moment. "How'd the press get wind of it?" There was a certain tightness in his voice that she didn't miss.

She knew he hated putting her in the spotlight–hated either of them being in the spotlight–but she couldn't help the little thrill she got thinking of the announcement being splashed across New Atlas. He was *hers*, and now everyone knew it.

"Oh, I have a feeling it was a certain meddlesome old man."

They both laughed. James tucked her closer and brushed his lips across her forehead. "I can't wait to make you Mrs. Kane," he murmured. Her heart leapt. She couldn't wait to be Mrs. Kane, either.

Emma froze as a thought hit her.

"What?" James asked. His expression turned serious, alert.

"I–He knows." She turned bewildered eyes to her fiancé.

"Who knows?"

"Kendrick." She stifled an incredulous laugh in her palm. "He said 'good luck with the wedding planning, *you two*.'"

James cursed softly.

"How did he figure it out?" Emma wracked her brain trying to figure out if she did anything obvious to show how attached she was to the Phantom, but she came up empty.

"Well, I guess he's just a good detective," James muttered. He stared out over the city.

Emma squeezed his hand. "Don't worry, we can trust him."

James cut his eyes at her. He smiled softly. "I know we can, Mrs. Kane."

She shivered at the name. "Not *yet*."

He kissed her head again. "I know, but I like the sound of it."

She did, too. She loved the sound of it. Emma Kane.

She settled her head on his shoulder as they both looked out at the skyline.

Hand in hand, they watched the sun rise slowly over New Atlas.

The night was over.

A new day had begun.

ACKNOWLEDGMENTS

This book has been a labor of love, which these acknowledgments will definitely show. It's going to be *long*. I'm sorry.

To Katie at Beta Reading Services for the invaluable feedback and encouraging comments, you helped kick this story off and get it where it is today. To Kristin Dwyer, my editor, thank you not only for your incredibly valuable and meaningful feedback that helped make this book perfect, but also for the sheer amount of unhinged comments and threats of lawsuits that made the process so fun. I know I paid you to work on this book but it doesn't even feel like it. Also, sorry for the emotional distress.

The biggest chunk of thanks goes to my original readers, back when this book was a fanfiction. To every single person who read it, commented on it, and sent messages or asks on Tumblr/ AO3, thank you thank you thank you.

I won't out your tumblr/ AO3 usernames but there are so many people to thank! I know it's been years since I started, but I still remember every single person who created a whole community around this story. To Fe, for your friendship and brainstorming and fangirling. To Caroline, for the fanart. To Shet & M, for being so cool, but mostly for the introduction to Tenet and for your writing–and especially for being writers I look up to. To Rosie, for using your awful camp wifi in 2022 to check in as you continued to read. To Lucy, for all the love and enthusiasm.

To Nina, my keyboard anon. I still can't believe you took a scene from a fanfiction and filmed it. Thank you for that, and for all of the long, long essays on each chapter.

Speaking of anons, to my bat anon whose name I still don't know as of 2025. I think of you often–your essays were the best. I love that even up to now, you occasionally send me long asks and check in.

To Rocky Maxwell: I can't believe my writing helped inspire a song. I still listen to The Knight sometimes and it makes me feel warm and fuzzy knowing I had even a small part to play in it.

To every single person online who enthusiastically and wholeheartedly encouraged me to reach for the stars and publish this. To everyone who commented, even if it was just to yell at me about Marie, thank you. Especially to those who have commented over and over again throughout the past three plus years, rereading and loving Middle of the Night through it all. I hope I did you proud.

Thank you to Matt Reeves and Robert Pattinson because, let's be honest, if I hadn't seen *The Batman* I would never have written this story. Can we maybe sneak a copy into the next film just for fun?

To Stephanie Drew Davies: Steph, this book would not be what it is without you. Hell, we wouldn't even be friends. Thanks for sending that first piece of fanart to me. I'm so happy I met you through this story and that we have continued to be friends. But mostly, thank you for being an amazing friend, confidant, artist, person, etc etc etc. And of course, THANK YOU for the amazing cover and everything else you designed. I still can't believe you did all of it just for me.

To Ariel, who became one of my best friends because of the original fic. Thank you, thank you, thank you for all the messages, texts, and general screaming over the years about this book. Thank you for becoming my sensei when it comes to publishing and for your endless advice and patience. I look forward to many more years of bitching about people together—and who knows, maybe we'll actually start that podcast. Now we get to be published authors together, which is the coolest thing ever. P.S. thanks for letting me borrow your world and make our stories part of the same multiverse!

I would like to thank my parents ~~Brain~~ Brian and Mala for always supporting me, my reading habits, and my writing. I'm sorry I kept this book a secret from you, but you guys had a lot going on in 2022 when I started this whole thing—and then I just needed to get it done by myself, just to know that I could. I already know your support is going to be massive, because that's how you both are.

To my cats, Oliver and Bria, who should basically get co-author credits on this (Oliver especially). They're the best kitties ever and they kept me company during all the weeks and months writing and editing.

And finally, finally, to my husband Andrew, who will undoubtedly say something about being last in the acknowledgments. Don't you know the most important ones go last on these things? Thanks for encouraging me and loving me and also for keeping the judging to a minimum when I wrote a huge book because of *The Batman*. Thank you for talking me out of my frequent overthinking and panics and telling me that I *can* do this. I hope I make it big so you can become a trophy husband. I love you so much.

SHELBY LEWIS was born and raised in South Carolina. She has a BA in literature and art history from Wofford College (not that she used it, but had a good time earning it). If she's not writing, she's usually found curled up with a good book with one or both of her cats or following her husband around to get on his nerves.

CONNECT WITH THE AUTHOR:
Instagram: @authorshelbylewis
Threads: @authorshelbylewis

Please consider leaving a star rating or a written review (even 1-2 sentences!) of this book on Goodreads, StoryGraph, or Amazon. It helps support indie authors!